W9-AAV-454

MYSTIC WARRIOR

OTHER WORKS BY THE AUTHORS

Tracy Hickman

(with Margaret Weis)
DRAGONLANCE CHRONICLES TRILOGY
DRAGONLANCE LEGENDS TRILOGY
DRAGONLANCE: DRAGONS OF SUMMER FLAME
DRAGONLANCE: WAR OF SOULS TRILOGY
DARKSWORD TRILOGY
ROSE OF THE PROPHET TRILOGY
DEATHGATE CYCLE SEPTOLOGY

THE IMMORTALS
REQUIEM OF STARS
STARCRAFT: SPEED OF DARKNESS

Laura Hickman

(with Tracy Hickman)
DRAGONLANCE: DRAGONS OF WAR
RAVENLOFT

(with Kate Novak)
DRAGONLANCE: LOVE AND WAR
"Heart of Goldmoon"

MYSTIC WARRIOR

BOOK ONE OF

The Bronze Canticles

By

TRACY & LAURA
HICKMAN

ASPECT®

WARNER BOOKS

NEW YORK   BOSTON

This book is a work of fiction. Names, characters, places, and incidents are the product of the authors' imagination or are used fictitiously. Any resemblance to actual events, locales, or persons, living or dead, is coincidental.

Copyright © 2004 by Tracy and Laura Hickman
All rights reserved.

Aspect / Warner Books

Time Warner Book Group
1271 Avenue of the Americas, New York, NY 10020
Visit our Web site at www.twbookmark.com.

The Aspect name and logo are registered trademarks of Warner Books.

Printed in the United States of America

ISBN 0-446-53105-7

Book design by H. Roberts Design

To our parents:
Dr. Harold R. & Joan P. Hickman
and
Clarence E. & Jennie L. Curtis

You taught us how to work, how to read, and how to dream . . .

TABLE OF
CONTENTS

Map of Aerbon   12
Map of Sine'shai   66
Map of G'tok   154

FOLIO I: The Dreamers   1
 1 Far Shores   3
 2 Galen   13
 3 The Forge   21
 4 Whispers and Ghosts   27
 5 Festival   41
 6 Blessed Coins   49
 7 Falls   57
 8 Dwynwyn   67
 9 Tatyana   76
10 Aislynn   83
11 Famurin Gamesmen   90
12 Tragget   98
13 Dark Waters   106
14 Bayfast   115
15 Hrunard   121
16 Mithanlas   130
17 Visions of Smoke   135
18 Demons   146
19 Mimic   155
20 For a Clock That Works   162
21 Up and Coming   169

FOLIO II: The Warriors 177

22 Whetstones 179
23 Common Ground 187
24 Bright Swords 196
25 Twelve Suns 204
26 Black Hope 212
27 A Private Walk 221
28 Nightrunners 228
29 Sympathetic 241
30 Master and Servant 251
31 Traveling Companions 259
32 Blind Eye 266
33 Obsessions and Confessions 277
34 Kyree 288
35 Beholder 297
36 Gynik 306
37 The Bargain 312
38 Deep Magic 319
39 Farther to Fall 329
40 Tower of Mnumanthas 337
41 Heretics 348

FOLIO III: The Mystics 357

42 Pieces in Play 359
43 True Blades 367
44 New Rules 375
45 Tin Soldiers 383
46 Small Sacrifices 392
47 The Warriors 398
48 Enmity's Fool 407
49 Destiny 414

Appendix A: Translation 419
Appendix B: Pir Drakonis 422
Appendix C: Mystics 429

Thrice upon a time
there was a world that was three worlds
One place that was three places
One history that was told
in three sagas all at the same time.

Thrice upon a time . . .
the gods foresaw a time
when three worlds would become one . . .
When the children of their creation
would face the Binding of the Worlds.

Thrice upon a time . . .
Three worlds fought to survive.
Their children would be armed
with the cunning of their minds
their fierce will to endure
and the power of newfound magic.

Thrice upon a time . . .
came the Binding of the Worlds.
Not even the gods knew
. . . which world would reign . . .
. . . which world would submit . . .
. . . and which world would die.

Song of the Worlds
Bronze Canticles, Tome I, Folio 1, Leaf 6

The Dreamers

Far Shores

In the 492nd year of the Dragonkings, no commoner within
the lands of Hrunard, nor anyone within the Five Domains
suspected that their world was already coming to an end.
The silent invasion moved as slowly and as inevitably
as a glacier, unmarked by the busy lives of the
ordinary inhabitants . . .

Only the fevered dreamers sensed the initial tremblers of the
Deep Magic; the vanguard of a glory and a doom they could
scarcely comprehend. They were the first of the
Mystics, these dreamers . . .

. . . and they were insane.

Bronze Canticles,
Tome III, Folio 2, Leaf 19

They watch me.

I feel their eyes peering through the darkness at the top of the falls. Each pinprick in the dome of night burns me, unblinking in its considerations. The stars try to speak—a murmuring of stardust on a wind that I cannot feel. I ignore them. They never say anything of consequence. They babble incessantly about the past and say nothing of the future. Their concerns, it seems, are too far above the lowly place that I occupy. They watch me with eyes of fire.

The stars are not the only ones watching me. Dark eyes, holes in the night, peer at me from under the black shadows of the forest around me. Their gaze is lust and hunger. Theirs are the eyes of the hunter, and I am the hunted.

I turn from them, stumbling in my flight beneath the low boughs of a pine tree. I might hide from the gaze of the stars here, but the other, unseen eyes are still on me, burning through the darkness. The whispered words between them drift past my ears, talking about me, talking _to_ me. The voices creak and groan like overheated metal: the hiss of steam and the taste of a forge. They are searching for me, licking their long teeth in anticipation. Their voices are more distinct now, chattering madly and incessantly.

Demons. They are dark spirits from the deep reaches of N'Kara—the belly of the world where all condemned sinners suffer unceasingly in the afterlife. They have come for me in my blasphemy and they are getting closer.

I know this place, these trees are near my home and yet so _different_ somehow. They can offer me no safety nor solace. I plunge headlong, mindlessly through the thick woods. Home is farther and farther from me with each panicked stride, but the demons stand between me and that place of solace. I am spinning, lost and confused by trees that I no longer remember. The branches move too slowly out of the way, marking my face and clawing at my eyes. The trees suddenly part . . . and I run headlong into the demons' encampment.

Four of the revolting creatures have their backs to me as I slide noisily to a halt. The demons are tearing at the flesh of a red-haired scholar, his arms and legs spread wide and staked to the ground. Books and parchment scrolls lie shredded and scattered about.

The haggard scholar looks up calmly from the tortured scene. "Would you be so kind as to help me?" he says in a quiet, patient voice despite the terror filling his eyes. "Please make them stop."

The demons follow the scholar's gaze.

Only my own life concerns me. I leap at once back into the woods, fleeing heedless of my direction.

Somewhere behind me, the demons scream, spurred into the hunt by the prospect of easy quarry. I hear their panting behind me. I sense the excitement in their squealing voices. They have caught me before—at other times and in other places—but not tonight, I swear! Not tonight!

The trees, enjoying the sport, now point the way for me, doing their best to come to my aid. But the rocks underfoot are friends to the demons, and one trips me in my headlong flight. I tumble painfully, rolling across the uneven ground. Fear conquers my pain, and, panicked, I push myself up from the dirt.

I can see them now. The metal that they wear flashes dully in the starlight. Their steel eyes stare unblinking as they bound through the underbrush toward me. Their skin, too, is green, even in the faint light of the stars. Their smell is an outrageous offense. Their long knives are drawn, dripping from the rending of a previous soul. They clang their blades against their armor as they approach. Hideous grins split their faces.

My feet struggle to find purchase in the dirt beneath me. Time stretches thin into an eternity. My legs will not move as they should. My body does not respond. The ground slides beneath me.

The demons rush forward, their screams echoing through the forest.

A massive vine suddenly lunges from the trees, wrapping around me. It jerks me upward, snatching me from the demons' outstretched claws and flinging me into the air.

I tumble slowly through the night sky, and then I am rolling gently into a meadow. No, not just *a* meadow—it is *the* meadow, the place where Berkita and I come on holiday afternoons. It is the stolen place, the secret place, the one place in the entire world that we claimed as our own, if not in deed then with our hearts. I drink in its peace, aching to keep frozen this moment forever, but the moment does not last.

The demons are already at the edge of the clearing. I flee once more, desperate to get to the falls that I know are beyond the far tree line. My breath, labored and hollow, rattles in my ears with each thunderous beat of my heart. The rushing of water calls me from beyond the trees. I heed its tumbling voice, weaving through the dark shadows of the forest at full gait. I can feel the heat of my pursuers on the back of my neck and taste their cloying stench. Cold, steely eyes still burn behind me. The chatter of their enraged voices rises with my every panicked stride.

A silence descends like a thunderclap. The eyes and the voices that are always at the edge of my mind have vanished. The peace is more unnerving than the pursuit. My rushed footfalls stutter to a stop. I stand gulping air at the top of the falls.

My breath smoothes out and my heart slows as I gaze into the river. The water rushes past on my left. There is movement in the water now—laughing, graceful spirits dancing across the rocks. I smile timidly at them and they smile back, waving their lithe arms, beckoning me. I watch their passage down the river until they leap gleefully from the crest of the waterfall, sparkling down the cliff face. They smash against the rocks below, shattering into smaller versions of themselves; hundreds and then thousands of them caught up in the foam. They rush among the rocks and then drift out into the still waters of Mirren Bay to the south.

A gentle breeze fills my nostrils, carried inland from the sea. From my high perch atop the falls cliff, my eyes follow the shore-line eastward beyond the river and the falls. There, cradled in the gentle crescent of the beach, are the glowing lights of Benyn Village—my village and the only home I know. Strands of smoke curl up from the chimneys of the town, weaving together toward the uncaring stars. The town sleeps deeply; secure in its slumber and oblivious to any world beyond its boundary wall. I wonder at the peace that resides here surrounded by a world infested with demons.

The hair on the back of my neck rises.

I know that _she_ is near.

I turn slowly to my right to face her, at once both dreading and longing for her visage.

Across the river, at the head of the falls, floats a woman on translucent wings.

I have seen her a thousand times before. Her dark, delicate features are achingly beautiful. Her large, almond-shaped eyes gaze at me — _through_ me — with curious questioning. Her hair is pulled sharply back from her oval face. Blue strands, two at each temple, are the only coloration in her otherwise brilliantly white hair. Her skin is dark yet lustrous, her features exotic. Yet it is her wings that are the most astonishing — long and intricate opalescent wings like a butterfly that float her above the common ground. They beat slowly, as though they were moving through water rather than air.

The river separates us.

I speak to her — as I have a thousand times before.

"Who are you, dear lady? Why are you here?"

Her eyes narrow with effort. Her smile dims slightly.

"Do you understand me?" I speak my words through a forced calm, desperate to be understood. "Can you hear me?"

She blinks and opens her mouth to speak.

It is happening again. I brace myself for what is coming.

The woman's voice drifts over the river as a song, and the water stops at its sound out of awe and wonder. The wind holds its breath. Even the stars cease to blink in the night sky.

The song moves through me, ringing in my mind and bones. I have heard the song before, but a thousand repetitions could never prepare me for the reality of it. The beauty of its sound shatters my being. The undeniable honesty of its feeling and passion overwhelms my mind with its grace and truth. Tears well up unbidden in my eyes from the joy and the feeling of ultimate loss—for I am small compared to this truth.

The woman stops her singing. She watches me weep and a depthless sorrow fills her visage. A great, glistening tear falls from her eyes and into the waters of the river.

The spirits of the river, now freed from the sound of her voice, see the tear as it falls. In a sudden frenzy, they fight one another for the tear as it melds into the waters now once more rushing to the sea.

I fall to my knees, weeping at the loss of the voice, wishing it would go on forever, rebounding in my soul.

"Pardon me . . ."

A human voice? Here? I leap to my feet in fright at the sound. My heart pounds once more as I turn.

Blinking through my tears, I confront a young man wearing the robes of a Pir monk—an Inquisitor, by the purple trim. The robe is slightly too large to fit well on his thin frame. The priest's light blond hair is wispy and short, cut in the rough manner of the Drakonic orders. His long face seems the longer for the turned-down corners of his mouth, and his pale blue eyes examine me suspiciously.

"Do you understand me?" the Inquisitor asks, his words coming slowly.

I nod, my mouth suddenly dry. I force my breath in and out, desperate to control my fear.

"Who are you?" the monk asks sharply.

The question strikes me as ludicrous, and I laugh nervously. "What do you mean, 'Who am I?' This is my dream—my night-mare. You should know whose dream you are in."

The monk arches his eyebrows in astonishment. "_Your_ night-mare? It's _my_ dream _you_ are in . . . not the other way about!"

The statement takes me aback. I gape at him, unsure how to respond. He continues to watch me.

"I'll tell you what," I say carefully after some thought. "What if we're <u>both</u> in someone <u>else's</u> dream?"

The Inquisitor blurts out a laugh. He tries to stifle it but this only causes him to laugh all the more.

I join him somewhat warily in my own joke.

"Perhaps so." The monk smiles. He moves slowly to sit on a rock near the falls. "Perhaps we are all just figments of the dragon-gods' dreams. I had never really considered that idea before. Tell me; have you seen her . . . that flying woman before?"

With dread and hope, I follow the monk's gesture toward the opposite bank. The winged woman considers us both as she floats in midair. "Yes . . . I have seen her many times before, here at the falls and elsewhere, it seems . . . but I cannot remember where or when."

"Intriguing, perhaps in this place there is no where or when," answers the monk. He leans forward suddenly, his eyes wide and desperate. "Listen, tell me, please . . . are we mad?"

I take a careful step back. "You are a monk of the Pir Inquis by the marks on your robe. The insane are your province. You see what I see here. If such dreams make me a madman then, perhaps, we both . . ."

The monk, however, is distracted. He stands up slowly, concern in his eyes as he faces toward the east. His gaze is fixed on the village . . . my village.

The smoke from the chimneys of Benyn curls over the sleepy rooftops. It begins to thicken until its darkness obliterates the stars. The smoke twists in on itself, coalescing at last into the form of a gigantic dragon, writhing over the village. The smoke-dragon's black wings beat downward upon the homes of my friends, family, all that means anything to me in the world. With each beat of its wings, another light is extinguished in the town. Another light . . . another life.

"Stop it!" I scream at the Inquisitor.

"It isn't me!" the monk responds, but his voice has changed, it screeches with the sound of demons. "What is it? What's wrong?"

The dark wall of the woods is suddenly alive with pairs of steel eyes. The demons, grinning hideously, advance toward me. The monk seems oblivious to the danger stalking up behind him.

I turn, plunging into the river. My bare feet splash into the icy waters, which sting them like sharp barbs. On the far bank, however, the winged woman beckons me onward, urging me quickly to cross, to save my village, to save my life.

A bitter cold grips my ankle. Too late, I glance down. It isn't the cold that stings me, but the icy grip of the water spirits. They laugh hysterically at my folly. I scream, struggling desperately to reach the opposite shore, but the water spirits are having too fine a game. More and more of them tear at my feet, my ankles. The malicious spirits foam and splash at my face and eyes and ears. I hear their voices gathering about me. "Come play! Come play!"

I trip over them, panicked, then slip on a rock, crashing flat in the frigid, gathering waters of the river. The spirits shout and roar with glee, their icy talons dragging me down with them toward the falls. They dance about my face, filling my ears and nostrils, blurring my eyes.

"We dance! We sing! We revel! Come play! Come play!"

I struggle for breath, choking on the waters. The water spirits, gathering in numbers by the moment, carom me against the rocks. The swiftness of the stream increases and the roar of the falls draws closer.

A hand suddenly grasps my wrist, pulling me up against the current. I reflexively clasp my hand tightly around the other's wrist, struggling to pull my head up and breathe. Shaking the water from my face, I gulp air as the water spirits rage against me.

It is the Inquisitor.

"Hold on, I've got you!" The monk's other hand strains to grip a rock on the embankment, as he pulls me against the current.

I frantically kick in the thunderous river, searching desperately for a foothold and trying to free myself from the hysterical water spirits.

"Come on!" the monk yells. "Hurry! I can't —"

His eyes widen as he sees the look on my face.

Behind the Inquisitor, and unseen by him, a silent line of grinning demons advances toward the riverbank. They creep patiently up behind the man but their eyes are on me.

I release my hold on the monk.

"No!" the monk shouts. He struggles to retain his grip but the water spirits pry at his fingers, splashing between them.

The Inquisitor's hand slips.

The river drags me backward. I roll among the water spirits, their voices laughing as they scurry about me. My body merges with the river and now I am clear as the stream, flowing with it, pulled helplessly down its course. Resigned to my fate, I am transformed. A spirit of the water myself now, I cascade over the crest of the falls. The water spirits leap about excited and triumphant. I tumble through the air and water, smashing against the rocks and exploding into a thousand drops of blood. Each drop is my shattered self, diffusing among the waters of the river and the foam of the water spirits. The crimson waters rush outward into the bay. I am scattered farther and farther apart — thinner and thinner until there is no more left of me to gather up. Nothing left of me to be me. Lost forever among the waters of the bay, lost forever to my home now dark under the smoke of the dragon . . .

BOOK OF GALEN
BRONZE CANTICLES, TOME IV, FOLIO 1, LEAF 4

2

Galen

Galen screamed, thrashing through darkness. He could not see, could not breathe, could not think of anything except escaping the awful place that was dissolving him into nothingness.

He opened his eyes.

An iron dragon, its maw gaping open, glared back at him.

Startled, he lurched backward, tumbling off the edge of the bed. He fell hard against the floor, his breath rushing out of his lungs. He lay there for a time, breathing heavily, his fear slowly melting into the smell of the fitted planks of wood and their reassuring solidness against his back. They were common and comforting sensations. They were so very real.

He lay still, stared up into the darkness pooled between the intricately carved beams overhead. The people of Benyn Township rarely closed off the ceilings of their homes, preferring the exposed space of the vaulting rafters to be as much a part of the expression of a room as the floor and walls. Galen was no exception. Dutifully he had carved the intricate patterns and icons of the Magnificent Vasska into the rafters of his house.

Vasska—Dragonking of Hrunard and all the region of the

Dragonback. His talons reached across the room, curving with the beam. Carvings of each of the four major aspects of Vasska—defense, conquest, glory, and spirit—adorned each of the vertical supports from the crossbeams to the peak of the roof. Many other faces—the lesser aspects of Vasska—stared back at him from the deep shadows of the ornate arches. They all seemed distant because of the haze created by his uncooperative fireplace flue.

"Galen?" came her sweet, sleepy voice, rising in concern. "Galen, what is it?"

He shuddered. Exposed to the early morning air, the sweat that had poured so freely moments ago now chilled him. Galen pulled himself up to lean painfully against the frame of their bed. He glanced ruefully up at the headboard where the iron dragon's head still hung as it had since he forged it for their marriage bed less than a year ago. Berkita had insisted on it, telling him that such an icon would bring fortune to their home and children to their bed.

He hated it, but Berkita would not be denied. He gulped in air, hoping to calm his thoughts. It would never do to upset Berkita.

"I'm all right," he said as evenly as he could. His words formed clouds in the cold of their one-room home. He glanced about, still upset. He had scattered most of their wedding pelts in his flailing.

He had hoped that somehow his marriage would have brought the dreams to an end. The truth was that he had little desire to think about anything but Berkita since their wedding. She had become his life and his breath. Yet just as each year since he was fourteen, the dreams were back. He simply had to find a way of keeping his dangerous secret from his beloved bride.

"It's just a dream," he muttered. "Just a bad dream."

"A dream?" Berkita was sitting up on the bed, pulling one of the larger pelts up around her to ward off the morning chill. The dawn was far from being born, it was only a hinted glow on the horizon, but he could still see her silhouetted form against the window beyond. He had ordered that glass for her, shipped across the Chebon Sea from Hrunard itself. Imperfect and rippled, the glass had cost him two months' profit from the shop. It offered little more than token resistance to the weather beyond its glazing, but it had made his Berkita happy.

Now, in the rising morning light, he gazed at her shadowy silhouette framed in that useless, glorious window. Her dark curls were a wild nimbus around the heart shape of her face. He needed no light to see her features, for he could see them with his eyes shut. Her high cheekbones so finely pronounced. Her violet eyes were jeweled treasures. If some thought her chin too sharp or her hair unruly, they were imperfections that Galen could not see. The sight of the firm sweep of her skin made him ache for her. She was all he ever wanted in life. Everything he ever hoped to attain was only to please her.

"A dream?" she repeated. "*Drak,* Galen! This is the third time in as many days!"

Galen shook his head. "Berkita, please don't swear."

He could feel her pout through the darkness. "I'm sorry, Galen. But . . . what's the matter?"

"Tell her, Galen."

Galen caught his breath, pretending to ignore the whispered words from the iron dragon's head. "Nothing. Truly. I'm just— I've just been so busy. The Festival's been bigger this year than most and I'm way behind at the forge."

"Tell her," insisted the motionless dragon heads from the hazy rafters overhead.

"Well, Father warned you when you first took up the forge." Berkita chuckled. "He always said Festival was the hardest time of year for smithies." The furred pelt lay draped about her, hiding everything, promising everything. "I can help you through the holiday. I've brightened a forge fire or two before."

"More than one as I recall," Galen chided, "though your father was always intent on settling you down to one."

"Not just any one," Berkita purred back at him.

"Most certainly not." Galen nodded. The local priest had apprenticed Galen to Ansal, Berkita's father, back when he was only twelve. The apprenticeship was one thing—winning his daughter, however, was something else entirely. Berkita was the only child of Ansal and his dear wife, Hilna. Ownership of Ansal Kadish's forge would be passed down to the deserving man who would win his daughter's hand. The competition for Berkita's hand in marriage became more than just a matter of idle speculation in the region. Aspiring blacksmiths all along the Dragonback may have had varying degrees of interest in Berkita, but all were quite moved at the prospect of inheriting Ansal's prosperous forge.

The matter of suitors was getting entirely out of hand until Ansal announced a smithing competition. It was never openly stated, but was implied that Ansal's appreciation of the winner's craft would also be something of a factor in determining who would earn the right to court his daughter and, subsequently, his forge.

Galen had loved her since the first day he reported to Ansal's shop for his apprenticeship. He had despaired of ever winning Berkita for himself until he had a chance meeting with a blind dwarf . . .

"Come on, Galen," Berkita said, shifting on the bed. "Don't be crazy, let me help at the forge."

Galen laughed—then shivered. Her voice was calming; sometimes he thought it was the only thing that kept him sane.

Sane. He *was* sane. He was not sure what was wrong with him. Whatever it was, if he was not completely cured, at least he was not getting any worse. Surely it was some sort of long, drawn-out illness. Perhaps he had eaten some blindlight berries by mistake years ago. Maybe it was something in the wind that would one day simply blow away. Whatever it was, he held on to the thought that it wasn't getting any worse. That, and the comfort of his cherished wife.

The iron dragon's head turned to gaze at him from its cold, dead eyes. *"Tell her!"* it insisted.

Galen only blinked. He had long ago learned never to acknowledge the objects and carvings that spoke to him. They, too, came more frequently with the dreams each fall—another emblem of his strange malady. Once, years ago, he had an entire argument with a particularly annoying walking stick while exploring the West Woods outside of town. Young Markin Frendigar happened to be using the stick at the time, however. Markin mistakenly thought Galen was angry with him rather than the stick. Since then, Galen made sure that whenever the statues, carvings, or pottery spoke to him he never answered back within anyone's earshot.

"No, there's no need for you to come to the shop . . . or your father either." Galen spoke gently to her. "Cephas is there and does twice the work of you and me put together. I honestly don't know what I would do without—"

A low trumpet resounded in the distance. Galen and Berkita both turned toward the window as a second horn joined the first in an even lower note. Their deep duet rumbled through the glass.

"Galen! It's Festival! Oh, come on! See?" She jumped from the bed, the curve of her firm back gloriously exposed through the folds of the pelt she held against her. She gestured urgently for him to join her.

The window looked south, down over the village as it sloped toward the shore a few miles away. The dawn was ablaze now in full earnest with red streaks crossing the sky from the east, bathing the town in a salmon brilliance. The polished dome of the Kath-Drakonis—by far the largest structure of the town—glowed under the fiery dawn. The smaller buildings of Benyn were dwarfed by its opulent expanse. Galen's thoughts went unbidden down the Vasska Processional to his forge shop and beyond, as the street continued all the way down to the docks. The towering masts of the fishing boats blushed crimson as they swayed in the morning swell. Farther still was the vast expanse of Mirren Bay. It glittered in the morning light. The Widow Isles lay just beyond the curve of the harbor. He thought he could even make out the Narrows more than twenty miles away through the morning, flame-streaked mists.

"It's a sign, Galen." Berkita smiled. "It's Vasska's blessing just for us!"

Galen stood up and crossed to join her at the window. He wrapped his arms around her, pressing himself against her smooth, warm back. The great horns atop the Kath-Drakonis once again rumbled, now joined by a third, even lower note, calling out the Dawn of the Scales and the Festival of the Harvest.

"They're trumpets of the Pir," Galen murmured into her hair. "They call to Vasska who reigns from afar."

Berkita giggled, wriggling in his tight grip. "Oh, really? Do tell!"

Galen squeezed her tighter and murmured into her ear. "The horns send a message to Vasska, beseeching the Dragonking's blessings on the harvest and calling his eye to fall upon his grateful servants."

Berkita turned her face toward him. "So you *do* believe the Articles of Pir!"

"No." Galen laughed darkly. "But I believe in results. The benevolent Vasska has kept the rest of the dragons at bay for over four hundred years. That's faith enough for me!"

"Oh, honestly, Galen!" Berkita turned away from him with a formidable pout. "You don't believe in anything!"

Galen folded his arms around his wife. "No, I am just careful about what I believe in. I'm a good and faithful member of the Pir, my dearest, but I prefer to offer my devotions with both my eyes open. Vasska saved us from the Mad Emperors of Rhamas—he saved us from ourselves. I sometimes think we celebrate the Festival more to be rid of the burden of the insane than to honor the Dragonkings."

Berkita stiffened in his arms. "What a terrible thing to say. The mad or the invalid or the weak-minded—they are all the Elect of Vasska. They are brought to the Festival and chosen out from the rest of us. The Pir Drakonis then takes them in and cares for them when the rest of us can't. It's the benevolence of the Dragonking that provides for those who are sick or different from the rest, and you're making it sound like something horrid!"

"Oh, I'm sorry, my love," Galen murmured to her. "It is a good and worthy effort by the Pir Drakonis. It's just that . . . have you ever noticed how those who are taken into the care of the church somehow never return home cured."

"Nonsense," Berkita sniffed. "Jasper Konal, the fishmonger, said it simply was the nature of their illness—that those with the Emperors' Madness could never be made well again and that was why the Election absolved them of sin and let them enter into the afterlife with Vasska."

Galen nodded. "That may be, but last Leavenmonth, Enrik

Chalker stood up in the Shoal and Reef and told all the men there that the Election was a sham and that he was going to expose the priests for the liars they were."

"You aren't serious!"

Galen nodded gravely. "I was there. I felt such shame for the man, Berkita. His own daughter had been taken in the Election the week before. Still, you must admit that the girl never returned—and Enrik's never seemed to be the same again. He still says it was all a mistake."

"How sad for him. Do you think they make mistakes, Galen?"

"I don't know, my darling."

Galen had worried over the years that he might be mistaken for one of those madmen, too. It would be a mistake, of course. He was not *really* insane; his "odd episodes," as he liked to think of them, did get worse in the fall around Festival, which was inconvenient, but otherwise seemed perfectly under control. All he had to do was avoid the Election in the town square each year. It often meant that he had to miss out on the more interesting parts of the Festival, but, he always told himself, at least it would not embarrass the church by accidentally carrying him off.

This year, he knew, avoiding the Election would be more difficult.

"Oh, Galen, let's not talk of such things, not today." Berkita closed her eyes, willing herself through the window and into the day of promise on the other side. "Vasska will touch us, and we'll be blessed."

Galen forced his smile. "So the coins will bring you your heart's desire, my love?"

"Don't you dare tell me you don't believe in that, too!" Berkita wanted the blessing of a child. She had talked of nothing but the blessing for months, and she expected Galen to be at her side for such an important occasion. Galen's concern was in avoiding the Election but managing somehow to show up for the blessing that followed.

"Yes, my beloved, I do indeed believe," Galen said. "I think a blessing from Vasska is exactly what I'm looking for today."

He felt her turn in his arms. The dawn lit her face in a halo of light.

"Well," Berkita said, looking up at him, her violet eyes flashing in the morning light. "If I'm to get *my* wish, I suspect I'll need a little more from you than a few coins at a festival!"

She let her pelt fall from her chest as she reached out. Berkita curled her hands around the back of Galen's neck, pulling him toward her. For Galen, the chill of the room vanished in her radiant warmth.

The resounding horns barely covered her bright laughter as they tumbled onto the bed.

The carvings of the dragons were, for the moment, silent.

The Forge

Galen's forge lay about halfway between Shoreline Road and the upper end of the Vasska Processional. It was a modest little shop set among other shops of various wares up and down the stone-paved street. The Processional, as the townspeople called it, was not the only street in town with shops on it, but it was, every day of the year, the most popular.

Now, with the brightening dawn, the street was unusually quiet. The fishing galleys remained moored to the docks, their early morning sailings for once forgotten. The streets were uncommonly deserted for this hour. The smoke was absent from the bakery chimney. The cooper's hammer was silent. Only the deep trumpets of the Kath-Drakonis broke the unaccustomed silence of the shops on the Processional.

Each shop was a unique and wonderful testament to the forces of the town that shaped it. Each strived for a balance between a recognizable individuality and a comfortable, common familiarity with the community. It was an impossible balance to achieve. The various influences that attempted to force their wild and tempestuous natures into some image of ideal perfection resulted in a town of glorious patchwork.

Benyn was, before all else, a seaside town with a modest fishing fleet. The sensible seafarers who settled here—where the Claris Branch of the River Whethril tumbled into the bay—had hopes for a future of grand destiny so long as it did not happen too quickly and did not disturb their way of life. This surface inconsistency was never questioned by its inhabitants. Such was paradoxical life in Benyn.

Nor was the sea the only influence on the town. In ancient times the Rhamas Empire folded Benyn into its might as well as its doom along with all the lands of the Dragonback. Throughout the myths of that fabled time, Benyn strove vigorously to remain unnoticed by the Mad Emperors whose names were terrible, but who were also gratefully distant. When the tyranny of Rhamas was at last overthrown by the five Dragonkings, the empire ebbed from the area, leaving the Dragonback to fend for itself. Its retreat conveniently left Benyn with a language that was common to much of the region. Over the ruins of humanity's failure to rule itself came the Pir Drakonis—a theocracy that brought a new law to the scattered towns and broken cities on the shores of the Chebon Sea.

Change was simultaneously helped and hindered by the theocrats of the Pir Drakonis. The "People of the Dragon" were exacting in their requirements and dogma. To a defeated and war-weary humanity, the order they brought with them was salvation. From that time on, they were the only government the people of Benyn knew. The Pir religion's roots grew deep in such fertile soil, reaching into every aspect of their common life, rule, and worship.

Thus Benyn was forged of fire, water, and dragon's breath into its unique shape. Its architecture was a mixture of shipwright craft, Rhamasian stonework, and Pir Drakonis icons.

Galen's shop was typical of those on the street. It shared a common north wall with Darlyse Kensworth's net-mending shop, nearly all of the shops having at least one wall adjoining another, and most sharing walls on both sides. It also had a second story where, up to just over a year past, Galen had lived in its sparsely furnished rooms. The rooflines of these adjacent shops all resembled overturned boats, their long, chalked planks running down from the keel-become-ridgeline in sweeping curves down to the eaves. The locals all liked to joke that if the town were ever turned on its head, it could just float away. These roofs were supported by fitted stone support columns—a legacy of the Rhamasian designs—that framed slightly thinner stone, wooden, or plaster walls running between these pylons. Everything, from the ridgepole of the roof to the foundation stones of its pylons, was now adorned with the icons of Vasska—the Dragon-king who occupied every aspect of the people's lives.

The blank eyes of the dragon carvings stared down on the doors of the Processional's shops. All were closed—except for one. The front of Galen's forge lay open. Iron castings of Vasska's many aspects stood as sentinels, their intricate features delicate and detailed. Down both walls were hung more ornaments of cast iron in various smaller sizes, interspersed with tools for every kind of trade.

A short set of stairs led up into the slightly elevated back part of the shop. Here hung bright steel, the brightest in all the Grand Basin. Not even the forgings from Hadran Head—imported from Hrunard itself—could compare to its purity and strength. This normally ample and assorted display, however, was sorely depleted. The Festival gift purchases had taken their toll on Galen's stock, even as they had enriched the fat ledger book locked in the strongbox at the far corner of the room.

Beyond all this, however, the back of the shop was cut off from the world by an iron, windowless wall. Many a child had pondered what lay beyond that wall, telling stories in the night to one another of hideous beasts and monsters chained in the service of the deceptively pleasant Galen. The adults enjoyed the lark of such tales and knew better. It was only the dark, hot heart of the shop: Cephas's forge.

Being a forge, the shop had some peculiar requirements, and none more peculiar than this particular forge. Fire was the greatest friend and fear in Benyn: a force to be respected and held carefully in check. Its blazing furnace heat could meld the carbon and iron of the Shunard Mounds into not just any steel, but the special steel for which this forge was renowned. That same heat could, if it were let slip from its bounds, ravage the town and put an end to its long and quiet history. So the forge, bellows, and furnaces were located here, in the back, its once-open arches now sealed off in iron from the adjoining alley to the south as well as the old storage yard to the west.

In this cavernous darkness, the forge in the corner glowed a deep red. The embers from the previous day's work had calmed overnight into an inviting warmth.

There, next to the forge, sat the old dwarf Cephas, his eyes bound tightly shut with cloth.

Cephas slept on the ground between the furnace and the bellows each night, despite Galen's repeated offers of the bed and rooms above the shop. He needed to feel the warmth of the forge, he politely explained each time, and to know that the stone was waiting for him each morning. With the coming of each dawn, the old dwarf would pick himself up from the ground and methodically change out the multiple layers of cloth over his eyes. Only then would he venture from the safety of his iron, pitch-black forge into the front of the shop, unlocking the shuttered doors and opening them onto the Processional before retreating again to the forge.

Cephas laid his hand against the forge and furnace for several minutes, pondering its temperature and the work to be done that day. Once satisfied with his plan, he turned and slowly started the process of bringing the forge to life. He moved about the forge room with confident steps and assurance. Though he was blind, he knew this room as only a dwarven smith could. He gathered up the charcoal from the bin, measured it in exact amounts, and then returned to the furnace.

All the while, in the darkness, he spoke to himself. It was a habit of which he was completely unaware and even denied when Galen chided him about it from time to time. Still, he reasoned to himself, when one is alone, one cannot be choosy about with whom one has a conversation.

"Temperature good er is," he said to the darkness. "The steel er good be today. Hallo, my dark fire, eh!"

He reached out, patting the furnace with a precise touch.

"Be a fury a'day, good friend. Er is want for the craft in the broad world."

He worked the bellows, carefully laying new charcoal atop the old coals, breathing blazing life back into the furnace. The heat rose quickly in the close room, but Cephas reveled in it.

"Er is some breaking-fast for you, pretty!" Cephas chuckled to himself, adding iron to the coals as he worked the bellows. "Into the furnace, er is! Out again pure and holy! Worthy of my, er is! Worthy of my clan! Worthy of my name, er is!"

His clan.

He grew silent at the thought as he always did, though he never missed a beat of his work on the bellows nor let his mind stray too far from the forging of the steel. He wondered where his clan was now. What would they think of mad old Cephas, wandering blind in the light? Would they understand his flight? Would they accept what he had done?

The thoughts always wove in and through themselves to the same conclusion: he would never know. He could never go back among them to find out. Cephas was dead to them—or at least he hoped so.

"No, sire." Cephas chuckled to himself. "Blind dwarf walks the world. Maybe visit the Shunard Mounds. Maybe cross the Dragon-back. Maybe see Palathina waters at night if the clouds hide the stars and moons. Maybe cross the waters there, too."

The steel pooling in the bottom of the furnace was nearly ready to be pulled.

Cephas smiled. "Yes, much of the world yet for a blind dwarf to see."

It was a litany he often spoke to himself, but in his heart he knew that he would never leave Galen. This strange human was more than a friend to him. Galen was a fair craftsman at the forge and a fine smith by human standards—such as they were. Yet there was something helpless about Galen that needed Cephas. The boy seemed to know a lot more about smithing than about life. Cephas had come to Galen's forge by accident, wandering from a ship docked at Hadran Head on the road toward Shunard. He had found Galen working his own forge, but while the boy had talent, he was obviously trying to do more than he actually knew how to do. Cephas had helped him forge his steel that day—and forged a friendship stronger than his own steel in the process.

They had been together four years. Several times a year since, Galen had offered—later demanded—that Cephas be his partner in the shop. Each time, again and quietly, Cephas had turned him down. Being a partner meant that the shop would own part of him, the blind dwarf replied. All he wanted was to make his wages, practice his craft, and enjoy the company of his odd human friend.

Cephas stoked the forge, felt its heat on his face, and then turned to the unshaped lumps of steel that were cooling on a large stone slab to the side. He felt the radiance of the heat and spat on each of the raw steel lumps, smelling the sizzle of his own spittle.

"Good steel er is!" He smiled under his wrapped, blind eyes. He pulled one of the lumps with tongs and moved quickly over to the forge.

"Good omen, this steel," he muttered. "Wonder what else this day forging er is?"

Whispers and Ghosts

Galen strode down Windward Road soaking in the daylight. The day was turning out to be uncommonly warm for early Leavenmonth. Although the leaves far to the west of the Margoth Wood had already turned to vibrant color, the grasses of the Grand Basin were still supple and green. The wind blowing off Mirren Bay had a chill to it as he walked, but the sunlight warmed his face whenever he stopped—which was often.

"Hail, Galen! Catching the sun, are you?"

Galen did his best to stifle a laugh. "Hail, Pontis! On a day like this, who shouldn't stop and smile at the sky?"

Pontis gazed back at Galen with kind eyes shining through the wrinkles of a dour face. Pontis had been fishing the waters of Mirren Bay for as long as Galen could remember. Early every morning Galen watched the old fisherman make his way down to the wharf. Pontis's craggy face had been carved by salt water, sun, and wind into leathery folds that were mistaken for scowls by those who did not know him. He was a weathered old salt of the Chebon Sea . . .

Who now was wearing the most outrageous costume Galen had

ever seen. Brilliant bands of yellow and purple alternated around the old man's body. A huge hat flopped over to one side, its crown ending in a silver bell. All of Vasska's domain—from Hrunard to the northern tip of the Dragonback—would be dressed in bright costumes today. For many, it was an opportunity to look striking and beautiful. For others, however, the effect was unintentionally the opposite. The sight of the wizened old seaman clad in this bizarre ensemble was the most incongruous and ridiculous thing Galen had ever seen.

"I see you're headed for the Festival." Galen spoke carefully, his eyes bright with the laughter he held tightly in check. He would not have offended his old friend and neighbor for all the lands of the Dragonback. He had built his home on the north side of town just because he knew the people like Pontis living next door were as good as they came within three days' walk—and three days' walk was as far as Galen ever wanted to go. Still, he was not sure how he would get through this conversation without laughing offensively at the ridiculous outfit. "Nice . . . weather for it."

"True as ever told," Pontis responded, his face relaxing into its more accustomed dog-faced frown. "Still, with a red morning sky, there will be a storm soon enough, mark my words, boy!"

Galen shook his head, his own enthusiasm undiminished. "Not clouds today, Pontis—it's Festival and I don't think the Dragon Priests will allow it."

"Vasska forbid," Pontis intoned grimly from under his yellow floppy hat.

"Vasska forbid," Galen responded in kind, then continued lightly down the slope toward the town.

Windward Road was quickly getting crowded. Farmers and fishermen alike had left their homes to join the excited and growing crowd toward the center of town. From the west, people were coming down the road all the way from Leeside to celebrate in Benyn. Galen did not doubt that before the day was closed, there would be many folk from Connis, Sharton, and maybe from as far as Delf just to join in the revelries.

It certainly seemed as though the entire Dragonback had decided to attend the Festival in Benyn. Galen was already having trouble making his way down the road through the pushing, excited crowds. The buildings lining Windward Road grew more elaborate as he neared the central square of the town. The intricate carvings of Vasska that ornamented the buildings were festooned with streamers of multi-colored cloth. Several of the more exuberant children were tossing dried flower petals from the upper windows of a few of the shops despite the halfhearted protests of their parents. The flower petals, saved since spring, were meant for the Reveler's Trump later in the day, but a few handfuls were already drifting down on the street from over-excited, anxious little hands.

Galen suddenly chilled as he stepped into the shadow of the Kath-Drakonis, the towering mass that stood to his left, blocking out the sun with its tremendous size. The great dome flashed with re-fracted light, casting small rainbows among the people in the shadowed street.

"Hail Galen!" called a voice from the crowd.

Galen glanced about for its source. "Hail!" he called out.

"Have you ever seen the like of it?" Galen could see her now. It was Chendril, the woman who owned the basket shop across and a few doors up from his own. Several of her baskets hung from a tall, carved staff she held as she made her way about the crowd. "It will be a grand day for the Pir, eh?"

"It won't do your purse any harm either!" Galen returned.

"How else will these good people get all their goods home?" Chendril laughed. Then she again began calling out, "Baskets! Strong baskets!"

The head of Chendril's staff turned and winked at him.

Galen turned his face, his broad smile dimming. Don't look, he thought. Don't look and it will go away.

He moved deftly around the perimeter of the crowded square. The young students of the Kath were performing the Supplicant Dance around the large fountain in the center of the square. Their parents watched in rapt delight, but most of the crowd took only a cursory interest in the traditional, occasionally awkward steps to the iron tempo of the drum. They spoke and laughed with one another in the press of the throng. At first Galen was able to make his way quickly around the periphery of the square by dodging through the numerous open storefronts, but one glance down Court Street—the road forming the south side of the square—and he knew that there would be no quick or simple way to get through to the Processional.

That left him with Barb's Lane.

Taking a deep breath, he turned right, put his head down, and walked purposefully along the stone-paved passage between the buildings. The going was much easier past all the weaver shops despite the narrowness of the street. The winding street tumbled down the slope of the town from the center of Court Street south until it ran into Cagger's Row. Barb's Lane was far too shabby for the name of "lane"—it was really more of an alley carved awkwardly between buildings competing for space. Still, it was a haven for the more creative and artistic pursuits of Benyn's business.

It was a place Galen studiously avoided, especially around Festival time.

"Galen's come to us!" hissed the carved poles supporting the awning to his left.

"Galen's day! Galen's day!" laughed a tapestry displayed on the other side of the road.

Galen kept his eyes forward and his gait steady.

"Hear us! Love us! Serve us, Galen!" the iron dragon fixtures attached to the gables murmured to him in a dark chorus. *"You called us into being—we own you!"*

Galen swallowed. Ignore them, he thought. Just ignore them and they will go away.

"They've come for you, Galen," a flute sang to him from a peddler's cart, the peddler taking no notice. *"You must flee . . . you must fly . . . you must tell your past good-bye . . ."*

The lane ended. A left down Cagger's Row and he was finally on Vasska's Processional, glad suddenly for the noise of the crowd drowning out the whispered voices that spoke with hushed urgency into his ears alone. He was only a few steps from his own shop entrance—glad to lose himself in its familiarity.

The twin dragon heads mounted on the corner of his shop turned and watched him as he entered.

"Ah, Galen," came the familiar rumble from the back of the shop. "You smell as strong er is!"

"You smell strong, too, Cephas," Galen said, returning the old dwarven greeting. He glanced about at the barren shelves. "It looks as though we've had a good morning already."

Cephas stomped out of the forge room and into the front of the shop. His leather apron was draped over his squat, powerful body. The dwarf's chest, shoulders, back, and arms were all so hairy that Galen had trouble knowing where his friend's hair and beard ended and his body began. He wore soiled cloth breeches—a concession to the modesty of human women, he said—and thick boots. "Aye. Steel's been flowing out er door. Gold been flowin' in. S'posing that what yer wanting er, eh?"

"I do, indeed." Galen smiled. Cephas was still rather fuzzy on the concept of trading one metal for another—especially such a useful metal as steel for such nonsense as a soft and useless metal like gold.

"Well, bags of it now er the strongbox," Cephas said, pointing with a huge, callused hand toward the forge. "Iron we got some. Steel mostly gone. Forging some now er out we."

"Thanks, Cephas." Galen glanced about the shop, then stepped past the blind dwarf and climbed up the short staircase at the back. "I . . . I think I'll take a few more turns at that inlay casting for the Kath."

Cephas reached up, gripping Galen's arm with terrible strength. The old dwarf never turned his head nor even seemed to look at the young smithy from behind his cloth-mask.

"Near time er Election," the dwarf rattled under his breath for Galen's ears alone. "The human priests look er you, friend."

Galen spoke quietly back. "They've never looked there yet—and the Pir monks never change. Every year they follow the same old search—and every year they miss me."

"Maybe this year change, er is?"

"No, the Pir are as predictable as the sunrise, Cephas. All I need to do is wait until the Pir monks and local Guardians finish their sweep and I'm safe."

"Maybe they catch you joining the crowd, eh? Maybe they catch you going in?"

"Relax." Galen smacked his hand hard against the old dwarf's back. He had long ago learned that Cephas only took it as a show of affection if he hit him really hard. "I've done this for years. Besides, they're looking to keep people from *leaving* the square—not from going in!"

Galen stepped past the dwarf and sat down at his workbench. The casting mold for the relief sat where he had left it yesterday. The tools remained next to the long stone mold where he had carefully arranged them the night before. Here is where his craft shown. His molds were intricate and beautiful, showing a delicate and artistic hand in a medium that was often more brutish.

"Short too is nose my!" squawked the third figure from the center of the mold.

"Sorry," Galen whispered. He picked up a burnishing tool and began shaving out the hollow for the nose, making it slightly longer. He never could understand why the reverse casting molds always spoke to him backwards. He was soon so lost in his work that he did not even see her approaching.

"Hey, craftsman—up here!" someone said.

"What?" Galen looked up somewhat confused. Who was speaking to him forward?

Berkita was laughing at him. She was already in her Festival dress, a beautiful pattern of rust colors that reminded him of the leaves turning. Matching ribbons streamed down her back from her hair.

"You cannot force the mold, you know." Berkita spoke mockingly as she repeated the words he had said far too often to her. "You have to let the stone take you to places that are—"

"Yes, that are bigger than yourself." Galen laughed, setting down the burnishing tool. "I thought I told you I'd meet you in the square?"

"So you did." She smiled crookedly back at him. "Still, I thought

I'd come and collect you. The Election is about to start, and the blessing is right after."

"I've had my blessing for the day, thank you." He chuckled, grabbing her and wrapping his arms suddenly around her waist.

She pushed him away halfheartedly. "Perhaps so—but you promised me, nevertheless— Hey, careful where you put that 'delicate hand' you're always bragging about!"

He released her with no small reluctance. "That's a delicate hand and an eye willing to see what is possible rather than what is."

"So you've said more times than I care to count." She tried to smooth out the wrinkles he had just put in her bright Festival dress. She stepped behind Galen, leaning her chin on his shoulder as she peered down at his work. "Still, this one looks like it's your best yet, my love."

Galen grunted his agreement, turning back to the work. It also helps when the stone talks back to you and tells you where you are making mistakes, he thought ruefully. Better not to mention *that* little secret.

Berkita, however, was not one to be easily denied. "Oh, leave it, Galen!" she said, tugging at his sleeve and bestowing one of her most formidable pouts in his direction. "We're going to miss it!"

Galen glanced at the street outside the shop. The crowds of the morning had noticeably thinned, and those people that remained were moving hurriedly toward the square.

"I've already told you, I'll be there as soon as I take care of—"

"Galen, please, just this once you could leave the work and—"

The gruff, familiar voice rumbled behind them both. "Your pardon, please." Cephas's voice sounded like gravel. "Galen, I have some trouble er forge. Give er hand, by a good lad?"

Galen glanced at the dwarf. Cephas had his head down, shuffling his large, booted feet.

"Ah, there, you see," Galen quickly said to Berkita. "Look, you run up and get us a place by the tall oak on the east side. I'll take care of this little problem and be there as soon as I can."

Berkita's violet eyes narrowed at him.

"You want a good spot for the blessing, don't you?" Galen said sweetly. "I'll be right there, I promise."

Her voice conveyed cold determination and a hot anger that were both barely controlled. "Galen Arvad, if you miss this Blessing of the Eye and Talon, I swear you'll be sleeping above the forge again, you hear me?"

"Yes, I hear you. Now stop wasting time and go get us our blessing place!" He swatted at her as she turned, and she was careful to only almost get out of the way. Her bright ribbons bounced with her beautiful dark hair. She smiled warily back at Galen and with a quick warning glance hurried up the street.

Galen and Cephas watched her go.

"Better you should tell her, eh?" Cephas sniffed.

"No." Galen shook his head sadly. "Better I should get well, and better you should get out of here before the Pir monks show up."

Cephas grunted, tugging at his forge apron. He hung it near the furnace, then disappeared into his little cavern at the back of the shop. Moments later he reappeared, pulling an oversized tunic over his head.

Galen could not help but laugh. "Where did you get *that?*"

The yellow-colored tunic was gaudily embroidered with white flowers and green vines. It was barely large enough to fit around the dwarf's middle, but the sleeves had to be rolled up to accommodate his short arms. He had pushed an absolutely mammoth brimmed hat on his head down to his ears. Three long purple feathers stuck vertically from its brim.

Cephas placed both fists on his wide hips. "What wrong ye? Festival er is, eh?"

"Yes, it is Festival indeed," Galen responded. Not for the first time did he question the wisdom of having a blind dwarf determine fashion for himself. "You look very . . . festive."

"Aye, festive is as er was!" Cephas responded proudly. "Gods of men no use to dwarves er is, but Cephas join for any dance or feast er is!" The dwarf clomped off to the opening at the front of the shop, touched the northern frame of the door, and pulled out his walking stick. He seemed almost sighted when it came to the shop itself, moving with confidence and working the furnace, forge, and bellows with ease. Yet he rarely left the shop, and on those occasions when he did, he had to make his way more carefully about town by feel and whatever other senses he relied upon.

Cephas was not truly blind, of course, no more so than any other dwarf, Galen supposed. Underground, in the dark tunnels of the dwarven realms, he could no doubt see as clearly as Galen could at noon above ground. It was the light of the surface that blinded him— even the stars, he said, burned his eyes. Galen wondered what had driven such a talented and amiable dwarf as Cephas out from among his own kind. Those times he had tried to broach the subject, Cephas had been very clear in not wishing to talk about it.

Occasionally, Galen satisfied this hole in his knowledge by making up stories. Perhaps Cephas was a merchant lost from his normal trade routes and too proud to admit his mistake. Perhaps he was a bandit cast out by his renegade brothers when he sought to go straight. To Galen, Cephas had a thousand histories all at once, and none of them true.

Galen sighed. Not much time to dwell on such things now, he decided. He hurried up the stairs to his old apartment, opened the package he had left there, and pulled out his own Festival costume. It was a light blue shirt with a rose-colored doublet. He thought he would cut quite a handsome figure in the outfit. Berkita, he knew, would be impressed.

The great trumpets atop the Kath-Drakonis were sounding. It was the call to the Election. There was not much time left.

Still, it wouldn't do to get his costume dirty. He laid it out carefully on the old bed and then hurried back downstairs.

The reversed carving Galen had been working on the table began to move. The figures turned their faces toward him, whispering. *"Closer come! Closer come! Tell to secrets have we!"*

Galen moved quickly to the forge and reached down, pressing against the eastern edge of a particular paving stone. In a moment, the stone door swung open in the floor. Cephas himself had designed the counterweight stone door. Its artistry was so good that when closed it vanished into the stones that blanketed the floor of the forge. With a last glance around the foundry room, Galen swung down through the opening, pulling the door closed above him.

It was not technically a cavern, or even a cave. It was more like a cellar that had been carefully hidden from the prying eyes of his neighbors. The pitch-black room had been carefully caulked by the dwarf to admit no light whatsoever. Galen had first thought that the dwarf wanted the space as somewhere to sleep without having to wear the blindfold that kept out the light of the upper world. Cephas, however, preferred to sleep next to the forge itself. What use the dwarf had for this room, then, was something of a mystery to Galen.

However, its usefulness to *Galen* was obvious. Here he could hide without fear of being discovered by the Pir monks. The room was not wide but it ran east under the floorboards of the storefront, allowing Galen to hear what was going on in the shop above.

He did not have long to wait. As predictable as the sunrise, Galen thought as he smiled to himself. The footfalls of the Pir monks shook dust down on him as they moved through the shop. He could even hear them fingering some of his wares. It was something of a game each year between the merchants and the monks. The merchants would purposefully leave out a few items, knowing that the monks would pilfer them. The monks, in turn, seemed to know where the line between offering and theft was drawn. There were occasional problems down through the years, but the local priestess was always good about moderating any hard feelings. As he crouched in the darkness, he could hear some of his own wares lightly clanging as they left his shop. For him it was rather like putting a bell around the neck of a cat: he could always tell when the monks were gone by the silence of his own gifts.

Through the floorboards, he heard the muffled sound of the horns, but their tune had changed. Now they sounded the Reveler's Trump. Somewhere up there, the parade was beginning. By tradition, the fools and jesters led the procession, symbols of the Mad Emperors of Rhamas. It ended with the Dragon Priest taking his position on the Kath steps. The Election would be next.

Galen waited a few moments, then released a quiet sigh of relief. The jingling overhead had receded along with the booted footsteps.

They were leaving. He visualized their robes moving down the street, checking each shop for anyone like him who actually was trying to avoid the Election. He purposefully waited longer still just to be sure, and then stepped gingerly back under the stone door.

He had performed his reappearing act before. Ever since he was fourteen and the voices started coming to him, he had feared someone would make a mistake and include him in the Election. At first he had gone unnoticed, hiding in the Whethril Woods or by the waterfall until it was all over. His mother had died when he was very young and he never knew what happened to his father, who was gone by the time he was twelve. The Pir monks had taken charge of him then and apprenticed him to a trade almost at once. The older he grew, the more difficult it was to escape the notice of friends and acquaintances in the town, but each year, with increasing skill, he had managed it.

Today, he knew, would be the most difficult of all, but he had been thinking about this a long time. Arriving at the Festival in the all-too-brief lull between the Election itself and the blessing was a fine hair to split. Nevertheless, for the love of his dear wife he needed to make this work. He knew that eventually down the years he would run out of excuses, but the voices, he was convinced, had grown less over the last year. He hoped that they would disappear entirely, thanks to the good influence of his beloved Berkita.

Galen tilted his head. There were no further noises from above except the distant rumbles of the crowd up at the north end of the Processional. The revels were almost finished—and there was no noise from the shop above. With a final careful pause to be sure, he pushed the stone trapdoor silently upward and climbed back into the forge room.

The shop front was still, as was Processional Street beyond. Not a soul could be seen in what had only a short time ago been teeming with activity. This was all going exactly as he had planned.

Galen gingerly climbed the stairs to his old rooms, pulling off his old tunic as he went. He quickly changed into his Festival costume, smiling as he pulled on his rose doublet. He tugged at it to straighten the seams and smoothed its heavily embroidered cloth.

"She's going to love me in it!" he spoke out loud.

"You look ridiculous in it!" said the doorknob.

"What do you know of fashion?" Galen did not mind speaking with the voices when he was alone. He simply considered it the same as when other people spoke to themselves. "You're just a doorknob."

"I can't keep them out anymore," the doorknob responded nonsensically. *"They're coming in and I can't keep them out."*

A deep fanfare rumbled through the walls, followed at once by a roar from the distant crowd.

"Sorry, no time to chat," Galen said, twisting the doorknob and opening the door.

He quietly slipped down the stairs. He needed to be ready for his dash up the Processional. Timing was everything. He might have tried to go back up Barb's Lane, but the thought of confronting all those voices made him physically ill.

"Galen! Back go!" said the stone figures in the carved mold. *"Darkness the in stay. Safe is it where stay!"*

The voices in his own shop were bad enough, he thought ruefully. Every remaining piece in the forge seemed to be talking to him all at once.

"Fly, boy, fly! There's a destiny . . . a fate that is your doom and your redemption . . ."

"Lost! Lost! All is lost!"

"Never go home again. The world is changing, madly changing . . ."

It was always worse at Festival, he reminded himself, tying the closure on the doublet. He turned the corner at the base of the stairs. It is always worse at—

Galen stopped suddenly, frozen in fear and astonishment.

A ghost was standing in his shop.

The monk from his dream!

"You!" Galen blurted.

"You!" the monk yelped back at nearly the same instant.

They both stood there, locked in an impossibly long moment, unable to move or utter another sound. The gaunt Inquisitor appeared to be every bit as astonished as Galen. He was identical in every detail to the man in his dream.

Slowly, the monk spoke.

"I . . . *know* you!"

Galen stumbled desperately backward, slamming against his workbench. His tools scattered in a loud clattering on the floor. The delicate mold shattered with a thunderous crack against the foundry floor stones. Galen clawed his way past the iron door into the forge room, then pulled hard at the squealing door into the empty storage yard beyond.

"Wait!" yelled the Inquisitor. "Come back!"

Galen turned to his left, dashing down the narrow alley south.

"Run, Galen!" the broken signs in the alley yelled. *"He's coming! He's coming!"*

"Stop!" the monk was shouting, his voice somewhere behind Galen.

Cagger's Row ran diagonally down toward the harbor. Maybe if he could get down to the harbor, then east down the shore, there were places where he could hide, places he knew that they would never find him.

A voice called from somewhere nearby. "Halt! Stand, in Vasska's name!"

The Pir Guardians! They were supposed to be up at the square — they were never in the town streets during the Election! He cast about, searching for some avenue of escape.

The shops about him were all open for the inspection of the monks, so he ducked into Dav Jekin's chart shop. In the back, he searched the racks of fishing and navigational charts that lined the walls, but an exit eluded him.

The charts all sang to him, their voices a jumble of sounds competing for his attention as he moved among them. *"Faraway lands . . . Exotic and frightful ports . . . The roads we take do not always lead us where we thought to go . . ."*

"No! Please stop!" It was the Inquisitor again! He had followed Galen into the shop.

Galen frantically dashed through the racks of charts. Suddenly he found it—the door to the back alley. If he could just duck into that alley and through a few additional shops, he might buy himself enough time to lose the monks and miss the Election as well.

"Dreams of places beyond the horizon . . . destinies not yet realized . . ."

"Please," the monk called out to him, "all I want is . . ."

"This way," the door called to him. *"This is the way . . ."*

Galen pulled open the door.

The Guardians were waiting for him on the other side. Their strong hands grasped him at once, pulling him out. They dragged him back down the alley and up the Processional past his own shop.

"You're late," a Guardian intoned flatly, "but not too late for the Election."

Glancing back, Galen could see the ghost from his dream standing before his own shop.

Festival

The Guardians' hands were rough and callused. Strange, he thought, that he should remember that detail. His world was crumbling around him yet all he could think of at the time were those rough hands against the fine cloth of his rose-colored tunic.

The disintegration of his plans was trumpeted with unheard voices the length of the street. The carved posts and pillars each cried out to him, wailing and warning. The rush of their sound filled his head. It came just as it had come every year, but he had never been this close to the Election itself. In years past, Galen had always instinctively gauged his safety in terms of just how far he could get *away* from the Election. Now the Guardians dragged him—nearly carried him—closer to the dread place.

The various carvings that adorned the shops of the Processional seemed to all be talking at once.

"Fight them, Galen! Give us a show!"

"Flee! Your life and your future . . . flee them both!"

". . . telling you once and for all . . ."

His life as a smithy had made him strong, but he was nevertheless no match for his captors. They were the Guardians of Vasska, both

41

feared and revered by everyone he knew. Even if he could somehow break free of them, he knew his own friends and neighbors would aid the monks of the Inquisition in hunting him down—if he were of the Elect.

If he were one of the Elect? As they neared the edges of the square, Galen snatched at another thought. Perhaps it would not be as bad as he feared. He had run from this black monster of the night for so many years, perhaps it would not be so fearsome in the bright light of day, faced down eye to eye and toe to toe. Perhaps it was just an irrational childhood fear that caused him each year to run and hide. Perhaps he was stronger than the doubting words that his illness whispered in his head.

"Galen! Woe and doom! Weep for our Galen!"

"Hail, Galen! Galen the Glorious! Galen the Conqueror!"

The Guardians heard nothing and said nothing. To remain stoically uninvolved and unyielding in the cause of Vasska was their defining characteristic. They neither knew nor cared to know who they held in their iron grip—all they knew was to take Galen from wherever they found him and deposit him in the place where he was supposed to be. They soon came upon a line of their brothers who had closed off the street ahead, who parted with eerie prescience as Galen was dragged forward. With a forceful shove, the smithy was launched into the seething mob beyond.

"Galen! It's about time, boy!"

Through the throng, Galen glimpsed the smiling, weathered face of Ansal, Berkita's father, a huge man who towered somewhat above the crowd. He still fashioned his silver hair after the traditional manner of the ancient smithies: pulled back from his tall forehead and bound into a long ponytail. It was a lifetime habit that he refused to give up, even though he had left the craft to Galen as a wedding present the year before.

"Galen! Where have you been!" Berkita demanded. "The processional is nearly over!"

For a moment, Galen had trouble concentrating on her through all the noise, both from the throng and from inside his head.

"Berkita," he said, at last being able to focus. "I need to ; . . I mean . . ."

"Galen Arvad!" Berkita's eyes narrowed suddenly at the sight of him. "What are you doing in that doublet?"

"What?" Galen blinked, trying to concentrate. "What do you mean?"

"You've known for a month my dress was going to be orange! How could you do this to me? We'll look terrible together!"

Galen sighed. "I just thought you would like it . . . I mean . . ."

"Well, what am I supposed to do now? The dance in the square is tonight!"

Galen gasped for words but nothing came out of his mouth. Berkita was working herself into a serious rage when her mother intervened.

"Well, I know a seamstress that may be able to help you out, my boy." Hilna laughed. She stood next to Ansal, trying to stay in the crook of her husband's arm. It was her protection from the jostling crowd pressing all around them. Hilna was a lithe woman from whom her daughter had taken her good looks. "The heralds have already finished and . . . are you sure you are quite all right?"

No, he thought, *I am entirely not all right.* He could feel the blood draining from his face, and a shiver passed through him. It was the voices, however, that were the worst of all. Their chatter and cacophony filled his head. His hands were wet with his own sweat.

"I'll be fine, Mother Kadish," he yelled over the roaring crowd. "It's just the noise . . . and the heat. I'll be fine in a few minutes."

"Well, I've cooked a special banquet for us all," Hilna replied. "I just want to make sure that you're feeling up to—"

"Quiet, Mother." Berkita spoke excitedly. "That's not our priest! There's someone else climbing up the Kath stairs. I don't think I've ever seen . . ."

Her voice trailed off as the entire crowd fell into a hushed silence.

Ansal's eyes suddenly went wide as he peered over the crowd. His whisper cracked with amazement. "By the claw! That's the High Priestess!"

Galen looked up at Ansal. He could feel the panic rising inside.

Calm yourself, he thought furiously. All you have to do is get through the next few minutes. There really is no reason to panic.

The masks in the crowd moved as their gaze passed over him. They laughed and cried. Each whispered dark noises, but he could not understand their words, so jumbled were their voices.

"The High Priestess, Father?" Berkita was thrilled. "Here? Are you sure?"

Ansal stood in awe. "I've seen tapestries in the Kath-Drakonis that depicted the High Priestess. She wore robes trimmed just like that. I . . . I think so, my dear."

"Galen?" Hilna asked again, her brow now wrinkled in concern. "What's the matter?"

Galen shook his head. He could barely stand up from the upset of his stomach and the dizzying whispered noises that whirled around him. A single voice suddenly caught his attention. He looked up.

"Good people of Benyn and all the folk of the Dragonback. I bring to you the grace and goodwill of Vasska. His eye sees you and his might watches over you. He has sent me, High Priestess Edana, to bring you his blessing personally."

A thunderous roar of jubilation and thanks erupted from the crowd.

"Hail-oorah!" Ansal shouted.

Berkita grabbed Galen, shaking him. "Can you believe it? It's Edana herself! Oh! I can't see! I want to see!"

"Hold on to me, Ansal," Hilna said, her eyes filling with tears. "I thought I would never know such a day! The Voice of Vasska herself—and right here in our own village! What ever is she doing here?"

"For you!" The masks shifted on the faces of the men and women who wore them. The jumble of voices was quickly resolving itself into a chorus. *"She comes for you, Galen! She comes for you!"*

Galen was ashen. "I . . . I don't feel well at all. I really must get back to the shop . . . I need to lie down."

"Oh, all right, Galen." Berkita looked at him with a strange combination of concern and annoyance. "Just as soon as the blessing is over . . ."

Edana, standing at the top of the broad stairs leading into the Kath-Drakonis, held her hands up, quieting the crowd quickly.

"You honor me as I hope I honor you in Vasska's name." Edana pushed back her satin hood, the purple lining flashing in the morning sun. Her hair was iron gray and cropped short after the fashion of the priestesses. Her eyes, deeply set above sharp, high cheekbones, were piercing even at a distance. She looked slight, even in her robes, yet her deep voice carried clearly across the large square. "Since the time of the ancients, each fall we gather together in thanks to Vasska for his benevolence and his diligence in behalf of you, his children— the Pir. We remember in song and story the dark days of the Rule of Man. Death rode across the land and the towers fell. Blood flowed in rivers that the sea itself could not contain. Those are the woeful songs and tales.

"But we know also other songs since then: songs of peace and songs of security; songs of faith and songs of law. We sing the songs of the dragon that forged in his fiery breath a new hope. We sing songs of that great creature whose flame forged a new faith and a new hope among the people of a troubled and broken land! We sing songs of the magnificent being whose wings spread across the sky and hold at bay the evil that stalks us beyond the Forsaken Mountains! His breath consumes the enemy that lurks in the caverns of Khagun-Fel! His claw crushes the hordes on the Plains of the Desolation! It is his songs we sing and celebrate here today."

The crowd erupted once more in cheering.

"No! Now! I've got to go!" Galen pleaded.

"But the Guardians! Galen, hold on." Berkita clasped her hands to his, her face filled with concern. "It will just be a few minutes and then—"

"You are a part of the Pir Vasska," Edana intoned, "and his Eye is on you in this Election! We begin!"

Edana turned to one of the robed assistants behind her. Galen vaguely noted that they wore robes trimmed differently than any he remembered seeing before, the robes of an Aboth. His head was throbbing but he held on to a single thought through the chorus of voices rattling around in his mind: just a few minutes more and everything will be right again.

The Aboth knelt down before a large trunk, opening it. In moments, he lifted a huge staff. The carving on the wide staff was worn smooth from use and blackened with the oil of uncounted hands that had wielded it. At its top, five long claws affixed a single, dull crystal globe. Galen saw something yellow or green flash inside the depths of the crystal, but he could not be sure.

Though he had never seen one, Galen knew the device at once— a dragonstaff. Each one held at its head a stone called the Eye of Vasska that was said to look out and discover the true souls of humanity. It was the central device of the Election.

The Aboth, still kneeling, presented the staff to Edana, who took it with deceptive ease and turned toward the crowd.

"Vasska calls to the Elect!" The sound of the staff's metallic cap rang across the square as Edana jabbed it onto the stone step. "He commands that you make yourself known as his Eye falls upon you! Enter the Elect into the peace of Vasska!"

Far across the square, a voice screamed over the silence.

"Blessed be the peace of Vasska!" Edana cried, pointing off to her right.

The crowd turned as one toward the sound of the screaming, and then erupted once more in a thunderous cheer. The mob lifted a woman, who continued to wail, over their heads. Galen did not recognize her—she was probably from one of the outlying settlements upstream along the Whethril. Still cheering, the throng passed her writhing body toward the waiting monks on the west side of the Kath-Drakonis.

The crowd was still cheering when another voice cried out in the center of the teeming rabble.

Edana pointed at the man and yelled over the crowd, "Blessed be the peace of Vasska!"

The roar once more thundered across the crowded square as the man was pushed up by the hands of his neighbors over their heads. It was Haggun Harn, Galen realized, an older man who had worked the fishing boats most of his life. The entire town knew that he had been acting strangely of late. His Election would be a blessing to his family—they would no longer have to care for him or be embarrassed by his occasional ravings.

Galen suddenly realized that the voices had stopped. He glanced around. The masks, the carvings, the ironworks— they were all silent and unmoving. More cries and more cheers filled the air, but Galen was no longer listening. He was going to be fine, he suddenly realized. The voices had stopped. He had nothing to fear from the Election. All those years he had hidden from this simple, harmless ceremony. Now he felt foolish for having avoided it—a child's fright that he should have long shaken with his coming of age.

He put his arm around his wife's shoulders.

She looked up at him.

He smiled at her as he spoke. "I'm sorry about the rose-colored—"

Sound exploded in his head.

He could not think about anything but the horrible keening in his head. It was the sound of a thousand death-cries at once, the outrage of uncounted spirits from the depths of torment. His hands instinctively came up to his ears, but the sound was not coming from outside and the action did nothing to diminish the pain.

He opened his eyes wide. Panic overwhelmed him.

The masks were all turned toward him. Their mouths were all open impossibly wide. They contorted horribly, shaking with their own resonance. The dragon carvings on the eaves of the buildings were turned toward him. They screamed.

Galen screamed, too.

The sound was drawn from him. He could not help himself. The noise in his head would not go away, wrenching a scream unwilled from his throat at the agony of it. He clawed at his head, trying to get to the pain that was inside, trying to pull it out, trying to do anything to make it stop.

He was only vaguely aware of the hands pushing him upward. The shouting mob was nothing compared to the shattering sound in his mind. He floated over the heads of his cheering friends and neighbors as though down a river. The pieces of his mind seemed to disintegrate. He was barely aware when the words rolled over the shouting crowd.

"Blessed be the peace of Vasska!"

Cheers, horror, laughter, terror . . .

The screeching noise in his head would not stop.

The more Galen struggled, the worse it became. Still, he would not give in to it—could not give in to it. He rode the crest of waving arms across the square, each one dragging him away from the life he loved. He fought against this human tide, struggled to tumble back into anonymity. In the end the tide was stronger than his desperate will. His strength failed him all too soon, sapped from him by the blaring voices in his own head and the well-wishes of his former neighbors and friends. Galen made a final desperate lunge. It was futile. At last, he succumbed to the voices. His mind collapsed into a deep and blissful darkness.

6

Blessed Coins

Berkita's screams were lost in the roar of the crowd.

It was impossible, yet there was Galen—her Galen—lifted off the ground and being pushed across the town square. Panicked, she searched the faces in the crowd for someone who might help her.

It was a terrible mistake—she knew this with her entire heart.

Berkita pushed against the crowd around her, desperate to reach her husband, but the mass of bodies yielded only a little. The square was so filled with people that it was impossible to move from one place to the next, and certainly there was no passage through to the other side.

Nevertheless, she fought against the wall of humanity, clawing madly at them in an effort to make them give way. Several turned toward her, their anger and impatience directed at her as if they thought she was just trying to get a better view. She gaped at the faces of friends as well as familiar patrons of the shop. Each in turn registered their quick, shallow sympathy and their impatience to get back to viewing the spectacle at hand, but no one would give way. With each moment her husband was being carried farther and farther from her.

Desperately, she turned to her father, tears streaming down her face. "Papa, what do we *do!*"

Ansal's face had fallen. His eyes were fixed in the distance on Galen as the roaring mob cheerfully propelled him toward oblivion. His breath was labored. He could not bring himself to look on his daughter.

"I . . . I don't . . . know," he stammered. "He is . . . is one of the Elect. He's been *Chosen!*"

"Papa, no!" Berkita screamed through the thundering noise of the cheering crowd. "It's a mistake, Daddy! There's nothing wrong with him! He's . . . he's not insane!"

Several others were being lifted up by the horde, riding a sea of hands toward their final destiny.

"Kita." Ansal had not called her by his pet name in quite some time, and he spoke it now with an emotional rumble deep in his throat. "The ways of Vasska are not known to us. Sometimes we just have to accept the will of Vasska. I . . . I can only believe that this is all for the best . . ."

"No, Daddy! It's a mistake! It's just some *stupid* mistake!"

Priestess Edana was lowering the staff of the dragon's eye now. The Election was over. Her words of blessing started flowing over the crowd. Everyone leaned a little closer to hear the High Priestess.

"Kita," Ansal said, his eyes unfocused over the crowd as resolve fought against the unthinkable. "I've come to the Election since I was four years of age. I've *never* seen a mistake. Not once."

Berkita looked back in anger and in shock. She glanced at her mother for some hope; some sign of support. Her mother, however, had turned away from her, burying her face in the dark safety of Ansal's costume.

Somewhere behind Berkita, Edana had reached the end of her blessing pronouncement. Berkita heard none of this.

Her father looked into her eyes at last. "No one has ever come back. And no one who has ever gone looking for them has ever come back either." Her father looked away from her once more. "Just accept it. As we all must."

Thin, golden coins flew out over the crowd.

Berkita suddenly saw the people around her with new eyes. Her parents could not—would not—help her. Her friends and neighbors, those she had grown up with and trusted and loved, stood about her suddenly unrecognizable, distant and frightening. They stood and cheered and shouted and laughed at her life being torn from her. In the packed throng made up of everyone she had ever known, she suddenly felt completely alone.

There was only one name that came to her; one soul that might, somehow, help her.

The crowd was reaching upward toward the sky, toward the golden blessing being showered down on them. A blessing which Berkita had not understood completely before now: the blessing that *they* were not among the Elect.

Berkita turned and ran through the crowd. Intent on getting closer, they seemed perfectly willing to let her move backward, away from the square. She pushed aside anyone not quick enough to get out of her way. She no longer cared for the faces that had suddenly become as strangers to her.

As she ran, the coins of the blessing rained down around her like golden tears. They brushed against her wet cheeks, slid down her orange costume, and rang slightly as they were left for others to pick up on the cobbled street behind her.

Priestess Edana, Mother of the Vasskan Pir and Exalted Speaker of Vasska, stepped into the cool shadows of the Kath-Drakonis and sighed.

The Aboth-Sek—her personal contingent of guards—had long ago learned the quiet signs of her command. They quickly came to bow before her, their arms outstretched to receive from her hands whatever she presented.

She removed the holy crown of her office with no small relief, tossing the dreadfully heavy relic to one of her Aboths. It gave her a headache each time she wore it to ceremonial functions, but it served a crucial purpose greater than simple adornment. It was a symbol of the rule of law—the law of Vasska, she reminded herself with a smile . . . and as such it was important that everyone who saw her knew that it was she, alone, who wore it.

"Thank you, Brother," she said with practiced humility as the monk gingerly handled the crown. Her words echoed slightly in the vastness of the main chapel. "See to its packing at once. Has all been made ready for the journey?"

"Yes, Our Holy Lady." The Aboth never took his eyes off the floor as he spoke. "The caravan is at your command as you requested. All is made ready."

"You have pleased me," she said, thinking the quicker they were out of this backwater fish-market the better. She longed for her own bed and the more mundane duties of her office. This trip had been a strain on her, but a necessary one, she had no doubt—no doubt at all.

Edana turned to another of her guards, speaking without preamble. "I would beg the presence of the Lord Inquisitor."

"Holy Lady, I shall bring him at once." The Aboth had heard such commands before and knew obedience was the better part of valor.

She glanced upward at the vaulted ceiling above her. Multi-colored light filtered down through the stained glass of the dome. She had been told this Kath-Drakonis was quite striking at midday, when the light filled the dual transepts, nave, and apse with rainbows of light. She hoped with all her heart not to be here long enough to see it.

It was a smallish Kath-Drakonis, after all, and not terribly well appointed. She had seen better in the larger ports of the Dragonback, not to mention the truly magnificent structures in Hrunard. It was all a bit depressing, really, to think that this building should represent the vast grandeur of Vasska to these people. The local Guardians and priests of the Nobis had been beside themselves when Edana arrived the night before—a feat of timing that had required that they spend a night in some collection of huts calling itself Leeside about twelve miles down the coast. It was all Edana could do to convince them not to vacate their own rooms on her behalf. She had been politic, of course, insisting that they not go to such trouble. The fact was that she had no intention of staying in their drafty, flea-infested cells. Still, it was all they had, she sadly reminded herself.

The Aboth was returning from the back of the apse. Beside him walked a taller, thin man in overlarge black robes trimmed in purple.

The thin man tugged at the front of his ill-fitting vestment, trying to straighten it out. Straw blond, wispy hair stood out from his head.

"Ah, Lord Tragget." Edana smiled into her words. "Our esteemed Inquisitor, welcome."

"I am blessed to be in your presence, Holy Lady," Tragget replied.

"May I congratulate you on your recent appointment," Edana said with a smile. "It was well earned and deserved, although I see that your predecessor left you with a mantle of office somewhat too large for you."

The perpetual frown on the young man's face broke into a momentary, awkward grin. "Yes, Holy Lady. It is a large robe to fill."

Edana smiled. "Well, we shall see to it that the tailors provide you a better one on our return to Hrunard."

The Inquisitor nodded his thanks.

Edana considered the Inquisitor for a moment and then spoke quietly to the Aboth-Sek. "Leave us."

The Aboths quietly moved away into the far corners of the Kath. Edana could no longer see them but she knew that they were there looking after her. Their oath bound them to silence and secrecy on her behalf, but a little caution was never a bad idea.

She slowly began to walk between the pews of the nave. The Inquisitor fell into step with her.

"Did you find what you were looking for?" she asked quietly.

The silence between them seemed longer than their echoing steps measured.

"I am not sure, Holy Lady," he replied.

"You are 'not sure'?" Edana's eyes narrowed dangerously. "What do you mean, Tragget? You dragged me across the Hadran Strait and into this shack-heap they call a town for 'I'm not sure'?"

"Revered Mother of the Pir," Tragget breathed out carefully. "The Elect are, of course, already on their way, but I'd like a little more distance between us and this place before I take a closer look. It would not do to examine this catch while we are still so close to town. After all, it was your reading of the dreamsmoke that started us on this hunt."

"Yes," Edana sniffed, "but it was you who brought us to this particular field. How did you know to hunt *here?*"

"It is my calling to know, Revered Mother," Tragget answered, his eyes cast down to the floor.

"Indeed," she coolly replied.

Berkita ran through the front of the shop and directly into the deserted enclosure of the forge.

For a moment, she stood in the place where she and Galen had stood so many times before. She could still feel a part of him there, smell his hair that was no longer there and feel the touch that was gone.

She wanted to fall to the floor and die. But Galen was still out there breathing somewhere in the world, and for that alone she had to keep going on.

Galen was lost—lost to a world suddenly far larger and more frightening than Berkita had ever supposed. The world beyond her town was the place of half-remembered names and shadowy legends. She had to go to him. She had to find him, save him, and she had no idea how to do so or where to even begin.

She knew only one soul who did.

"Cephas!" she cried out, her throat raw from screaming. "Cephas, where are you!"

The ting of metal swinging in the breeze.

"Cephas! By the Claw, answer me!"

She was shaking now.

Suddenly, the stones of the floor swung upward. Berkita leaped back out of the way, astonished at the opening suddenly appearing at her feet.

"Ell, so much for secret caverns, eh?" Cephas pulled himself quickly out of the hole. "No needin' *that* hidin' hole now, er is?"

The dwarf had changed with astonishing swiftness. Berkita had glimpsed the strange little man at the edges of the crowd in the square; he was hard to miss in his outlandish clothing. This had all disappeared, however, in favor of his brown leather vest and a massive traveling cloak. His bedroll—a human invention to which Cephas had taken a fancy—was slung over his shoulder and across his wide, hairy chest. His hair seemed to stand out straighter than ever in every direction from his head.

"Sorry for ye, er I." Cephas began stuffing his traveling sack. Feeling his way about the back room, he pulled several strips of dried meat from where he had stashed them and pushed them into the oiled leather pack. "Sorry for Galen er I. Do er I can fer the lad. Bring his bones back home er I may."

"Where are they taking him?" she demanded.

"Far," Cephas said flatly, still feeling his way down the items on a shelf and occasionally dropping one into his sack. "Galen be riding the Blood Road now. Flows like a vein er is. The heart be in Hrunard. Bleeds out in Enlund. Cephas smelled the iron in er spilled blood come the Enlund Plain."

"Hrunard?" she gasped. "Across the strait!"

"Strait? Aye," the dwarf chattered on, never stopping his intent work gathering items about the shop. "That the beginning er is. This dwarf walked the land, Lady Arvad! Under the burning stars, this dwarf walked! Beyond the ruins of Mithanlas, beyond the Desolation itself this dwarf walked! Yer talk of dragons were not tales in those lands er is. Their wings burn clouds in Hrunard! Their breath breaks stone in Hrunard!"

Berkita sucked in a breath. "How do we get there?"

The dwarf stopped his work. A long moment passed and then he began to shake with a deep, rumbling laughter. "We? *We* don't get er is, Lady! *Cephas* walks the roads!"

"No, Cephas." Berkita stepped forward, more determined with every word. "No! I will walk the road, too."

The dwarf turned slightly toward her. He could not see her, but the dwarven custom was that watching the words coming from an elder's face had more meaning. "The old Empire Road Cephas walks. The *long* road down Dragonback! Around the wide Chebon Sea, Lady! Dangerous road by day. Deadly road by night. Five bright moons pass 'til Mithanlas er is! Blind old Cephas save Lady Arvad trouble of dying?" He laughed again and resumed packing. "Joke good as er is!"

Berkita swore under her breath. Her only hope of finding Galen was a blind old dwarf who didn't want her help.

She saw what she needed in an instant. She pulled the large, heavy ax off the wall, startling the dwarf. She turned and swung it over her head, putting all her strength and speed into the blow.

The dwarf leaped back at the sound of the blade through the air. "Wait! Lady!"

Too late. The heavy ax smashed down through the strongbox chained to the floor near Galen's table. Gold and silver coins spilled out onto the floor.

"Argh, you've dented the blade sure er is!" the dwarf moaned.

"You walk at night, dwarf, but I ride by day: ride the caravans, freight wagons, ships—ships across the straits, Cephas! I can buy you a lot shorter road than you can walk!"

Cephas shook his head slowly. "You buy a shorter road, perhaps, Lady. Perhaps you buy a quicker death?"

Berkita looked at the coins on the floor and then back to the dwarf. "Then if I die, you will bring my bones back, too."

Cephas thought for a moment.

"Done!" he said, and held out his massive hand.

Falls

First, he was aware of the pain—an overwhelming, pervasive pain like an aura encompassing his entire being. His mind had retreated from it several times, but now he knew from somewhere at the bottom of thought that he must face it or die. There was a press in the back of his mind demanding that he awake—a sense of danger that—

He opened his eyes wide.

The sunlight was low on the horizon—lower, certainly, than he remembered it being at the Festival. Unless the sun had somehow reversed itself, it was late in the afternoon. He must have been unconscious a long time. Some awful stench bothered him, although he could not quite place the strange smell. The sunlight flickered through the woven pattern of wicker bars that—

Galen suddenly scrambled to his feet, slamming at once into the barred walls of the cage. He railed against them, his muscular arms shaking the crossed pattern of the ironreed strands under his white-knuckled grip. Dried rawhide secured the strands and refused to break. Galen's feverish eyes darted wildly, taking in the gently rocking vista of his homeland that lay torturously outside his reach. The trees of the Margoth Wood that he had grown up in were drifting by slowly. The tall oak trees were just starting to turn their autumn colors, their broad leaves a brilliant splash of color on a warm and sunny day. The grasses beneath them were still supple and green, not yet having heard the call of a new season as they basked under a glorious sun.

Galen pushed himself away, then lunged once more at the cage wall. He screamed with a gravelly voice, like an animal filled with mindless, blinding rage. His full weight smashed again and again against the ironreed lattice but it yielded only enough to absorb the force of his blows. At last, spent and frustrated, he turned and slid his back down the cage wall until he sat panting amid the soiled and filthy straw that covered the floor.

The large woven cage swayed gently back and forth with the deliberate, pounding strides of the torusk underneath. The massive creature was the most common beast of burden in all the Pir provinces. This one appeared to be nearly ten hands high at its shoulder plates, with the dual ridge of flattened plates running from just behind the large crest bone that protected its neck down to its wide, flattened tail. Their docile spirit, powerful legs, and gentle gait made the torusks ideal beasts of burden.

Galen shared a large cage on this creature's back with about thirty other people. Straw was strewn in a thick layer on its bottom. He looked into the faces of his companion travelers. Some of them he recognized—there was Haggun Harn that he had seen taken at the Election. Epheginia Gallos and her mother, Miural, were also huddled together in one corner. He knew them all well, but none of them would meet his gaze.

The others were strangers. Each was dressed for the Festival but must have been taken in other townships—Whethrin or Shardandelve farther up country in the Dragonback. Some rocked back and forth on the hay, others had cried their eyes red and dry, while still others, their eyes bright or glassy, sat staring toward a horizon that only they could know.

Galen did not care. His world was outside the cage, and getting farther away by the moment. Still panting, he dragged himself around the crossed ironreed, looking longingly back down the road. The torusk on which he was carried was only one in a long line of beasts, all making their way down the coastal road toward Leeside. In the distance beyond, he could still make out the wisps of smoke from the evening fires of Benyn. There, the families of his hometown would be fixing their Election feasts, preparing to settle in at the close of a satisfying and joy-filled day.

Somewhere among those thin columns should have been smoke from his home fire. Somewhere beyond the tree line, Berkita should have been helping her mother with their feast, laughing happily at their own blessed fortune and smiling with hope for a future. Somewhere beyond the distant ridgeline, Galen should have been sitting next to Ansal by a blazing hearth, talking of the good business at the forge while Berkita smiled at them both. Somewhere under the dimming sky was a life that should have been his. Somewhere down that road was everything that he ever wanted.

His hands on the wooden lattice, he pulled himself around to look forward. Several more torusks preceded them, their long, slow stride gracefully conveying them over the crest of a small hill. He could see the road winding down among the shoreline rills. The forest continued down a ways on his left toward the coast but had given way to the gentle climb of grassy knolls on his right. The trees of the forest cast long shadows in the lengthening sunset under a salmon-colored sky. It was toward that sunset that he was traveling: away from the life he loved toward lands that he had only heard named in whispers . . . or not named at all.

Hot tears stung Galen's eyes. Blinking, he saw a Pir monk walking below him along the side of the road next to the cage.

At once, Galen pressed forward, his hands gripping the strands of the ironreed as he yelled. "Help me! There's been a mistake made! I'm not one of these people! I don't *belong here!*"

Next to him, another man pressed forward, his hair unkempt and his eyes red. "Help me!" he called out to the monk as well. "Let me out! I'm not mad!"

"No!" Galen growled at the monk. "Listen to *me!* You've got to help me—I'm not one of the Elect!"

Several more of the prisoners saw the monk as well. They all rushed forward, making the cage sway precariously.

"Help me, kind sir! I've never harmed anyone . . ."

"Let me out! I demand that you let me out . . ."

"Vasska save me! Vasska hear my prayers!"

Galen reached out through the woven reeds, the noise of the denials around him mounting by the moment. "No! Don't listen to them! I'm a faithful member of the Pir!"

"I'm a faithful member of the Pir, too!" a woman shouted.

Galen pressed on. "*I'm* the one who is sane!"

"No, *I'm* the one who is sane!" the wild-haired man next to him cackled.

The monk turned, and it was only then that Galen saw that he was holding a staff.

"No!" Galen screamed. "You've got to listen to me!"

The monk turned the eye of the dragonstaff toward him.

"You've got to listen to *me*, too!" the crazed man shouted, just as the horror of the dragon's eye filled Galen's head and robbed him once more of conscious thought.

She hovers there before me, just beyond the glistening strands of the spider's web.

I lie within a tiny glade. The web glistens by the light of a round moon, blue-white in a still night. It is a place that I have never been before. The chill of the night bites into my bones as I rise from the frigid ground.

Wondrous as all this is to me, I cannot take my eyes off the winged woman. I fear her and love her all at once. Her beauty is unlike anything I have ever seen, yet there is something distant and removed from me that I cannot understand. There is no warmth in her. I still fear her voice; a sound filled with more terrible longing and sadness than I can possibly recount to you. I cannot understand her words, yet their passion and power are capable of stopping the birds in flight and the rivers in their courses. I know that she weeps and that her tears are more than the world can bear — but does she weep for me?

As I weep for myself?

I come to stand before her now, my feet breaking the frozen grasses as I walk. Each blade shatters with the sound of smashing crystal beneath my bare feet.

She gazes back at me through the frozen web strands with sorrowful eyes that mirror the breaking of my own fragile heart. Can she read my thoughts? Can she read my heart as well? I cannot know, for she is gratefully silent this night, and were she to speak, her voice might shatter the world and me with it. Yet there is something in her eyes that calls to me, speaks to me with some understanding beyond words.

I reach out toward her. The iced strands of the web cut into my fingers with a razor's bite. My blood runs down the webbing, clotting soon in the chill. I taste the iron in my own blood as I suck on my split fingers.

The winged woman drifts closer to the web that stands between us. She reaches forward with her delicate fingers. I hold up my bleeding hands, shaking my head.

She wonders at my gestures but halts for a moment. Her face contorts at my words. A question seems to form on her thin lips. She is staring at the glistening web between us. Her large eyes narrow for a time as she considers the patterns before her, then she reaches forward once more with her delicate hand.

As I watch, the strands begin to thaw, the warmth of her approach melts away the bitter chill. The ice turns to water and the strands become supple. She pushes the weave of the web strands easily. They separate.

I smile at her in awe.

She smiles back at me, beckoning me toward her.

I step through to the other side, my feet and hands numbed by the cold.

BOOK OF GALEN
BRONZE CANTICLES, TOME IV, FOLIO 1, LEAVES 6–7

Galen awoke.

He tried to rise but his limbs were stiff. He rolled over, his back against the cold, hard ground.

He was staring up at the large cage harnessed to the back of the torusk, almost ten feet above him. Several of the Elect inside the cage were staring back down at him, muttering to each other in astonishment.

Galen suddenly realized that it was he that had amazed them.

He was lying outside the cage.

He clambered to his feet. The great caravan of torusk beasts had stopped next to a river. Each of the beasts was taking its fill before continuing the journey. Galen could not place the spot exactly in the darkness, but he suspected that it was the Whethril River east of Benyn.

It did not matter. Galen was somehow free of the cage. How he was free or why were all questions that were best examined later and in a place far from here. All that was important now, he knew, was to get away as quickly as possible.

The river, he knew, was his best hope, but the Inquisition monks accompanying the caravan were intent on the watering of the torusks. Escape first; river later. Galen moved quickly and as quietly as he could toward the line of trees bordering the road. He paused only a moment in the underbrush, glancing back to see if anyone had noticed his leaving.

The wild-haired man with the red eyes, outraged that he was still in the cage, was screaming at the top of his lungs and pointing directly toward where Galen crouched. Some of the monks were being bothered enough to start paying attention.

Galen did not wait for them to become curious; he turned at once and ran heedlessly into the forest. All he could think of was getting away—putting distance between him and the monks. Then he could take the time to think. Then he could formulate a plan.

The trees were black shapes against the moonlit shadows of the forest. Galen crashed through the underbrush, the trees raking his skin as he ran, cutting into his flesh.

The ground beneath him suddenly fell away. Galen stumbled,

tumbled down a steep embankment and over a precipice. He fell for what seemed an eternity, then slammed into black water. The icy cold shocked the breath from him. He flailed, frigid needles seeming to prick his skin everywhere.

He broke the surface of the river pool, sputtering and gasping for breath. The river was carrying him farther away from the torusk encampment, but was rushing toward an ominous roar downstream. He churned through the waters, desperate to keep his head above the waves and find some way back to shore.

At last, one of his feet smacked painfully against riverbed stone. In several bounding steps he managed to push himself into shallower waters of the opposite shore.

Then, over the sounds of the rushing river, he could hear shouting. He could not understand the indistinct words but he understood their intention, that the voices were upstream and getting closer.

Galen, dripping wet, launched himself once more into a full run down the riverbank. It was the clearest way out of the woods and the easiest landmark for him to follow in the darkness. The cut of the river gorge soon opened into a wide, wooded slope.

The roaring he had heard earlier was getting louder as he ran. He suddenly knew where he was! This was the Whethril River after all and he was just above the falls! There were caves at the base of that cliff—the dark hiding places of his youth. He knew them well, the woods were full of food, and fresh water would not be a problem. He could hide here as long as necessary, then make his way back to Benyn and find a way to put his life back together.

The crest of the Whethril Falls was suddenly in sight. Galen could make out the Sentinel Rock jutting up from the top of the falls. Mirren Bay glittered beyond in the moonlight. There was a narrow trailhead next to the Sentinel that ran down the steep cliff. He had never navigated it in the darkness before, but he would find out if he could now.

He was within ten steps of the Sentinel when he noticed the darker figure standing before the jutting rock.

Galen tried to change direction, but he skidded across the smooth river stones on the shoreline. His feet slid out from under him, and he fell backward into the shallow water.

"Wait!" the shadowy figure called.

Galen knew the voice. He slowly stood up, dripping freezing water.

"Who are you?" Galen huffed through labored breaths.

"Someone you have met before, I think," the hooded man replied. He held up both of his empty hands. "All I want is to talk with you."

"I don't have much time for talk."

"Then we should speak quickly," the shadow said.

Galen considered for a moment. "Am I dreaming?"

The shadowy man slowly lowered his hands. "No . . . not unless I am dreaming."

"Or unless we're both in someone else's dream." Galen sighed.

The shadowy man drew back his hood and laughed nervously. The face, the cropped, light blond hair, Galen had seen them so clearly in his mad dreams. He had wondered if he were somehow dreaming that same face in his shop just before the Election. Now he was standing here at the top of the falls, talking to a man from his nightmares.

The waterfall rumbled in the night.

"We really haven't much time," the Inquisitor said, his eyes flashing in the moonlight. "It is the most extraordinary thing . . . us talking here like this."

Galen drew himself up from the riverbank and stood. His rose doublet was soaked and ruined but he barely noticed. "Yes . . . yes it is. I dreamed about you just the other night. Odd, it was in this same spot where you and I met in my dream."

"Perhaps not so odd as you think," the Inquisitor replied carefully. "I dreamed that same dream, except that there was a woman standing by that stone . . ."

"Yes!" Galen exclaimed. He took a step closer to the priest. "Yes! A woman with wings . . ."

The Inquisitor smiled. "She floated above the ground . . ."

"Yes! And her voice sings the most exquisite pain . . ."

". . . And joy," they finished together.

Galen took several anxious steps closer to the monk. "Please! I don't understand any of this. What has happened to me . . . what is happening to us?"

"It is simple: you . . . you've heard the call of the Elect," the Inquisitor said sadly. "You are insane. You are a threat to the church of Vasska and a danger to the faith that keeps the peace throughout Hramra."

"No, please!" Galen cried. "I'm not insane . . . no more than you are, Father! I'm no danger to the faith! All I want is to go back to my old life. I wouldn't harm anyone or bother anyone . . . especially the church, Father!"

"I am sorry, my child," the Inquisitor intoned.

"But you were *there!*" Galen begged. "You were in the dream and you *knew* that it was real . . . real as anything here!"

The sounds of the pursuing monks rose in Galen's consciousness for the first time. They were near now.

"Come back with me," the Inquisitor intoned quietly as he took Galen by his shoulders. "We'll take care of you."

"No!" Galen screamed. He grabbed the monk and tossed him aside, knocking him to the ground. "No! I don't want your care! I want my life back!"

There was a whirring sound somewhere behind him and a blinding thump at the back of his head.

Galen pitched forward. Darkness closed over his mind as he fell for a seeming eternity into unconsciousness. His final thoughts were of the beautiful winged woman at the top of the falls watching him tumble into the darkness with tears in her eyes and his own words rattling through the blackness . . .

"But you were *there!*"

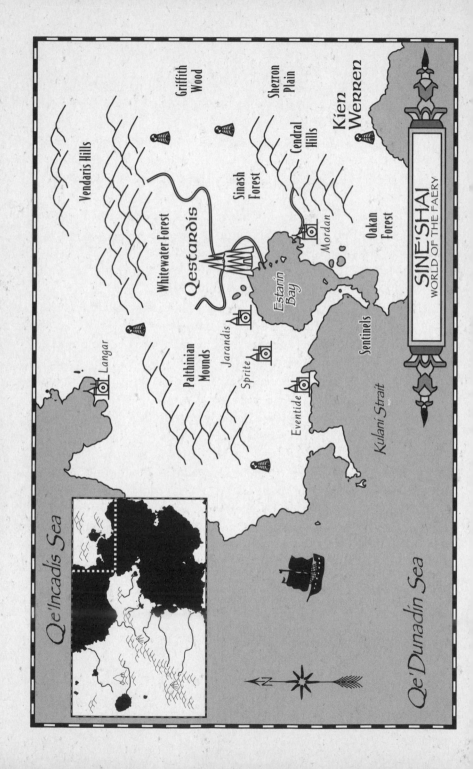

Dwynwyn

O nce upon another time, in a distant land of myth . . .*
There was a Seeker faery by the name of Dwynwyn.

Seeker Dwynwyn floated toward the top of Brideslace Falls, a puzzled expression on the delicate, sharp features of her face. She preferred solitude to the crowded halls of the royal court, where she felt constantly reminded of the differences that separated her from every other caste in the kingdom. Even if she were of a more common caste, she knew that she was not the most desirable of the faerykind. Her nose was too short, turned upward at the end slightly as though someone had come along and pushed it there. Her skin was a deep chocolate tone, the darkness considered very becoming in a faery of the Qestardis, but her large eyes were set too far apart for the likes of most of the faery suitors at court. Her hair was brilliant white, carefully accented with two blue streaks at each temple denoting her rank and her calling at court.

She hovered at the top of the falls, considering. Perhaps it was her

---

* All faery stories begin with this line. It is a designator for the listener or reader effectively saying that what follows is a lie—that it is something like real events but altered by limits of perspective and words. Faery stories were invented for the benefit of communication with humans, who require story structure for communication. They are for all intents and purposes useless to the faeries themselves.

calling at court that drove the male faeries away. Seekers were always thought of as being set apart from the majority of faeries. It was the Seekers' job to search the face of Famarin—their world—and find new ways of bringing things together. Combining truths into greater truths: that was the calling of a Seeker. It was a calling which was utterly required in the faery courts and completely frowned upon by any potential in-laws.

Yet despite the discomforts of those differences, she would never have considered her station as anything but her fate dictated by Grand Truth that governed the lives of all the Fae. She was Dwynwyn, simple as that.

Dwynwyn spread her wings—a glorious pattern of deep violets and cobalt blue whirled through a transparent expanse—and floated silently over the crest of the waterfall. Next to the falls, a tall pillar of rock jutted toward the darkening sky. Alighting, she curled her wings about her protectively, shielding her from the night that was falling over the shore.

"He is gone now," she said to herself, the whisper of her voice echoing beautifully among the trees.

"Who is gone, m'lady?" spoke an impatient voice into her ear.

Dwynwyn turned toward the sound. In all her deep reveries, she had forgotten her sprite that came to perch on her shoulder. Cavan was a good and loyal assistant, one of the brightest of the third caste servitors she had ever met, but his impetuousness often tested her calm. His nose was long and pointed. His wings favored the mothlike patterns of his kind. He had already started to glow in the twilight.

"You well know who I am speaking of," she replied.

"Ah, the strange man-creature!" Cavan spoke quickly. Cavan, like every other caste of the Fae, found the ways of all Seekers to be an unfathomable mystery; therefore anything out of the ordinary gave him hope. "Does he still trouble your visions?"

"He does trouble my second sight, Cavan," Dwynwyn replied. "Not just my sight but sounds, tastes, and smells."

"Unique!" the sprite cried out in excitement.

"Unique, yes," Dwynwyn said calmly, considering the light of the setting sun as it sparkled across Estarin Bay to the southeast.

"Then perhaps he is the key—the key to the new truth* that you seek?" Cavan replied quickly. "He must be the answer! There is so little time left to us . . ."

"I am well aware of the time, Cavan." Dwynwyn glanced sideways at the sprite. "You cannot rush a Seeker. New truths are not uncovered with each hour of the day. They come to us; we do not go to them."

"But you've said yourself that everything depends upon discovering a new truth." Cavan's voice spoke with an annoying whine. "Without it, the fate of all Qestardis is sealed to our doom!"

Dwynwyn held her anger carefully in check, just as she did so often with the rest of her emotions. Icy calm had served her well in her calling. Her voice was glacial. "No one is more aware of my responsibilities to the queen than I am, Cavan. This man of my vision may well be the key to the new truth that I seek—but he also may not. A Seeker cannot dictate when or where a new truth may come."

Cavan lapsed into an uncharacteristic silence. Dwynwyn could see that she had offended him.

"Would it delight you to learn that I saw him in my waking hours as well?" she said quickly.

"Here?" The sprite leaped from her shoulder, flitting anxiously before her face. "Tell me! Tell me the truth of it!"

"I walked the woods today for reasons that I cannot say in truth," she replied. Indeed, Dwynwyn knew that she could not speak her motivations as a fact, for she herself was not sure of them. It was always like that for her; she never quite understood the deep forces within that drove her toward uncovering new truths. Those few other Seekers she had spoken with found it as much an unknown as she herself. What had brought her to the woods this day and why this particular path? What causes had foreshadowed and destined her to

---

* Faeries believe only in fact; they quite literally have no imagination. They believe that anything that does not exist in their experience is a lie. They believe that all truth that now exists has existed since the beginning of creation. "New truth" consists entirely of uncovering a truth that was previously unknown either through investigation or, more often, through the combination of known truths to uncover a "new truth." The uncovering of such previously unknown truths is the calling and province of the Seeker caste.

this place at this time? She could not name the causes of her coming, nor could she fully ascribe the fortuitousness of her journey to strictly random events. It was an undiscovered truth, and as such, should not be voiced. "I was compelled by forces which I do not recognize or explain. Yet I did come here and I did bring my tatting lace. As I sat in the glade near the river, I spied the man from my dreams in the eye of my mind, as a memory of fact experienced for the first time.* There, floating in the air above the glade, this man knelt weeping. His voice called to me from the lace in my hands, as though the lace itself were holding us apart."

"Did you understand him, m'lady?" Cavan asked, eyes wide. "Did he tell you a new truth?"

"No." Dwynwyn looked to the ground. "His words sounded harsh, like rocks tumbling down a hillside. I knew that the voice came from beyond the lace. Somehow my lace was hurting him, though how I could not say. Unbidden, I pulled apart the tatted lace, opening up the pattern in my hands."

"Did you relieve his suffering, m'lady?"

Dwynwyn smiled slightly. "I am not sure, Cavan, for as I pulled a hole in my lace, he fell from the air."

Cavan flashed with surprise. "You plucked this creature from the sky!"

"I did not pull him," Dwynwyn repeated. "He suddenly fell."

"Through a hole in your tatting lace?" Cavan arched his brows at the thought.

"I cannot say in truth," Dwynwyn replied. "But he did fall in the eye of my mind. In this strange memory, I thought he traveled down the River Sandrith to these falls where I have seen him before."

Cavan darted about the top of the falls, his light reflected in the rushing waters. "I do not see him, m'lady!"

"Nor do I, Cavan." Dwynwyn folded her arms. The night was deepening. She should return before she was missed. "He is out of my mind once more."

---

* Humans might describe this experience as "imagining" a hallucination or a daydream, but this trait is completely unknown among faeries.

"Perhaps that is his gift, then . . . to disappear?"

Dwynwyn shook her head. "I do not believe he has a gift, Cavan."

The sprite stopped in midflight. "No gift? All the creatures of Famarin are known to have a gift . . . a gift of the gods! Perhaps he had wings?"

"No wings, Cavan. He does not fly."

"Gills, then . . . perhaps he is of the merfolk?"

"No. He walks the land."

"Serpent, then?"

"No . . . and the time has come for us to return."

The sprite landed once more on Dwynwyn's shoulder. "It is not possible. All creatures of Famarin have a gift."

Dwynwyn looked down the coast to the northeast from the falls. The shoreline curved around gently from the cliff below. In the distance, she could make out the crystal towers of Qestardis, the greatest city of all the Sine'shai lands. Its broad avenues radiated inland from the shoreline of the bay. Its magnificent, delicate towers reached toward the stars emerging in the sky above, aglow with their pastel, inner light.

"Please, Seeker," the sprite asked, his voice anxious once more, "is this creature the answer you are looking for?"

"No, Cavan, he is not," Dwynwyn replied, her eyes still gazing on the incomparable beauty that was the center of her nation. "Would that he were! For unless I discover some new truth . . . some unique combination of truths that has not occurred to us before . . . then I fear that all we hold dear will be destroyed before the season is out."

With that, Dwynwyn spread her wings gracefully and floated up into the night sky. Her eyes never left her home.

Qestardis was older than the oldest of the faery—and that is old indeed. Its foundations stretched beyond memory of any living faery. Its roots reached deep into the Seven Lords and all the trouble those origins implied.

The memories of the Fae—as they often refer to themselves—are long indeed. The faeries' histories tell of the eternal nature of the Fae and of their immortality. It is one of their gifts from the gods, spoken of in the ancient texts. They spend their lives on Famarin moving from one truth to the next as they attain their different levels of enlightenment—all strictly held within the bounds of their castes. The search for truth is the center of all the faery existence. Indeed, it is generally known that when a faery reaches an understanding of the absolute truth, then that faery passes into the Grand Truth wherein the spirit is dissolved from the body and the faery becomes one with the gods.

This aspect of enlightenment, however, is a rare event in the recorded annals of the Fae, for only a few legendary members of their kind actually lived long enough to achieve that blessed state, and none within the direct experience of any living Fae. Death visits the delicate faeries often and in many forms. The roc of the air hunts them both for sport and for their meat. The barbarian kraken—wild nomads of the Qe'tekok Sea and wanderers of the De'Phenith Ocean—regularly attack the faery ships that cross whatever waters they inhabit at the time. Disease, illness, and accident all take faeries long before their enlightenment. The Fae have long been hunted by creatures of nature and have hunted them in return with greater effect.

Such dangers, however, were nothing when set against their two greatest enemies: the Famadorians and their own brother clans.

The Famadorians were of the lowest caste—the fourth caste as reckoned by the Fae, a large group which included races as diverse as mermen, selkies, centaurs, satyrs, and minotaurs. The Fae considered all of them to be of a single caste: barely civilized, barbaric, uneducated, and incapable of much learning. Each of these races considered themselves to be the true eldest of the elder races—and despised the faeries for asserting otherwise. The unshakable belief in the superiority of the Fae over the Famadorians—which essentially included any race that was *not* Fae—made relations with Famadorians occasionally strained and far more lethal.

Yet deadly as the continuing wars and conflicts with the Famadorian races were, they were nothing compared to the wars among their own kind. In the elder days, the Seven Lords ruled the Fae with a unified voice. They banded together millennia before, defeated the

Famadorians, and established the supremacy of the Fae over all of Sylani'sin—the Fae lands. Yet not a hundred seasons passed before the Seven Lords fell into bitter dispute over the true path of the Fae and their destiny. The Seven Lords shattered the Circle of Truth and prepared for war, each knowing with absolute conviction that theirs alone was the true path for the future of the Fae, that the gods were on their side, and that they were destined to establish their truth, by force if necessary.

And force, of course, had been necessary.

The War of Seven had ground through the centuries like an endless millstone. Its grist had been the bones of successive generations of faeries from all the Kingdoms of the Seven and the various castes and families of which they were a part. Its harvest had yielded only a precarious and deadly balance, with none of the Seven gaining supremacy over another.

It was a balance that had sustained Qestardis, her faery queens, and her castes for over a thousand years.

It was a balance that was coming to an end.

Seeker Dwynwyn smiled softly at the sight of her beloved city as she approached it through the evening sky.

The seven towers of the encircling wall glowed with brilliant light in the evening. Each spire had been drawn up from the foundational rock beneath and compelled into its spindle shape. The towers were each meant to honor the Lords and the hope for reconciliation of the Seven, for which successive queens had long given up hope. The circular outer wall was formed after the ancient tradition of the faery, reminiscent of a time when the faery ring was both an enticement and a trap for the Famadorians who should cross one. Now this great wall of smooth-shaped granite protected the Qestardan Fae. It reached out from the slopes of the Forest Basin into the waters of the Estarin Bay. Here, above the long docks of the city, rose the tallest of the towers. At its peak shone the light of Qestardis, a beacon to the returning fleets and a light calling all the Fae of Qestardis home in the deepening night.

The cool evening was filled with faeries, their soft natural light swirling softly about the great city as each flitted home from their various tasks in the outlying woodlands. They formed a glowing cloud about the city center, illuminating the streets below and the delicate buildings in their collective light.

"It seems busier than usual," Cavan murmured on Dwynwyn's shoulder.

Dwynwyn nodded, her wings beating in slow, graceful arcs. "The Fae of Eventide and Bay Narrows have been called into Qestardis. The queen fears for their safety."

"Then our doom may be closer than I knew." The sprite sighed. "Did not the queen dispatch the militia?"

"She did," Dwynwyn replied. She turned slightly in her path to avoid a rushing pixie, then returned to her course. The great tower grew closer with each beat of her wings. "One legion from Kien Magoth moved toward Eventide this morning. A second legion from Kien Werren reinforced the Sentinels to the south."

Cavan scoffed. "One legion each! Does the queen expect two legions to stop Lord Phaeon and his fleets?"

"No, Cavan. The queen expects them to die. We cannot stop Lord Phaeon. I know this. The queen knows this. Moreover, Lord Phaeon knows it, too."

Beyond the wall tower, the great Sanctuary of Qestardis came into view. The cobalt blue minarets of shaped crystal reached with graceful majesty above the city shining below them. The formed domes of amber color glowed above the great Hall of Audience. Dwynwyn drifted carefully through the increasing mass of faeries, pixies, and sprites as she drew closer to the keep.

The sentry faeries moved aside at Dwynwyn's approach. Once past them, the Sanctuary came clearly into view. She saw the wide balcony adjacent to the Audience Hall and moved quickly toward it.

"Mistress," Cavan said quietly. "If our cause is lost, why has the queen ordered two legions to their death?"

Dwynwyn sighed. "She has done it for me, Cavan. They will die so that I might have time to find something new that may save us, some combination of truth that has not been anticipated by Lord Phaeon nor our Queen Tatyana nor either of our respective courts."

Dwynwyn alighted on the balcony as gently as a feather. The

sentries guarding it recognized her at once, bowed, and moved aside to admit her.

Cavan whispered in her ear, "So their lives buy you time. Do you know where you may find such a valuable truth?"

"No, Cavan," Dwynwyn whispered back. "I do not."

Tatyana

The Sanctuary brought some measure of peace to Dwynwyn's troubled thoughts. She could not help but feel comforted here, even in the most distressed of times, for the very nature of this place precluded anything but peace.

She stepped through the archway into the enormous open space beyond. The trunks of goldwood trees, nearly fifteen hands in diameter, rose in ordered columns high overhead. The boughs, nearly out of sight in a soft glowing haze, arched gracefully into a woven lattice as delicate as any lace created by faery hand. Each trunk had been carefully nurtured and coaxed to form shapes from the history of the Qestardan faeries. The legacy and sundering of the Circle of Seven was depicted there in living, delicate detail. Sprites flitted about each of these trees, constantly correcting their shape for growth and nature, lest the tale itself be lost. Dwynwyn knew that there were duplicates of these in shaped stone lining the Avenue of Delights below the Sanctuary Gates, yet these living monuments always spoke to her of a continuing history of which she was a part.

A delicate carpet of grass ran between these trunks, the height and shape of each blade prescribed by royal decree. Flowers and shrubs lined this grassy path, their flowers open in perpetual brilliance, with alternating morning, evening, and nighttime flowers each taking their turn during the revolutions of each day. Thus each part of the day brought a different aspect to the Audience Hall. Nighttime was, in fact, Dwynwyn's favorite time here, with the blue night flowers smattered with brilliant white Bride's Lace. To the second sight of the Seeker, it seemed as though the stars themselves were flowering in the garden at the behest of Queen Tatyana, although such a connection was lost on all other faeries. To them, it simply seemed a pleasant effect for the time of the day.

Dwynwyn made her way gently down the garden. Looking up, she could see that the amber panels set among the lattice of the dome had faded to clear—no doubt at the queen's command—and the stars appeared overhead now. Queen Tatyana was powerful indeed, but she did not command the stars. Indeed, the limits of her powers were altogether too obvious now.

Dwynwyn saw the courtiers at the central dais. They surrounded the concentric circular steps of shaped granite that led up in steps to the throne. Queen Tatyana held open court here three times during the governmental seasons: morning, afternoon, and night. Each of these sessions was heavily attended, but this meeting, in the darkening evening, was neither regular nor crowded. The names of the few gathered in the room were well-known to each other. So, too, was the purpose of their gathering in this, the most cherished place in all Qestardis. Their voices, however, carried through the hall with a loud fervor that might have been understood in the farthest reaches, even if the hall had been completely filled.

In the center of it all, Queen Tatyana sat on the Qestardi throne. Her robes shimmered in their own light, accenting the ebony tones of her smooth skin. Her almond-shaped eyes looked sleepily over the assembled masters of her domain. High, sharp cheekbones gave her a cool, severe look, although those who knew—and few there were who could truly make such a claim—knew her to be warm and compassionate. Her long black hair was pulled back into her ornate crown, exposing the high hairline of her forehead. Her long delicate hands rested on the throne's armrests, but Dwynwyn noticed that they were moving nervously over the intricate carvings of the throne.

"The reports from Kien Yanish are that Lord Phaeon landed earlier this day at Langar," spoke Kivral, the Voice of the Watchers. He was a pixie whose clear voice rang through the hall. "He asked only passage for himself and his aides to Qestardis. This was granted as per your orders, Highness."

"From Langar?" Queen Tatyana spoke the words with detachment. Her voice was a sultry deep song, even in times of trouble. "Then he intends a land campaign against us from the northwest?"

"No, Your Grace," answered Newlis, Voice of the Warriors. "He does not land in force at Langar. His main fleet remains at anchorage across the Kulani Strait at various bays from Sail's Rest to North Haven. He will land either at Eventide or east along the seawall, and then march north. It is the quickest way for his army to both occupy *and* fortify our land while deposing Your Grace."

"This fortification would not be necessary if the Famadorians were not marching against us from the Vendaris Hills," snapped Krival.

"Which, of course, is why Phaeon purchased their attack in the first place," Tatyana intoned coolly. "It is his armaments that are in the hands of the Famadorian warriors, his gems paid for their food. Such knowledge does not alter the truth of our condition, Voice Krival."

"You speak truth, Grace," the pixie replied.

"Lord Phaeon sees a lesser truth, Your Majesty," said Evys, a dryad hovering near the trunk of one of the trees. Dwynwyn recognized her as the Voice of the Forest. "His thoughts are not those of Qestardis and his truth is foreign to us. He comes to establish his truth over our own. Were destruction his objective, his fleets would be sailing the waters of Estarin Bay this same night."

Krival shook his head sadly. "He wishes to replace the soul of Qestardis without destroying its body. Conquest is always better when one does not destroy the thing one is trying to take."

Queen Tatyana's eyes flashed. "Where *is* the value in Qestardis if it is not in its soul and its truth? Lord Phaeon may as well bring the walls of Qestardis down to dust if he were to rob us of our heritage and our truth. Voice Newlis! Where is this conqueror Phaeon now?"

"He awaits your pleasure in the Hall of Wisdom, Queen Tatyana . . . do you wish him admitted?"

"I do *not* wish it!" Tatyana snapped, and then drew in a long, deep breath before she continued. "It is a terrible truth that is imposed upon me. Can you offer me no hope, Voice of Warriors?"

"Your Majesty." Newlis sighed. "In war there are always events of nature which defy known truth. In evaluating the war before it's fought, it is impossible to know any outcome with certainty. So much is dependent upon the chance small things that are unseen and unaccounted for until viewed afterward." Newlis straightened and looked his queen squarely in the eye. "Yet there are times when a truth is so abundant as to defy such unknowns. I cannot defend Qestardis from the Famadorian armies of the north and the incursion of Phaeon from the south. As I weigh it, Your Majesty, the preponderance of success lies on Lord Phaeon's side of the scale. I would give my life as I stand before you to make it otherwise."

"Very well," Tatyana said evenly, then turned to the Voice of the Sanctuary. "Weldin, please call on Lord Phaeon and beg his entrance into the Hall of Audience."

The well-groomed sprite bowed in the air and then flew straight toward the northern doors, a sharp line of glowing dust trailing behind him.

"So, it seems that we must hear Lord Phaeon's terms after all," Tatyana intoned. "Or we must discover something new that will tip your very heavy scales back into our favor . . . Ah, Dwynwyn, I see you have returned."

"Yes, Your Majesty," Dwynwyn said, folding her wings around her and bowing low.

"How goes your search?"

"It continues, Your Majesty."

Tatyana merely nodded in response.

The doors at the northern end of the Hall of Audience slammed open with a resounding boom. The startled advisers each jumped in shock and surprise at such an abrupt intrusion into the peaceful hall.

"I see Lord Phaeon wastes no time," Tatyana observed.

Lord Phaeon marched with a quick military stride down the

length of the hall, his four aides following in strict formation two steps behind. His eyes never once left Queen Tatyana or her throne as he moved. The towering trees and the delicate lace of the canopy overhead were of no interest to him. The grasses under his booted feet bent and broke with his every step, a deliberate insult since he could more easily have flown over them. His leather armor slapped against him in a precise rhythm as he moved; a deliberate sound to fill any hollow and quiet that might affront him.

Dwynwyn eyed him warily. His hair was a golden color, falling in long, waving locks down to just below his neck. His skin was tanned under a campaigner's sun, but Dwynwyn could see that given enough time it would assume a natural color far lighter than those of the Qestardi. The man's ears curled upward and forward slightly at their tips, something she guessed had to do with his Argentei lineage. His pearly white wings were tightly folded behind him. He was, indeed, a beautiful specimen for a faery.

Like the sirens, Dwynwyn thought: beautiful and deadly.

Lord Phaeon strode through the councilors without giving them a single glance. He stopped abruptly at the foot of the dais, then made a quick bow.

"Lord Phaeon, you are expected." Tatyana smiled.

"I should have thought myself expected for a long time, Queen Tatyana," Lord Phaeon said, his tenor voice smooth in the Sanctuary air. "Must we fuss with polite protocol or may we get to the business at hand?"

Tatyana's eyes narrowed. "I observe that being politic is no longer fashionable in Argentei."

"Nor is it required in conquest." Phaeon shrugged. "Sister Tatyana, we can banter words all night, but it does not change the truth of your position. The Famadorian armies are prepared to take your land from the north. They are well equipped, I can assure you—"

"I would think so, since you equipped them."

"Of course, but do not interrupt!"

Tatyana nodded her consent.

"They are also up to the task. The centaurs are reasonably well organized for Famadorians and make excellent warriors: fast and ruthless. My own armies are in a position to oppose them—and our armies combined could defeat them, increasing the landholdings of Qestardis manyfold northward beyond the Vendaris.

"However," Lord Phaeon continued, absently adjusting a troublesome strap on his breastplate, "as I am sure your advisers have informed you, if the landing of my armies is opposed by your laughably inadequate legions, you will either so weaken your northern border as to invite the Famadorian hordes to take your capital or—"

"Or your own legions will land on my unprotected flanks and steal my nation from under me anyway," Tatyana concluded impatiently. "You speak the obvious, Lord Phaeon. Why this tedious discourse?"

Lord Phaeon fixed his strap, turning his gaze back on the queen. He smiled crookedly. "Why? To propose a union, Your Majesty."

Tatyana shifted on her throne.

Phaeon's tone grew colder. It was not a request. "Your Majesty will abdicate the throne of Qestardis to me. I, in return, will take your daughter, Princess Aislynn, to wife, thus reassuring the populace of the continued line of the Seven Lords. Argentei and Qestardis will remain two separate nations so far as the rest of the Seven are concerned, but they will have *one* ruler—myself. You get to keep your precious heritage intact and I get to challenge the other five kingdoms in turn."

Queen Tatyana stood suddenly from the throne, her voice quivering with rage as it boomed through the hall. "How dare you dictate such terms to me? Me! I am the daughter of the Seven! I will not barter away my daughter or my throne!"

"Your throne is already lost, madam!" Lord Phaeon snapped back. "Your ancestors are dead, your armies will soon be dead, and you may join them for all I care! It is all past and gone . . . you alone have not yet realized this truth! Marriage of your daughter to me and the abdication of your throne is *all* that may save any of these things you hold so precious and valuable to your so-called heritage."

"What is my daughter to you, Argentei?" Tatyana spoke through clenched teeth.

Phaeon laughed in derision. "Your daughter? Why, nothing at all, madam, I assure you! I could not care less for your daughter. I'd bed *you* if I thought it would produce an heir and keep the rabble cowed."

Phaeon glanced once at the shocked expressions around the room and then shrugged again. "Your daughter, however, should do well enough from what I have heard. Oppose me and you and your nation die. Consent and you may live. Either way . . . you are mine."

With that, Phaeon turned and marched confidently from the hall.

Aislynn

Aislynn, Princess of Qestardis and Daughter of the Eternal Light, sat at the window of her tower rooms and sulked.

Her rooms were in the upper reaches of the southeast tower of the Sanctuary, connected by crystal halls to her mother's residence and those chambers reserved for the extensive royal family when they came calling. The exterior landings and access shafts[*] for the royal concourse were all scrupulously guarded by the Qest-hai, the personal guard of the Qestardi queen and her family. Under their careful eye, the servants of the queen flitted through the apartments bearing in their glittering arms every possible item that might delight the whim of the royals.

Aislynn's own rooms were situated in the most advantageous part of the tower and were richly appointed. Her bedchamber was soft and luxurious. The bedframe had been shaped from ash trees whose boughs crossed into a canopy overhead, and the mattress was that perfect combination of plump and firm that gave her the best of rest. Its coverlet was a silken cloud filled with goose feathers. Next to her bedchamber, her sitting room was no less lavishly appointed. Several

---

[*] There are no stairs in faery architecture, as all faeries fly. The access shafts are primarily used to control comings and goings among the faeries.

fainting couches—her favorite type of furniture—were carefully situated about the oval room. A long window seat against the southern curve of the wall was almost completely concealed in pillows. Her windows looked out over Estarin Bay, their view chosen for its serenity and beauty.

It was among those pillows that Aislynn sat. Her dark face was drawn into a studied frown. She hugged her knees to her chest, arranging her wings into what she believed to be the epitome of heartbroken form. She was basking in intense misery.

Far below her, the gentle waves of Estarin Bay broke against the rocks at the base of the tower. The comforting sound had been a constant lullaby to her since she was a child. Now she wished it would be silent and leave her alone to be tragic.

"Mistress Aislynn!" called the high-pitched voice. "I bear ominous news!"

Aislynn rolled her large, almond-shaped amber eyes. How could she be truly devastated with the servants flitting about? "What is it, Starlit?"

"I'm most distressed to inform Your Glory that . . . oh! Mistress, this sitting room is completely out of order! I'll see to it at once!"

Aislynn glanced around. It was true: pillows were cast all about the room. The princess had earlier been experimenting with being tempestuous before turning to melancholy. Now Starlit was darting about the room, glowing more than usual with her exertion, and struggling to put the pillows back to order.

Aislynn surreptitiously kicked another pillow from the window seat to the floor when Starlit was not looking. She then turned back to the window and sighed as best she could. "You said you had news, Starlit?"

"Oh, yes, Your Glory! Lord Phaeon has come to the Sanctuary!"

"Indeed?" Aislynn said with measured interest. The news certainly had a dreadful element to it that might assist her quest for gloom. She had known Lord Phaeon, Lord of the Argentei, for uncounted years as she matured. He was a fool whose view of truth was far different from that of the Qestardan Fae. He saw only that might and conquest were the destiny of the Seven. He took what he wanted because that was his truth. Aislynn detested him as much for what he stood for as for his insults to her mother, and considered him barely better than the Famadorians no matter what his birthright caste. Still, she could not see how the news affected her. She had nothing to do with the brute. "I can only hope that he leaves, soon, as well."

"Yes, Your Glory," Starlit answered quickly. "And so he has!"

"He came . . . and then he left?" Aislynn considered kicking another pillow to the floor, but then thought better of it as it would only keep the sprite here longer. "My," she said dryly, "that *is* news, indeed."

"Yes, Mistress," Starlit continued, still carefully organizing the pillows, restoring the room to its perfect, pristine state. "The Seeker Dwynwyn has begged an audience with Your Grace to tell you the particular truths of it. Indeed, she awaits your pleasure without should you—"

"What?" Aislynn turned in sudden interest, completely spoiling her calculatedly morose pose. "Dwynwyn is here? Don't just flit about, Starlit! Show her in at once!"

Starlit was so startled that she nearly dropped a pillow on her own. "Of course, Mistress! At once!"

Starlit expertly tossed the final pillow back in its place just as she flashed through the oval of the doorway to the antechamber beyond.

Aislynn stood quickly, smoothing out her delicate nightgown in her excitement. She nearly forgot the dressing coat, hastily snatching it from the back of a nearby fainting couch and tugging it on quickly. Aislynn panicked for a moment when her wings momentarily got caught in the vents at the back of the coat. She managed, however, to free them just before Starlit drifted into the room in as stately a manner as the small sprite could manage. The tall Seeker floated in behind her. Starlit tried to make a proper announcement, but Aislynn would not wait.

"Dwynwyn!" the princess shouted with a laugh. She ran across the room, quickly folding the Seeker in a warm embrace.

"Mistress Aislynn, how good it is to see you." Dwynwyn carefully placed her arms around the young faery in return. "Is this a new pattern in your dressing coat?"

"It is, indeed, Dwynwyn—how very clever of you to notice! I've been ever so excited to show it to you. A Shivash trader brought it last week, and no one here has seen anything like it."

Starlit, interrupted in her introductions and now completely forgotten, flared briefly in her frustration and then drifted back toward the anteroom.

Dwynwyn glanced at the retreating sprite. "Do you think I may have damaged that friendship?"

Aislynn laughed heartily. "Oh, I certainly hope so! Starlit is a good servant, I suppose, but she can be just so . . . chipper."

"Maybe we should be grateful for the cheer while we still can." Dwynwyn's thin smile dimmed slightly at the thought. "Which reminds me; I was told you were up here brooding?"

Aislynn turned and walked them both into the room, her arm still around the Seeker's waist. "I *was* brooding . . . or at least trying to brood. I thought that brooding might lend me a more serious aspect which the courtiers might find interesting."

"I take it you have settled on one particular courtier to torment." Dwynwyn raised a knowing eyebrow.

Aislynn smiled shyly, biting her lower lip. "Yes . . . there is one in particular, as you well know!"

"Deython, of course." Dwynwyn nodded. "How is your Qest-hai friend?"

"Well enough, thank you . . . though not as attentive as I would like."

"He *is* of the second caste, Your Highness," Dwynwyn said evenly. "There is only so much attention he could pay you without causing considerable scandal to you both."

Aislynn pouted. "I know. But I enjoy his attentions all the same, and a little scandal might liven things up around here."

"So you tempt him with your melancholy." Dwynwyn shook her head as she smiled. "And how far into sadness did you find yourself?"

The princess frowned. "Not very far. It is difficult for me to sustain a really good melancholy. Were the truth of my existence more desperate, I might have some cause for depth and a more serious manner. But look about—my life conspires against any true brooding and condemns me to a shallow joy."

"Mistress Aislynn," Dwynwyn said, her eyes turning away from the princess. "The truth of what you suggest may be your undoing. Take care where your heart leads your mind and your words."

"I shall take your advice, Wyn, as always," Aislynn replied, gesturing to the Seeker to sit next to her on an overstuffed couch.

Dwynwyn smiled. "You haven't called me that for a long time, Your Glory."

"Your Glory?" Aislynn smiled. "You used to call me . . . let me see . . . 'Slim,' was it not?"

"Oh, please, Your Glory, that was many years ago!"

"Yes, but not so long that we are no longer friends." The princess once again patted the couch, this time with more insistence. "Please, Wyn—let's be with one another as friends. The reality of our stations may wait until another time."

Dwynwyn sat down next to Aislynn. She looked carefully into the deep green eyes of the young princess. Both of them were about the same age so far as the cycles of the seasons were counted, but Dwynwyn knew she had seen far more truth in the world than her friend. "Truth ages," went the old Fae saying. If this were so, then Dwynwyn was feeling very old in that moment. The burden she carried with her was one which she was loath to share with Aislynn . . . for as the old faery saying went, a shared truth can never be recalled.

Dwynwyn mourned her friend's innocence, for the Seeker would soon be an instrument in its death.

"Where is Cavan?" Aislynn asked brightly.

"What?" Dwynwyn said suddenly, as though waking from a sleep. "Oh, pardon me, Aislynn, my mind was distracted."

"How delightful," the princess exclaimed. "I don't often get to see you perform your powers as a Seeker. Is this how it often is for you? Does your mind leave the present in search of the new truth?"

Dwynwyn smiled. "Yes . . . and no . . . All truth is observed by the Fae, Princess. All truth already exists, so in that sense there are no 'new' truths: only truths we have not yet uncovered. This ability is in all the Fae. The only difference is in the abilities of the Seeker to discover new combinations of truth. We take truths that are known or discovered and put them together in new ways so that we might uncover deeper truths that have previously been hidden. That is where the Seeker excels; by using what is called a second sight to see that truth which had not been seen . . . Are you following this, Princess?"

Aislynn held perfectly still for a moment, her large eyes focused intently on her friend. Then, she said, "No. I don't understand you at all."

Dwynwyn sighed. "Perhaps my words are unable to convey it clearly."

"No! No! I'm sure you said it perfectly." Aislynn patted the Seeker's hand. "I'm just, well, it is a truth for which I am unprepared as yet. Were I prepared, I would understand it."

"Yes, Mistress, that is so." Dwynwyn took the young princess's hand. How cool and smooth her dark skin, Dwynwyn thought. How beautiful she was sitting here in her pampered cage. How Dwynwyn hated what she had to do. "There are other truths which you must understand now, whether you are prepared or not."

"I certainly accept that," Aislynn replied. "So may I ask again, where is Cavan?"

"I have sent him to my home," Dwynwyn replied with the truth—as all Fae are compelled to do. The Fae know nothing but the truth as they observe it. Some truths were greater than others, however, and Dwynwyn could not be distracted by lesser questions. "Your mother has sent me to you. There are truths of which you must be made aware."

Aislynn's green eyes blinked. "If this is the queen's truth, why has she not come to tell me?"

"She would have come herself," Dwynwyn replied directly, "but she believes that I will better be able to answer your questions and convey the full reality to you in a way for which you have been prepared."

It took the better part of the evening to explain it. To the Fae, truth is an absolute. It cannot be summarized or outlined or compacted. Truth required a full accounting in the mind of any Fae. They believed themselves immortal and therefore they had all the time necessary for the full truth—until now.

Dwynwyn recounted to Aislynn every particular relating to the situation, all the while searching for the boundaries of the princess's knowledge. When her own recitation of facts connected with Aislynn's understanding, then the Seeker would move to another aspect of the truth, searching again the boundaries of Aislynn's awareness. From history, legend, reports, and observations, Dwynwyn wove a truth of doom, a truth of fear, and a truth of the unthinkable as though she were working with her bobbin lace.

The last strands of truth were eventually laid. Lord Phaeon had come boldly into the House of Qestardis and demanded the surrender not of the nation alone, but of Aislynn herself to him as the means to unite their kingdoms under his crown.

At last, when her recitation was complete, tears were streaming down Dwynwyn's cheeks. "Now, my dear friend, you should have no trouble finding cause to weep and despair . . . as I weep and despair."

Aislynn looked up. Her face, too, was streaked with tears. "So either I am to be sacrificed to this hideous Phaeon or our entire kingdom is to be torn apart by the dogs of the Famadorians and the dogs of House Argentei?"

"It is the truth plain to all the court of Queen Tatyana," Dwynwyn replied.

"Then I must accept my fate." Aislynn spoke through choking sobs. "I must be ruined. It is destined truth."

"No," Dwynwyn said resolutely. "It cannot be the only truth in the world."

"There is another?" Aislynn asked tearfully.

"I don't know," Dwynwyn replied heavily. "*That* is what I have been called to discover."

Famarin
Gamesmen

Dwynwyn's quarters were on the northern, land side of the Sanctuary above the main gate. The Queen's servants, third caste servitors of the first estate, populated this section of the glorious structure. Maids, butlers, cleaners, servers, washers, dyers, tailors, cooks, chamberlains—in short, anyone who served on the floors of the queen—were all quartered in this section of the Sanctuary. Each felt the privilege of their caste deeply. They honored their ancestors for providing it and they honored their children with its inheritance.

The happy caste of royal servants could look out from the shining crystal panes of their quarters and down on the busy populace of Qestardis that was, in every way, below them. The laborer castes and trade castes of the second and third estates were all of lower rank. The servants looked from their windows and gave thanks that they were not among them. Of course, there were other castes *above* them—scholars, warriors, and a host of castes related to the royal lineage—which all looked down on the servant caste from their higher rooms of the Sanctuary. But to the servants, this was as it should be.

Only the Seekers upset their carefully ordered view of the world beyond the crystal.

Seekers, such few as existed, were included among the serving caste, although with some peculiarity. The abilities of the Seeker for the second sight mysteriously flowered outside of caste. Thus, Seeker talents might suddenly be evidenced in lower castes. When brought to the attention of the court at Qestardis, these rare and prized individuals were tested and, if found with this peculiar gift, elevated often far beyond their former caste stature.

Thus the other servants looked on the Seekers with a great deal of suspicion and not a little envy. Seekers were "out of their place" in the great scheme of the faery gods. It was all unjust and somehow unnatural. So the others of their often new peer caste shunned the Seekers, tolerating them to the letter of royal decree and not a degree further.

Dwynwyn ignored their disdain. It had become to her as a vague but persistent sour smell in one's own house, something bothersome at first but, in time, blending into the background of daily experience. She knew their contempt but no longer registered it in her mind.

So it was that when Dwynwyn alighted on the Grand Servants' Balcony, she took no notice of the scorn tossed her way with such a studied casualness. She crossed the polished marble floor of shaped inlay and down the long curving hall teeming with her fellow faeries in the service of the queen. She spoke to no one, and no one spoke to her. She could not have been more alone had she been at the top of the Star's Throne peaks themselves.

She passed a succession of oval doorways shaped into the ornate wall. Each held a unique pattern coaxed from the wood from which it was formed. At last, she came to a door whose pattern was happily familiar to her. She touched her hand to its surface. The fibers of the wood warmed and twisted at her touch, separating as they pulled back into the framework of the oval.

Dwynwyn stepped quickly inside and gestured at the door for it to close immediately behind her. She just could not bear to explain the condition of her quarters to someone from the housekeeping caste that might happen to pass by her door. One glance around the room assured her that the sight might cause one of those obsessive pixies to faint and die on the spot.

Her quarters were decorated in an early-period bedlam—which is to say, they were not decorated at all. True, the outlines of the original furniture—endowed by the queen—were still discernible to the trained eye. They were nevertheless obscured by an explosion of colors, fabrics, objects, paintings, carvings, scrolls, clothing, bedding, scrawled notes, haphazard stacks of vellum, a menagerie of toys, and, especially, games.

Cavan flew raggedly into the room under a stack of Dwynwyn's clothing. He strained against its weight, puffing his words out in short breaths. "I see . . . that you have . . . have been working."

Dwynwyn winced. This always happened when she was under some pressure to discover a new truth. She always started her search with clean chambers—pristine, in fact—and then it all fell apart as she focused single-mindedly on the application of her skills to her work at truth-seeking.

She sighed. "Yes, I *have* been working. But I'm too troubled to concentrate just now. I need to relax."

"Relax! With all the trouble in the kingdom you want to lie down and—"

Dwynwyn's eyes locked on Cavan with a stare that froze him in midflight.

"It will take a few minutes"—Cavan bobbed again beneath the stack of clothes—"but I can have your bed ready for you."

"No, I'm not tired," Dwynwyn said testily, her gaze going out into the deep night. The city below her had quieted down into sleep. The glow of the city militia drifted through the still streets under her gaze. "I just want to think for a while."

"Thinking *is* work," Cavan huffed, dumping his burden into a large basket in the corner of the room. "How about a game? Something mindless?"

Dwynwyn chuckled. "Mindless games? That would be just fine, Cavan, but just for a while. How about sylan-sil?"

"What?" came the muffled response under yet another pile of clothing bobbing across the room.

"Never mind . . . I'll set up the game," she said as she removed the long mantle of her office from around her shoulders and tossed it onto the floating stack. It dipped downward under the added weight. Cavan groaned in the air but made no other sound.

Dwynwyn grasped several stacks of parchment from off the table in the center of the room and shifted them over to her desk near the window. There actually was no clear space on the desk either, so she simply stacked those papers on top of previous stacks with the mental note that she would need to separate them out again sometime later. In short order, she had cleared the low table as well as the chairs that faced each other across its surface.

"Do you know where I put the game?" she called out to Cavan, as she searched through several wooden cases stacked in one corner.

"I do not!" Cavan replied as he returned to the room. His glow had a decidedly rosy hue to it from his exertions. "How many times have you told me never to disturb your things no matter where you set them?"

"I know. It's just that I thought you might have seen it while you were— Oh, never mind, I've found it." She pulled a large case made of polished rosewood from behind an avalanche of scrolls.

"Wonderful," Cavan groused. "Our kingdom is about to be conquered and I get to stop and be bested by your superior play."

"You never know." Dwynwyn smiled, pulling an inner box from the sleeve of the outer case. "The fates may favor you this time."

"It is your skill that I fear, not the fates." Cavan drifted down through the air and settled onto the chair's cushion opposite the Seeker. "Still, if it will help you rest, then I am happy to oblige."

Dwynwyn opened the hinged outer case completely and laid it flat on the table, revealing the inner playing surface now framed by the sides. Beautifully intricate carvings formed grids and curving lines across its surface in a pleasing array. It was the beauty of the board that had attracted her to the game when she first saw it in a strange little shop in Bay Narrows. The shopkeeper there had told her he had purchased it from a merchant trader from Shivash but that he did not know anything else about its origins. There was something special about it, however, which had attracted her to it. The only problem she had was finding someone willing to play it with her. Playing a game with the royal family would be outside her place. No one of her own caste would have anything to do with her. That left her servant, Cavan, who, she had to admit, was tiring of losing to her so often.

"I'll let you choose your colors," Dwynwyn said politely as she opened the inner case. Four sets of eleven worn stones, each of a different color, lay within. Each was cut into regular facets with different facings, and each facing had a different symbol.

"You *always* let me choose my colors," the sprite replied with a frown.

"After the throw?" Dwynwyn offered.

The sprite's glow increased with his smile. "Now *that's* more like it! I'll take four and three."

"And I'll take all eleven." Dwynwyn smiled. She pulled all eleven of the speckled gray stones from the case. "Are you ready?"

"Just a moment," Cavan said. The small pixie had managed to pull three of the black stones and four of the yellow stones from the case but was having difficulty holding them all at once. "It's just that . . . very well, yes, I am ready."

Dwynwyn nodded. "Ready? . . . *Now!*"

They both tossed the stones into the frame of the board. The tokens bounded about, careening off each other and bouncing inside the frame. In a few moments, each piece had settled to a place on the etched surface. Dwynwyn made a few minor adjustments to their placement, setting them more squarely on the board's markings, then looked up quizzically at the pixie.

Cavan smiled. "I believe I'll take the gray!"

Dwynwyn nodded. "A strong starting position, I'll grant you. Perhaps the fates will be kind to you after all, Cavan."

"Perhaps," the pixie said, his wings fluttering as he came to hover over the board, inspecting it. "But the fates always seem to be a mixed blessing with a humor all their own. They are just as quick to rob victory from a sure bet as they are to grant victory to a lost cause."

Dwynwyn sat back in her chair, considering Cavan's words.

"That is rather profound for a sprite. Have you been of the scholar caste all this time and not told me?"

Cavan smiled as he moved a large piece down a carved line of the board. "Why, no, Seeker! I'm just of the third caste . . . but I'm open to a better offer."

The Seeker chuckled. "That's well and good here, Cavan, but I wouldn't go repeating that outside these rooms. I have enough trouble on my own without having to pull you out of it, too."

"What was it like?" Cavan asked, settling back onto his chair. "I mean before you came here."

Dwynwyn considered her own move on the board. "Oh, I don't know. It's been so long ago, I don't remember very well."

"Well, yes it has but . . . but you changed castes. What were you before?"

"Cavan, I'm sure I've told you this before."

"Perhaps, but I'd like to hear it again."

"Very well. I was of the sixth caste, strictly second estate." Dwynwyn spoke absently, moving two of her smaller stones in response. "My father was a shaper in the Griffith Wood just a short way east of Kien Yanish. Mother was in the trades, too. She was a linen weaver— at least that's what I remember her doing. I don't remember much about her, actually . . . except that she seemed very sad."

"So, what truth leads a girl of the sixth caste from the Griffith Wood to the second caste and Seeker for all Qestardis?" Cavan replied, frowning as he spoke at the results of his opponent's move.

"Strange fates, indeed." Dwynwyn leaned back from the board, gazing out the crystal window once more and into the darkened world beyond. "My gift was obvious at an early age. It was hard on my parents since I obviously was not to inherit their gifts, but they had hopes for me of bettering my life as a Seeker. A Wanderer of the fourth caste, unsanctioned, really, took me on to work passage to Qestardis for the testing. I toured with her for a time. We were performing new combinations in Rivadis when Seeker Polonis first saw me. Do you remember Seeker Polonis?"

"I do," Cavan said, finally making his own moves on the board. "She was unpleasant and rude. I never liked her."

"That's because you never knew her," Dwynwyn replied. "She took me in for the testing, helped me find my inner sight, and taught me the more practical truths of the Fae courts. That is how I came to know Princess Aislynn and her family. Then Polonis was gone and Aislynn's mother ascended the throne at about the same time. Fate does, indeed, deal a mixed blessing to—"

She stopped, staring at the game board.

Cavan looked up. "Seeker?"

Dwynwyn spoke in hushed tones. "The pieces on the board, Cavan, there is something different about them."

The sprite looked carefully at the stones arrayed before him. "No, Seeker . . . they look the same to me."

"They seem to me as though the board itself were all the land of Sine'shai," Dwynwyn said, her eyes narrowing. "The pieces are as people on that land, each poised to find one another."

"They are only stones, Seeker," the pixie asserted.

"This one"—Dwynwyn pointed to a large gray stone with a low caste symbol—"this one is the wingless man I met atop the falls! He journeys across the waters toward his fate. These others"—she pointed to the other side of the board—"they pursue him to his benefit. But these stones drive the creature toward . . ."

"Toward what, Dwynwyn?" Cavan spoke in awe, his eyes wide. "I don't see anything!"

Dwynwyn's finger drifted across the board toward its near left corner. It stopped, pointing toward three red stones, one large with a low caste symbol on its upturned face, and two smaller showing much higher caste designs.

"Toward these," she breathed. "They are driving him toward these."

Dwynwyn abruptly stood up, snatching the stones from the board.

"Perhaps I have been looking for my answer with the wrong eyes," the Seeker said, excitedly looking at the game pieces in her hands. "Perhaps the truth I seek is found not in our world's truth."

"Perhaps, Dwynwyn"—Cavan raised his eyebrows gleefully as he looked at the upset board—"this means that I've finally won a game after all."

Dwynwyn whispered to the large gray stone in her right hand: "What truth do you hold, man with no gift? And what danger are you running toward?"

She gazed long at the red stones in her left hand. One was warm, one was cold, and one of them seemed very familiar to her.

Tragget

I am a sinner.

My soul is harrowed with guilt. I plead for the purifying grace of the dragon's eye. I cry blood-tears at the anguish and torment that awaits me, for I have strayed from the light and my mind wanders in dark and awful places, hidden from the sight of the dragon.

It is not the eye of Vasska that is upon me now. My soul lies under the gaze of an enormous giantess. It is the winged woman! It is her beautiful, terrible eye that looks upon me now as she examines me in silence.

Her beauty is temptation incarnate. The dark, smooth skin torments me with thoughts and desires that are outside my vows. She beckons me away from my faith, from my teachings, from all that is holy and good. She draws me toward her darkness. Her voice is a song of longing more painful in its beauty than my words can give utterance. My prayers beg that I never hear that voice again. My heart cries that I would forfeit my life to hear it only once more.

Vasska protect me! Vasska come to my aid! Dragon of strength and spirit of creation incarnate, do not leave me here alone in my torment!

I stand in the palm of the winged demon-woman's hand. She stands taller than mountains, her glorious head among the clouds of the sky. From her hand, I look down on the face of the world far below. The coasts of the Dragonback and the Chebon Sea stretch toward the sunset, and the lands of my home—of Hrunard—are barely visible through the obscuring haze of distance. It appears to me as though I stand above a map. Yet it is not a map, for I look down on it as though from the tops of the clouds.

Is this how the dragon-gods view the world in their flight? Is this the vision that Vasska carries with him? If so, is this not also a forbidden sight and do I not also blaspheme even as my eyes drink in the wonder of it?

I sojourn in blasphemy. I travel the paths of the damned. Were I not in sin, would I not be mad?

Vasska strengthen me!

I turn in the hand of the woman. There is Vasska! Has he come to me for my deliverance? Has he interceded through my prayers?

There, too, is Mother Edana arrayed in her ceremonial robes. I call out to them, begging them for help, but they do not hear! I confess and beg for absolution, but they do not respond to my cries! I try to run toward them, to make them listen and understand, but the dark, winged demon that holds me has other plans.

Her hand turns slowly over.

I tumble into the air, screaming, and clawing at the rushing wind. I fall through the clouds toward the waters of the Hadran Strait, frantically looking about. Mother Edana tumbles unconcernedly through the air. Even Vasska falls, his wings inert, immobile. The winds of the winged she-demon's breath catch them as they fall. Edana and Vasska tumble in the gale, tossed and buffeted by winds toward the far shores of Hramra. In moments I lose sight of them in the clouds as they fly farther and farther from me.

Am I then damned? Has even Vasska turned his eye from me? Is the power of this demon-woman greater than that of the gods of our world?

Despair clutches at my heart. I do not resist my fate. I fall knowing that I am lost. Why has my faith failed me in my hour of its need? Why has my faith failed me in this terrible place?

Wherein did I sin?

The black waters of the sea rush up toward me. I can now discern the ships of the Vasska fleet, carrying home the harvest of condemned souls from the far reaches of the empire. I fall toward the ships, their tall masts point as daggers toward me in the sky. These deadly toys below me grow larger by the moment.

As I watch, the ship below me groans and contorts. Its railings shift, and the planks of its deck warp horribly. The masts curl back on themselves. The ship is horribly deformed into the face of a man — of _that_ man!

The man that walks in my dreams . . . and now haunts me by day as well. Was I asleep when I saw him by the waterfall? Now again he appears as a contorted ship tossed on rough seas. The ocean waves break against his face, running off at the corners of his eyes like great saltwater tears. The eyes gaze up blankly toward me, the wooden face filled with torment. Its mouth groans open, a black void beyond it. It gapes toward me in a silent scream. My own scream cannot fill the void.

I fall into the maw of the man's wooden face and an eternity of blackness . . .

The Confessions
Bronze Canticles, Tome VI, Folio 3, Leaves 14–16

Tragget awoke with a start, shivering in the darkness of his ornate litter. The torusk beneath him, to which the compartment was mounted, continued to sway gently. The pillows and cushions of the enclosure held him in a comforting embrace but did not alleviate his panic and dread.

The Inquisitor pulled the curtains aside. The salty tang of the shore assailed his senses on the predawn mists. They had journeyed all through the night, rushing to beat the dawn. The darkness was already thinning, however, and they were not yet at their next stop.

Tragget leaned out slightly, hoarsely whispering to the handler who sat on the neck of the torusk just forward of the litter. "Gendrik! How long before we can embark?"

Gendrik turned slightly in his saddle. He was a practiced handler, his long, crooked guide pole held with a steady touch against the torusk's right tusk even as he spoke. "We are making good time, Lord Inquisitor. We shall have our charges on board before the sun breaks." Gendrik turned to face forward. It was not the first time this night that Tragget had asked him this question. "You should rest, my lord. I will wake you when we approach the port. Get some sleep."

Tragget drew back into the litter. Sleep, he thought. I would avoid it if I could. He rubbed his hands across his face, and then pressed them against either side of his forehead. Perhaps, he thought wildly, if I pushed hard enough, these tortured visions would leave me. I could force them out of my mind and be pure and holy once again. I could stop living this nightmare and make everything right, the way it used to be.

But the face still haunted him. He had seen that same face weeks ago, dreaming his wicked dreams in his own quarters deep within the Temple at Vasskhold. It was the vivid images of those dreams that had driven him across the sea to the Dragonback in the first place—visions that led him with unnerving accuracy to a forgotten, unimportant little speck of a town. He remembered wondering at the time just what the face symbolized in his dream. He was sure it was some sort of metaphor or analogy for some other problem that he would find there and solve. That, at least, is what he told himself on each step of the fated journey.

Then, horribly, he had found that the face was not some figment of his fevered dreams but flesh and bone in the waking world. Now he flitted about the image of that face like a moth about a fire, knowing it would destroy him but unable to leave his fascination with it all the same.

There was only one thought that offered him hope. If he *understood* these horrible episodes, he reasoned, then he would no longer *fear* them. Children hide from monsters in the darkness. Shine the light, however, and the shadows vanish, the darkness flees, and the monsters are discovered to exist only in dreams. His monsters *did* live in his dreams—and if he could shine the light of understanding on those, perhaps he could banish them and his sins as well.

It all had something to do with that shadow-man of his nightmares now, somehow, made flesh. So the flame comes with the moth, Tragget thought. This time, the moth will study the flame from safety, and when it is properly understood . . .

. . . Then the flame will be extinguished.

South of the Begoth Rill, the plain sloped in rolling undulations down to the north shore of the Chebon Sea. The South Shore Road wound its way across these gentle hills. It continued on toward the large port of Hadran Head and more interesting destinations farther along on the western coast. The road had been packed and hardened over the years by the travelers, merchants, and their assorted beasts that regularly passed down its familiar path, beating a wide furrow into the ground.

Gendrik knew that road well, but he knew other roads, too. In the gray predawn, he wrapped the crooked end of his long pole around one of the tusks of the torusk and pushed it. The torusk obliged by turning its head and lumbering off the highway down a barely discernible trail. The other torusks of the caravan followed suit, their great clawed feet churning up dust in the darkness. They moved in this dim cloud through the darkness, down to the sea.

At the back of a long finger cove nestled a forgotten and unimportant backwater known as Stoneport. The fishing was poor here and the waters were generally exposed too directly to the sea to be much of a safe harbor.

Disadvantage, however, can be turned to profit, given the right circumstances. Because local business was poor, the town residents were appreciative of whatever money came their way. They were grateful enough for the largesse of the church to keep their mouths conveniently shut.

Moreover, the bay may have been exposed, but it was also deep—deep enough for great Pir ships to anchor unnoticed by anyone who might care.

Tragget watched the town as they approached. The shacks and hovels had all dutifully shuttered their windows and closed their doors. No one cared to know what was passing by their meager homes. No doubt they told themselves it would be a grievous sin for good members of the Pir Drakonis to question the questioners of the church. Besides, the great rust-colored ships with their folded wing sails would be gone soon enough and the town would be all the richer for its turning a righteous blind eye.

The muddy road wound down to a large clearing east of the fishing docks. Tragget saw the fishing boats of the village already waiting at the shore, each manned by crew from the Pir ship. Tragget smiled. He had heard about the efficiency of the Pir Elar, the secret operatives of the Kardis order, but rarely got to the outlying areas to see it function firsthand. The villagers apparently did not mind having their boats assist the Elar in their work—most likely for an added fee. In turn, so far as the church was concerned, the fishermen more or less were maintaining boats the Elar only occasionally needed for their own purposes. It was a wonderful arrangement, benefiting everyone . . .

Except the Elect, of course. Tragget's smile waned at the thought. Yes, except for the Elect.

The monks of his own order alighted from their litters at the end of the column. They had kept a watchful eye on their charges throughout the night. For the last hour or so, the prisoners had gotten quiet, lulled by the motion of the torusks and drained of hope. Now, with the change of rhythm, they were slowly becoming active again. The monks of the Inquisition would need to watch them more closely now.

"Would Your Lordship wish to board now?" Gendrik asked from his perch.

Tragget remained in his litter, peering furtively out from between its curtains at the activity in the caravan. "No, Gendrik, thank you."

"But, my lord, the jollyboat is alongside the pier and awaits your pleasure."

"No, Gendrik!" Tragget's voice carried more impatience than he intended. He brought it under control at once. "No, thank you. I'll board in good time."

"Yes, my lord."

One by one, the torusks were led down into the water at the shore. The individual cages of the Elect were in this manner brought next to the gunnels of the shallow-draft fishing boats. Each was then grappled and pulled roughly onto the deck, its occupants tumbled one on top of the other. They cried out, rousing the others in their cages to start shouting and screaming as well.

There were no concerned ears to hear them.

Tragget watched from the security of his litter as each of the cages was pulled aboard. Soon one of the ships' deck was crammed with cages. The Aboth-Marei pilot stood in the pilot's cage on the ship's prow and called out into the waters below. The placid surface of the water roiled suddenly with movement as an enormous merdrak serpent—a dragon of the deep—butted against the ship's bow from beneath and swung it out into the harbor. In a few minutes its place was taken by another waiting ship and the process was repeated.

Where was the man? Tragget thought nervously. Where was that face? Was he dreaming yesterday or was it real? No, it *had* to be real. He had seen him twice and . . .

There he was. Tall and lanky, his hair was disheveled and his face was red. He still wore that ridiculous rose-colored doublet. They had managed to get him back into the wicker cage and had even posted a series of monks in shifts to watch him. No one had figured out how he could have escaped from the cage—yet another mystery in a man who held far too many for Tragget's peace of mind.

Peace of mind, he thought. Maybe that's what I seek.

He watched intently as the young man's cage was pushed sideways onto the next boat. He did not take his eyes off it, afraid that it might vanish somehow with the morning mist. Other cages were dragged onto the deck as well, but Tragget took no notice of them. His eye was fixed on the man. He watched until the little fishing boat made its way out to the larger, anchored ship. He watched until all the cages had been hoisted up onto the deck. He watched longer still without seeing anything but the haunting face of the nightmare man made real.

He saw in his mind a moth carrying a flame.

He saw the ship swallowing him in its distorted maw.

He closed his eyes. He had seen enough.

"Gendrik," Tragget called out with a heavy voice, "I believe I would like to go aboard now."

Dark Waters

Galen lay miserably in the narrow bunk that was too short for him, held fast to the bunk rail, and closed his eyes.

He had never traveled on the water before. In all his life next to the sea, he had never ventured out on any of the boats that daily set sail from his fishing town. His travels had always been limited to what distances his feet traversed from time to time. Galen was a creature of the land with no desire to sample any other means of transport.

Now, deep within the hold of the massive ship, he was surrounded by a world completely alien to him. The motion of the ship through the long swells of the sea beyond was disorienting. The sounds all around him were strange and ominous. More than that, however, was the closed, stifling darkness of the hold where he lay clinging to his bunk. Closing his eyes seemed to help for a time—but only for a time.

He was not alone in his discomfort. The ranks of narrow wooden bunks, which filled the long deck up to its low ceiling, were often crammed with two or three people each. Galen's fragile stomach, however, had convinced others who might have tried to push their way into his bunk to stay well clear of him.

Sick as he was, he still had enough presence of mind to count himself among the lucky ones. Those who could not find a bunk were forced to stand bent over under the uncomfortably low ceiling, there not being sufficient room vertically to stand or horizontally to sit. The poor ventilation made everyone else's discomfort a shared experience. Many were vomiting loudly, the acidic smell rolling through the hold and inspiring others to follow in due course.

Galen opened his eyes. Keeping them shut for too long made him feel distinctly as though the entire ship was about to turn over in the water and retch them into the sea in disgust.

He craned his head around and pressed his face up toward the ventilation grate above the bent crowd next to his bunk, as close to the free air as he could get. He could see several grates beyond, passing through successive decks. With each swing of the boat, he caught a glimpse of the deepening clouds overhead. It would rain soon. He would be soaked where he lay, but better to be wet than to give up what precious air drifted down occasionally through the grate.

Someone fell back against the bunk, jostling it badly. Galen growled angrily into the face of the offending man, who just shrugged and nodded behind him. Only then did he notice the yelling and wailing. A madman was lashing out at the crowd around him, screaming for them to get out of his way though there was no space for them to give him.

"Back away, you sons of darkness! Back!"

The packed crowd surged once more away from his blows. The force rippled through the mass of people, shoving them hard against the surrounding bunks, bulkheads, and hull. Galen's head bounced painfully against the overhead.

"Demons! Demons! Get back from me or I shall use your own powers against you!"

Galen could see only flashes of the man's face through the crowd. He was bald except for a ring of disheveled white hair circling from ear to ear. His nose was large and hooked on the end. Heavy brows extended over his feverishly bright blue eyes.

The packed crowd around him swayed back and forth, trying to get out of the bald man's way. Some in the crowd shouted at him. Some laughed hysterically.

Only one person made a move to stop him, however. Galen could not quite make out who it was from his bunk, but their hands kept reaching for the crazed man, trying to calm and comfort him. They were long hands, with delicate, smudged fingers.

A woman's hands.

"Drag me down into the pit, will you?" the man screamed, his voice raspy with overuse. "I won't go with you, I tell you! I won't go!"

Suddenly the old man lashed out, knocking the woman senseless as she fell back.

The crowd pulled violently away from the dangerous berserk lunatic, the sudden press spilling everyone from Galen's bunk down among the crowd. Galen fought his way to his feet and was at once crushed against a bunk support behind him. Someone has to stop him, he thought as the air was pressed painfully out of his lungs, before this fool kills us all.

He quickly pushed himself through the intervening captives. Quite all of a sudden, he found himself in a small clearing amid the mass of people. The balding man, his breath ragged, was standing directly in front of him.

Having reached the man so quickly, Galen suddenly realized he did not know what to do.

The maniac turned his face upward toward Galen, his bright eyes trying to burn through the smithy's soul.

Galen held up his hands, palms open.

The madman blinked.

"Please, no one wants to hurt you," Galen said more calmly than he felt. "I'll help you . . . Just . . . be calm and it will be all right."

Tears welled up in the lunatic's eyes. "Master?"

Galen glanced around. No, he realized, the man was indeed talking to him. "Sorry . . . I . . ."

The features of the bald man softened as he suddenly reached forward, clasping Galen's hand in his own bony grasp. "You've come for me? You've come to my aid at last?"

"Sir? Please, I don't . . ."

The man collapsed in front of Galen, racked with sobs. He clung to Galen with his head bowed, his hot tears running down over their clasped hands.

Galen found himself moved by the man's obvious pain. He knelt down, reaching out with his free hand, trying to help the man back to his feet. But the man only sobbed the louder, wailing either in pain or in joy Galen could not tell.

Another hand reached out. The long, smudged fingers Galen recognized, but the deep voice was new to him.

"Maddoc," she said quietly. "Maddoc, I am here."

Maddoc looked up. There was a rapture on his face, a sublime peace that struck Galen as idiotic. "Rhea? Is that you, my beloved?"

"It is," Rhea responded. Galen turned toward the voice. She was a short woman with a broad, pleasant face. Her light hair was cut short—an unusual style for women anywhere in the Dragonback. Her wide-spaced eyes gazed intently down on Maddoc, warily studying every move the man made. "I am here."

"Rhea!" Maddoc's eyes filled once more with tears. "He is here, Rhea! He is come! I have found him at last!"

The woman glanced at Galen for a moment. "Yes, my dearest. You have found him. Now that you have found him, you must get some rest."

Carefully, Rhea peeled the madman's fingers from their viselike grip on Galen's hand.

"Yes," Maddoc replied. "Yes, I would like some rest."

"Rest from the troubles of this world?" Rhea asked.

"Yes." Maddoc smiled foolishly. "Rest from the troubles of this world."

Rhea turned toward Galen. "Sir, please help me. He must lie down somewhere soon. If we can find him a place to rest, he won't trouble anyone again tonight."

Galen looked around. His stomach was lurching and he longed once more to crawl back into his bunk and hold tightly to the cool wood, but he could not see anywhere to lay the tired old man. "He can have my . . . my bunk, if he . . . that is, if he wants . . ."

There was someone else already in his bunk. A stocky, overweight man with thinning hair was just settling between the rough side rails.

"Excuse me, sir," Galen offered.

The man in his bunk gave no response.

"Pardon me, sir," Galen said louder, assuming that the man must not have heard him properly.

The man did not stir.

Galen, annoyed, tapped him forcefully on the shoulder. "Please move, sir! You are in my bunk."

The man turned his round, flabby face toward Galen, his quivering cheeks already flush with indignation. "Do you know who you are talking to? Go away before you find yourself in serious trouble!"

Galen glowered. "You are in my bunk—please get out!"

"I am the guildmaster of Shardandelve!" the man screamed, his face purple with rage. "This is *my* bunk now—mine by right!"

Galen stared at him for a moment, only then realizing that the madness in this ship took many forms. He turned to Rhea, who was struggling to support the swaying Maddoc. "Any suggestions?"

"Toss him overboard," Rhea replied with a chill smile, "if you think it will help. I've got to lay Maddoc down before he has another episode."

Galen quickly sized up the guildmaster of Shardandelve, shrugged, and then grabbed him by his tunic.

"Hey! What do you think you're—?"

"Sorry," Galen said. "I'm afraid that you're in the wrong bunk."

The blacksmith pulled the heavy man clear of the bunk's frame in a single motion.

"My lady." Galen sighed. "Will this do?"

Rhea nodded as she helped Maddoc slowly toward the narrow bed.

The rain cascaded down through the ten-foot-square overhead cargo grating well into the night, but Galen did not mind. The light cascade felt like it washed his soul as he sat under the grate. Most of the people on board considered him to be insane anyway, so his behavior was easily dismissed by the others in the hold. They believed themselves to have enough sense left to stay as dry as possible.

Galen, on the other hand, cherished the space it afforded him and the air that it brought into his lungs. He preferred being wet to choking and suffocating.

Rhea sat on the edge of the bunk next to Maddoc. The wild man rested now with a peaceful look on his face, his breath slow and easy. For a long while, however, Rhea's sad eyes were not watching her sleeping charge, but the rain-soaked Galen sitting with his back propped against a wooden brace.

She spoke to him so quietly that she had to repeat herself.

"Who *are* you?"

Galen turned toward her, his hair wet and matted. He chuckled. "*That* is a good question, lady."

"Rhea," she responded.

"Excuse me?"

"Rhea . . . just call me Rhea," she said quietly, "and my husband's name here is Maddoc."

Galen turned his face up toward the falling drops.

The woman would not give up on conversation. "So, who are you?"

"You can call me Galen, Rhea."

The woman thought about that for a moment. "Galen, is it? It doesn't seem like much of a name."

Galen smiled wearily into the dripping water. "Sorry . . . maybe I'm not that much of a man."

Rhea frowned, then moved carefully closer to Galen as she spoke. "Oh, I doubt that. I doubt that sincerely. Maddoc is, as you can see, quite ill. He believes everyone he meets to be a dream—all phantom demons who are trying to keep him from some blessed other world."

"Sounds nice." Galen spoke with complete lack of interest.

"Yes, it does," Rhea agreed, kneeling as close to Galen now as she could without being directly beneath the drizzle. "This other world of his sounds very nice, indeed." She paused for a moment, then whispered, "Have you been there?"

Galen turned to look at her as though she, too, were as mad as

Maddoc. Then he shook his head and turned away. There was a slightly patronizing tone in his voice when he answered, "No, Rhea, I've never been to Maddoc's 'other world'—"

"That's really odd," Rhea cut him off, "because he has seen you there."

Galen turned. "What?"

Rhea smiled as much to herself as to Galen. "Why, yes, didn't you know? Maddoc told me that he saw you."

"Well, I don't recall ever having seen *him* in this world, let alone any other, so could you please just leave me—"

"So who is this dark woman with the wings that you meet so often at the falls?"

Galen glared at the woman.

"Ah, so Maddoc *has* seen you before!"

Galen looked away. "I don't . . . I don't know what you're talking about!"

"Oh, of course you don't," Rhea said in thinly veiled sarcasm. "But you see, if you *were* the rose-colored man who spoke with the winged woman, then we might well be able to help each other."

"Rhea . . . Lady, look—all I want is to get back home."

"And I want to help you find your home," Rhea said with sudden determination. "Look, there is more to this so-called madness than is seen in Vasska's eye, if you know what I mean. It's true that some of the people who are here truly are insane, but most of the people who are of the Election all exhibit extraordinary symptoms with common themes and delusions."

Galen raised his head. "What the *drak* are you talking about?"

"Think about it," Rhea continued. "It is like a plague of some sort but without a discernible cause. None of the symptoms are life-threatening or even directly harmful to anyone else. Some of these people may have even demonstrated extraordinary abilities—yet they are included in the Election and are crated off into the dark heart of Hrunard and never heard from again."

Galen snorted. "So you're saying the Election is some sort of illness?"

"No, that's not it at all." Rhea shook her head. "We've been studying this for a long time. We felt sure that the people in the dream represented *real* individuals. You're the first one we've met that confirmed that this experience is one shared with others. There must be a common reason behind— Have I said something funny?"

Galen sighed through his smile. "No, not really . . . I'm just listening to the observations of a madwoman."

"I am not one of you," Rhea snapped.

"Not one—of *us?*" Galen sneered.

"No, not . . . That's not what I meant!"

Galen turned toward the woman, his dripping face moving uncomfortably close to hers. "Then just what do you mean, *Rhea?* What could you possibly say to me that would bring me one *step* closer to going home, *Rhea?*"

The woman did not budge an inch. "That if we work together we might have a chance of understanding *why* the Election takes place at all. If we understand that . . . we can use that knowledge to free ourselves—you, Maddoc, and me."

Galen's eyes narrowed. "How?"

"I . . . I don't know yet . . ."

Galen sat back against the post in disgust.

". . . But it has to be better than dying separately!" Rhea continued. "There is something amazing happening here . . . to nearly all of these people, to Maddoc and to you. If we could only figure out—"

"Hold a moment." Galen held up his hand. "Maddoc and me? What about you?"

Rhea stopped for a moment, her jaw working, but the words did not seem to want to come out.

"You . . . you didn't see me by the falls, did you?"

Rhea looked away as she spoke. "I was with Maddoc . . . I've been with him since . . ."

Galen turned his gaze steadily on her now. "Yes, but you *weren't* with him by the falls. *You* didn't see the winged woman, did you?"

Rhea locked her eyes with his gaze and answered him directly. "No, I did not."

"You've never been there, have you?"

"No," she said stubbornly. "I have not."

"Because you are *not* insane, are you?" Galen intoned.

"No," she whispered hoarsely.

"By the Claw, lady!" Galen could not decide whether to be horrified or giddy at the thought. "You faked your own Election? Are you out of your—"

"Out of my mind?" Rhea countered. "Wouldn't being out of my mind *qualify* me for the Election?"

Galen laughed, trying to think through the twisted logic of her statement. "Why?"

"Love." She shrugged the word as though it were as much a burden as a blessing. As Rhea spoke, she turned her gaze back toward the man still asleep on the hard bunk. Her voice filled with a quiet warmth that reminded Galen too much of his own loss. "Maddoc is my . . . well, *used* to be my husband. We've been trying to avoid the Election for years, but these last few months Maddoc's condition has worsened. He was caught in this Election and my heart had no choice but to follow him. You can understand that, can't you? Even if we were no longer married in the eyes of— Are you all right?"

Galen's eyes filled with tears, barely noticeable among the rivulets of rain still cascading down from the grate above. "So much had happened, so quickly that I . . . that I had forgotten," he said with choked words. "The Elect of Vasska have no ties to the world of the flesh. They are freed from all mortal bonds. All contracts and marriages are dissolved in the eyes of the Pir Drakonis."

"Yes, Galen," Rhea said, all the while still holding her husband's hand. "To the world, we are all dead."

14

Bayfast

The storm swept down from the northwest, a Teeth-weeper, as the local shipmasters termed them. They were not uncommon in the latter months of the year, an old and blustery friend that visited itself down from the northern climes of the Shandisic Ocean. It whined through the stays of the trade ships searching for safe passage through the Dragon Teeth Isles. It ruffled the waves of the Northreach Sea into frothy caps. It then vented its fury through the Hadran Strait before finally spreading itself thin on the Chebon Sea. The Teeth-weepers were always the harbingers of the chill part of the fall season. In time, as the seasons ripened, the winds would shift and the Teeth-weepers would be replaced by the White Gales of winter. But for now, the gentler winds of Vasska's realm held sway.

The trader *Fairwind's Fortune* drove hard through the water under the great towering clouds that sped low over the sea. The crew had shortened her sail so as not to overtask the rigging. Speed was her friend, as with any trade ship, but too much wind could cripple her if handled improperly. As it was, the wind sang through the back stays, driving the prow into the waves with determination.

The wind was at Berkita's back, too. She stood on the forecastle, heedless of the occasional spray that bounded up around her. Her hair flicked around her face as she stood in the gale, her lined robe pulled tightly about her. Her attention was not on the ship beneath, nor the wind that sang about her, but on the far shore of a land she had never known except in stories.

Galen was there, she knew. Somewhere before her, walking paths she had not yet put a foot to, seeing sights she could not yet see, but still under the same sky and the same sun. That thought warmed her faintly.

The wind at her back drove her ever closer to him, and that was all that mattered. Despite the spray that surged up around her as the prow broke against each ocean swell, their progress felt agonizingly slow. She would use force of will alone to move the ship faster if she could. The sea and the winds seemed to side with her, yet there were limits to their gifts.

So all she could do was pray—pray to the spirit of Vasska across this same sea for the deliverance of her husband from this cruel mistake. Her mouth whispered the words into the wind, asking that it carry her heart's desire to Vasska's will, pleading to see her husband once again, begging to hold him once more.

"Kindly wind er is," rumbled the voice beside her.

Berkita shook with a start. In her fervent prayer she had not noticed the fur-encased dwarf clomping up to stand next to her. Her voice belied her surprise. "Cephas! Oh, I am so sorry. I . . . I didn't . . ."

"Me spirit by yer words ne'er troubled, Lady Arvad," the dwarf intoned. His hand gripped the deck railing like a vise. His feet were set wide upon the deck. "Hkoolien's breath push us to Hrunard er is. Favored of the earth-gods Lady Arvad er is! Two suns pass and Cephas tastes no land. Know ye er is, Lady Arvad?"

Berkita peered into the horizon. "No, Cephas, I do not and the captain has tired of my asking. You might ask him for both of us where—"

Cephas harrumphed. "Ask the captain er I did! Captain asked back, 'What need a blind dwarf to know er is! Blind dwarf already lost. Know er is and *still* lost er is!'"

Bertika turned toward him with disgust. "He spoke to you like that? We've paid our passage in full, he has no right to—"

"Aye, no right er is," Cephas said, putting his hands up, trying to calm his companion down. "The Khalan ways er strangers to the light er is. Humans fear dark. Hide from it. The Khalan clans from the dark er is. Humans fear and hurt what they know not." The dwarf sniffed the wind as the boat broke another wave. "Still, we be closing to Father Ground. Lady Arvad be making port by evening tide er is."

"Are you sure?" Berkita asked, straining forward against the wet rail, searching the horizon in the distance.

The dwarf smiled from behind the wind-whipped fur of his hooded cloak. "Captain the blindest er is. Cephas sees better er he with different eyes." He tapped his forefinger to the bridge of his nose. "Cephas knows the smell of Father Ground. That smell calls to me bones. We be in port er sundown, Lady Arvad."

"And then?" Berkita asked anxiously.

"And then"—the dwarf turned his head, seeming to look at her through the heavy binding tied over his eyes—"then the hunt begins er is."

Bayfast stood silhouetted against the thinning twilight. Berkita, whose farthest travels from her home door had been the forty miles to Hadran Head, was at once in awe and dismay at the port they approached.

Quite suddenly, the captain issued a flurry of orders through his first mate. The *Fairwind's Fortune* slowed well beyond the outer coral reef that bounded the inner harbor. To Berkita, it seemed as though the ship had stopped altogether, though they were simply moving at an agonizingly cautious pace. Stones and structures had been added to the reef to create a formidable seawall. There appeared to be only one passage through to the harbor beyond, and it was marked by two watchtowers on either side of the harbor entrance. At the tops of these towers signal fires constantly burned in great cauldrons.

"The Pillars of Rhamas!" Berkita breathed in awe. "They are magnificent!"

Several merchant seamen working the foredeck overheard her remark. In a moment they were winking and nudging each other.

Cephas sputtered, "Lady Arvad . . ."

"I've heard the stories, of course, but I never thought that I would actually *see* them! Imagine the cursed fleets of the Fallen Empire, sailing out from between these very towers to do battle against Vasska's sea serpents!"

The merchant seamen were barely able to contain their laughter.

Cephas rumbled under his breath. "Them not the Pillars of Rhamas er is."

"What?" Berkita's face, too, flushed.

Cephas mistakenly thought Berkita had not heard him. He spoke louder, but this only added to the unintended merriment of the crew. "These towers er not the Pillars of Rhamas. Them the harbor lights er is."

"Oh," Berkita said with embarrassed quiet.

"No need to fret er is. Them cauldrons a history of their own er is. Them were salvage from Azhelanthas . . . ruins er is far a-south. Part of yer self-same Old Empire once er were. Forged by dwarves er were. Beautiful, too, I wager. Cephas smells the rust from them. Metalwork long corroded in the salt-spray, Cephas guesses. Shame to lose the past er is."

Berkita only nodded. She felt ashamed and awkward. How much more of the world do I not know? she wondered.

It was not the known world that worried her. She had grown up next to her father's forge and had always believed that something of the qualities of his steel had become part of her; strong, tempered, sharp-edged, and with just barely enough flex so as not to break.

No, it was not the known, but the unknown, that frightened her, and the world she was entering was a dark mystery. She gazed across the expansive harbor toward the large port city. The spindly towers capped with domes seemed so foreign and forbidding, and Berkita felt herself become small and insignificant. How would she ever find Galen when the world was so wide and she was so small?

The ship moved with slow care into the harbor, heightening Berkita's anxiousness. She tried desperately to maintain her calm, telling herself over and over that slow or not, the time would pass and she would be walking the same shores as her husband. She knew that their marriage was dissolved so far as the church was concerned, but she could not bring herself to think of her beloved any other way.

She was surprised, therefore, when the ship suddenly dropped anchor well away from the harbor shoreline. "Cephas, have we stopped?"

"Aye, so er is!" Cephas said with dwarven finality. He began gathering up a pair of sacks he had set on the deck at his feet.

"But . . . why are they stopping? Why aren't they going in to shore?"

"Aye, calm ye, Lady!" Cephas said as he slung both sacks over his shoulder. "Look ye the quay. Tell Cephas what er is!"

"The quay?"

"Aye, Cephas eyes ye be. What see er is?"

"Well, there are a lot of boats . . . ships, really. I've never seen so many in all my life. There's everything from fishing boats to trade ships."

"Any serpent ships?" Cephas demanded.

"I don't know. I've never seen one before and—"

"They be odd to your eyes," Cephas interrupted. He, too, was anxious. "Back-swept prows er is . . . raked masts, too. They be moving but no sails er is."

Berkita spoke quickly. "I see them! They're everywhere! How do they move without sails?"

"The Pir monks speak merdrak serpent. Serpents wear the hull like hat. Push through seas er is. Faster than winds. Where er is?"

"Well"—Berkita squinted into the sun setting beyond the harbor city—"I think there are about eight ships tied to the wharf. In fact, they're the only ships moored there."

"Aye," Cephas grunted. "Business good for the Pir er is."

"I see three more looking as though they are waiting their own turn at dock. They just move back and forth."

Cephas chuckled. "The serpents don't like to wait. Restless they be! Any others?"

"There are five more leaving the harbor now," she said. "They're nearly out to sea."

Cephas grunted, then turned, bent over with the sacks on his back. "Then time is expensive, Lady Arvad. Them ships unloading the Elect er is. If Galen among them, good chance we to free him."

"If?" Berkita snapped, following the dwarf down the ladder. "What do you mean if?"

"Bayfast closest port to Benyn er is. Most likely Galen be getting the land under his feet here." He stretched his free hand before him. Berkita reached out, taking it and placing it on the railing. Cephas nodded his thanks, then began feeling his way down the ladder to the middeck below as he spoke. "Other-thought, this closest port we make from Hadran Head. Best chance to get to Galen before Mithanlas . . . Ah, harbor boat alongside er is, Lady? Cephas already packed your sack so we go er Bayfast now!"

He was about to lower himself over the side of the boat. Berkita saw at once, however, that the small craft was not yet below the ladder. She hastily reached forward and pulled the heavily laden dwarf back aboard.

"Not yet, Cephas," she said insistently. "What did you mean by *if* Galen's among them?"

The dwarf sighed, then placed his free hand atop Berkita's still gripping his shoulder. Her small fingers were buried beneath his huge hand. "Many ports of Vasska on the shores of Hrunard er is. Bayfast one only. Lankstead Lee er is. Vestuvis, Southport, too, er is. Maybe others north shore Cephas never walked. Serpent ships know them all. Cephas know them not."

"Then if he isn't here," Berkita asked in a low voice, "where do we look for him?"

Cephas raised his face. "The sun no longer warms me back. See you the failing light of your day, Lady? Beyond Bayfast, beyond the Hynton Hills, there where the sun sleeps, Mithanlas er is."

The dwarf turned his blind, bandaged eyes toward the sun he could not see.

"There where the sun dies go all the Elected dead of Vasska. We live among the dead . . . there we find Galen er is!"

15

Hrunard

W here are we?" Rhea breathed.

Galen shook his head. He had no idea.

He had anxiously watched the sun pass over the cargo grate twice more before the serpent ship slowed, its motion shifting to a more pronounced roll. The hull then lurched slightly and a rumbling trumpet from below shook the keel, setting off a new round of fearful wails from the terrified prisoners around him. Then the grate had opened and the Pir monks, each armed with a gnarled staff, had beckoned them topside. Galen followed several others of the Elect up onto the deck, with Rhea helping Maddoc just behind him.

The brightness of the harbor surprised him. It took a moment for his eyes to adjust to the light. When at last they did, they were looking on a land he had never known.

The reef arched around the turquoise waters of the bay. It certainly looked smaller than Mirren Bay, and everything was out of place. The land itself was low, with only a slight rise from the shoreline that circled around first west and then north. On that side ran a long stretch of brilliantly white beach. There were a few smaller ships in the harbor, their brigantine sails flashing under the midday sun.

Several other serpent ships were also there, moving gently about the bay as they awaited their own turn at the docks.

There were more pressing matters, however.

There were double cages on the deck, with a harness slung between them exactly like the ones that had brought them to the ship in Stoneport. The Pir monks herded the Elect in line just in front of Galen through the openings in the torusk cages. As each cage was filled, the stevedores heaved it aloft using the braced yardarms of the ship and cables as a hoist. One by one, the filled cages were then lowered over the side to the backs of other waiting torusks. Beyond the ship's railing, a ragged line of torusks wound its way down the long wharf to which the ship was moored. Where the quay met the shore, a town of squat buildings sprawled outward. The bright colors of the shops and homes were faded and badly weathered from a perpetual battle between the inhabitants and the sea. Beyond the town, there was a gentle rise that was crested by the main road. On that road, Galen saw a stream of torusks, each burdened with a full cage, winding southward. Where their destination lay, however, was difficult to see. The billowing clouds that still raced ashore from the north blended into a deep purple and dark horizon to the south.

Galen shivered as he moved forward on uncertain legs. Each step is farther from home, he thought desperately. The road I travel has no end and each step is farther from my home.

With an anguished howl, he suddenly bolted toward the bay-side railing of the ship. He had to get away—anywhere and anyhow. Blind with fear, he plunged toward the starboard side, the open waters of the bay beckoning him on.

He did not even see the Pir monk standing between him and the ship's railing. The startled monk, lulled inattentive by the repetition of the caging, was unprepared for his onslaught. Galen ran squarely into him, sending him sprawling to the deck.

Galen's feet tangled momentarily among the monk's robes, but he did not lose his balance. All he could think of was getting off the ship, away from the Elect, and somehow fleeing for home. He gripped the railing with both hands, pulling himself forward over the bulwark.

Light and pain exploded in his mind.

I stare up. The masts of the ship sway above me. There is uneasiness about everything, as though I have somehow forgotten part of my life.

Far above me, the winged woman drifts amid the ship's rigging. She gazes down at me with a smile that breaks my heart. I long for her and am at once ashamed for the longing.

"Galen! You are here!"

Groggily, I turn my head. I am lying with my back against the middeck of the serpent ship. The cages are still here but the monks, the Elect, and Rhea are all gone.

All except Maddoc, who stands on the deck, leaning casually back against one of the cages.

"What a delight to see you here!" Maddoc smiles graciously. "Can you stay?"

"I . . . I don't think so," I say. My head is throbbing. Now I can hear another voice from far away. It calls to me from the shadows, summoning me back to another place.

"Oh, I am disappointed," Maddoc says, shaking his head. He sits down on a capstan. "I would so very much like to get to know you. I think we have a lot in common, Master, you and I."

The throbbing in my head is getting worse. The clouds overhead are slowing down as though the world around us were a spindle toy winding down just before it falls. I desperately want to close my eyes, but not yet. I point upward. "Can you . . . do you see . . ."

"The winged woman? Of course I can see her!" Maddoc looks up casually, his arms crossed over his chest as he considers the dark beauty floating above us. "Indeed, I would think she would be rather difficult to miss."

I struggle to remember something that drifts just beyond my thoughts. It is something important—something I want to do here—but all I can think of is this winged woman. I glance up toward her again. Her large, shining eyes gaze back down at me, seeming to look through my soul. I swallow hard. "Well, at least she isn't speaking today. I can never make up my mind whether her voice is too painful or too beautiful to endure."

"Perhaps she simply has nothing to say," Maddoc says. "But even without her glorious voice, she is beautiful to look at, isn't she?"

"Yes," I say carefully, remembering suddenly what I wanted to ask this madman in my dreams. "Beautiful as Rhea."

Maddoc looks back at me sadly, then turns away. "No . . . no one was as beautiful as Rhea."

"She is trying to help you, Maddoc." My words are quiet and reassuring.

Maddoc draws in a painful, shuddering breath. His face is a mask of tortured pain. "I would have thought that you of all people would understand! She's lost to me! I see her shadows and I know what might have been."

"She is trying to understand," I say, but the look on his face betrays his disbelief. I must try some other way to reach him. I must try to help him. Perhaps I am trying to help myself, so I change the direction of my words. "I am trying to understand. Help me to understand as you would have helped Rhea."

"My dear, sweet Rhea!" Maddoc sighs. "No one was as beautiful as Rhea. How I miss her!"

The voices in the back of my head are more insistent now. The pain in my head becomes an overwhelming noise. It washes over me, engulfing me . . .

BOOK OF GALEN
BRONZE CANTICLES, TOME IV, FOLIO 1, LEAF 8

"Galen! Galen, wake up!"

Galen opened his eyes and groaned. Now he could sense the gentle sway of the woven cages on the backs of the torusks plodding along beneath them. "We're back in the cages."

"Yes we are," Rhea said as she sat back, her words tinged with sarcasm. "Although some of us managed to get into the cage without being clubbed senseless. How is your head?"

Galen tentatively touched the back of his head. There was a rather large knob under his hair that had not been there before. He hoped it was smaller than it felt. His hand came away sticky with his own blood. "I believe my head will remain attached to the rest of me, more is the pity for the pain."

"Well, at least you're still here," Rhea replied, sitting back on her ankles.

Galen lay curled up uncomfortably in the corner where he had apparently been dropped. He struggled for a moment, trying to get to his feet, but the throbbing in his head decided otherwise. He slipped back down and looked around.

The cage was more crowded than it had been in Stoneport. Several of its occupants were once more raving loudly. Others rocked themselves back and forth. One young woman was tearing methodically at her clothing while she sang quietly to herself. Beyond the woven reeds, he could see undulating grasslands drifting quickly past under the long strides of the torusks. He could still smell the sea, but that was quickly giving way to the aromas of earth and sun. It was still morning. By the position of the sun he guessed they were moving roughly south and perhaps a little toward the west. He could not make out the beginning or the end of the line of torusks making their way down the heavily trodden path beneath them. He had absolutely no idea what awaited him down the road that stretched ahead. Galen looked at her. "Yes, I'm here . . . wherever that is."

Rhea shrugged. "I read some of the signs in town as we were passing through. The port was someplace called 'Fehran' somewhere on the northern coast of Hrunard, I think. Have you ever heard of it?"

"No." Galen shook his head carefully, lest the motion add to the considerable pain he already felt. "I mean, I know about Hrunard and all, but, well . . ."

"I know." Rhea smiled wearily. "We all know about the Empire of Vasska. We sat in the pews and listened with rapt attention to the legends of this distant land. It was no more real to us than our own dreams and nightmares."

"Only now we're here"—Galen sighed—"in the land of dreams."

"Or nightmares."

"Yes, nightmares," Galen agreed.

Rhea moved slightly closer to him. "Do you have dreams, Galen of Benyn?"

He looked up at her sharply.

"Yes, Galen, I have to know." Rhea's voice was insistent, quietly demanding. "Do you have nightmares?"

"Sometimes, but everyone has nightmares!"

"But these are special nightmares, aren't they, Galen? Special dreams?" Rhea's eyes were bright, desperate. "You see things and go places that you have no knowledge of otherwise. Sometimes you meet people and speak with them in your dreams."

"Yes . . . no . . ."

"Tell me, did you dream earlier today?" Rhea moved closer to him, her eyes holding his gaze in thrall. "After your desperate flight and the Pir monk dropped you onto the ship's deck like a sack of wet wheat, did you dream?"

"Yes." Galen's voice sounded heavy in his ears.

"And did you meet anyone there?"

"Please." Galen shook. "Just leave me alone!"

"No. Just tell me." Rhea's voice was quiet but would not let him go. "I'm trying to help you. There is a mystery in all this and I think I can help you if you'll just help me. So tell me: did you speak to anyone in your dream?"

"Yes."

"Who?"

"Maddoc . . . your husband."

"Ah, and what did he say to you?"

"Say? It was only a dream . . ."

"Of course, but what did he *say?*"

"He said . . . he said he was glad to see me there."

"And what did you say to him?"

"What? Are you insane?"

"That's supposed to be why I'm here." Rhea smiled again but an edge remained in her voice. "Humor a crazy woman for a moment. What did you say to him?"

"I don't . . . I told him that I was trying to understand what was happening to us . . . just as you were trying to understand."

Rhea looked away thoughtfully. "And what else did he say?"

"He said that he missed you . . . that you were more beautiful than—"

"Than the winged woman?"

Galen blinked. His chest felt heavy and he found it momentarily difficult to breathe. "What? How . . . how do you know about what we said? What do you know about—"

"The winged woman? Dark-skinned, with two blue streaks in her long white hair?"

"By the Claw!" Galen gulped.

"Maddoc," Rhea said smugly. "He told me."

"*He* told you?!"

"He was surprised to see you there, wasn't he? He's seen the winged woman, too, although only since meeting you, as nearly as I can tell. You were both on the deck of the ship. The winged woman was above you."

"Yes," Galen said. "She was drifting up among the masts and the rigging. And Maddoc *did* say you were more beautiful than the winged woman."

Rhea blushed faintly. "Thank you. It's . . . it's nice to hear him think of me that way."

Galen glanced over at Maddoc. He stood swaying slightly, his eyes fixed in a distant stare. He was humming softly to himself. "He really does love you."

"Yes, I believe he does." Rhea nodded, her thoughts in a different place and time. Then she returned to the present. "Did you see the hooded monk?"

"What?"

"In the dream. Maddoc told me he saw a hooded monk standing behind you in the dream. Did you see him?"

Tragget sat leaning forward out of the front of his litter, the curtains thrown open. His gaze longingly swept southward with the clouds riding the prevailing winds. There, in the distance, he made out the forest-cloaked foothills of the Mithlan Range. Beyond that rose the purpled outline of three towering mountain peaks. They were the Lords of Mithlan, and he smiled to see them. At their base, though he could not see it yet, lay the great city of Vasskhold, still gloriously being purged and purified of its former, ancient blasphemy. It was the center of the Pir Vasska, the heart of his religion and the pinnacle of authority in all things under Vasska's eye.

It was his home.

The road unwound slowly beneath him. The area was not as familiar to him as the eastern ports and northeastern territories of the Hrunard. He would have expected to have made landfall in either Bayfast or Lankstead Lee as was customary, but finding this vision made flesh dictated a little more urgency in his return.

The thought of Galen made Tragget uncomfortable, but the fact that he had found him demanded a quicker return route home, which was the only good aspect of his present business.

They had traveled westward to Fehran across the trade winds rather than south to the standard ports. Fehran usually handled all the ships ferrying the Elect from the Dragon Teeth Isles and the northwestern edge of the Dragonback. However, it had the advantage of being the shortest land route to Vasskhold, and the quickest way for him to bring a close to this sorry mystery.

By noon the caravan had reached Jonsbridge, a town that was little more than a way station servicing the caravans. Tragget was grateful they did not remain there long. The Lords of Mithlan called him, and he was getting impatient.

The afternoon wound down as the mountains grew larger and larger in the Inquisitor's eyes. They passed into the Northwatch Wood where the towering trees hid the Lords from his eyes for a time, but he felt no concern. These were the woods in which he had played as a boy. They were familiar to him, and he could feel himself nearly home.

The long caravan of torusks crested a ridge where the trees of Northwatch gave way to a long meadow. Tragget leaned forward, excited once more.

"Stop!" he cried. "Stop at once!"

The guide for his torusk obeyed, touching the great beast gently behind the forelegs. The torusk quickly moved off the flattened dirt road and halted among the tall grasses, out of the way of the continuous caravan behind them.

Tragget stepped to the small platform at the front of his litter, stood up, and smiled.

The Lords of Mithlan towered before him: great granite mountains thrust out of the earth, standing spectacularly before him in the setting sun. Brideslace Falls tumbled from a crevasse between the two lesser peaks on the north, cascading down a cliff face. It fed the River Indunae, the lifeblood of his city.

Vasskhold shined in the reddening light of sunset. To the ancients, it had been known as Mithanlas, a city that ruled the northern provinces of the Rhamas Empire with an oppressive hand. It had nearly been destroyed by Vasska in his righteous anger, but instead was spared in Vasska's mercy to become his throne and footstool. The seven rings of the city walls shone in the dying light of day. At the nexus of the rings, the Temple of Vasska reached skyward with its magnificent towers and central dome larger than any in the known world.

Tragget smiled. Soon he would learn all he needed to know. Soon he would fulfill every wish his mother had demanded of him. Then, when he had done all he promised he would do, Galen's life would end and Tragget's could begin. Soon the nightmare would be over.

Mithanlas

Galen's face pressed against the woven reeds of the cage.

He had never imagined such a place.

The long caravan of torusk beasts lumbered quickly down the ancient highway. The outlying farms gave way to a wide avenue over four cart lengths wide, running straight as an arrow's flight eastward toward the mountains. Here and there, patches of broken paving stones pushed up through the hard trampled dirt of the roadbed. Those stones, Galen thought with wonder, were probably as old as the ancient Rhamas Empire itself—laid there no doubt by craftsmen over four hundred years dead. First homes, then the commerce shops of guild craftsmen, marketplaces, and tradesmen lined the magnificent avenue. Their architecture shared one common theme despite all its diversity: all the buildings adopted, adapted, and utilized the ancient ruins that remained standing as part of their structure. Galen watched as they passed an obelisk column, its ornate and intricate lettering still vivid after all these centuries, now used to support the corner of the ramshackle cooper's shop.

"Weep for the spirits of the lost."

Galen turned toward Rhea. "What?"

"That carved column." Rhea nodded toward the shop. "The

130

ancients of Rhamas believed that their spirits lived on in the memories of those they left behind. They carved their great deeds into stones so that the memory of the departed spirits would never be lost." Rhea shook her head as she sighed. "But in the end, the city was lost and most everyone perished. What great deeds did that obelisk once herald, Galen? Are the honored spirits of the dead lost now that their glory is being used to hold up the corner of an apprentice tradesman's shack?"

Galen looked at her curiously. "You *know* this place?"

"I *am* something of a scholar . . . or at least my husband is," she replied. Then she smiled, pointing ahead of the torusk. "But I dare say even you could recognize that."

Galen turned to look forward along the length of the torusk's back.

He caught his breath.

A long curving wall rose above the tops of the buildings. The machicolations of the parapet, an impossible fifty feet above the level of the ground, were broken in most places but still recognizable. The northern part of the wall was fallen completely, its gigantic stones pulled down and crushed into a small mountain of rubble. Farther to the north he could see the rampart rise again just before joining a tall tower. Another curving rampart arched still farther beyond the tower, before it, too, was partially collapsed.

"They came from out of the setting sun."

Rhea and Galen turned sharply at the sound of Maddoc's quiet voice. The old man gripped the reeds of their cage fiercely. Tears were streaming down his face.

"Can you not see them, Galen? Are your eyes so closed? Mithanlas stood alone. The Beautiful, some called it . . . others, the City of the Seven Circles. She was the last, however. The last of the ancient cities to stand against the dragons. Rhamas was no more. Her warrior legions were no more." Maddoc turned suddenly, his eyes focused far off, as though gazing at a different time. He pointed down the avenue toward the walls. "The sun blinded the sentries on watch that evening. The dragons were upon them quickly, but not before the alarm was sounded."

He looked wildly up and down the avenue. "They screamed and ran for the gates to the inner circles of the walled city, but the gates were already closed. Their homes were already ablaze under the dragons' breath, the smoke from the ruins extinguishing the sun before it set."

Galen stared out on the busy street. Merchants made their way past the caravan, never looking up at the faces of the Elect. No one gave any sign of the horror and blood that once ran down this street. If Rhea was right, then the dead had truly been forgotten.

The great wall was much closer now. Galen could see that enormous scaffolding now stood against it. Stone guild craftsmen swarmed over the structure, pulling great stones up out of the rubble beneath and reshaping and fitting them to repair the wall. Even Galen's untrained eye could see where the old construction ended and the new repairs began. The new work lacked the perfect symmetry and precision of the ancient craft.

The torusks' progression brought them between the towers flanking Mithanlas's main outer gate. Immense statues had once stood before each of the towers. They had been pulled down, their parts scattered or carved into other uses. Only the broken legs remained to identify the spot where once they had looked down on the avenue as a symbol of power and dominion.

A dark shadow fell over the travelers as they passed into the tunnel between the towers. The massive gates of the city stood open on either side, their wood black with oil and age.

"Here!" Maddoc pointed at the base of the gates as they passed through. "Right here thousands perished, caught between the conflagration of the dragons and the pitiless guardians of the inner circles."

Galen shuddered. He could hear the screams of the dead in the shrieking wheels of a passing trader's cart. There was a damp cold here that seemed to reach into his soul. Death clung to this place.

Red light bathed him as their torusk emerged once more under the evening sky. Rows of kneeling men carved in stone lined the avenue now. Most were shattered to rubble, but those that remained intact seemed to bow toward them in homage. Beyond them, a field of ruins stretched back toward the broken outer wall. Grasses and brush choked the fallen structures. Yet even through the obscuring weeds and rubble, now and then, Galen glimpsed the delicate art of a craftsman now centuries dead.

The ancient streets of Mithanlas were sliding past with every long, deliberate step of the torusk caravan, yet Maddoc's words summoned a different vision into Galen's mind. Galen could almost hear the thronging people fleeing back in panic among those labyrinthine roads and see the ancient architecture standing for one last moment before it fell to the dragons' onslaught.

"The ramparts were of no avail. The dragons would not be denied. For three days they clawed at the wall . . . them and the army they led. In the end the second circle was breached . . . just there"—Maddoc jabbed his finger forward—"and the armies streamed into the open streets beyond."

Galen shook himself, trying to pull free of the images that Maddoc's words were calling into his mind. He tried to concentrate on the here and now—on the ramshackle shops and buildings that were encroaching on the devastation of the ruins. The new construction was a sprawling chaos of immediate need, designed for no purpose higher than the next sale, profit, or meal.

"They were the 'Dragon-Talkers,' the People of the Dragon as they fashioned themselves, and before them the guardians fell back in panic to the towers of the Seventh Circle. It was too late . . . the city was lost and with it all the ancient ways." A tear coursed down Maddoc's cheek. "Mithanlas . . . the Beautiful."

Galen turned to follow Maddoc's weepy gaze. Down the straight avenue, past the ramshackle buildings and the never-ending torusk caravan, he could now make out the inner wall of the Seventh Circle. Nine towers—towers that he had thought of only as legends when he was growing up—rose shining in the setting sunlight, with a single great tower of the Temple dwarfing them all. They were the glory of the ancient city, captured intact in the siege four centuries before.

"One among the Dragonkings claimed it as his spoils. From that day it became the place from which he ruled. The 'Pir'—the people—became his subjects, and from that time he has ruled from this place of shame and death."

"Vasskhold!" Galen breathed, shaken to his soul.

Even as he spoke the word, a great shadow crossed the sun behind him.

Galen looked up . . . and was shattered.

The leathery wings were a reddish blackness against the red-orange brightness of the clouds. They scooped the air in long, sweeping arcs, pulling the huge mass of the creature through the air in pulsing thrusts. It was impossible to tell the size of the behemoth at first, for there was nothing near enough by which to gauge its distance. Yet its wings must have spanned over a hundred feet, judging by the dust from the street and ruins that each downward thrust whirled into the air. The barbed tail was fanned out in its flight, trailing the creature's body in undulating waves. Its shadow rippled across the ruins of the city.

"Vasska!" Maddoc yelled, shaking his fist at the creature as it passed overhead. "Damn you!"

Instinctively, Galen fell back against the cage. It was Vasska, the holy center of his religion—the dreaded and terrible Dragonking of Hrunard—and the god of his world. The words of the Pir monks had suddenly been made flesh before his eyes.

Galen was too awestruck to speak, too terrified to scream, and too astonished to look away.

Vasska took no notice of such small attentions. The immense dragon soared over the city, pulling itself into a wheeling turn around the central Temple tower. Its horned and bristling head craned around, inspecting the Temple. The spiral of its flight tightened and it rushed upward, its great clawed appendages extended toward the mounts at the top of the Temple tower. There, after a furious beating of its leathery wings, Vasska perched in the failing light of day, surveying the prize city below as it had through countless sunsets for nearly four centuries.

Next to him, Galen was dimly aware that Maddoc had continued to rail against the sky.

"Damn you for what you have stolen! Damn you for my life!"

Visions of Smoke

Encompassed by the nine towers with their banners flying in the evening breeze, the center of Vasskhold looked much as it had during the ancient rule of the Mad Emperors. The broad Avenue of Tears passed through the Broken Gates—the only name anyone could remember for the passage. Pilgrims would choke this passage each day, emerging from the gates in a river until they came to the Pentigal. In reality, it was the intersection of three roads, rather than the five the name implied, but no one questioned the juncture's imperious nature, however, as it was the true crossroads of Vasska's rule. Here all roads in Hrunard were said to end—at the very foot of the Temple of Vasska.

Pilgrims would stand for long moments before the still reflecting pool, lost in awe. The mirror image in the water seemed to elongate those blackened spires that remained towering above them. The toppled spires and shattered stone gave testament to the fall of the city four hundred years before. The damage, however, did not detract from the magnificence of the central keep, the soaring heart of the city.

Nor would the damage be too long-lived. Scaffolding stood against the Temple's surface. Nearly three hundred pairs of hands, a mixture of Pir craftsmen and devout pilgrims, each day struggled to lift the broken stones from the base of the structure back into their former positions—or into positions better suited to the Temple's new purpose. With as much speed as the stoneworkers could manage, the ancient keep was being reshaped in the image of the Pir Drakonis.

These same pilgrims would then walk between two great colossi. These ancient statues once represented the images of Thon and Kel, the brothers of legend who had forged the city. With hammer and chisel, however, the Pir Drakonis had eradicated them: their heads had been reshaped into two of the aspects of Vasska. The dragon heads looked down at the pilgrims from atop the bodies of men now long- and, so far as the pilgrims were concerned, gladly forgotten.

Within the Temple doors, the pilgrims were once again struck by the majesty of the building itself. The main entrance brought them into the first of four naves: enormous open spaces of worship that towered overhead to intricate arches of incredible workmanship.

At the transept, the nexus of the four naves, stood the Iconograph. It was a massive iron structure, nearly sixty feet in height, representing all the different aspects of Vasska peering outward from its center axis. All the history of the Pir Drakonis was said to be represented in its intricate workings. Great oak beams radiated from its base. The pilgrims would each wait enraptured for their solemn turn at the great spokes, to push the Iconograph in its constant revolutions, to whisper their prayers and supplications to the Dragonking, and to keep the eye of Vasska on all parts of his domain at once.

Far above the Iconograph, part of the ceiling was missing, a casualty of that war so long ago, but it had been reworked with long arches. These met directly over the transept, forming a partially completed dome. It was the central feature of all Kath-Drakonis throughout Hrunard. The Vasska Dome, though not yet completed, promised to be the greatest and most magnificent of them all.

Through the glass and still-empty panes overhead, the pilgrims' eyes could rise even farther to the top of Kel's Keep, a tower which, even missing a full quarter of its original height, still inspired tears in the true believers. Every pilgrim knew that tower as the home of Vasska and its portal into the mortal realms.

Still they would come and weep for joy as they pushed against the smooth oaken beams and turned the Iconograph as it rumbled in its eternal revolutions.

To them, this was holy ground.

Tragget passed quickly by the pilgrims, giving them little heed as they struggled against one another to get out of his way. An Inquisitor of the Pir was not someone to be hindered. They separated before him as he walked purposefully through the first grand nave. He took little notice of the magnificent building or its inspiring surroundings. The prayers of pilgrims were of no interest to him. His purposes were his own—as was warranted by his office.

He smiled to himself momentarily. No doubt the pilgrims thought he wanted a turn at the wheel in another example of the Pir clergy stepping to the head of any line. Let them think what they will, he thought as he turned right and quickly walked to the side of the nave.

Two Pir monks who stood watch parted quickly at his approach. The doorway they guarded was invisible to any untrained eye, crafted as it was to blend into the intricate architecture of the nave itself. He stepped quickly through the opening, closing it immediately behind him.

His mind took little notice of the wide landing of the spiral staircase he had trod numerous times before. The stairs spiraling up to his right were old friends. He instinctively knew the halls, chambers, rooms, and spaces to which they led overhead. But they were not his destination yet. He turned to his left and descended the steps.

He passed two more similar landings before following the exit of the third. The rumblings of the Iconograph overhead had actually increased the farther down he walked. Now the squealing sound grew louder with his every step down the hall. Somewhere in the back of his mind he was aware of the arrow slits staggered on either side of the wall—and the eyes that were watching him from the darkness behind them. It was of no concern to him; it was not his death that they sought.

The iron door at the end of the hall had no latch, for it could not be opened from this side. Tragget did not lessen his stride, for he knew the unseen eyes would take care of it for him. Indeed, as he approached, the iron door screeched as it opened wide.

The deep rumbling sound assaulted him through the open doorway. In the center of the room, the iron shaft from the Iconograph above rotated in its mountings. A large wooden wheel was attached to the shaft, its thick vertical pegs meshing with those of a vertically mounted wheel. Behind this a more intricate collection of wheels, meshed pegs, and broad leather bands swung in purposeful motion.

"Pir Mondrath!" Tragget shouted. It was impossible to be heard otherwise in the room. "My scribe gave me instructions to report here at once. The Lady's instructions were—"

"The Lady is below," Mondrath returned, his voice booming through the thunder in the room. "She said you were to join her. I've brought the cage up. You may descend at your pleasure!"

"Descend? No one is allowed below except the High Priestess—"

"Actually, Lord Inquisitor, lots of people go down," Mondrath replied in his booming voice. "It's just that the High Priestess is the only one who ever comes back *up!*"

"You're sure she asked that I join her below?" Tragget responded. He was shivering despite the stifling heat in the room.

"Yes, Lord Inquisitor! She was most emphatic!"

"Then let's get this over with."

"What?" Mondrath shouted, putting a hand to his ear.

"See you shortly!" Tragget shouted.

"We'll see!" Mondrath shouted back with a wicked smile. He pointed to an archway past the screeching wooden cogs, then stepped over to the maze of cogs and pulleys.

Tragget walked down a short arched hall into the adjoining room. A flaming brazier illuminated an ironreed cage suspended by a thick rope over a roughly chiseled opening in the floor. The rope passed up through a smaller hole in the ceiling. Tragget snatched a torch from an iron framework and lit it in the brazier. He then quickly stepped through the open side of the cage, latched the latticework door behind him, stuck the lit end of the torch out through the ironreed, and held tightly to the woven bars with his free hand.

Mondrath glanced down the hall, gave Tragget a nod, and then pulled a large wooden lever. The Inquisitor heard the squealing of the leather belts against wood pulleys as the cage began its descent toward the heart of the beast.

The beast? he thought darkly. Yes, the Temple of Vasska was something of a beast after all and not unlike the Dragonking himself. The Temple was the center of the faith. It was toward his great tower that all Hrunard turned, from beyond the visible horizon, in their prayers and recitations. The exterior was at once magnificent, awe-inspiring, and terrible in its colossal size. In all the public places, it was alluring, compelling, and powerful.

But get too close—get down into its veins—and you find just how cold its heart really is. The stained, rough-hewn walls of the lower corridors lacked any of the pretenses to glory or beauty that one might find above. There was a palpable blackness that flowed through its corridors that thickened with each step. Get to its heart, Tragget knew, and you find mystery more frightening than any children's tale. It was the beating heart of that chill secret that had sustained the Pir over the centuries.

It was the same mystery that drew Tragget into the darkest reaches beneath the Temple.

Smoky torch in hand, he dropped past labyrinthine halls. The cage's shaft was carved straight down through the ancient halls of the original tower. He passed the levels where long-dead priests once spent their days in worship of the forgotten Rhamasian gods. He left behind him the halls that once quartered the Mithanlas army in their last desperate attempt to hold the city. He descended past untold rows of cells in the dungeon, now gaping open in testament both to their ancient use and their current abandonment. Spirits of the long-dead seemed to linger here. He left them all behind . . . his focus on a destination that descended below them all.

The shaft plunged ever downward. Soon he passed even the lowest depths of the old tower, into the carved rock of the mountain roots themselves. A chill radiated from the nearby walls. They were slick and glistened in his torchlight, their hewn surfaces glazed over in leached limestone and sediment from occasional cracks on either side.

The shaft at last broke through the ceiling of a cavern—one last antechamber to cross. The cage slowed perceptibly as it neared the bottom. Mondrath was good at his job. It came to a stop just a foot above the cavern floor. Another iron brazier, like the one above, burned to one side of the shaft, and beyond it Tragget could see a slick staircase ascending into the darkness. In former times that long and treacherous path would have been the only means of reaching this place. It was a path he hoped never to have to take . . . and at the same time he was fearful that he would not have the opportunity to take it at all. To climb the fearful distance he had just descended would have been torturous, but few there were who entered this place that lived long enough to face that prospect.

In any event, he knew his path lay in the opposite direction.

Tragget remembered his training as a Talker. It was one of the Rules of Five, the primary tenets of the Dragon-Talkers, never to approach a cavern with light. He snuffed his torch in a sand trough next to the stairs, then set it carefully by the brazier. Then, reluctantly, he took a breath and turned around.

His eyes slowly grew accustomed to the darkness and shapes began to emerge against the dim red light coming from the opening before him. The stalactites and stalagmites rimming the cave brought to his mind the image of razor teeth. The glazed stone flooring seemed to be a slick tongue arching slightly down toward the dark gullet at the back. It was like walking into the mouth of a dragon, he thought. A premonition, perhaps, for those who were brought here with more finality of purpose—and for whom a torch to ascend would not be needed.

He stepped gingerly toward the gullet at the back of the antechamber. He could see already the steady red light beyond.

Down the long throat, he thought. Down to the heart of the beast.

He emerged into a colossal cavern. The narrow passage opened onto a great peninsula of stone, jutting out over a black and unplumbed abyss. At the end of the peninsula, however, lay a large, flat expanse atop a pillar of stone. Four columns of red light shone upward, shuttered behind iron housings. Silhouetted against this light, Tragget could see the back of the throne. It seemed dwarfed by the enormity of the space around it.

The Throne of the Seer. Edana's throne.

He stepped quickly across the crest of intervening stone. No matter how carefully he trod, his booted footfalls echoed loudly against the distant walls.

A shadowed hand extended from the throne, signaling him to stop.

Tragget obeyed at once. He tried not to breathe.

The arm signaled him to continue.

Tragget moved forward once more, this time with far more care. At last, he stood next to the throne.

Edana sat calmly, her eyes almost sleepy in her repose. She gazed out between the dim, illuminated beams.

"It is all right, son," she said calmly. "Vasska is nearly asleep."

"You should never call me that . . ."

"Who is there to hear?" Edana chuckled as she gestured into the darkness. "Where else could you call me mother?"

Tragget looked down. He could not take his eyes away from the horror sleeping across the gulf before them. "P- please, you *know* that we can't—"

"No? How about just 'Mom' then, eh?" Edana chortled.

The mammoth form of Vasska, Dragonking of Hrunard, lay in an immense hollow of rock atop a vast stone pillar. Its curled body lay entirely in shadow, beneath the level of the shuttered fires. It was a terrible darkness against darkness: a palpable horror that lurked just beyond Tragget's ability to see. The Inquisitor was gripped by the ridiculous desire to open wide one of the shuttered lamps and throw a stark beam on this shadowy, lurking menace, but he knew better than to give in to it. The light was not meant to shine on the dragon, it was meant to illuminate other things.

He had seen Vasska before—but never this close.

"You sent for me . . . M-m-mother?" Tragget spoke quietly, his mouth suddenly dry.

"Ah, now isn't that much better?" Edana replied. Her voice was far away, as though she were distracted by other thoughts. "Mother and son: just as though we were real people with real, little lives. Yes, I sent for you. Vasska is nearly asleep. Then we can begin."

"High Priestess—"

Edana raised her finger.

"M-mother . . . it is forbidden for me to even—"

"I will determine what is forbidden, son." Edana smiled slightly. "You *are* a Dragon-Talker, are you not? I trained you myself. I would think you would appreciate the opportunity to practice the art on an actual dragon. Besides, I thought you should be here to read the smoke tonight."

"I may be a Talker . . . b-but I am not a Visionary," Tragget said as he shuddered involuntarily. He could not seem to control his stuttering. "I d-do not know the art."

Edana glanced up at him. "I think you may not need much training tonight, my boy. The smoke has been most— But wait! It is starting!"

Tragget's eyes remained fixed on the black mass below. The darkness shifted perceptibly. The dim form of the immense dragon shrugged to the hollow sound of scales scraping against the rock. So mammoth was the beast that Tragget, in the dim ambient light of the cavern, could not make out where it ended and the darkness of the abyss began.

"There!" whispered Edana. "See!"

Smoke curled upward from the shifting blackness, wisps emitted from the dragon's nostrils as it slept. It wrapped around itself in the stillness of the cavern, twisting and turning, separating and recombining. It writhed like a living thing.

Tragget swallowed. The dreamsmoke of the dragons. The first of the Dragon-Talkers had discovered its prophetic qualities more than four centuries earlier. Since that distant time, it remained the hidden heart of the Pir Drakonis's power.

It was the darkest and most closely guarded secret of the Pir Inquisitas—a secret which, though he had known about it, he had never witnessed.

"Watch carefully, boy," Edana murmured. "Watch and learn."

The smoke wove in and out of itself, rising higher into the cavern above. In moments, the curls and eddies drifted into the upturned light of the hooded fires, exposed in sharp illumination against the blackness beyond.

The smoke twisted in on itself as though from some unseen current of air.

Tragget caught his breath. His words were but a breath. "A man!"

"Yes." Edana smiled thinly. "The man I seek. The man who has appeared in the smoke each week since Fivemonth. And his clothing, what do you notice?"

Tragget squinted at the shifting smoke. "A commoner . . . no, a fool. He wears a fool's cap."

"A symbol for a liar," Edana corrected. "He is a liar . . . a keeper of secrets . . . a pretender."

The smoke broke into two figures.

"Who . . . who is that?" Tragget's words nearly caught in his throat.

"That is you," Edana said smoothly. "See? The figure wears robes that are too large for him. It is you."

"I don't . . . I don't want to see any more," Tragget said as calmly as he could. He knew the color had drained from his face.

"Do not fear the dreamsmoke, child." Edana's words were as much a command as an assurance. "There is more concerning you."

Tragget heard a second, hearty exhalation from the dragon. A wide fan of smoke arched upward into the light. Demons danced among the eddies, then dissolved. Warriors congealed, only to die and dissipate in battle. There was a winged woman . . .

Then there was Vasska. The fan of smoke formed into the likeness of the great dragon, arching above the two figures. The ephemeral wings spread wide in the red upturned light. The head condensed atop a curling neck of smoke. It craned down menacingly over the two smoky figures, its jaw hanging wide as though to eat them.

The fool figure reached out for the robed figure. It held a long, smoky knife over its head, ready to plunge it into the figure of the smoke-dragon. At the last moment, however, the robed figure turned. It reached out with its hand, plunging it into the chest of the fool, tearing out the fool's heart. The fool shriveled up, its own smoke drawn suddenly into the robed figure.

The robed figure then stood alone beneath the great smoke-dragon. Its momentary arms drifted upward as though reaching for the beast. The dragon figure, looming above, suddenly collapsed downward, its smoke twisting around the robed figure and dissipating completely at its feet.

Vasska, still shrouded in the darkness below, snorted.

Tragget suddenly realized he was shaking.

"The smoke of dragons never lies," Edana said simply and quietly.

The dark mass below them slowly unwound from its curled position. Great leathery wings stretched upward into the red light. Tragget could see the scarred holes from past battles sharply illuminated. Higher and higher they rose until Tragget felt sure they would fall forward and crush him.

Then, with agonizing slowness, the long neck craned up into the light. The spiked head of the dragon shook over them. As its mouth yawned wide, Tragget knew that he had been mistaken: Vasska's maw was much larger than the antechamber cavern.

The Inquisitor could not move.

The dragon twisted its head downward. Its wings beat twice to steady it, whipping a sudden gale across the area of the throne.

Tragget blinked against the sudden storm of dust.

The dragon spoke as quietly as it could, but the cavern shook under its voice.

The sounds were so foreign to human ears that it took training just to recognize them as a form of speech. The sound was not conveyed just from the voice box of the dragon but also from the sounds it made by shifting its scales, the peculiar clacking of its claws, the sucking or blowing sounds of liquid pressed between the tongue and the palate.

Yet it was not just the challenge of the horrific sounds of the dragon speech that made communication so difficult, as only the Dragon-Talkers knew.

Dragons thought in completely different terms than humans. Many of the preoccupations of humanity—life, death, love, and wealth—were completely unfathomable to dragonkind. So different were their lines of thought and reasoning that neither dragons nor humans considered the other to actually be thinking creatures at all—until the Dragon-Talkers found their common ground.

Dragons understood greed, power, survival, and pride.

"Edana! Portend dreamsmoke Vasska now wager Satinka outcome future query?"

The wager! Tragget had understood! Vasska wanted to know about the outcome of his bet with Satinka, the dragon-queen from the west. It was their wager that was to be decided next. The loser would be forced to mate. As dragons only mate when driven to do so, it seemed only reasonable that Vasska would be curious about the outcome.

Edana stood up from the throne; she spoke with difficulty. The human voice box is a remarkable instrument, but some of the sounds were physically beyond her race. Still, she was well practiced, and Vasska had long ago gotten used to her terrible accent.

"Vasska Lord! Portend dreamsmoke tell I. Sighting flight dragons two!" Edana rasped. *"Sky single. Field wet-red blood human Conquest Vasska blinded bright . . . dragon Satinka humbled low blinded bright."*

Tragget's eyes widened. He understood Edana's words all too well.

Vasska was a Dragonking, descended from the sky, and a creator of the world.

The High Priestess was lying to their god.

Demons

The sound of the doors closing behind them was still echoing through the upper gallery when, at last, Tragget spoke.

"You lied," he said simply.

He had kept silent all through Edana's voluminous recitation of visions and portents to the dragon towering before them. None of it had anything to do with what he had witnessed in the dreamsmoke. When the towering creature seemed at last satisfied with Edana's depiction, it had settled back down into the darkness. Edana had then turned and gestured for the young Inquisitor to follow. He had maintained his silence during their entire traverse of the cavern, the ride back up in the wicker lift, and throughout their long walk past the naves and into the ceremonial hall.

Now, entering the upper galleries of the Temple and the private domain of the High Priestess, he spoke.

"You lied . . . to the maker of worlds?"

"I most certainly did not." Edana spoke with mock petulance, amused by the young man's concern. She turned, walking with confidence down the hall. She assumed the sharp and easy manner of a cat playing with a mouse it has just caught. "I told Vasska a true vision. Indeed, it was a vision interpretation from just the other day. I just did not tell him about *this* particular vision, is all."

Tragget followed her, their footfalls echoing across the polished floors, rattling between the long sequences of arched alcoves running down into the distance. The ornate stonework in the frieze carved into the ceiling looked down on them with seeming interest. Tragget almost thought the eyes of the figures were following them down the hall, and not for the first time. Perhaps it was just the nearness of the Aboths that almost certainly were hovering nearby, unseen and unheard. They saw everything. They heard everything.

Tragget's hands quivered under the long sleeves of his robes as he quietly spoke once more. "But the vision . . . I saw it . . . you saw it . . ."

"Yes, of course I saw it, Tragget!" Edana snapped as they neared the end of the hall. "Master your nerves, will you? You are the Lord Inquisitor of the Pir, not some simpering pilgrim whelp. It's about time you learned something about your position in the world and the responsibilities that go with it!"

"Yes, Our Lady," Tragget said quietly. Yet his hands still shook when he reached out to open the large door at the end of the hall.

Edana eyed him critically as he stood holding the door for her, and then she stepped through. Tragget followed, carefully closing the door behind them both.

The sitting room was spacious and ornately decorated. The coffered ceiling overhead was ornamented by a beautiful fresco of the sky. A large fireplace filled nearly the entire opposite wall. The other doorways led to Edana's private quarters.

Most of the pieces about the room were antique Mithanlas furnishings that had somehow found their way into the High Priestess's private collection. Here and there, however, were things from more distant lands beyond the boundaries of Hrunard: a dwarven helm said to come from the mountains beyond the west, a pair of ancient, shining tapestries from the south beyond the Desolation, and three charts looted from a derelict Indraholm corsair depicting the coasts of lands that not even the knowledge of all the captains of the Pir merchant fleets could place. Each of these unexplained items Edana had shown to Tragget on countless occasions, telling him how she had come by them and speculating for hours on their meaning and the lands from which they had come. The pieces both frightened and fascinated Tragget, for they spoke of a world beyond the boundaries that caged his life. He longed for the freedom they represented, and feared it even more.

"Sit down, Tragget," Edana said, gesturing to a large chair opposite her own as she seated herself before the fire. "It is time that you exercised your office."

"I have always done so, Lady, in whatever task or calling the Pir have required," Tragget responded as he sat.

"But never in an office with so great a capacity. Never with so much required of you, I think," Edana returned. She gazed into the fire next to them, its flames reflected in her eyes as she spoke. "I have met with the Pentach Conclave. They have a question which, I believe, you alone can answer for us."

"The Pentach convened? Why was I not informed?"

"We did not wish to attract attention to ourselves." Edana shook her head. "Five Dragon-Talkers, each one the voice for a different dragon, all getting together at once? No one knew; especially not the dragons."

Tragget leaned forward in his chair. "The Pentach has not seen fit to convene since the Council of Harquan. That was over three hundred years ago. Why now?"

Edana turned back to him, her eyes flickering with the firelight. "You know something of the history of the Festival, do you not?"

Tragget sat up, stiffening in his chair. "Somewhat . . . yes. It is our oldest custom, as old as the Pir itself, I believe."

"Quite right," Edana replied, settling back into her own chair. Her elbows lay on the armrests, her hands folded together with the index fingers pressed against each other as though pointing toward the focus of her thought. "The records of that time are fragmentary at best. The land was a chaos of death and anarchy in that time. The five divisions of Hramra—Hrunard, Enlund, Bayway, Dragonisle, and the Forsaken Mountains—these were not settled by the Pentach until the hundred and seventeenth year of the Dragonkings."

... and peace was our-
... another season."

... the natural order of things. It is how we honor the
...ngs." Tragget was sweating now. He could not understand
...e Edana was going with this line of reasoning.

"Yes, a perfect balance of harmony and peace. Down the centuries we have simply counted its costs, paid its price, and reaped its reward. Each of the Pir from under the five Dragonkings has kept careful records since the Council of Harquan. Each of us has come to the same conclusion. Since our records began, the number of the Elect has increased each year. Since four fifty-three, the number of the Elect has increased at an even greater rate. The price has been going up and it is getting steeper each year. The reasons for the ceremony were lost to us, but the process specifically elected those who suffered from the madness. Why the Election of the Mad at all?"

"I still don't see what this has to do with the office of the Inquisitor," Tragget said flatly. "It seems to me the easiest way to deal will all of this would be to ask Vasska yourself. You are the Dragon-Talker, after all. Vasska was there."

Edana chuckled. "A direct, if inelegant, solution. Pir Oskaj, Talker for Satinka, actually *did* forward that same proposal to the Pentach. We each asked."

"And?" Tragget prompted.

"And we each were told the same thing: 'The mad kings must die.' Nothing else. Just 'the mad kings must die.' No dragon would give any further information on the Election or answer any question pertaining to it beyond that simple response."

"Then," Tragget said, still puzzled, "I suppose 'the mad kings
die.'"

...nking...

Tragget d...

Edana l...

Pentach wants you...

"What?" Tragget...

"If the dragons will not tell us why they... perhaps the madmen can. The Pentach wish you to stu... ness—find out what it is about these madmen that the drag...

Tragget stood up, the color draining from his face. "You c-ca... be s-serious! This is . . . is b-blasphemy! To have the madness is... s-sin against Vasska and the Pir!"

"Your emotional outbursts are becoming tiresome, boy!" Edana's eyes narrowed as she spoke. "You presume to lecture me—High Priestess of the Pir Vasska—on the nature of sin?"

Tragget breathed heavily, struggling to control himself. "Your Grace, do not ask this of me! I find the m-madness repulsive and vile! I am not well suited for this task at all!"

"Sit down, boy."

"But, p-please, Your Grace, I—"

"I said *sit down!*"

Tragget dropped at once onto the chair. He faced Edana but his eyes were focused far away.

Edana reached forward, grasped Tragget's jaw. "Look at me, boy! Now!"

Tragget set his teeth and focused his eyes on the face before him.

"I've done all this for you, son. It has taken years." Her hand closed tighter around his jaw. Her grip was surprisingly powerful. She pulled his face forward as she spoke. "I will *not* have the entire glory of Hrunard taken away from us because a gutless, whimpering son ...es not have the courage or vision to see his own destiny!"

"Mother! I've done everything you've—"

"...ou've done! You're a child of fate, Tragget! Your future was ...in the dragonsmoke before you were born! I saw you there

Tragget shrugged. "The Pentach itself did not exist until the fifty-seventh year by any reckoning."

"Precisely!" Edana emphasized the word by tipping her pressed index fingers toward the Inquisitor. "And yet the Festival, the Election of the Chosen, predates all of these events. Some of the earliest records we have are conflicting and fragmentary. The Election itself was a crude and cruel process, but in the end it was the same. The dragons were honored by it, the price was paid, and peace was purchased for the land for another season."

"That is the natural order of things. It is how we honor the Dragonkings." Tragget was sweating now. He could not understand where Edana was going with this line of reasoning.

"Yes, a perfect balance of harmony and peace. Down the centuries we have simply counted its costs, paid its price, and reaped its reward. Each of the Pir from under the five Dragonkings has kept careful records since the Council of Harquan. Each of us has come to the same conclusion. Since our records began, the number of the Elect has increased each year. Since four fifty-three, the number of the Elect has increased at an even greater rate. The price has been going up and it is getting steeper each year. The reasons for the ceremony were lost to us, but the process specifically elected those who suffered from the madness. Why the Election of the Mad at all?"

"I still don't see what this has to do with the office of the Inquisitor," Tragget said flatly. "It seems to me the easiest way to deal will all of this would be to ask Vasska yourself. You are the Dragon-Talker, after all. Vasska was there."

Edana chuckled. "A direct, if inelegant, solution. Pir Oskaj, Talker for Satinka, actually *did* forward that same proposal to the Pentach. We each asked."

"And?" Tragget prompted.

"And we each were told the same thing: 'The mad kings must die.' Nothing else. Just 'the mad kings must die.' No dragon would give any further information on the Election or answer any questions pertaining to it beyond that simple response."

"Then," Tragget said, still puzzled, "I suppose 'the mad kings must die.'"

Edana nodded. "Yes, I suppose they must. Yet always I have wondered . . . why? What do the Dragonkings have to fear from a few madmen?" She suddenly looked straight into Tragget's eyes. "What *do* the Dragonkings have to fear from a few madmen?"

Tragget did not answer.

Edana looked up at the ceiling and continued. "That is what the Pentach wants you to find out."

"What?" Tragget blurted out.

"If the dragons will not tell us why they fear the madmen, then perhaps the madmen can. The Pentach wish you to study the madness—find out what it is about these madmen that the dragons fear."

Tragget stood up, the color draining from his face. "You c-cannot be s-serious! This is . . . is b-blasphemy! To have the madness is a s-sin against Vasska and the Pir!"

"Your emotional outbursts are becoming tiresome, boy!" Edana's eyes narrowed as she spoke. "You presume to lecture me—High Priestess of the Pir Vasska—on the nature of sin?"

Tragget breathed heavily, struggling to control himself. "Your Grace, do not ask this of me! I find the m-madness repulsive and vile! I am not well suited for this task at all!"

"Sit down, boy."

"But, p-please, Your Grace, I—"

"I said *sit down!*"

Tragget dropped at once onto the chair. He faced Edana but his eyes were focused far away.

Edana reached forward, grasped Tragget's jaw. "Look at me, boy! Now!"

Tragget set his teeth and focused his eyes on the face before him.

"I've done all this for you, son. It has taken years." Her hand closed tighter around his jaw. Her grip was surprisingly powerful. She pulled his face forward as she spoke. "I will *not* have the entire glory of Hrunard taken away from us because a gutless, whimpering son does not have the courage or vision to see his own destiny!"

"Mother! I've done everything you've—"

"*You've* done! You're a child of fate, Tragget! Your future was written in the dragonsmoke before you were born! I saw you there before you were in my womb, child! I knew your greatness then. I nurtured you, saw you raised by the Pir Nobis from your youth. I kept your parentage secret for your own protection. I brought you to your position over the opposition of the Aboths and the Kardis order. I have done all this for us both and I will *not* have you toss it all aside because you are too pathetic to face your destiny!"

Edana's grip was powerful. The pain shot up from his jaw into his temples.

"I *have* seen it!" Edana sneered, her stare burning down into Tragget's watery eyes. "I've shown it to you just as it was shown to me! Do you think you have found this fool which the smoke has portended or not?"

Tragget was on his knees before Edana. Tears spilled over his cheeks from her crushing grip. He nodded as best he could within her grasp.

"Then you will find out why the dragons fear him. You will discover the power that the madness holds. You will wrest this power from his beating heart and master it, do you understand me!"

Tragget closed his eyes against the pain, pressing the tears from his eyes. He nodded once more.

Edana suddenly released him.

And stroked Tragget lightly on the cheek.

"That's a good boy," she said sweetly, her entire demeanor changing within a blink of the eye. "I knew that I could count on you to do the right thing, Inquisitor."

"Y-your servant," Tragget breathed a shuddering of air through his aching jaw.

"Ah, you look tired, Tragget." Edana looked down on him, a concerned face framed around two chill eyes. "Your journey has been a long one, no doubt."

"Yes . . . yes it has," Tragget said, staggering to his feet. "My apologies, Our Lady, I am indeed fatigued."

Edana stood up, taking him by the arm. "Then come, let me see you safely to your rest."

Tragget only nodded. He knew the way well, though few others breathed who knew it also. They walked arm in arm through the northern door and into back hall storage. It was, in a way, comforting to him. The secret latch mechanism and the counterweighted stone door were friends from his distant childhood. The thin corridor led to the rooms of his youth. It was here that Edana had passed the days of her confinement, unknown to anyone. It was here that he was born. It was here that he had lived his secret life. The rooms were dark and dusty now, as forgotten as the days he had spent there. Down another corridor they walked and through another hidden door to his apprentice rooms, now reclaimed by him as the apartments of the Grand Inquisitor.

"Thank you, Revered Mother," he said as he stood next to the bed. "I . . . I just need a little rest."

"Of course. We'll speak more of your assignment tomorrow."

"Very well," he replied.

Edana nodded, then quite suddenly turned and pushed her way back through the hidden doorway. She closed it carefully behind her.

Tragget stared at what suddenly had become a blank wall, and then collapsed on the sumptuous bed.

Vasska, what am I to do? he thought to himself. I'm fighting the madness myself and they want me to research it? I'm trying to get rid of the demons and they wish me to invite them in?

He closed his eyes. The sleep was already overcoming him despite his desire to fight it. Already the demons of his sin were dancing around the edges of his mind, threatening to overwhelm him and drag him into their land of flame and darkness. As he drifted off, he could see the Lords of Mithlan, the great mountains behind the city, towering up into a flame-red sky. The mountains were broken, sundered through their peaks with a great cleft. Fire and brimstone gushed from its maw, cascading down into a great plain of molten stone.

Directly before him, at the crest of a hill, lay a great warrior-giant. His armored head alone, lying against the ground nearby, was fully thirty feet in height.

The warrior had been overcome by the demons. The vicious little creatures were dismembering him, dragging off pieces of him for their own dark and terrible purposes. Tragget feared them more than death itself, for he knew that they would take him apart if they could. There was one in particular who seemed to always take an interest in him, a scrawny little demon wearing an oversized cap and a ragged, dirty orange shirt. He could see the little demon climbing out of the fallen warrior's nose.

Tragget screamed silently in his sleep. He stood in the middle of a great fire. Its searing flames leaped all about him, consuming him, destroying him. All the while, the demons danced frantically in a circle around him.

The madness was getting worse.

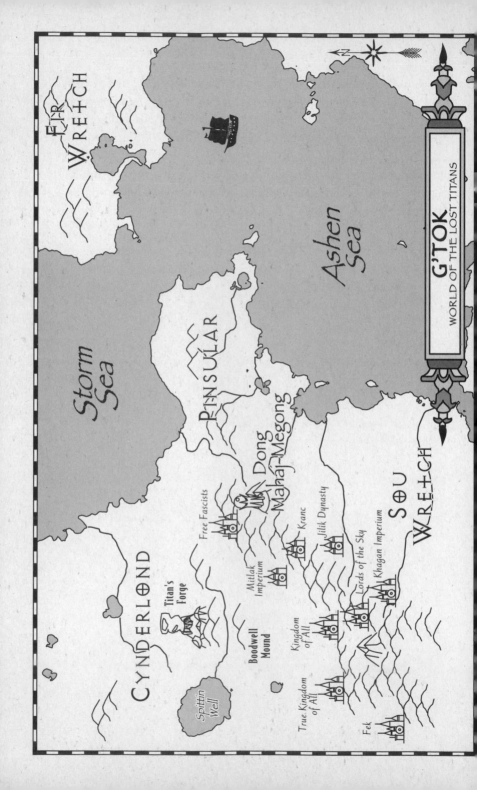

Mimic

imic climbed down from the Titan's nose, wiped his already filthy sleeve across his own nose, and sat on the rock with a pronounced thud.

Mimic was a goblin—the goblin engineer fourth class in the service of Dong Mahaj-Megong, King of the Goblins. It should have been a wonderfully illustrious and prestigious title, and might have been except for two things: first, there were only four engineers in the service of Dong Mahaj-Megong, and second, there were no fewer than twelve recognized and uncounted unrecognized claimants to the title "King of the Goblins," each of them less than a hundred miles from his master's august throne. Mimic decided that these facts tended to put a damper on the majesty of most honored titles.

Mimic himself had few illusions as to his current status on the great bureaucratic totem that sat above him. He was short for a goblin—barely over four feet tall*—and not very good-looking. His ears were not long enough and their points were somewhat rounded—a physical fault he had lamented on more than one occasion. Worse, his

---

* The original manuscript indicated this measure as being "five feet," but the measure was according to goblin feet. Throughout this translation, however, we have converted most measures of time, weight, and distance for both convenience and clarity.

left ear tended to droop more than his right, giving him a rather disconcerting off-balance appearance of little appeal to symmetrically minded goblins. The last stroke of bad grooming fortune involved his hair. His single tuft was bright white and completely uncooperative. No amount of coaxing would get it to stand straight up. Occasionally, when he happened upon some black grease from one of the derelict Titan machines, its application to his hair seemed to sharpen his image. Yet the grease was getting scarce, and a particularly unfortunate mishap involving the Megong Bonfire Dance had nearly left him bald.

Since then he had worn his old cap with the hole in the top and used it as best he could to hold his pathetic hairlock in something close to a respectable vertical position. Even though Lirry smacked him around every morning yelling about "that stupid hat ain't regulationatory," Mimic knew different. So long as he wore his shirt of office—the orange shirt of the engineer fourth class—he was within the established and well-defined dress code of his class.

Besides, Mimic thought, Lirry would just find something else to beat him up for anyway. It was better to know what to expect. So every morning Mimic wore his hat and every morning Lirry smacked him around, and Mimic took it quietly because, for one thing, the beatings never lasted very long.

And for another thing, Mimic silently knew that one day—he didn't know when—*one* day, things would be different.

Mimic said little to his fellow engineers but thought plenty to himself. He would envision wild stories about making a Titan fully functional one day—just by accident—and having it step on Lirry. Or he would be working on one of his little clockwork experiments and he would imagine it suddenly would start actually working—and it would blow a hole through Lirry's head. Or he would find a gigantic tree-cutting machine of the Titans and find a way to start it again just as Lirry—

"Hey, Mimic!" It was Lugnut Lipik, the second class engineer. He had joined G'dag and Zoof leaping around the fire. "Look at us! We're summoning the fire spirits!"

The rest of the Expeditionary Force had built a huge fire nearby.

They would need the warmth as the night progressed, since Mimic was sure that Lirry—the expedition boss—would never allow them to leave their prize for even nearby shelter.

This particular Titan they had found nearly whole. It was filled with lots of gears and wheels and even a couple of belts still intact. It was quite a prize, and Lirry should have been pleased, but he seemed just as sour as ever. "Nothing works!" he had said after they had climbed all over the hulk, half buried as it was in the hillside. "How am I gonna get outta this job unless you rock-knotted tar-poopers get one of these things to *move?*"

The first engineer shrugged, the second engineer shrugged, the third engineer shrugged, and then Lirry smacked Mimic. All of this seemed perfectly equitable to the first through third engineers.

Mimic stood up with a deep sigh, turning his back on the fire. The ripple of its light flickered against the huge form of the fallen Titan, its metal still shining in places. The right arm was missing and the rest was buried in the hillside. What must they have been like when they walked the land! he thought. Their strides were over a hundred feet in length. Did the ground shake under their footfalls?

This Titan had nearly crested the Norvald Ridge before it fell for the last time. Beyond its shattered form, the range dropped down to the west into the Cynderlond. A great battle had taken place there, long before his memory or the memory of anyone that he knew. Through the mists of distance, he could make out the Forge, the broken mountain which still hurled the molten blood of G'tok from its wound.

The view inspired Mimic with both awe and sadness at once. Did they live there? he wondered. Had his own people lived with them? Did his ancestors worship the Titans as gods? Why had the gods died?

"Hey, Mimic! If you're not going to dance, then at least make yourself useful! The fire's dying already!"

It took a moment before Mimic realized someone was yelling at him. He turned back to face his companions by the fire.

"Eh? What do you want?"

"I said the fire's dying already here!" Lugnut said, stamping his foot.

"Oh, right!" Mimic could see that the flames were quite low. "Be right with you."

He reached down with both arms and filled them with as many books as he could carry. Staggering over to the blaze, he dumped them quickly into the flames.

The fire roared and crackled back to life.

Mimic shuffled back to his rock and flopped down once more. These book-things were everywhere. A lot of Titans seemed to have a number of them inside. Sometimes they found entire buildings containing these books—stacks and stacks of them. Sometimes they had artlike pictures inside that showed machines—especially the ones they found inside the Titans themselves—but otherwise they were not very pretty. Lots of angular designs in lines on the page, but after a while one lost interest because the angled lines didn't mean anything and weren't all that pretty.

They did, however, burn extremely well.

Mimic had begun to grow a bit uneasy about these books. Somewhere in the back of his mind, he wondered if there wasn't something more to them than ornate fuel for bonfires. He honestly didn't think the Titans had created them with that purpose in mind. So, if not bonfires, what did the Titans think the books were for? Why bother keeping so many of them around everywhere they went?

Maybe, he thought by the light of the burning books, maybe they were holy icons of the Titans' gods! Maybe the Titans thought the symbols would protect them or bless them in battle.

Maybe.

If so, then they didn't do a very good job, he thought, gazing up at the broken iron face rising behind him from the hillside.

Mimic took in a long breath. It had been a hard day and the next would prove no easier. There was more of the Titan to salvage. Dong Mahaj-Megong would want as many trophies from this expedition as possible, and Lirry was no doubt determined to more than please his own superiors in the Ministry of Acquisition and Theft.

The flames of the fire danced before him. In their waves of heat and light, there appeared to him a face—a thin, tall face with ugly, tiny ears. Its skin appeared pale and terrifyingly smooth. It looked vaguely like some sort of horrid flesh-Titan—a ghostly spirit perhaps haunting this hilltop since the War Days.

Mimic knew that face. He had seen it in his dreams many times before.

Did this spirit come in the night through the flames of the fire? Mimic had handled books often. Perhaps the books were tombs for the spirits of the Titans and they had freed them in their burnings! Perhaps the spirit came to kill them even as they watched!

But the spirit made no move. Its image disappeared as quickly as it had come.

Perhaps it comes to kill Lirry?

Mimic smiled. With a sigh that made his left ear droop uncontrollably, he curled up on the rock and went to sleep . . . thinking of the spirit chasing Lirry through all time.

> I say this as an engineer first. As I have explained before, to be an engineer one must begin with the position of the argument and then find the facts that fit it. When the discovered facts do not fit the argument, one knows there is something wrong with the facts. One then needs to go out and get new facts that work. If this proves impossible, one may be forced to modify the original position of the argument with the sure knowledge that the new argument was actually the old argument all along, only remembered incorrectly by everyone else.[*]
>
> This is science: the truth is only what we believe it to be. Life is merely a question of ignoring those facts that do not support your viewpoint.

---

[*] Readers and scholars of the Bronze Canticles have often noted the striking difference in the apparent eloquence of this text as compared to the other, third-person accounts from the goblin realms. This oral history, dictated and passed down by memory due to the lack of any formal writing system known by the goblins, was embellished linguistically over the years. This passage from Mimic's oral history is the only known source of Mimic's firsthand experience. However, as it is highly self-serving and has certainly been heavily embellished to improve Mimic's image as an educated goblin, the accuracy of the account is highly suspect. It is most improbable than he—or any other goblin—ever actually spoke this way. This is, nevertheless, typical of all goblin oral histories.

It is important to understand this, as it has direct bearing on my arguments and the extraordinary circumstances of my life afterward.

Before this time, each of my encounters with the Creature was in my dreams. Dreams are constructs of our imagination or the manifestation of spirits intruding into our perspective viewpoint or the result of underdone meat. In any event, I found that in this particular dream, I was standing near the bonfire of my companions. They had all apparently fled, for I saw none of them nearby.

The hideous Creature stood in the midst of the bonfire. His form was made entirely of the flames. His face was smooth and pinched, while his ears were rounded as though by some terrible accident, as I have heretofore detailed to you. His robes glowed as though they were the embers of the fire itself.

I thought about how I might help him. He was constructed entirely of flame, and so I sought to encourage the fire by throwing another set of books into the conflagration. This I was making ready to do — but through his gestures he plainly forbade me. I felt thereby encouraged in my suspicion that there was something more important in the book than its burning.

I opened the book in my hand. The strange, angular designs that lined the page began to glow. As I watched in amazement, they drifted upward from off the surface of the pages and circled around the fire. As each spiraled up around the fire — and I must be perfectly clear on this — the angled designs pulled flame from the creature until they, too, burned.

Then, when the designs were burning white-hot in the air, they flew over my head. Different designs branded themselves to different parts of the Titan. Each glowed for a time then faded, absorbed by the metal of the fallen giant, only to be replaced by more designs. The pages of the book began to turn over, leaf after leaf, in my hand. The burning sigils flew faster and faster until the last of the pages was empty and the book slammed shut with a sound like the clap of thunder.

The last of the symbols faded against the iron shell of the Titan. I stood in unreserved amazement. I adjusted my cap and tried to straighten my recalcitrant hair to a more respectful vertical rise.

The sound was low at first but unmistakable. Ancient metal was moving.

As I watched, the great Titan began to rise.

Its hollow, metallic eye winked at me.

An Oral History of Mimic, Bronze Canticles, Folio 1, Leaf 32

For a Clock That Works

The first engineer shrugged. The second engineer shrugged. The third engineer shrugged.

Mimic closed his eyes.

Then Lirry smacked Mimic across the head, sending the goblin down to the ground. A puff of dust billowed where Mimic hit—as close to a comment as the goblin engineer ever got.

Lirry glared down at Mimic, seemingly offended at his very presence. Lirry was Mimic's superior, a fact that Lirry never tired of reminding Mimic or any of the other four engineers under his command. The difference between them may have been only a single, fading black band around the middle of Lirry's orange tunic, but it was a difference that Lirry beat into Mimic every day.

Lirry was shorter than any of his crew but he had a wide, barrel-shaped chest and fists that could fracture granite. His shiny yellow eyes were set far back in his head and looked too close together. His wide mouth could show plenty of teeth, but Lirry never smiled unless it was at the discomfort, misfortune, or pain of someone else. His ears were his best feature, rising quite high on either side of his head—a vanity that he never tired of talking about.

Lirry was known without any trace of affection as "Chief" to anyone with the misfortune of working under him. It was an endearing nickname he had chosen for himself, and woe betide any of his crew who forgot it. His official title was "Chief Engineer," which meant he was one rung up from the bottom and an uncountable number of rungs from the top. Not that any of that daunted Lirry in the least. He was absolutely convinced that the next discovery or the next lucky throw of the bones could be parlayed, traded, or leveraged into the next step up that same ladder. Results were measured entirely by his progress in the eyes of his superiors. Lirry's status before the Dong Mahaj-Megong was the only reason any of the engineers beneath him had for breathing. Every unenthusiastic response from his crew was a personal insult, every missed discovery a deliberate act of career sabotage.

"You call yourselves engineers?" Lirry spat as he spoke. He always spat when he was really mad or excited. "I find the most complete Titan since the Great Leg of last year and *you* cannot get it to work?"

Actually, that was not entirely true: it was Mimic who had led them to this remote side of the Norvald Ridge, guided by the inexplicable promptings of his friend from the fire. Still, as Lirry often reminded them, they were supposed to be a *team*. As such, anything the team discovered should rightly belong to him.

"Disloyal maggots! Stupid idiots! What rock-brain called you engineers anyway?"

"Oh, I know! *You* say we engineer!" It was Engineer Third Class Zoof. Zoof was a tall, scrawny goblin with an ample tuft of white hair at the ridge of his head that made Mimic mildly jealous. Zoof was a good engineer, too, but had no understanding of when to keep his mouth shut.

The tips of Lirry's ears quivered with rage. Zoof was too big for Lirry to smack, so he kicked Mimic instead. "You get back into that Titan! No more slack work! You won't embarrass *this* chief! You find me something that works!"

With that, Mimic knew that the morning morale meeting was

fortunately at an end. He could safely get up from the ground now and resume his exploration of the Titan where he had left off. Lirry assumed his accustomed position, sitting outside the Titan and eating while the four of them entered to work. The three other engineers were clambering up through the lowest ear of the great head, somehow convinced that if they were near one of their fellow engineers when the "big discovery" was made, they would share in it, too. None of them actually expected that *they* would be the ones to find it, but they were willing to gamble that someone else just might.

Mimic groaned to himself, unconsciously tried to straighten his scraggly strands of hair, and headed up toward the nose where he had left off the night before. The metallic face of the Titan had weathered considerably over the years since the War Days. There were plenty of hand- and footholds etched by nature in the face now. He quickly climbed the upper lip and came to the opening.

Mimic glanced to the east. The sun was rising with a lustrous pink into a clearing sky. He could almost see the ruins of Farval to the east and the purple mountains of the Sanctuary Range beyond. The sun would provide good warmth this morning, and that cheered him. Goblins could see the differences between hot and cold in the dark. The chill of the previous night and the warmth of the sun on the Titan would make his job much easier this morning than it was yesterday afternoon when the Titan had warmed through the day to an even temperature.

With that, Mimic put both hands on opposite sides of the nostril and pulled himself up.

Making his way up the short passage, he then turned at once to his left. The smooth, round shaft of metal snaked downward into the lower parts of the great machine. He knew this way well, for he had traversed it yesterday with great delight. The long, snaking brass fittings were elegant and mystical to him. The chambers below held great collections of sprockets, worm gears, flywheels, and other wonders that he had only heard about in the recitations of the talemasters.

The tale-masters spoke of such things, of course, because that was their job, instructing the youth in the ways of life and what was expected of them. In the most ancient of days, before the War Days, the goblins and their kind served the great Titans as slaves, tending their machines and treading the very same narrow corridors of metal that Mimic walked at that moment. Then came the War Days and the Titans fell in some terrible conflict. The tale-masters said that the Titans fell because Dong Mahaj-Megong the First banished them from his great kingdom and brought destruction upon them with fire and death. Then the goblins were free to be ruled by the Dong and had been ever since. Still, the Dong was sorry for the loss of the Titans' great machines. In truth, the goblins were not entirely certain as to whether there was any distinction between the Titans and their machines. Most believed that the Titans *were* the machines. Regardless of which was true, since that time, it has been the dream of every goblin to reclaim the glorious machines of the lost Titans.

This Titan was like walking into a dream.

Mimic frowned. Perhaps it was better not to think about his dreams right now. He had work to do.

He worked his way through a maze of passageways both large and small. Several times he had to squeeze his slight body through an opening that appeared too narrow even for him. He could both see and feel the walls get cooler as he moved farther and farther down. The differences in temperature between the metal plates were getting less and less down here, for the sun had not penetrated this far yet. It was getting hard for him to see. Yet there was one passage that he had noticed the night before that he was most curious about. He could not have explored it then—the temperature was too even by then to see well—but this morning he might have more luck.

He was right. The corridor was much brighter.

He entered it and traversed some of the distance before stopping for a moment. The corridor before him had buckled, and jagged edges of metal stuck out. Then the passage became narrow and difficult, still he continued downward through the twisted, wrenched metal. Much to his surprise, things seemed to be getting easier to see now, as though there were some source of heat from below. The shaft was now nearly vertical, so Mimic spread his hands and feet in all directions, pressing against the sides of the metallic wall as he continued downward.

At last he came to a round door with a large latch. The latch was much the same as others he had encountered on numerous other expeditions, but for some reason this one seemed more stubborn than most. He pushed and pulled, and shook it, but it moved only a little. Finally, desperately worried that he would run out of contrasting heat as the day wore on, he stood on the hatch itself, grabbed the latch handle with both hands, and pushed with his feet.

The latch suddenly released, and the hatch fell away under him.

Mimic tumbled down through the opening, falling against a smooth, cold metal plate. The air rushed out of him. He lay there gulping for a few moments, trying painfully to regain his breath. He could still see the open hatchway above him, which was a good sign. At least he knew the way out.

He rolled over and looked around the chamber.

"Oh, no . . . books!" he moaned.

A great curving surface conformed to the arch in the slick wall. All along its surface were a number of books carefully set in square boxes in the wall. There were several that had been left out of their special little square holes. One now lay directly underneath the goblin engineer.

Mimic rolled over and picked up the book. "Well," he said with a sigh, "at least there will be another fire tonight."

Without thinking, he opened the cover of the book. Well, there they are, he thought, all those strange angled lines and dots. They are not even all that pretty to—

Several of the symbols flashed with a momentary, dull heat of their own.

Tick.

Mimic blinked. What was that? His ears quivered for a moment, straining for some sound. He remained completely still for several moments.

Nothing.

Mimic looked back down at the book. As he looked down on the page, the same symbols flashed again with dull heat.

Tick.

Mimic's head turned sharply. His left ear straightened completely in his excitement.

Somehow, he had missed it. Perhaps it was the disappointment at finding books again. Perhaps it was the even coolness of the chamber itself. Whatever the reason, now he sat on the floor frozen with hope and anticipation.

There, on the end of the curving bench, was a single, intact machine.

Mimic set the book down without a thought. He moved carefully and reverently toward the machine. He tried not to make any noise, as though somehow he might frighten it into disappearing. It was a device of the gods themselves—not some broken hulk but an actual complete mechanism—and he wanted to worship it.

It was a delicate square framework, a cube about the length of one of his hands filled with intricate cogs, gears, drives, and shafts. There was a large, round plate on one side of the framework with several angle symbol markings radiating from its center. A protruding shaft in the center was attached to three extended arms. Each arm ended in a flattened arrow and pointed at strange symbols radiating away from the center. One short arm, one medium-length arm, and a third long and thin arm.

Then Mimic's heart sank.

Several pieces of the mechanism appeared to be scattered both on the bench itself and on the floor around it. A large, coiled band of metal lay nearby that might have once been part of it, too.

So it was not complete, as he had originally thought. Dejected, Mimic turned back once more and picked up the book from the floor. Maybe there was some value in a book that glowed, he thought. He flipped open the page once more, found the symbols, which glowed as his eyes read them and

Tick. Tick.

Mimic wheeled around, the book still in his hands.

The mechanism had made a sound!

Mimic was an engineer, and an engineer is above all else observant. There is little detail that manages to escape their attention. It is the changes in detail that shout to them.

The arms on the shafts had moved!

Mimic glanced down at the symbols on the page.

They glowed under his eyes.

Tick.

The long shaft moved.

Mimic looked down at the symbols, but he did not stop at the first few. As his eyes moved, more of the symbols afterward glowed, each in their turn.

Tick. Tick. Tick.

He glanced up. The mechanism was indeed making the sound. The arm was moving, being rotated by the shaft in the center.

Tick. Tick. Tick.

Mimic was no fool. He knew exactly what he had found the moment he found it. Here was the greatest treasure any engineer had ever discovered. Here was the sort of thing for which every goblin yearned and dreamed.

Here was something that could really get you killed.

He sat down in front of his prize. There was a lot to be done and thought through. There was a lot he had to learn.

He did not understand the meaning of the symbols before him on the pages, but they were unimportant and entirely irrelevant so far as he was concerned. All he knew was the cause and effect. So he kept looking at more and more symbols in the book and observed as each set glowed how they affected the device. He carefully noted in his mind the changes that each produced. All the while he thought and thought and thought.

He only hoped he had enough time.

Tick. Tick. Tick. Tick.

Up and Coming

The first engineer shrugged. The second engineer shrugged. The third engineer shrugged.

There was no Mimic to smack.

Lirry was livid. "He knows it's time to report! Sun going down already. Three days and no treasure. First day, Mimic says he's close to treasure. Does Mimic bring treasure? No! Second day, Mimic says he's *very* close to treasure. Does Mimic bring treasure out the second day? *No!* Today, Mimic says treasure stuck but will come out today. Does Mimic even bother to come to morale meeting? *No!* Who does he think I am, keeping me waiting?"

Third Engineer G'dag held up his hand, eager to please his boss. "I know! I know! I know who he thinks you are! He tells me many times!"

Lirry was so wrapped up in his outrage that he ignored the second engineer. "If he doesn't bring me treasure tonight, we burn him with the books! There's no room for slacker-deadbeats in the elite engineer force of Dong Mahaj-Megong! I'll find *new* fourth engineer when we get back to—"

A clang echoed down out of the nose of the Titan.

Lirry's yellow eyes narrowed as he turned toward the sound. The remaining engineers all took several careful steps back down the slope, unsure whether Lirry was going to physically explode or not.

A yelp echoed from the nostril, followed by a succession of three more quick clangs.

Mimic tumbled out of the nose head over heels. His entire body was curled around a large sack. He landed with a soft *ooft* in the sand.

Lirry stalked up the slope to where Mimic lay. "No one authorized a rest period, you loafing pile of pond scum . . ."

The chief engineer's invective trailed off into silence.

The other three engineers raised their brows in surprise. Lirry's anger might end when he choked on his own words—which was never often enough. It might end when he ran out of horrible things to say—which would take a long time. More often, it might end when Lirry got tired of talking and simply smacked the object of his displeasure.

It never ended in stunned silence.

Mimic lay with his back against the great fallen Titan. His orange shirt was more smudged than usual. His face was glistening with sweat. His sparse strands of hair were bent over nearly sideways.

There, in the sand between his legs, lay the Device.

"This . . . this is the treasure?" Lirry murmured, for a moment unsure. He reached forward, picking up the mechanism with both hands.

A cog fell out as he lifted it. It landed with a soft thud at the chief's feet.

"This . . . this piece of *junk!*" Lirry's green, mottled skin went suddenly pale with rage. "I waited for you three days for this trash!"

Mimic's eyes flickered open as consciousness dawned once more in his mind.

Lirry screamed, his eyes wild with rage. He lifted the Device over his head with both hands. Mimic was going to get permanently smacked this time, smacked so hard that there would be no point in smacking him again. Lirry would beat in the head of the fourth engineer with his own joke of a treasure just for the pleasure it would bring to him.

Suddenly, Lirry froze, the device wavering slightly over his head.

Tick. Tick. Tick.

Lirry looked up, his eyes wide with wonder.

Tick. Tick. Tick.

Lugnut, G'dag, and Zoof all fell to the ground, their faces pressed into the sand in homage.

Tick. Tick. Tick.

It was as though the Titans had returned.

Lirry slowly lowered the Device. He forced his fierce grasp to relax. Now he gently cradled it in his long, pointy fingers. His eyes, which flicked over every detail of it, were always drawn back to the great round plate and its moving arms.

Lirry turned around. His grin nearly split his head. He held the Device in front of him, cradled it in his arms as though it were a child more precious than any ever born to the goblin realms. He stroked it gently, then screamed shrill and long with joy.

"Look what I found!" Lirry crowed.

He staggered down the slope toward the three prone engineers. Each of them was awestruck by the magnificence of the find. Lirry was going to be rich!

"Throw some more books on the fire tonight, boys! We're gonna celebrate big!" Lirry screeched. "We're gonna dance in my honor, eat all the food and . . ."

Tick. Tick. Click! WHIRRRrrr . . .

The Device suddenly stopped.

Lirry's eyes went wide. The visions and hopes of his entire life had been floating before him. Now, suddenly, they were fading. He wanted desperately to hold on to them, but with every passing moment of silence they grew dimmer.

"I can fix it," said the small voice from just up the slope.

Lirry and the other engineers looked up.

"I can fix it," Mimic said, picking himself up off the ground.

"You?" Lirry said, his voice squeaking with incredulity. "You can fix the mechanisms of the gods?"

"Well, maybe not all of them, but I can fix *that* one," Mimic replied.

Lirry took an uncertain step toward Mimic. "Well . . . well of *course* you can fix! What kind of engineer would you be if you *couldn't* fix!"

"Do you want me to fix it for you, Chief?" Mimic said quietly.

"Uhh . . . Well . . . yes! Yes, I want you to fix!" Lirry replied. "Unless another engineer of higher rank wishes to try and . . ."

Lugnut, G'dag, and Zoof had taken a sudden interest in dirt, plants, and the sky, in that order. None of them wanted to catch Lirry's eye.

"As you command, Chief," Mimic said. He stepped down the short slope and stood before the chief.

Lirry held the Device out in front of him. He would not let it go completely—would *never* let it go completely. Mimic glanced here and there around the Device. He considered it for a time. With a judicious nod, he then poked a thin finger into the mechanism. He closed his eyes and spoke to himself for a moment.

Tick. Tick. Tick. Tick.

Lirry visibly relaxed.

"There," Mimic said, "fixed."

"Of course! As was your duty," Lirry sniffed. "Now, get back inside! Find many other discoveries and treasure! Bring back and make my mission more glorious still!"

"Your wish is to be obeyed." A slight smile played on Mimic's thin lips as he turned and walked up the hill toward the fallen metal giant. He was just climbing up the face of the Titan once more when—

Tick. Tick. Click! WHRRRrrrr . . .

"Ah! Ah! Ah!" Lirry squealed as though physically stuck. "Mimic! Mimic! Come! Come! Come!"

Mimic turned. His face was all casual innocence.

"Fix it! Fix it! Fix it!" Lirry was leaping up and down in fear.

Mimic walked down the slope. At his approach Lirry calmed himself down long enough to hold the Device still. Once again, Mimic considered the Device—though for longer this time. Finally he touched it in two places, closed his eyes, murmured once more, and . . .

Tick. Tick. Tick. Tick.

"There you are: all better! Of course, I don't know how long it will continue to work. I would think that the best thing to do would be to show it to as many of the goblin leaders as possible while it still functions." Mimic nodded with a satisfied smile. Then he spoke in terms he knew Lirry could understand. "Device working: very valuable—bring much power. Device *not* working: just more junk. Still, *you* are chief, Lirry. You know best. Now, if you excuse me, Chief, I'll get back to work."

Mimic turned back toward the slope.

Smack!

Lirry knocked Mimic to the ground with as hard a blow as he had ever landed on the small goblin. Mimic rolled over, gazing through watery eyes back at the chief. The leader of their expedition stood over him, the Device clutched fiercely in one hand and his fist shaking at Mimic with the other.

"No one goes back inside! I say this expedition is over!"

Lugnut, G'dag, and Zoof immediately cheered and began to dance.

"The Holy Device of the Titans stays in my hands. As expedition leader it is *my* great discovery!" Lirry pointed his sharp, long finger down in Mimic's face where he still lay on the ground. "And *you*, engineer, will never be far from me either!"

They crossed the burned-out valley directly south of the Norvald Ridge, from which they could see Rune Farval, the ruined city to the east, as they descended the slopes. A thin line of gremlins from a nation calling itself the Free Fascists were moving between the ruins and their claimed homeland at the foot of the Esvald mountain range. The shortest path to Mimic's own homeland lay directly through the land of the Free Fascists, but no one encroached on that territory even under the direst of circumstances. The Free Fascists were on what they called an ethical crusade to one day rule the world. Unfortunately for them, they could never agree on a single set of ethics between them, so they determined that each of them, in turn, would take the post of Truth Determinate, the highest position of authority in their system. That leader would determine the current correct ethics, religion, and viewpoint for their freethinking kingdom. All viewpoints were therefore tolerated, but only in turns. Since the position of Truth Determinate changed at irregular periods—often as the result of violence—one could never enter their lands for fear of being put to death for breaking new and unpredictable laws.

For this reason, the road taken by the Expeditionary Force and their leader Lirry took them south-by-southwest toward the Boodwell Mound. There was an ancient watchtower there that could provide shelter, but more importantly, it was the field headquarters for Lirry's immediate boss, a sniveling little goblin who was the Lower Controller of the Ninth Division of Northern Expeditionary Forces for the Ministry of Acquisition and Theft.

He was otherwise known as Philt.

Philt, when shown the Device, was so excited by the discovery that he felt compelled to claim it as his own. Knowing that Lirry would sooner part with his head than the Device, Philt determined to have Lirry executed on a charge of treason, sedition, and blasphemy. The execution might have gone through except that Lirry still would not give up his hold on the Device and the goblins set up to execute the Expeditionary Force were so astonished at the Device that they refused to do so. This left Philt in an awkward position, which was cleared up by having Lirry and all his engineers awarded a metal rod of honor instead of being executed. Philt constantly reminded Mimic and his fellow engineers of his name during the brief ceremony on the execution field so that his own superiors might remember that he had played some part in recovering the marvelous Device.

Lirry was then ordered to take his group southeast into the foothills until they came to the River Clar, which they were to follow eastward up into the Tovald Mountains.

At each outpost, they encountered the next level in the great bureaucracy that was the kingdom of Dong Mahaj-Megong. Philt led to Klach. Klach led to Blek, who tried to steal the Device. He was running with it when it suddenly stopped working, which distracted Blek long enough for Lirry to catch up to him and beat the little goblin nearly to death. Blek's smaller brother, who took over Blek's job, then sent them to Milch, Blek's superior.

Each step they took up the mountain led them closer to the great mountain fortress of the goblin king, Dong Mahaj-Megong. At each stop, their fame and honors grew. The marvelous Device was, indeed, the treasure that Lirry had sought for all his life—that every goblin had sought for all their lives.

And Mimic was beside him every step of the way with a book hidden in his sack and the face of the tall, thin man in his dreams.

The Warriors

Whetstones

The sword rattled in Galen's hand, sending the shiver of the metal running up the length of his arm. He stumbled backward, his feet threatening to tangle under him. The former smithy found the steel suddenly heavy and awkward in his hands, but there was no time to think about that or much of anything else except deflecting the slashing blade of the opponent in front of him.

The massive crowd of Galen's fellow "Elect" looked down into the circle of bloodied hard-packed dirt from five separated sections of tiered benches surrounding the arena. Each of them by section would take their turn against the other four in a rotation strictly enforced by the Pir monks standing along the upper perimeter of the area's great bowl. For now, however, they were an audience of the mad to a blood-drenched spectacle. Some wept, some cheered, some screamed, but all in their way contributed to the thunderous roar that engulfed the combatants below.

Galen did not hear them. His world had quickly shrunk to two people, himself and the man in front of him who was trying to kill him.

Galen's section had drawn the second rotation. He could barely watch the first groups as they faced off against one another. The

"Elect" of the first two groups stood facing each other with awkward swings and unsure steps. Fear filled all their eyes and none of them moved.

Then the Pir monks, each holding a dragonstaff, turned their staves and the Eye of Vasska was upon the floor of the arena.

It was enough. Death would have been preferable to the torture of the Eye.

Each of them had trained through the morning on the practice fields. They were taught the nine basic defenses, followed by the nine basic attacks. One man with a wide girth had fallen to the ground from exhaustion during that first morning. The Pir monks quietly slit his throat. His body had left a long bloody streak across the practice field as they dragged it off. Practice resumed at once. Galen's arm was numb and his legs shaking beneath him—but he stayed on his feet until the end of the session.

Now, in the afternoon, it was his turn on the floor to test what he had learned in the morning against one of the other Elect. Some of the other pairs were tentatively trading blows in the practice sequence. Their neat patterns of attack and defend, so polite in rehearsal, collapsed into vicious chaos with the first glance of the Eye.

Now Galen could not think of anything but the wild-eyed maniac in front of him who was intent on burying a blade in his head. What the madman facing Galen lacked in talent he made up for in raw and mindless determination. He probably did not see Galen at all—his pupils seemed fixed on something just beyond his target. He was only slightly taller than Galen and perhaps a good ten stones heavier. His curly hair lay in flattened waves down his head, dripping with sweat. Days ago this man might have been clean-shaven, but now his beard had emerged into strong stubble. He might have been a storekeeper or a shepherd or a cooper in his former life, but no longer.

Now the man was berserk with rage, driven beyond thinking by his own inner darkness. His sword flashed through the air, fast and strong, and it was all Galen could do to keep up with the blows raining down on him.

Galen stumbled backward once more, his feet kicking up dust

from the hard-packed dirt of the arena floor. At least ten other pairs of combatants battled one another in the large circle, while a wall of screaming Elect were held back just beyond the confines of the arena floor. The time had not yet come for their blood to be spilt.

Worse still, Galen was not sure that the advice his sword was giving him was helping.

"One! One! Two! Four!" the sword was shouting into his mind. "Too slow! You'll never kill anyone this way!"

"I don't want to kill anyone!" Galen shouted over the crashing steel. The berserk man was closing on him again.

"By the gods! Another coward," the sword sang back over its own breath through the air. "A sword of the Rhamasian Guard . . . Two! Four! . . . a blade of the old kingdom guard . . . One! Two! Three! Six! . . . and they put me in the hands of a coward! Six!"

Galen obeyed just as the madman lunged toward him. The sweeping arc of Galen's blade in front of him pushed the attacker's thrust aside, bringing Galen in close to his opponent. The smithy took another step in, smashing his free hand into the face of his foe.

The madman reeled backward, blood suddenly running from his nose.

"Well met!" the sword cried with glee. "Two steps back now and reset your stance! He's coming back at you."

Galen stepped back, but did not get his feet under him before the madman, having dropped his weapon in his rage, slammed into Galen, lifting him completely off his feet.

"By the gods," the sword spat at him. "I told you about your stance!"

The air rushed out of Galen as he fell back flat against the ground, bright lights exploding in his vision. By now, however, the madman's momentum was against him. Though he was pressing down on him still, Galen caught his opponent with both feet, then flexed and catapulted the wretch over his head.

The madman howled as he rolled through the air, then crumpled against the hard clay of the arena floor.

"Get up!" the sword screamed in his mind. "Get up and set your stance!"

Galen scrambled, kicking his legs in a panic to roll over and get off the ground. He quickly turned toward where his opponent had landed. His breath was ragged as sweat streamed down over his eyes. He blinked, trying to clear his vision.

Galen's foe lay still on the ground, a stain slowly reaching out, feeling its way into the dirt around him.

Galen stared in abject horror. His mind wished and willed the man to rise, to move, to make some sound. He would not—could not—be the cause of this.

"*By all the gods of Mount Helista!*" The words of the sword rang in Galen's ears. "*I had forgotten how good that feels!*"

Galen blanched. In knocking Galen to the ground, the fool had pressed himself down on Galen's upturned sword. His blood had run down the length of the blade, coating it in a dark sheen. The crimson river had continued in its torrent, flowing down past his grip into a long rill curling around his forearm. The sticky red liquid had bathed him up to his elbows in the man's stolen life.

"*We'll make a warrior out of you yet, Galen!*" the sword sang with confidence.

Galen dropped the blade.

It would not come off.

Galen knelt over the long water trough, which lay just outside his assigned barracks—one of more than a dozen ancient buildings all on the verge of collapse. It was here that he fell sobbing at the end of the day. It was here he remained into the night.

The stars looked down on him from the blackness above, but he turned his back on them in shame. The folk of Benyn had long believed that the stars were the eyes of their ancestors looking down on them through the Veil of Sighs. It was their whispers that were heard by Vasska, their pleadings that brought prosperity and protection to their descendants still trudging through the middle lands below.

He could not face them. He could not contemplate their judgments on him.

"Galen." The voice was distant and hollow.

He once more scrubbed and scraped his skin, but even in the darkness he knew the stain was still there and would not come off.

"Galen . . . can you hear me?"

It was dark and he did not care. It was night and he did not notice. The Pir monks would discover him outside the cramped barracks, and only Vasska knew what they would do to him when they found him. Whatever it was, it could not be bad enough.

"Galen, please, you've got to listen to me."

He wished she would leave him alone. What did she care, the wife of a man as insane as Galen was himself? Why could she not just leave Galen to his own demons? Did she not have enough of her own?

"Galen! Let it go!" Rhea grabbed his arm, shaking him and pulling at him.

Galen pulled savagely away from her. "Let it go? You were there! You saw! Everyone *saw!*"

Rhea pulled her hand back slowly. She looked at the ground, considering, as Galen struggled to control himself.

"This place isn't life. It isn't you," she said at last. "Think about someplace that is real! Think about your wife! That's what is real!"

"My wife?" Galen stopped. He gazed down into the murky water of the long trough. He held up his right arm, dripping wet, the skin raw from the scrubbing. "I have no wife; by the law of the Pir! Even if we could start again, how can I return to her now? How can I ever touch her again with this stain on my hand?"

Rhea knelt next to him. Her eyes regarded him sadly. "It's gone, Galen. The stain is gone."

"Gone?" Galen cried. His words were choked with pain. "How can you say that? It isn't gone, it will never be gone! It's burned into my eyes . . . my heart!"

"But you didn't put it there, Galen!" Rhea's eyes held steady with Galen's as she spoke, her words strong and even. "You didn't take up the sword, Galen . . . they put it in your hand! The Pir, the Festival of the Harvest, the Election . . . that is what put it there! *That's* what we have to understand and conquer! *That's* what we have to fight!"

"What? Fight the church? Fight Vasska himself?" Galen barked back at her from behind tear-blurred eyes. "That is the *world*, Rhea! You want to fight the entire world?"

"No, Galen, no!" Rhea said evenly, her voice calming. "The Pir are not the entire world. Vasska is not the entire world. They are immense, they are powerful, and they have ruled since before our memories, but they are *not* the entire world."

Galen shook his head in disgust.

"There is more to the world than you know, Galen." Rhea sighed and then leaned back against the trough. "There certainly was more to the world than I knew. You and I are a great deal alike in this, I think. The Pir was my world, too. Then my daughter contracted this so-called Madness of the Emperors. She was clever, a great deal like you, I believe. Maddoc thought she could be cured of it no matter what the Pir taught. Then my beloved Maddoc fell into the madness, too, but did not master it as Dahlia had done. He withdrew from both of us to find solace in another place . . . another realm. Dahlia, my daughter, and I took Maddoc and fled before the next Election. We've been traveling ever since and we've seen a lot of the Dragonback in that time. Dahlia was convinced that there was a power to the madness; a power even greater than the Dragonkings. I think it may be a power that could take on the world. It may be our greatest hope."

Galen looked at her for a moment. "You *are* mad, after all."

Rhea laughed. "Perhaps I am. If I am, however, I wonder if I am the only *truly* mad person here."

Galen shook his head. "There is no hope in the madness, only a curse. The Dragonkings saved us from ourselves when the Rhamas Emperors went mad."

"So the dragons tell us," Rhea said, letting irony season her words. "Look, Galen, all I am trying to do is to bring my husband back to me and get back to my child. You can understand that. Dahlia taught me to observe what I see and try to find some meaning in all of it. You and everyone else are here because you are the 'Elect,' but no one seems to have any real idea as to *why* you are the Elect, let alone why the Pir Drakonis brought you here to learn to fight. Until we know the answers to those questions, we'll never have *power over ourselves,* let alone the world."

"Children's stories," Galen sniffed.

"But good stories, Galen, good stories! Believe me or not if you wish, but I need your help if I'm going to get the answers that we both need!" Rhea leaned forward, her voice more urgent than he had heard from her before. "I think we can find the truth about it all—the Festival, the Election, the madness, all of it—but I can't do it without your help. You can go there, to this other place where my husband finds refuge from the world of the living. *That* is where the secret is buried, I am sure of it. *That* is where the truth can be found and where you can find your answers, too. I know it, Galen! I just *know* it!"

"How can you know that?" Galen snapped. "How can you know anything that I am going through?"

Rhea looked down sadly. "Because Dahlia believed it and she is still out there searching, too. I have to know it, Galen, because finding the answer is all I have left to believe in."

"You saw me out there today . . . you see me tonight." Galen laughed sadly. "The great warrior! I won't last long enough for you to find your answers, Rhea, not for you, your daughter, or your husband."

"You won," Rhea said flatly, "didn't you?"

"My sword won," Galen spat. "It told me what to do!"

"The sword *speaks* to you?" Rhea said, her eyebrows rising in surprise.

"Yes, it does. Crafted objects just . . . I don't know, they're always talking to me, and look what it got me!"

"It bought you life for another day," Rhea replied. "It sounds to me like you should listen to what your sword is telling you. You could learn a great deal about surviving all of this."

"Why? Why should I survive at all? Why should I live and not that man who died because of me today?"

"As long as you live there is the possibility of living another day and finding a way out of this horror." Rhea's voice grew more urgent. "If not for you then keep living for your wife! If not for her then keep living for Maddoc and Dahlia and me! We can figure this out, Galen, I know we can, but I cannot do it without experiencing what happens in that strange place you both share. I can't go there myself. I need you to go there for both of us! I need you to learn what it is in that place that the dragons fear—fear so much that they kill all who have been there. Then I think we will know how to free us all and get back to my husband, my daughter, and my life!"

Galen shook in the darkness.

Rhea held out her hand. "Please, Galen! Help me bring my husband home."

Galen took a great, shuddering breath. "And me? Who will bring me home?"

"If there is a path home for you, Galen, we will find that, too." Rhea pushed her hand forward once more.

Galen looked down once, nodded, and then took her hand.

He could still see the stain on his hand.

He knew it would never come off.

Common Ground

I walk through legions of the dead.

The low clouds blanket the sky above me in a vibrant salmon color. No hint of breeze moves in this place. No sound disturbs it. All is as still as the dead about my feet.

The corpses blanket the rolling plain, their blood flowing in quiet rivulets across the landscape to gather in rank, coagulating ponds. The bodies themselves are blackened, whether with fire or decomposition, I cannot tell. They number like the grasses of the meadow. Some scythe has laid them down forever on these fields to rot and be forgotten.

It is a place that I have never seen before. I know not whether it is a real place or a place existing in the madness only. Nor do I know whether it is a vision of times past or of times yet to come. To me it is a place and a time of its own.

My hand is coated in blood. I look at the crimson stain prominently discoloring my arm, and the smell of the dead overwhelms me. All I want to do is to fall down, hide my face, and hope for the dream to end.

I cannot. I have a purpose here in this terrible place. Somewhere in this madness I must find Maddoc, that strange, crazed man. I must learn what he has learned and understand the

madness as only a madman can. It may be the only hope I have
of finding my own sanity and of returning home.

"I know this place," says a voice next to me.

He is here; the strange monk who so often enters my dreams. I
turn to him, still curious as to the enormous devastation of this
place. "I don't. Where are we?"

"The name is not important, Galen," says the monk. "It would
be meaningless to you. How is it you know this place?"

"I don't." His question annoys me. "I thought the Pir Inquisitas
had all the answers."

"We do," the monk says, smiling roguishly under his yellow, unkempt hair. "It's just that we forget them when it is convenient."

I shake my head. This is my companion in my madness? A
monk with questions I cannot answer and answers that I can only
question.

I turn away from him. Small demon creatures move across the
dead that cover the hills, picking at their armor and scavenging
anything that they can carry. They do not seem to take much
notice of us.

I wonder for a time what the winged woman might think of all
this death, and in my wonder she appears! She floats in the distance above a delicate and beautiful white tower, while between us
runs a great crimson river. She does not seem likely to leave the
tower, for at the foot of the tower another battle is joined.

Terrible beasts—beasts out of some nightmare whose names are
not known to me—are tearing at the stone and mortar. Their
claws gouge great chunks from the limestone, shaking the tower
and threatening its collapse. The winged woman looks at me and
even at this distance I can see her dark eyes widen with pleading
and fear.

I am ashamed under her beautiful gaze, for I do not know how
to help her in her terrible predicament. I am helpless as I wander
among the dead.

Through the silence, a voice drifts toward me from the distance.
"Halloo!"

The monk turns with me toward the sound. "Do you know him?"

"Yes," I respond simply. I have been thinking of Maddoc, and in so doing, the madman has also appeared. I see him at the top of a gentle rise, waving at me, his face split with a great smile.

"Who is he?" the monk asks.

"His name is not important," I retort through a twisted smile. "It would be meaningless to you."

The monk scowls at me.

I stride up the slope, leaving the monk to brood below me among the dead. My footfalls are unsure on the blood-slicked grass. I pick my way upward between the bodies of the fallen, coming at last to the crest of the hill.

"Quite a sight, isn't it!" Maddoc speaks with a satisfied nod.

"It is indeed," I reply. I have found him easily in this place of dreams. I have done what Rhea asked thus far. Now that I have his attention, what am I to ask? It seemed so important in the other world. Here, however, its urgency is lost, and there is a feeling that things are as they are supposed to be. Even with the appalling images all about me, I stand calmly in the midst of the carnage and speak with this man as though we had just met on the street at home.

"Such a waste, however, wouldn't you agree?" Maddoc says with a shake of his head. "Here they are, painting the landscape red and black and not a one of them has any idea as to why they are doing it."

"Yes, that is a waste," I reply, my eyes fixed on Maddoc. "Why are they doing it?"

"Why?" Maddoc is bright-eyed but suddenly sad. "Why do men do anything? Someone beats a drum, sings a moving song, and marches the rest of the cattle off to the slaughter. There is, of course, a lot of talk of duty and honor and loyalty. Then, when enough people have died, the demands of duty and honor are met and the blood can stop flowing for a season."

"There are some things worth standing for, worth fighting for . . ."

Maddoc looks at me suddenly with interest. "Defend, conquer, glory, and spirit, eh? Nonsense! Vasska is the Dragonking of the Pir, a god incarnate of this world. The dogma and the doctrine are repeated in their Kath-Drakonis to every child old enough to understand the words. The din never stops, my friend. And when at last you die, they use the same words to sew you into your shroud and drive you into the sod. You are born, live, and die for defense, conquest, glory, and spirit, and none of you—not one— ever thinks to question it. No one wants to really know _why_ all these men litter this field of battle or _why_ this battle was essential in the first place. No; let us all recite defense, conquest, glory, and spirit as we march down the length of someone else's sword and give our lives for someone else's ideals!"

I look once more over the long rolling fields of the dead. "So this is your vision?" I ask.

Maddoc raises his head once more and smiles. "Yes . . . I suppose it is."

I shake my head sadly at him as I speak. "What terrible thing has the world done to you?"

"The world only did me two favors," he replies, his voice rough and shaking. "Both of them are lost to me now."

"I spoke to her, you know, to your wife," I say. "She believes there is a way for us to escape this place and return to . . . return to her."

Maddoc looks down. As the moments pass, I believe that perhaps he might agree with me. "No," he says at last, looking up at me with a deeper sadness than I have ever seen before in any man's eyes. "She is wrong—she is dead."

"How can you say that?" I ask. How do I convince this crazed man to help me? "I just spoke with her this evening! She is trying to help you in every way she knows how. She even has convinced the Pir she herself is mad just to be with you and care for you! If you'll only just—"

I do not see it coming. Maddoc swings backhanded in a stinging blow across my face, knocking my head sharply to the side. When I turn back, he is pointing his finger at my face in warning.

"Do not mock me, boy!" he growls.

Mock him? What in Vasska's name is he talking about?

Then I see her.

Up near the crest of the hilltop, she lies unceremoniously atop a heap of corpses.

Rhea stares back at me through the fogged, vacant eyes of the dead.

"I come here when I can." Maddoc sighs. "Most days I cannot face it. Still, I hate to think of her here without me among all these strangers."

"What is this place?" I ask urgently as I stare at the dead form of his wife. "Is this the afterlife?"

"Afterlife? That place of rest beyond the Veil of Sighs that the Pir promised all those mortal fools? No, it most certainly is not!" Maddoc answers. "It is the place of dreams, the place of the past, the place of the future—all these and none of them. It is a place of the possible, the probable, and the entirely improbable. It's a bridge or an ocean and often both."

"That means nothing," I say, shaking my head.

"No? Perhaps it means <u>everything!</u>" Maddoc turns, walking back down the hillside toward the wide river.

I step carefully among the corpses, picking my way down as I follow in his path. The monk, seeing us coming down from the hilltop, moves quickly along his own course to intercept us.

"Sir!" the monk calls out as he approaches Maddoc. "I require a moment of your time!"

"All of life is a moment of my time," Maddoc responds as he walks purposefully toward the river of blood. He barely acknowledges the monk as he speaks. "I don't think I can afford giving it to you."

The monk is caught up short. He addresses me as I pass him. "Is <u>everyone</u> in this place so difficult?"

I look at him and laugh. "Apparently!"

The monk glares and then falls in line behind me.

The three of us come at last to the wide, sluggish river. Ahead of us I clearly see the tower of the winged woman. The great stones are being torn down in earnest now. The terrible beasts, creatures with the bodies of horses yet the chests, shoulders, and heads of men, have by now nearly collapsed the structure. I clearly see the lust in their eyes, desires that cannot be contemplated.

"She is yours, you know," Maddoc says as I come to stand beside him. "I have seen her often, of course, but she pays little attention to me. She is always looking for you."

I gaze up at the winged woman.

She holds her hands cupped before her as though holding something protectively, and rays of light break out in long streaks from between her fingers. It must be a great and precious possession. The exquisite expression on her face seems to say that her own heart means less to her than the glorious treasure she holds in her hands.

Then I experience an understanding as though it were placed in my mind. It is not like hearing her voice, which I know is both beautiful and terrible. This is a communication beyond words. I understand her need—and what I can do about it.

I kneel down by the crimson river, plunging my stained hand into its depths. As with the thought of her communication, I know what is there. My hand closes around the slippery, smooth object and I pull it from the river.

The blood drips free of its surface. It is a black, polished stone about half the size of my fist. I carefully set it down on the bank of the gory river and reach once more into the dark red depths.

"What are you doing?" the monk hisses, panic or fear in his face.

"I think . . . I think this is what I came here to do," I reply, not having any better explanation myself. Time and again I reach down into the horrible stream, pulling more stones out and setting them down next to me. When at last I feel I have enough, I stop.

A cry rends the air, shattering the dead stillness like glass breaking. I look up in fear. The winged woman has fled her tower, her wings fluttering with great speed. The creatures, howling, run after her but are too slow to catch her.

She is flying directly at me!

I stumble backward, lose my footing, and fall painfully onto the riverbank.

The winged woman approaches, drifting above the ground, and collects the black stones, a puzzled look on her face. She flies around me where I lie, dropping the stones one by one into the sand. I count them as they fall. Thirty-six stones in all now form a circle in the riverbank sand around me.

Almost without thought, I move to touch one of the stones with my bloodied hand. I hesitate, for a moment unsure. Then I reach beyond the circle of stones and grasp the hand of one of the dead. I pull it toward me. The gruesome corpse drags lightly across the ground at my touch. I lay the dead hand atop one of the stones, withdrawing my own hand at once.

The bony hand closes around the stone of its own accord.

I scramble to my feet in shock. As I watch, the corpse rises, coming to stand before me a gory visage; its broken sword still in one hand and the stone in the other.

The roar of the beasts approaches behind us.

The winged woman looks anxiously at me.

The monk stares at the revived corpse in abject terror.

I glance at Maddoc. I see him smile and nod at me.

One after another, I quickly set the hands of the dead on stones, and each then rises to stand about me. Within moments I create a circle of the horrific dead. There are thirty-three of them in all by the time I have formed a full circle, with myself in the middle.

Three stones remain.

"May I join you?" Maddoc asks.

I shiver as I nod. I reach down, pick up the three stones, and then toss one to him.

Maddoc reaches up and catches the stone, then smiles again at me. "One more . . . just for luck?"

I toss a second stone in his direction. Once more he extends his hand to catch the stone, but in flight it transforms into a sword. Maddoc grasps the handle deftly, swinging the blade in a quick arc before reversing his grip. Blade down, he presses the hilt of the sword to his chest in salute.

The pommel of his sword is fixed with a large black pearl.

Suddenly, all the dead of the circle move as one. They all turn to face me—with such faces as remain—and strike the hilts of their swords against their chests. In the dark chaos all around me, I see the pommels of their sword hilts flash. Each shines with a large black pearl.

With this salute, the fields of dead behind them rise of their own accord. As a great wave, they stand radiating from me beyond the hilltops. Their grotesque visages are suddenly transformed with light and power.

They turn as one and charge across the river. The terrible beasts are challenged at the river's edge.

The winged woman radiates with joy.

BOOK OF GALEN

BRONZE CANTICLES, TOME IV, FOLIO 1, LEAVES 12–15

Once upon another time, in a land of deepest myth . . .

Dwynwyn dreamt a strange dream.

Dwynwyn stood atop the towers of Qestardis, gazing out onto the sea. While she thus stood and contemplated the future of her beloved queen and nation, the waves of the ocean pulled back from the shore. The black rocks of the sea were thus exposed and among them she dreamt of a strange creature, a wingless faery without talent, whom she had seen in her other dreams.

She drifted downward from the tower toward the man. She spoke no word. She uttered no sound. In other dreams she had harmed the giftless faery with her gentle songs and knew not the truth of it. So she approached him in silence.

He nodded toward her and extended his hand. He dared not to touch her but dropped the pearls into her outstretched hand. They were some thirty-six in number, and their beauty was powerful and caught her eye. Within them, Dwynwyn saw a new truth[*] that had not before been known among the Fae folk of all the kingdoms. There, within these unique pearls, was the power to protect her beloved princess.

The waves of the ocean once more closed over the shore, hiding the strange, wingless faery from her again.

Yet there below the beautiful towers of Qestardis, Dwynwyn wept openly, for the strange, wingless faery had given her the pearls but had not instructed her in the fullness of their truth. She knew within her that they held the power to protect and save her beloved princess.

But she knew not how.

FAERY TALES
BRONZE CANTICLES, TOME VIII, FOLIO 2, LEAF 37

---

[*] Faeries believe that all truth already exists but that many truths have not yet been discovered. It is the search for these undiscovered truths that is the sociological obsession of the faeries.

Bright Swords

The horns of the Temple summoned morning once again to break over the towers of Vasskhold. The morning sun had not crested the tall peaks to the east and would not do so for several more hours, yet the day would not wait. Vasskhold rose with its early supplication to the Dragonking's benevolence. It breathed through the day to the rhythm of the Dragonking's tasks. It would lay itself down only when the Dragonking's glory had been satisfied.

The Elect were also summoned by those same horns but into a world that was terrible and new. Its boundaries were measured by the great walled crescent of land just east of Vasska's Temple, which from ancient times had been known simply as the Garden. The name conjured up images of lords and ladies strolling through verdant landscapes of carefully tended lawns, trees, shrubs, and hedgerows. Any remnant of such a vision was remanded to the distant past, however, for no such glory remained in the Garden. The arch of the long enclosure was now a prison. Long rows of ill-kept barracks housed the Elect along the sweeping remnants of the ancient avenues. The ruins of an ancient cathedral to forgotten gods served as their mess hall and general gathering place. They called it "the Hall" for lack of anything grander. To the north were the practice fields. The arena stood to the south. The Pir monks watched over it all from the Eighth and Ninth Towers of the Inner Circle and from the great sweeping walls that were the boundaries of this new world.

It was back into this world that the horns also summoned Galen.

"Galen, please! Wake up!"

Rhea's voice.

"Come on, Galen. I need you. We have to face the day."

Galen rolled over on his thin, hard bedding. His shoulder scraped against the boards of the bed above him as he did. Face the day? he thought. He didn't want to face the day. He didn't want to face anything. His body ached. Stiffness gripped his joints. It was all going to begin all over again.

"Please, Galen, something's happened to Maddoc."

"I'm coming, Rhea," Galen replied, his voice sluggish as he tried to form the words. He forced open his eyes. For a moment, he stared up at the rough-hewn boards just inches from his face. Then he remembered: his little stone home still waited for him somewhere. His comfortable forge existed *somewhere*. More than anything, he remembered that *she* was out there. Berkita still lived and breathed somewhere in the world. There were reasons to face the day.

He rolled out of the narrow bunk, barely avoiding a gibbering idiot who was trying to pluck apples from a nonexistent tree. His name was Otris, came from someplace called Waystead and now occupied the lower bunk directly across from Galen. Otris had grown worse over the last three days. Galen doubted he would survive two more.

Galen stretched, looking about as he tried to twist the knots out of his lower back. Rhea had long since vacated her upper bunk, the third in a stack of four. He spoke to her as he stretched. "So Maddoc had another rough night?"

Rhea was glancing up and down the rows with distraction. "He got a bit restless at one point . . ."

"Yeah, I remember." Galen yawned.

"Oh . . . I had hoped he didn't disturb anyone. The thing is—"

"Well, I think that pretty much ended when he started screaming about the demons climbing up his nose and tearing his heart out." Galen shook himself, trying to wake up.

Rhea was defensive. "He doesn't know any better, Galen."

Galen shook his head. "It's all right, Rhea. I don't sleep much anyway as it is. When I *do* sleep . . . well, it isn't always restful."

"Did you dream last night?"

"Look, could we not go into that just—"

"Galen," Rhea was insistent. "Did you see Maddoc last night in your dream?"

Galen shivered. "Yes, I saw him."

"What happened? Where did you see him?"

Galen slid out from his bunk. The masses of the Elect were heeding the call of the trumpets to their morning feed. "Look, Rhea, can we talk about this a little later? It was not pleasant . . . I just need a little time."

Rhea followed after him as he turned to shuffle out of the barracks. "Time? We don't *have* a little time, Galen! Maddoc's gone."

"Gone?" Galen looked back at her. The throng was pressing them toward the door. "What do you mean he's gone? It's a prison, Rhea, they don't just let you wander out for a stroll. He can't have gone very far."

"I know . . . but I've looked for him. He was gone from the bunk when I awoke this morning. I've been all over the Garden but—"

"You didn't mention this to the Pir, did you?"

"No, of course not!" The press of the crowd was worse as they neared the exit door.

Galen and Rhea emerged from the barracks into the soft light bathing the wide avenue. The sun had not yet crested the Lords of Mithlan to the east although the morning was already deep. The street was packed with the Elect, all making their weary way down toward the Hall.

"Look, we'll find him." Galen spoke over his shoulder to Rhea as she walked behind him, his breath forming clouds in the chill morning air. It was true that Maddoc might well have disappeared for good. He would certainly not be the first to vanish from his bunk and never be seen again. But Galen saw little sense in upsetting Rhea at this point and decided that a comforting lie was better than a stark possibility. "He's here somewhere . . . he'll probably just turn up on his own."

Rhea suddenly stopped. Galen looked at her quizzically for a moment before he realized that everyone else had stopped, too. They were looking at something behind Galen.

Galen turned. His jaw slacked in astonishment.

He stood at the center of a circle that had suddenly opened in the crowd. At its perimeter stood men of the Election, each already holding a sword from the weapons racks of the arena. They stood at attention in the circle, the hilts of the swords pressed to their chests in salute. He recognized Mikal Feathrin and Thais among them from his own town of Benyn, old Haggun Harn, too, but the rest of them were unfamiliar.

They were saluting Galen.

Rhea stepped up to him, speaking quietly over the suddenly hushed crowd. "Galen? What's happening?"

Galen turned around in the open space. "I . . . I don't know!"

The pommel of each of the swords was shining in the morning light.

Each was a polished black stone.

"This cannot be happening!" Galen said, his breath pounding out in clouds with each beat of his racing heart. Their faces and their bodies were whole, but several of them he recognized from the dream.

He counted them.

They numbered thirty-two.

His mind raced. Can that be right? Thirty-two? He had counted thirty-six in the dream. Could the dream have been wrong? If so, then could his dreams be wrong about other things as well?

Someone suddenly pushed his way into the circle.

It was Maddoc. He, too, raised his sword in salute—another sword with a black, polished pommel stone.

Rhea ran to Maddoc, brushing aside the sword and throwing her arms around him. She buried her head against his chest, closing her eyes in relief.

"Nice to see you again, Galen!" Maddoc smiled, taking no notice of his wife.

Galen blinked. "Maddoc! What's going on? Who are they?"

"We are all your men," Maddoc said brightly.

Galen moved forward, grasping Maddoc's sword hand and pushing the sword down out of sight. He spoke urgently under his breath as his eyes darted about. "But I don't *want* any men!"

Maddoc shook his head, a mad smile on his face. "But you called us and we came! We are your men and we'll serve you to the last! We are a circle of brothers forged by your will! We call ourselves 'The Circle of Brothers Forged by Galen's Will.' Admittedly, it isn't a very *good* name for a warrior cadre, but it will just have to do until we come up with a better name."

"Maddoc, you've got to get these men to disperse! If the Pir see this . . ."

"But, Galen, *I* didn't assemble these men! They came at *your* calling from the dream."

"I don't care *who* called them here or *where* they came from! They've got to break up! The Pir will see them like this and think they've got some kind of uprising on their hands!"

"Ah! I get it!" Maddoc winked at Galen. "You want them to be a *secret* cadre!"

"Yes, fine," Galen said, exasperated and desperate. "Anything to get them to break this up! Just . . . Hey, where did they go?"

The circle was gone and the crowd was filling in the space, quickly erasing any trace of what had just happened. All that remained was an intense murmur running through the crowd in the street, and the suspicious looks they often cast in Galen's direction.

"They move like the shadows in the night!" Maddoc intoned in a voice filled with conspiratorial drama. "They are everywhere and nowhere . . . watching! They are the *Secret* Circle of Brothers Forged by Galen's Will!"

Rhea shook her head sadly. She took her husband's arm and turned him back toward the Hall.

"Don't you worry, Galen!" Maddoc shouted as they moved into the crowd. "I'll come up with a better name soon!"

* * *

Galen tried every other sword on the rack.

None of them would have him.

He stood facing the one sword that did not scream at him with a sound that made his teeth hurt. It was also the one sword that he was loath to touch.

"You did this, didn't you?" Galen said to the sword at last.

"Of course I did," the sword replied. *"It was all a matter of convincing the other swords that you are mine. To be honest, it was not that hard. They don't see the potential that I see in you. It isn't every season that I get to enjoy training a true warrior!"*

"A true warrior?" Galen scoffed. "You must not be a very sharp sword after all."

"Clever," the sword replied, *"but sharp is the one thing that I am. With my help, Galen, you'll acquit yourself well in the wars. You'll be a true, tragic hero who—"*

Galen straightened suddenly. "Wars? What wars?"

The sword sang with the thrill of its memory. *"The Dragon Wars, of course! The armies of Vasska and the other four dragons meet in fierce battle on the Enlund Plain! Oh, it is glorious to see, Galen! The forces of the great dragons colliding in armed combat. Desperate deeds and heroic sacrifice! It makes me proud to be a part of it!"*

"What are you talking about?" Galen protested, folding his arms across his chest. "We aren't at war!"

"But the Dragon Wars have been going on since the fall of Rhamas," the sword protested.

"That's over four hundred years!" Galen could not grasp it. "No war can last that long!"

"Ah, yes, more's the pity," the sword replied. *"I'll admit that it is difficult to sustain a really good war for very long. One side or the other so often runs out of supplies or money or will or just people to fight. Then, too, the life of a sword is all too often a short one. Only the heirlooms have much chance of being taken from the field of battle and preserved. Of course, those swords never get to see much action, either. I suppose I've really got the best of both: I've seen a lot of action over the centuries and am still around to cut an edge."*

Galen took a step back, studying the sword. "So you do. We killed a man yesterday, you and I."

"*Him? Well, I beg your pardon, but that one hardly counted! He fell on me! It's actually rather embarrassing. All the other swords are laughing at me, but that's not your fault. I mean, how were you supposed to know the ox was going to impale himself on——*"

"Shut up!" Galen said.

The sword went silent.

"You talk too much for a sword," Galen said at last.

"*Yes, I suppose I do,*" the sword replied, "*but you have to understand that I don't talk to just* anyone. *You're only the fifth 'Craftis' I've met, and each of those was so crazy that they didn't make any——*"

"Craftis?" Galen squinted. "What is a Craftis?"

"*Someone who can speak to crafted objects. You know, things made by hand?*" The sword seemed excited as it spoke into Galen's mind. "*I think that the makers must imbue something of themselves into everything they make. It takes someone special—someone even special among the Elect—to hear and speak to that something. I remember every life that I have taken, too, and sometimes I wonder if each of them imbued me with some of themselves as well. I don't know about such things, I'm just a sword, but I am a sword that can help you stand out in the war!*"

Galen sighed. "Well, if I need a sword, I suppose it might as well be you. Do you have a name?"

"*A name?*" the sword responded. "*What? You mean like 'Doombringer' or 'Human-cleaver' or something ridiculous like that?*"

Galen shrugged. "Look, I was just asking . . ."

"*S'shnickt.*"

"S'shnickt?" Galen frowned.

"*Yes, you can call me S'shnickt,*" the sword moaned. "*It wasn't my idea.*"

"Very well . . . S'shnickt," Galen said, reaching out for the sword at last and taking it from the rack. It felt cold to his touch. He loathed holding it but knew that if he were to survive to get home, he would need the sword's help. "I guess we're partners."

The metal rang with joy.

"Get me safely through the war, S'shnickt," Galen murmured. "I've got to return home."

"Return home?" the sword said. *"But,* no one *survives the war! You'll die valiantly, but that's about as much as you can hope for."*

"No one ever comes back?"

"No one . . . just us swords."

It was then that Galen noticed the pommel on the sword.

It was a shining black stone.

Twelve Suns

"Y ou say this Galen has formed his own followers? Are you *absolutely sure* about this, Gendrik?"

"Yes, my lord," Gendrik replied, swallowing hard. His throat was choked and dry. He did not understand any of this. Lord Tragget had summoned him to the Hall of Truth before dawn and he had barely had an opportunity to wake up before he found himself being ushered into the Garden, of all places, on a secret mission for the Inquisitor.

Now that same Inquisitor, his master, was leaning so far forward in the Judgment Throne that the servant feared for a moment his master would fall off. Tragget's face looked nearly purple and his eyes blinked furiously. "Gendrik, by Vasska, I'll send you to the wars myself if you're so much as making up a single lie . . ."

"I saw it myself, Father," Gendrik squeaked. "You *did* ask me to watch this particular Elect, as you may recall. I was following your instructions when it happened."

Tragget leaned slowly back into the Judgment Throne. His long, narrow hands reached forward, gripping the ends of the throne's arm rests until his knuckles were bright white.

Gendrik tried to swallow again. He never did care for the Hall of

Truth. It was the domain of his master and his work required that he visit it from time to time, but that did not make the doing of it any easier. The hall was long and narrow, with windowless walls crafted out of polished obsidian and a ceiling that closed to a pointed arch twenty feet overhead. One entered the room through a large double door in the west end, and the Judgment Throne sat on a dais at the east end. From where he stood before this throne, Gendrik could see two arches on either side of the dais. One led down to one of two side exits from the Temple. The other archway led directly to the jailer's chambers. It was a unique feature of the Hall of Truth that one never knew which archway led to safety and which led to destruction at the whim of the Inquisitor. Great vertical drums in both hallways pivoted at the same time, causing a left turn to become a right turn or vice versa. One's fate before this throne, therefore, was known only to the Inquisitor until it was too late to question the sentence.

The Inquisitor was as much a mystery as his room. Tragget pressed his fingers together, touching them to his lips in thought before he spoke. "Go on, Gendrik, omit nothing."

"Y-yes, my lord." Gendrik was sweating despite the chill in the windowless room. He could not help himself. "Well, this woman woke Galen up—"

"Rhea Myyrdin."

"Yes, my lord, Rhea Myyrdin."

"Go on."

"Well, she was upset about her husband—Maddoc Myyrdin—having gone missing from the barracks. It seems he had a difficult night last night and had not slept well."

"I don't doubt it," the Inquisitor murmured.

"Excuse me, Your Lordship?"

"Never mind . . . continue."

"Well, let me see . . . Galen replied that he hadn't slept well either. Then this Rhea wanted to know if Galen had seen her husband in his dreams."

"Wait," the Inquisitor said abruptly, leaning forward. "Say that again!"

"This Rhea asked Galen if he had seen Maddoc in his dreams. I remember it clearly as it seemed like such an odd thing to ask. His reply was just as strange: he said he *had* seen him."

Tragget's eyes were intent, his voice quiet but strained. "Did he say he saw anyone *else* in his dream?"

Gendrik thought for a moment.

Tragget waited out the silence.

"No . . . no, my lord, he didn't mention anyone. It was about then that they were leaving the barracks. I had some trouble staying with them and following their conversation. This Rhea woman said she had looked all over the Garden for her husband. Galen said that she should not be too worried about the whole thing as Maddoc would probably show up soon enough, being as they were in a prison and there wasn't much chance of him going very far. It was about then that the circle formed up."

"The circle?"

"Yes, my lord, the circle of mad warriors. They seemed to come out of nowhere. They just appeared out of the crowd, opening a space around this Galen Arvad fellow. Oh, the space was twenty feet across—is that important?"

Tragget relaxed his grip on the chair long enough to reach up and rub his eyes. "Go on."

"Well, sire, I managed to get to the edge of the circle just as they all saluted this Galen Arvad with their swords. It was about then that Maddoc Myyrdin arrived with his own sword and started jabbering on about how they were all Galen's men and Galen said that he didn't want any men. Not that thirty-two men are much of an army—"

"Thirty-six," Tragget corrected.

"Your Lordship?"

"You mean there were thirty-six of them," Tragget said with growing impatience.

"Oh, no, my lord! There were thirty-two of them in the circle . . . well, thirty-three if you counted Maddoc Myyrdin. I remember that quite clearly because of the swords. Each sword had a different blade and handle but they all had a black stone fixed to the end of the—"

"A *what?*" Tragget asked sharply. "A black stone?"

"Why, yes, Your Lordship . . . didn't I mention that before?"

"A polished black stone at the pommel?" Tragget was leaning forward once again, his blue eyes wide, the look on his face dangerous. "At the bottom end of the handle?"

Gendrik gulped. "Why, yes! I remember counting the swords because it was so unusual. I checked with the weapons master later about it. He said that I must have been one of the madmen, too, because there were no swords with a black stone in the handle in his armory. I was worried for a time, sire, that they might not let me out of the Garden after that one!"

Gendrik watched Tragget anxiously. The Inquisitor once again was rolling things around in his mind, his gaze fixed on some distant place. It unnerved Gendrik. He had been much more than Tragget's torusk master; for several years now he had been the eyes and ears of his master in the streets and towns they visited. He knew from experience that the longer an Inquisitor thought, the worse it could be for the people standing before them. "Sire, if it pleases you, may I go now? I've much work ahead of me . . . all in your service, might I add?"

"Gendrik, quiet! I know full well that you have more than a month before the caravans leave for Enlund."

"But Your Lordship, one of the Aboths informed all the torusk masters yesterday that the caravans would be leaving twelve suns from now."

Tragget looked once more directly at Gendrik. The torusk master tried to swallow but found he could not. His mouth had gone completely dry.

"Twelve suns!" Tragget snapped. "That isn't nearly enough time!"

"Well, no sire! That's why I've got to beg your leave and get back to work right away! Fear not, sire; twelve suns is a short time, but the caravans will be ready to take them."

Tragget furrowed his brow. "You are *absolutely* certain about these swords?"

"Certainly, sire; thirty-three of them, all with black stones in their handles . . . Is it important?"

Tragget leaned back into the throne. "No, Gendrik, it is not important but you have done well. Take the arch to my right and go with my blessing."

Gendrik stared at the right archway, hesitating.

Tragget stood up, stepping purposefully past Gendrik down the hall. The Inquisitor called after him as he departed. "Do not worry, Gendrik! You are still of use to me."

Tragget stood as Edana entered the sitting room.

"I was in audience," Edana complained, angrily pulling the holy crown of the Pir from her head and tossing it in a chair at the side of the room. "The hall was filled with petitioners! They are there still for all I know, wondering—as I am—why the Voice of Vasska had to suddenly leave."

"My apologies, Mother of the Pir, but this could not wait." Tragget stood near the large hearth, his hands clasped together nervously. "Are the caravans to Enlund leaving in twelve days?"

Edana stopped brushing back her crown-tangled hair, looking curiously at the Inquisitor. "Yes . . . yes, they are. I see that you are taking the duties of your office more seriously. It is true; the caravans will be leaving after twelve suns have passed. It is the will of Vasska."

"The will of Vasska? Holy Lady, it is not enough time!" Tragget pleaded with an angry undertone in his voice. "The Council has tasked me—you have tasked me—to discover what the dragons fear in these madmen. I've made some great progress in this regard. Just today, in fact, there was an incident—"

"That disturbance in the Garden?" Edana said easily.

"Well, yes. I was not aware that you had heard of it."

"The Elect are always forming groups." Edana shrugged, lifting the mantle of her office from her shoulders and draping it over the crown and chair. "There have even been a few insurrections organized from time to time. The dragonstaffs always quell them. Besides, the Chosen Elect are always dead in the war before anything substantial can come of it. You think this is different?"

"It was different, yes. It involved a unique man among the Elect. He is the reason we went to that Festival in the Dragonback."

Edana raised her eyebrow in interest as she settled into her great chair. "Indeed? Then you think that he *is* the man of the visions?"

"I believe he may well be," Tragget returned anxiously. "I . . . I don't know but . . . well, there has been some evidence that he is exerting . . . extraordinary powers."

"Evidence? Really?" Edana's eyes narrowed. "What evidence?"

Tragget looked away, his hands working nervously in front of him. "It's . . . it's difficult to explain. The Elect who appear to serve him all wield swords that are somewhat alike. They all have a black stone in the handle. Now, before last night we have no record of any such swords in the armory, yet now they exist."

"And you think this man—"

"Galen Arvad," Tragget urged.

"Yes, you think this Galen Arvad had something to do with these strange weapons?"

"I do."

"Why?" Edana asked quietly.

Tragget turned, slowly pacing the room. "Well . . . I th-think that it is s-significant that each of these w-warriors has an identical change in each of their s-swords and that they all give their allegiance to Arvad. It is clear that he is the focus of this strange phenomenon."

"Black stones, eh?" Edana mused. "Where did these black stones come from? Why are they significant?"

"I d-don't know where they c-come from," Tragget responded, "nor do I know why they are significant. That is why I need more time! Twelve days is simply insufficient for me to learn what I need to know!"

Edana pondered for a while before answering. "Tragget, this change in the caravans was neither my doing nor the will of the Council. Vasska ordained it directly. There is urgency in the war that must be satisfied at once. There is nothing I can do about that; it is out of my hands."

"I am making progress, Holy Lady," Tragget responded with deliberated words, "but I do not believe I can get what I need in only twelve suns' time!"

"Do not question the will of Vasska! We are all a part of the Pir and we will all of us do our duty," Edana replied coldly as she stood. "I am not interested in hearing about your weaknesses or deficiencies. You have twelve days to get what you need from this Galen Arvad before he falls before his duty to the Pir. It was in the vision, Tragget, and it *will* happen as prophesied, but only if you stop complaining and find a way to make it happen."

Edana turned toward the door, resettling her mantle about her. "We are destined to rule even Vasska—it is up to you to find a way! Make it happen and don't bring me any more excuses."

With that, she snatched the crown from the chair and exited the room.

"What do you think, Lord Inquisitor?" the master stonecutter tentatively asked.

Tragget stood before the colossi, considering them in the failing light.

The two statues were once of Thon and Kel. Now their faces had been replaced. Where once the brothers had watched over the city, now the long snout and horned mane of the Dragonking cast its cold gaze westward down the Avenue of Triumph.

"The heads seem smaller than they ought to be," Tragget observed critically.

The stonecutter quailed noticeably. "It was the original stone, Your Lordship. We had to work with what was left. I assure you that the utmost care was taken—"

"Yes . . . yes, I'm sure it was," Tragget responded quickly. He feared that if he let the man twist much longer on his words, he would hang himself. "You have done well. You may continue with your work."

"Thank you, Lord Inquisitor!" The master stonecutter bowed several times as he stepped backward. No doubt the man was anxious to get back to his work; even more anxious to get out of the dangerous proximity of the Inquisitor.

Tragget continued to gaze on the statues. Outwardly he was as hard and unmoving as the great figures before him. Within, however, was another matter; his thoughts tossed tempestuously about as he sought answers to questions he barely understood.

After his encounter with Edana, the walls of the Temple had felt confining and its air oppressive. He desperately needed to get out and find some space of his own in which to think. The examination of the stonework being done on the colossi was an excuse readily at hand, so he had exited the Temple at once. He ignored the fountains, gardens, and shops of the inner keep in his hurried step and did not stop until he had passed out of the Conqueror's Gate.

Now the statues were staring back at him. How appropriate they seemed; the head of a dragon and the body of a man! The priests of the Nobis order had sanctioned the change, stating that it was symbolic of the relationship between the Pir and their Dragonking. Far better, they said, than to perpetuate the fallen glory of humanity.

The head of a dragon and the body of a man: that is the Pir, Tragget mused. Emasculated and decapitated humanity. We do the work while Vasska and his kind think for us. The Dragonkings have a future and a destiny of their own. Humanity has none. Our destiny is the same as the body's—the grave.

Not I, however, Tragget reminded himself. The doom of the Dragonkings is written in my destiny. I've seen it in the smoke; my fate is bound to the power of the Mad Emperors. It is written in prophecy.

He knew his destiny, but what course should he take to fulfill it? This power—this mystic force—was the key. It called to him seductively toward sin and blasphemy against the Pir. He longed to embrace it, flee into it and turn his back on the Pir and his guilt forever. Yet his reason, his duty to his mother, and his duty to the order that had given him everything held him back from that abyss.

He had a destiny, but did that destiny perforce include the Pir? If the dragonsmoke foretold the fall of the dragons, did that not include their religion as well? Was his fate with the Pir—or completely without them?

The head of a dragon . . . the *heart* of a man. Tragget did not know which road would lead him to his destiny, but one thing he did know; neither road would avail him if Galen died before Tragget could learn what he knew of the power. The heart or the head— either way he had to keep Galen alive.

Black Hope

Dwynwyn awoke with a start. She quickly sat up on her bed, her flailing foot knocking several scrolls littering her rumpled bedsheet to the floor. She sat there for a moment trying to catch her breath, feeling as though she had been flying at great speed from some distant place.

Cavan burst into the room. "Mistress Dwynwyn! I heard you cry out!"

"Did I?" Dwynwyn responded. She was disoriented, as though she had been in one place, blinked, and then found herself entirely in another. The surroundings of her room, though familiar, only confused her.

"You did!" Cavan fluttered quickly over to her. "Are you well, Mistress?"

Dwynwyn did not hear him, her mind still preoccupied with the sudden transition from her dreams to the waking world.

A world of dreams? It was far more real this time than any of her previous experiences. She remembered standing upon the tower of Qestardis, though it stood in a different place; a place of rolling hills she had never been before. A fog had blanketed the lowland, obscuring a field of—a field of what? She could not remember it clearly. In her mind she recalled the clouds washed over against the hillsides below as though they were waves of some vaporous sea. The dark wingless man was there, standing at the edge of this fog. There was another wingless man standing with him . . . thin with fevered eyes. The dark one was beckoning to her, urging her to come down to the tower's base.

There was something there at the base of the tower. The answer to her search. The end of her quest. The key to their salvation. She floated down from the tower, down toward the shore of fog, toward the glinting treasure that could protect them from the doom that threatened them. Dwynwyn looked carefully in the fading light as she neared the ground.

She saw it clearly. It was the wingless man's gift to her. It was his power given to her. It was a new truth to which he was leading her.

"Dwynwyn!" Cavan was shaking her by the forewing vein of her left wing. "Talk to me! Are you well?"

"Oh! Cavan, stop! Of course, I'm well!" Dwynwyn swatted absently at the sprite, who quickly dodged out of the way. "It's just that . . ."

No, she suddenly realized, she *did* know that place . . . or somewhere much like it!

"Cavan! Quickly! We must leave at once!"

The sprite flickered uncertainly for a few moments. "Leave? Leave for where, Mistress?"

Dwynwyn was already out of her bed, kicking aside several scroll sheaves that had somehow managed to fall between her and her crowded closet on the opposite side of the room. "There isn't time to explain . . . just *hurry!*"

Cavan had never before questioned his mistress—but he was seriously thinking of doing so now.

They had been together for many, many seasons. Cavan had met Dwynwyn while she was still undergoing her apprenticeship under Seeker Polonis and Cavan had been stationed in the court as a servant to Princess Aislynn's entourage. Cavan was no longer sure just why he had poured the wine into Dwynwyn's lap when the Seeker was first presented to the princess. Perhaps it was something Polonis had said that distracted him, or maybe the old crone had managed to give him a shove. Regardless of the cause, Cavan had been certain he would be dismissed from the halls of Qestardis for such a grievous error and thereby become nameless* in his own caste. Dwynwyn, however, had asked that Cavan become her servant and took the young sprite in under her own name. Since that day, Cavan had served her with unquestioning loyalty and devotion.

At least, he had until this moment.

Dwynwyn floated above the waves that rhythmically washed up onto the sands of the beach and then withdrew back into Estarin Bay. The walls of Qestardis were well behind them as they drifted above the shore west of the palace. Cavan preferred the safety offered by those walls. He always considered the world beyond them to be something of a dangerous place: filled with Famadorian creatures of infinite diversity and ferocity. He particularly never trusted the sea. Its merfolk occasionally traded with the faeries, but were mercurial in their disposition and occasionally raided faery ships regardless of the treaties they had pledged.

Now he glanced about uncertainly. "Mistress, perhaps if you could tell me what you seek, I could requisition a group of the third class to come out and retrieve it for you?"

"I'll know when I see it, Cavan," Dwynwyn replied, "which is, incidentally, why we cannot send someone out here to get it for me; I don't know what it is yet. Do you still have that basket?"

Cavan was more confused than ever. "Yes, Mistress, I have the basket, although I can only hope that it is fit to hold your clothing again when we return home. We *will* be returning home, won't we?"

Dwynwyn said nothing. She slowed over the waves, whose waters had turned a brilliant turquoise color. Cavan could easily see the bottom as though he were gazing down into a reflecting pool in the palace. It seemed clean enough and not terribly deep. There did not appear to be any of the merfolk around, but one could never tell. He

---

* To be "nameless" in the Fae classes is to be unrecognized by the other members of one's caste. In most cases it is a virtual death sentence since most Fae refuse to accept a lower station than their born caste, and no station above their caste will support them.

had heard that they were terribly quick in the water. The shore was not far away, but certainly too far for Cavan's liking.

"Mistress, I really think that we should be getting back to . . . Dwynwyn?"

The Seeker had stopped. She hovered just a wing's width above the surface of the sea, her eyes wide as a smile played about her lips.

Suddenly, her wings collapsed.

Cavan was ablaze with light. "Dwynwyn! No!"

The faery fell, crashing down into the surface of the sea.

Cavan flitted, desperate and helpless. The water churned below him, opaque now with the froth and agitation of Dwynwyn's sudden plunge, hiding all evidence of her.

"Dwynwyn! Come back! Come back!"

The roiling surface began to calm, and Cavan could make out a shadow moving beneath the turquoise water fractured by white bubbles. The sprite glanced frantically about, wondering what he might find nearby that would help Dwynwyn out of her mortal danger but seeing nothing of immediate use.

Why had she done this? His mind raged in anger and frustration. He felt certain nothing had damaged her or driven her from the air. Maybe she was sick or poisoned. He should have asked sooner, should have been more attentive and questioned her course of investigation earlier when it might have done her some good.

The surface was nearly calm once again. Cavan could see a dark shape struggling just below the surface. Panic contorted his face.

Suddenly, the dark shape moved and rushed upward. Cavan darted back away from the explosion of water as it broke the surface.

Dwynwyn stood shoulder deep in the water. Her white hair lay flat between her wing veins. The wings themselves sagged behind her. They were hopelessly wet and lay heavily on the surface. The Seeker coughed furiously, water spraying from her mouth.

"Cavan, I must . . . remember to . . . breathe *out* through . . . my nose when . . . under water," she sputtered.

Cavan was livid. "Ah, so *that* is the new truth you have discovered, Mistress? We came out here to discover *drowning?*"

Dwynwyn smiled between convulsive coughs. "No, Cavan. We came to gather these."

The Seeker thrust three dark shapes up from the water.

"Those are the ugliest things I have ever seen," Cavan replied, and faeries never lie or exaggerate their opinions. "What are they?"

Dwynwyn gazed at them. They were, indeed, ugly to the eye of the faery. Even though they were natural, something the faery value above all, they were irregular and roughly crusted disks. More than anything, they looked like dirty, wet rocks.

"They are a new truth, Cavan," Dwynwyn replied with a smile as she dumped her find into Cavan's basket. "And there is a lot more of them, too!"

"More of them?" Cavan responded in alarm.

Dwynwyn pinched her nose with her left hand and once more disappeared beneath the surface in a frothing churn of bubbles.

"How *many* more of them?" Cavan yelled down through the water.

He only got more bubbles for an answer.

Dwynwyn slogged back into her apartments. Her wet wings sagged uselessly from their veins, and her white hair—crusted with the sea salt—hung down around her eyes. Her outfit for the day, a flowing gown, clung to her tenaciously, its hem stained dark from the long walk back to Qestardis.

The palace guards who had strained to lift her back up to the level of her quarters had made it perfectly clear that she stank.

But she was happier than she could ever recall being.

"Mistress." Cavan spoke from the depths of his misery. He was struggling with the weight of the basket. "The stewards are gathering in the hall. They are dismayed at your appearance."

Dwynwyn moved quickly across the floor, the occasional drip from her dress marking her path across the litter-strewn floor. "Shut the door and they won't have to look at me."

Cavan obeyed as he always had. The portal closed decisively behind him on the gathering and disapproving faces peering in. "The eyes of the queen's servants are now shut, although I doubt the same can be said about their mouths. What do you want me to do with these—what *are* these things?"

"Seashells . . . I think. At least that is how they appeared to me," Dwynwyn replied from her adjoining bedchamber. "Just put them down on the table!"

Cavan cast about the cluttered and disheveled room. "*What* table?"

"The big one by the window."

"There isn't any place *on* the table to put them," Cavan replied. There wasn't any place to put them anywhere in the room so far as he could see.

"Such a bother!" Dwynwyn replied, emerging from her bedchamber, where she had changed into her comfortable, faded lounging robe. She quickly surveyed the carnage on the table, threw her arms around a large stack of bound books, and lifted them clear. She then pushed aside several boxes on the floor with a foot and, having gained some territory, set the books down on the floor.

"I wish you'd let the servants clean your apartments," Cavan groused.

"I know," Dwynwyn replied, still absorbed in her tabletop reclamation project, "but after they cleaned, how would I ever find anything?"

"How do you ever find anything *now?*" Cavan responded.

"There!" Dwynwyn said, happily ignoring his comment as she sat down on the far side of the table. The sun was high in the sky behind her, shining down through the large window. "Set them down right there in front of me."

The sprite set the basket down, then collapsed back onto a stack of books still remaining on the table. The basket had grown increasingly heavy throughout the morning and their long walk back toward the city. It had been an exercise in both endurance and patience, and Cavan was exhausted.

"I need a knife," Dwynwyn muttered as she pulled the first of the grotesque shells from the basket. Despite the encrusting outer growth, there was a beautiful symmetry to the underlying shell and something more, she was certain, beyond. "Cavan?"

"Yes, Mistress," the sprite replied wearily.

"I need a knife?" she repeated. The inflection was a question but the tone said otherwise.

"Yes, Mistress . . . at once." Cavan sighed, then rose from his resting spot on the books. He flitted once more out the main portal. The sudden opening apparently caught several of the servitors outside speaking among themselves in hushed tones. Startled, they jumped back as the sprite flashed past them. In the next moment, each of them turned away as though distracted by their ordained tasks. The portal closed on the tableau in the next heartbeat.

Dwynwyn smiled. Let them gawk and talk among themselves. She was a true Seeker, and this was a new truth. Something extraordinary was happening, something she had not come across in all the studies and searches of the ancient knowledge. This was what she yearned for all her life and was the heart's blood of her existence: the revealing of a new truth.

She turned once more to examine the crusty shell. There was a thin line she could see running around its perimeter, which she assumed was the gateway. The fact that she was sure of this thrilled her, too. It was not a truth she had learned in her books or scrolls nor discovered through experiment and trial; this was a truth that she knew beyond those truths of experience. That, in itself, may well be a new truth, she thought.

As Cavan reentered the room, she noticed that the crowd outside had grown in the last few moments. Cavan was clearly frustrated, his normal radiance decidedly shifting in color toward the red.

"I told the servitors that you wanted a knife," Cavan said in a huff. "Half of them were afraid that you wanted to kill yourself, and the other half were afraid that you *didn't!* Either way, they were more than willing to provide the knife."

"How good of them," Dwynwyn remarked with a wry smile. She took the knife—a dagger from one of the house guards—and set the shell against the polished wood top of the table. Leaning down closer, she carefully inserted the blade into the thin line, sawing back and forth down the length. Then, fitting the long edge of the blade into the cut line between the upper and lower halves of the shell, she twisted the dagger, prying the halves apart.

"Mistress!" Cavan said, drawing back in disgust. "What in the queen's name is *that?*"

A gritty, white-colored sluice spilled from the open shell down onto the tabletop. The interior of the upper shell was a glorious array of colors, while the bottom half still held the remaining thick liquid.

Dwynwyn cocked her head to one side, then dipped her finger in the fluid and drew it to her lips.

"Mistress! *No!*" Cavan whispered urgently.

"Salt," she replied. "How extraordinary a truth!" She then reached forward, her fingers searching through the runny sludge for a moment. A smile once more brightened her face. "Cavan! Some water in the washbasin! Quickly!"

The sprite rushed to the sideboard and poured water from an urn into the basin. He brought it back at once, setting it next to the spilled sluice before flitting back to watch over Dwynwyn's shoulder.

Dwynwyn pulled something out of the milky liquid and washed it in the basin.

It was a large black pearl shining with a blackness that seemed to shame the night. But as she turned it in the light, variations in its midnight coloring were revealed which gave depth and complexity to its darkness. The pearl was perfect in its roundness and, somehow, difficult to look at for any length of time.

Pearls, the most prized of which were white, were known to the faeries, who often bartered for them with the merfolk at the trade docks of the quay. However, their origins had always been a mystery.

"I have never seen its like, Mistress." Cavan sounded breathless and troubled.

"You will," Dwynwyn said in wonder. "Each of these others contains a brother to this one."

"Each one?" Cavan squeaked. Black pearls were certainly not unheard of, but none such as this. "There must be dozens in the basket!"

"There are thirty-five more of them, Cavan."

The sprite was in awe. "Mistress! How can you know?"

"I just know, Cavan." Dwynwyn smiled, her brow nevertheless furrowed with puzzlement. "I have seen it in my mind."

"There is something unnatural about this, Mistress!" Cavan said with increasing distress. "We should call in the scholars to consult."

"No," Dwynwyn replied, holding the exquisite pearl up to the light streaming in from the window behind him. "I need you to call the royal jeweler. I have a very special task for him that will not wait."

A Private Walk

D
wynwyn fluttered hurriedly through the archway, quickly pulling her white hair back and binding it tightly. There had not been time for any more formal styling and it was still damp from the quick rinse she had given it to get out the sea salt. Dwynwyn knew she was barely presentable at court as she was: her robe was shabby, and she had forgotten her slippers entirely in her haste. It would have to do.

The Sanctuary was in more turmoil than Dwynwyn had ever seen it. Faeries, pixies, nymphs, and dryads dashed purposefully between the great trees and congregated around one or more of the central courtiers near the throne, to whom they would speak in earnest, hushed tones. There was so much activity in the enormous hall that Dwynwyn felt the air currents whip into a frenzied breeze swirling its way between the trunks of the trees.

Tatyana sat attentively at the center of this storm, leaning forward with interest, her right hand absently stroking her smooth chin. The queen's large amber eyes were bright and alert, yet the Seeker could see weariness in the lines of her face.

Dwynwyn drifted to a halt just beyond the circle of the courtiers. She floated slightly to her right, drifting intentionally into the line of the queen's sight. Their eyes met in recognition for a moment. It was just enough. Tatyana nodded slightly in the Seeker's direction. It was their understood signal between them that the Seeker had need to counsel with the queen as soon as possible.

Tatyana the Glorious raised her hand slightly. Voice Newlis, who had been speaking to her in earnest, did not see her signal, however, and continued to speak hurriedly.

"Enough!"

Tatyana rarely raised her voice. When the occasion required it, however, she could give it a timbre that carried to the farthest corners of the Sanctuary. The very sound could make even the highest courtier submit. Some of the servitor class believed that if the queen was in any real distress, her voice would be heard from the highest of the royal apartments to the farthest foundations of Qestardis itself.

That same voice echoed through the coves of the Sanctuary even as she stood imperiously before her throne. Everything in the world within the view of Tatyana had frozen in its place.

"Who dares bring disorder into my Sanctuary?" Tatyana thundered. "The anarchy is what we fight; I will *not* submit to it in my own house. *Here I will have order!*"

Only the Voice of Warriors, frustrated and desperate, dared answer her. "But, Your Majesty—"

"This is still *my* Sanctuary, Nevis! *Mine!* I will have order, is that clear?"

"Yes, Your Majesty!"

She gazed imperiously over the assemblage, a slight disdain edging her voice as she spoke. "I will take counsel with my Seeker for a time. It is my command that the Sanctuary be cleared of all else until I command otherwise. Nevis?"

"By your will, Your Majesty!"

"Admit no one without my permission—*no one!*"

Tatyana glared about her. The entire court held still in uncertainty.

"Must I repeat myself? Clear the Sanctuary *now!*"

Suddenly, the frozen courtiers, servants, and messengers sprang to life. Color exploded with their rushed movements, desperate as they were to flee the huge hall. A new wind suddenly whipped a wet strand of Dwynwyn's hair across her eyes, which blinked closed. As she wiped the strand away, she heard a succession of thunderous booming sounds from all parts of the hall as portals slammed closed.

When she again opened her eyes, only Tatyana and herself remained among the great trees of the tower Sanctuary.

Dwynwyn spoke quietly. "Your Majesty, I—"

Tatyana held her hand up for silence, her head cocked to one side, listening. She remained there, motionless for some time, searching for some sound among the towering ornate trunks whose branches supported the lacelike structures of the crystal domes overhead. After a time, apparently satisfied with the silence, she lowered her hand and turned to face her Seeker.

"Dwynwyn, I have been hearing a great deal about you today," she said, sitting down and resuming her placid, regal pose on the throne of Qestardis.

"Yes, Your Majesty." Dwynwyn nodded quietly. "I would imagine that you have."

"The captain of my guard tells me that you walked . . . just imagine it, *walked* back toward the city from the Estarin shore as you were apparently incapable of flight."

"That is accurate, Your Majesty."

"Furthermore, my chief steward tells me that you arrived at your apartments in a frightful condition, that your clothing and wings were completely wet and that you smelled strongly of fish!"

"The reasons for which, I would be most relieved to explain, Your Majesty!"

Tatyana laughed heartily, relaxing back into her throne for the first time. "Oh, please don't, Dwynwyn—at least not yet! The Seekers constantly amaze us. You are one of the few delights that remain in this world. You are always finding things that are *new* and *unique*. These things delight us to no end. To take the facts that have been laid before me and to try to fit their pieces into some reasonable explanation of its truth is a joy to us. Oh, I know you do this all the time in your caste, Seeker, and perhaps combining truths in new ways—the discovery of further truth—no longer holds interest or mystery for you. Yet for an old royal such as myself, it is a delightful game to play, even for a short while."

"Your pleasure is mine, Your Majesty." Dwynwyn bowed with a slight smile. "If I may be so bold, the discovery of new truths remains my passion and joy, second only to my service to you and your court."

"Both clever and politic, I see." Tatyana rose from her throne. "You would have been a great courtier had life not ordained you to a different fate.* Come, Seeker, take a turn with me through my little garden."

Tatyana stepped down from the dais, drifting slowly back across the trim grasses behind her throne. Her magnificent detailed wings barely moved as she floated among the carefully shaped flowers and shrubs. Dwynwyn quickly fell in next to her, trying as carefully as she could to gauge her distance. She wanted to hear everything her queen was quietly saying without touching the royal personage.

"It is a beautiful day, isn't it, Dwynwyn?"

"Yes, Your Majesty, I quite agree."

"Yet the night is coming, Dwynwyn, and an end to our day; the end to uncounted thousands of days and into a night whose end I cannot see." Tatyana thought for a moment before she continued. "The Famadorians are pressing us harder from the north. We hold them still just north of Kien Yanish. Voice Newlis tells me our warriors could break their line with a sustained attack and perhaps even push them back into the Vendaris Hills except—"

"Except Lord Phaeon has assembled his armies to the south," Dwynwyn finished. Such impertinence would have brought the queen's wrath down on any other courtier's head, but in this, as in so many things, Seekers were different.

"He has done more than assemble, Dwynwyn." Tatyana sighed. "We have had word that his fleets have sailed. They approach our western shores, most likely landing somewhere south of Kien

---

* Fate is a preoccupation of the faeries. They believe that just as there is an ultimate, all-encompassing truth, also there is an all-encompassing fate. That fate exists, however, does not make the faeries "fatalistic." They believe that part of their purpose in life is to discover what their fate is through their own actions and decisions.

Magoth, or possibly at Eventide. They will then encamp and prepare for their final march on us here."

Tatyana stopped and looked up at the beautiful trunks, each shaped with the history of her people.

"My courtiers can offer me no saving truth by which we may escape the fall of our will to Lord Phaeon," the queen said as she turned to look directly at Dwynwyn. "Can you?"

Dwynwyn looked into the amber eyes of her queen. "That, Your Majesty, is why I smelled like fish this afternoon."

Tatyana raised her eyebrows. "Now you must tell me all."

There, beneath the towering trees of the Sanctuary, the queen of the Qestardi listened to her court Seeker. Dwynwyn rehearsed for her, from first to last, all her experiences of relevance.* How the wingless man without a gift had shown himself, and how strange circumstance had led her that very day to return from the waters of Estarin Bay with thirty-six unique and otherwise inexplicable black pearls.

And when she had finished, Tatyana turned to her in astonishment. "Is this the full truth of it?"

"It is, Your Majesty."

"But it is incomplete!"

Dwynwyn nodded, studiously ignoring the implied insult. "Yes, Your Majesty, it is indeed incomplete. I have these thirty-six perfect and entirely inexplicable pearls that were shown to me by a wingless man who, so far as I may explain, does not exist."

"Then perhaps you are ill or fevered," Tatyana responded with concern. "Perhaps I have asked too much of you."

"Seekers are often dismissed as ill or fevered," Dwynwyn replied with a calm chill in her voice, "but mental derangement cannot explain the truth of the pearls that now reside in my chambers. No, Your Majesty!" Dwynwyn felt the truth of it resonating through all her being "I know what I know! There is a truth here . . . a truth

---

* ". . . rehearsed for her, from first to last": This is a common faery construction meant by the original author to shorten the hand-copied text. Faeries are exacting in their telling of their stories and histories. This phrase allows the faery chronicler to save himself the trouble of duplicating text that has already been copied by referring the reader back to previous records.

beyond any truth we have known before! I see only pieces of it at one time. They are like threads in a tapestry, gathering in my hands. I am weaving them together, and when I do, then a great truth *will* emerge, I know it!"

"This new truth you seek, Dwynwyn," Tatyana said heavily. "Will it save us?"

Dwynwyn shook her head. "I do not know, Your Majesty . . . but I know of nothing else that will."

The queen cocked her head to one side. "What do you need, Seeker?"

"Time. I need time."

Tatyana looked long into Dwynwyn's eyes and then turned, resumed her flight back across the garden. "The Famadorians press us from the north; Lord Phaeon approaches from the southwest. It seems our Argentei brother is anxious to stand my house to stud, and with about as much dignity as that implies. Time is a commodity that is in short supply in Qestardis."

They came once more to the throne dais. Tatyana settled into her throne once more, the mantle of her authority clear in her posture. "Though your truth is incomplete, I accept it, Seeker Dwynwyn. You are charged to undertake a journey. You shall prepare with all haste and depart for Kien Werren, our tower-keep on the southeastern shore. You shall take a phalanx of my personal guard with you and such servants as you deem needful to transport whatever materials you shall require."

"Yes, Your Majesty; at once—"

"I am not finished," Tatyana snapped. "You will also take with you the Princess Aislynn, Daughter of the Eternal Light, and remain at Kien Werren until such time as you either discover your new truth or I send for you."

"Your Majesty?" Dwynwyn blinked.

Tatyana's voice suddenly softened. "I cannot protect her here, Dwynwyn. This may buy you some time, but a few days only. Protect her if you can; that is my charge to you."

"I shall do all that is possible, Your Majesty," Dwynwyn replied. "I accept your charge."

"Remember," Tatyana said, her face a mask. "If you fail, there will be no one left alive of my court to give you another charge."

"A gift for me? Is it from Deython?"

"No, Your Highness, it is from me; a most special gift," Dwynwyn said quietly.

"Why, it's . . . it's . . . what *is* it?"

Dwynwyn pulled out a plain box from behind her back. There had not been time enough to fashion anything more ornate. The Seeker opened the lid of the box as she presented it to the young princess. "They are pearls, Your Highness, from the waters near Qestardis. It is a necklace that I had commissioned especially for you."

"They are rather plain, are they not?"

"Yes, Your Highness, they are indeed. I asked that they be made plain."

"Why?"

"They are not to make you pretty, Your Highness. You are already pretty. They are to protect you."

"Protect me? Protect me from what?"

"I do not know," Dwynwyn replied. "Perhaps from the rigors of the road. We are leaving tomorrow as soon as preparations are complete."

Aislynn's face fell. "Where are we going?"

"As far as we can, Your Highness," Dwynwyn replied.

Nightrunners

I t was the very soul of dark morning; the bottom of the well of night.

It was under its cloak that the five faery nightrunners slipped quietly from their hidden moorings near the Sanctuary and drifted out through the great eastern gate.

The nightrunners were a special type of cloudship—a common transport in Qestardis. Faery shaper artisans had discovered the truth of the cloudships nearly a thousand seasons before this tale. Crystals were first coaxed into thin, rigid spheres between fifteen and twenty hands in diameter. These transparent globes then had their breath drawn from them by the artisans until their essence sought the sky. Several of these globes were then bound under lace netting which, in turn, was bound by stay lines to gondolas suspended beneath. The result was a small ship that, when properly balanced, would drift neutrally between earth and sky.

Floating was one thing, but flight was a different matter. While the cloudships could lift great weight, they were difficult to control and required considerable strength to move over long distances. The altitude of the ship over the ground was maintained through the use of heavy ballast bags hung by ropes over the sides of the ship. These were added or discarded as the cargo required for neutral buoyancy. Horizontal control was exerted through harnesses attached to the lacework over the globes. That allowed faeries strapped into the harnesses to turn the cloudships in the desired direction.

Moving these ships, however, required great effort, and it was the dryads that provided the best solution by enlisting the aid of the forests. The dryads spoke to the trees, and the trees obliged them by pushing the crystal globes of the cloudships along with their leafy branches. For this reason the gondolas suspended under the cloudships, with some irony, normally hovered just feet above the ground, under the canopy of their powerful and protective forests.

The nightrunners were special cloudships of the royal house designed not for cargo but for speed. Three crystal globes strained against the intricate lace netting above thirty-foot-long gondolas. These gondolas were ornately decorated with the symbols of Tatyana and the histories of the Qestardi, but they were carefully inlaid into jet black hulls broken with dark green swaths. The lace netting over the spheres was also the color of night.

These were ships of the night whose passage was meant to be only in shadow and starlight.

The nightrunners, propelled by dark-cloaked members of the Queen's Guard both in steering harness and at the push-bars on either side of the gondolas, drifted quickly over the eastern fields. Phalanxes of guards flew in formations nearly fifty feet from either side of the ships, their heads turning slightly every few moments as they kept watch over their path.

At the aft end of the central nightrunner's gondola, two figures sat, their faces turned back to gaze once more from whence they came.

The shining towers of glorious Qestardis illuminated their faces, a beacon in a black world. The spires, impossibly thin and graceful, drove upward into the darkness, cutting it like sharp knives. It was achingly beautiful in the night, making the darkness toward which they rushed seem blacker still.

Aislynn's tears shone in the light of her homeland. "Will we see the Sanctuary Trees again, Dwynwyn? Will there yet be a home to which I may return?"

Dwynwyn, too, watched the great city as it rapidly fell farther from their sight. "I cannot see that truth, Your Highness, but if my search bears fruit then we may yet again dwell with joy in the towers of Qestardis. At least I managed one convenience for you, Your Highness: your friend Deython was appointed captain of your guard for this journey."

"Deython?" Aislynn brightened somewhat at the thought. "You *are* good to me, Dwynwyn!"

The city's rays illuminated their path for a time as the nightrunners sped eastward across the River Thenis. The effort was taxing on the guards. Those who had set out from the city were exhausted by their efforts either in pushing against the long handles protruding from the gondola or from the harnesses attached to the lace netting overhead. At the river, the guards who had been patrolling exchanged places with those who had been pushing the nightrunners. The ships then pressed east once more in a new burst of speed. This was the dangerous time, for the glory of their beloved city was their enemy now, their shapes silhouetted against its brilliance.

They craved the cover and assistance of the great forests to the east. The truth of their passage needed to be kept hidden from the eyes and minds even of their own people.* So their journey was hastened this night, pressed to the limits of their endurance.

As morning twilight grew brighter over the Cendral Hills, the nightrunners passed into the western borders of the Sinash Forest. Ashi and Emli, two dryads who were part of their company, spoke urgently to the trees from the lead gondola. Though it was well into the fall season, the ancient maples responded. They awoke from their deepening slumber, their branches reaching out tenderly toward the

---

* Faeries do not lie, as they are obsessed with the truth of all things. The closest that faeries come to deception is to keep the truth of something hidden for a time that suits their purposes. However, if asked directly, they will answer with whatever they know to be true. For this reason, it appears, everyone who knows about the nightrunners' flight from Qestardis is with the caravan itself, with the single exception of the queen.

crystal spheres of the nightrunners, shaking loose in their movement a flurry of brilliantly colored leaves. With relief, the guards posted a diminished watch and withdrew to rest on the second and fourth gondolas.

The awakened trees passed the nightrunners between them, gently propelling them toward the southeast. Over the course of several hours, the silent nightrunners thus journeyed well to the east of Rivadis, unknown by any except the sleepy trees, all of whom favored the dryads.

There, in an enclosed glade deep within the forest, the maples of Sinash let the nightrunners rest for a time. The Fae in the company took their meals and rested as well as they could. At Aislynn's insistence, Dwynwyn arranged for Deython to accompany the princess on a walk in the glade, her delicate feet brushing through the carpet of fallen leaves. Even with this distraction, it was obvious to Dwynwyn that Aislynn was already weary of the road. The princess and her Seeker took their meals in silence.

As afternoon lengthened, the dryads spoke once more to the trees of their need to move. The nightrunners were again loaded and pushed into the tree line. Once again, the maples spread their leaves and gently brushed the globes along the treetops. Aislynn occupied her time gazing at the lush forests drifting beneath and about them. She had never before been so far from the halls of her Sanctuary home and was heartsick for her lost comforts.

As the evening softened, the trees responded to the dryads and allowed the nightrunners to drift to a halt. They had reached the southmost reaches of the Sinash Forest. In a deep ravine below them, the River Kush ran in frothing whitewater rapids westward toward Estarin Bay. To the south, they could clearly see the lights of Mordan nearly seven miles away, twinkling through the silvery leaves of Suthwood.

"Do we make for Mordan?" Aislynn asked in a hushed voice.

"No, Your Highness," Dwynwyn answered. "Our truth is our own and not for the good subjects of Mordan, nor are the faeries our only concern."

"No?" Aislynn looked at Dwynwyn with surprise.

"No, but the trees also." Dwynwyn sighed. "The maples tell our dryads that Suthwood is mostly comprised of, well, elms. The maples say that they are not to be trusted."

Aislynn sighed. "I would have granted a large boon for a decent bed."

"Another night, Your Highness." Dwynwyn spoke quietly. "Another night."

They crossed the River Kush well to the east. The great dark mass of the Cendral Hills rose on their left as they skirted around the range's foothills. The guards traded their positions more often now, their haste to pass Suthwood evident in their straining wings and taut muscles. The nightrunners rushed silently over the tall grasses, their gondolas barely making a whisper in the night.

Aislynn's gaze remained on their wake across the landscape. For a moment, as they rushed through the night, the Kush gorge cut a break between Suthwood and Sinash Forest. There, across an expanse of Estarin Bay, glimmered the lights of Qestardis more than twenty miles distant. To Aislynn, the enormous and beautiful city had shrunk to her thumbnail, and she wept quietly into the night.

The night was long under the stars. The clear sky cooled quickly. Dwynwyn covered Aislynn with her cloak, the young princess having finally cried herself into a fitful sleep. Dwynwyn moved gently forward in the gondola searching the landscape under the bright stars.

The rolling foothills unwound in their path. Dwynwyn could smell the spicy scent of fading foliage and wild mint from the edge of Suthwood on their right. The tall grasses beneath them barely rustled at their passage. There was a beautiful serenity over the landscape.

Dwynwyn flitted off the deck of the gondola and flew quietly forward of the caravan. Glancing about in the night, she saw the captain of the guards on a nearby hilltop. She changed her course and was soon drifting next to the sentry as he floated in the shadow of a great oak tree near the crest of the hill.

She could see that Mordan Township was now well behind them. Qestardis was but an earthbound star on the northwestern horizon. She could easily see the nightrunners drifting quickly past them at the base of the hill below.

"Good evening, Deython," Dwynwyn said in a hushed voice.

"It is, Seeker," the captain replied.

"You may address me as Dwynwyn."

"My thanks to you—both for the compliment of your name and for suggesting me for this posting."

"I accept gratefully—although the princess's preferences were an influence in your appointment."

"That is glad tidings, Dwynwyn," the captain confided. "The princess often keeps silence with me."

"She holds her counsel well." Dwynwyn smiled.

"Indeed . . . it is one of many things that I admire greatly in her."

Far ahead of them, Suthwood gave way to a larger, darker mass of forest. It must be Oakan, Dwynwyn thought as she surveyed it. Its nether cliffs, far beyond her sight, fell directly into the Qe'Dunadin Sea. It was Qestardis's southernmost boundary. Their objective was still a full day beyond its borders, but Oakan offered safety and rest. Kien Werren awaited them off the southern tip of the Cendral Hills on an outcropping of rock that overlooked the Qe'Dunadin Sea. It gazed out across the Shezron Plain to the northeast. It was the farthest tower of the Qestardan realm and the most defensible.

Dwynwyn also knew that it could very well be the last place where the light of her nation might be extinguished.

"Will we make it to the Werren?" she asked the captain.

Deython either would not reply or did not know.

"Why do you play these games, Dwynwyn?"

The Seeker looked up from the game board, her thoughts drawn from the patterns that moments before had so absorbed her. "Pardon me, Your Highness, I was distracted. What did you say?"

Aislynn repeated her question with slight annoyance. She never liked repeating herself. "I asked you why you play these games."

Dwynwyn smiled as much to herself as to her charge. "My deepest apologies, Your Highness. I play them because it is my duty to do so, Your Highness. The games are part of my gift and my calling."

Aislynn lay back on her cushions, the gondola swaying slightly with her motion. The towering trunks of the oak trees drifted past them in their passage. The oak foliage drifted down around them in a vivid display, made all the more vibrant by the red-streaked sunset overhead. The soft creakings of the stay lines were the only sounds intruding on her thoughts.

"I think," Aislynn said at last, her gaze fixed on nothing in particular in the deep woods, "that you bring your books and scrolls and games and toys with you simply because it amuses you to do so. *I* believe you do it to annoy the stewards who are forced to pack your things whenever you travel."

Dwynwyn smiled once more to herself as she moved her pieces down several lines of conflict and retreat. Aislynn was restless. "And you believe this to be a complete truth?"

"No," Aislynn answered absently. "I suppose not. It is just that it is what I would do if I were you."

"I shall remember that when next we travel anywhere else, Your Highness. It may seem strange to you that such a thing could—" Dwynwyn sat up, suddenly alert and concerned.

Those guards who were not on watch suddenly fluttered from their gondolas, rushing quietly outward among the trees.

"We've stopped?" Aislynn said. "Are we there?"

"No, Your Highness, we are not." Dwynwyn stood up, moving quickly to the front of the gondola. "Ashi! Emli!"

The dryads appeared quite suddenly from behind two of the trees.

"Why have we stopped?"

Ashi responded first. "The trees, Seeker . . ."

". . . They sleep . . ." Emli rejoined.

". . . And they will not awaken!" they both finished as one.

"How odd," Aislynn said.

At that moment, Deython flew with driving purpose between the trees. "We must get out of these woods at once."

"But how, Captain?" Dwynwyn asked quickly.

"We are not far from the forest edge, and Kien Werren is just beyond. We should be able to fly the distance."

"No, Captain! I have to have my things."

"With all my respect, Seeker," Deython said harshly, "but lives are more important than a few comforts that you—"

"Deython, a great deal depends on these mere 'comforts.' A great deal more than you know! We've got to find a way to—"

The leaves crackled.

Instantly, the faery guards appeared from the trees, encircling the nightrunners. The long, thin blades of their swords slid from their sheaths.

"Are you wearing your pearls?" Dwynwyn asked quickly.

"I don't know why you insist on my wearing them," Aislynn responded through a pout. "They're dreadfully large things and not all that pretty against my skin—"

"Are you wearing them?" Dwynwyn snapped angrily.

Aislynn blinked, her already large brown eyes wider still. "Well, yes . . . of course! Why?"

The leaves on the ground suddenly exploded upward. A screeching chorus shattered the silence of the wood.

"Satyrs!" Deython cried out.

The powerful hindquarters of the satyrs propelled them in a sudden rush toward the nightrunner, their cloven hooves digging into the soft earth of the forest floor. Hair completely covered their legs and backs, their exposed skin a clay red color. They measured only three or four feet in height, but their passionate ferocity was feared by creatures many times larger. Their large hands could tear a creature limb from limb. The black eyes of the creatures shined beneath their heavy brows crested by a pair of short, spiraled horns.

The satyrs rushed the nightrunners from all sides, but the faery guards were fast and had the advantage of their swords. The shining arcs of their blades cut into the charging line of satyrs with terrible effectiveness. Even so, momentum alone had carried several of the satyrs all the way into the circle of guards. Several of them were grappling with the terrible strength of the satyrs, who had managed to drag them to the ground.

The circle of the guards, however, still held.

The satyrs, their initial charge having thus been repelled, fell back slightly, shifting about the circle of the guards, screaming at them with now bloodied faces. Again and again, they suddenly launched attacks against the guards at one point or another in the circle. The guards would collapse backward at each assault, fall on the charging satyrs, and then push them back. So quick were the satyrs, however, that the guards could not disengage from the battle. They were locked in combat and neither side appeared able or willing to withdraw.

"What do we do?!" Aislynn squealed.

Dwynwyn shook her head frantically. She was a Seeker!

What could she do? What *should* she do?

A new sound ripped through the air, closer and more frightening.

Dwynwyn fell backward away from the sound.

A long, narrow shaft suddenly ripped across the gondola inches from her face, slamming with terrific force into the trunk of a tree.

Suddenly the air was filled with sound. The deadly bolts battered against the hull of the gondola like heavy rain. They crossed over the sides in a blur of deadly motion.

Lying in the bottom of the gondola, Dwynwyn pulled Aislynn down beside her.

"Dwynwyn . . . please!" Aislynn cried. "You're hurting me!"

The arrow impacts rattled the sides of the gondola. Dwynwyn could hear the cries of the wounded and the continuous clang of metal beyond the hull. She longed to know what was going on but dared not lift her head to see.

Suddenly, a bloodied figure vaulted over the gunwales, landing heavily next to them.

Aislynn screamed.

It was Deython. Thickening ichor coated his face, and his bloodied sword was clasped in his hand. He yelled, his voice barely carrying over the din of battle beyond the hull. "Centaur bowmen! They're using the satyrs to keep us occupied while they pick us off at a distance!" Another volley tore through the air over the gunwales of the gondola. Deython flattened himself against the floor planks, then urgently continued. "We must fly, ladies! The guards are ready. At my word, we will take flight together, the guards surrounding you as we gain height. That should protect you long enough for us to get out of range!"

"But my books! My things! What of them?" Dwynwyn shouted.

Deython was adamant. "On the ground, we die! Fly and we have a chance at life! We'll return for your things later if we can!"

"*No!*" Dwynwyn shouted savagely. In a single motion, she took the sword from the surprised captain's hand and stood.

The arrows flashed past her. She was vaguely aware of the dark, thundering shapes moving through the woods just beyond her vision. The satyrs, seeing her, screamed once more, the sight of a faery female stirring a mindless lust and desire within them that they could neither understand nor control. Several of the faery guards lay motionless on the ground, but her attention was fixed elsewhere.

The weights of the gondola hung suspended by cords on either side of the hull. Desperate and afraid, Dwynwyn swung the sword with both her hands. Her fear gave her strength. Her blows did not land where she had intended, but close enough.

"Lady Seeker," Deython cried from the bottom of the nightrunner. "What are you doing?!"

Aislynn gazed on in frozen astonishment.

The cords snapped under her blows. One by one the weights holding the nightrunner to the earth dropped heavily to the ground. The gondola rocked unsteadily for a moment, listing heavily down toward the final suspended ballast weight. Dwynwyn barely took notice. She drew back the sword once more and swung it with all her might.

The gondola jerked suddenly, knocking Dwynwyn completely off her feet. Her wings fluttered frantically to right her. In the next moment she was aware of her feet once more pressing against the deck planks of the nightrunner.

The cloudship was vaulting skyward. Free of its restraining weights, it rose past the sleeping branches of Oakan Forest, each moment gaining momentum and speed as it rose majestically into the failing light of the sky.

The sky was haven. The Famadorians below were entirely earthbound. The sky was safety—but now the nightrunner rose freely into that same sky, faster and faster.

Dwynwyn was suddenly very aware that she might have cut too many of the ballast weights. She watched in amazement as the roof of the forest fell away from under the nightrunner. The brighter stars appeared in the deepening twilight. To the south stretched the vastness of the Qe'Dunadin Sea. Turning around, she saw the dark mass of the Cendral Hills to the northwest. The blackening Shezron Plain stretched beyond the edge of the forest far to the northeast.

She turned and looked down along the coastline. In moments she saw it, the great tower of Kien Werren less than a mile away, now silhouetted against the shining sea under the twilight sky.

"We were so close!" Dwynwyn muttered in amazement.

"The guards," said Deython as he gazed down over the side. The guards below had been caught by surprise when the nightrunner launched into the sky but were nevertheless grateful that they were now released from the deadly ground. Those who could rose quickly to protect their princess as was their sworn duty.

Only then did Dwynwyn notice the shredded membranes of the captain's wings. He could not have flown up with them on his signal, nor could he fly now. Blood pulsed from the wound, a dark stain growing under where he lay. Dwynwyn wondered for a moment if Deython knew how badly he was hurt but then realized that he most probably did.

A sudden gust of the evening breeze pressed the nightrunner sideways. Dwynwyn gripped the side as though to steady the ship. They were being carried quickly eastward by the breeze, out past the edge of Oakan Forest. The guards, such as remained, were still in pursuit, trying desperately to reach their captain and the princess.

On the ground below them, Dwynwyn was aware of motion. The centaurs were galloping under them, their bows still in hand. They know we will come down, Dwynwyn thought. They are stalking us. Faeries can only fly so far.

"We've stopped rising," the captain said heavily, his breathing labored. "We're going back down."

"Why?" Dwynwyn questioned, glancing about the nightrunner. Then she saw it. The foremost crystal globe was cracked. An arrow must have fractured it.

The centaurs continued to gallop under them, waiting for them. Dwynwyn took a shuddering breath. She and Aislynn would have to fly for the tower after all.

"Aislynn," Dwynwyn said calmly. "Do you think you can fly as far as the tower?"

"I . . . I don't know," the princess replied. "I suppose if I must . . ."

"You must." Dwynwyn then turned and looked sadly down on the injured guard lying at her feet. "Captain, I . . ."

"You must fly, ladies!" Deython said simply. Then he smiled. "My men will come for me, then I'll take care of you."

"Dwynwyn! Wait!" Aislynn called out. "Look! Look to the tower!"

Dwynwyn turned and was astonished.

The tower was erupting with flight. Figures rushing into the air from the courtyard below streamed toward them.

"The tower guard!" The captain sighed with relief as he looked over the side of the nightrunner. "They've seen us! Mother of the Glade be praised!"

Aislynn cried out loudly from the gondola, waving her arms frantically. "Here! We are here! Oh, Dwynwyn, perhaps I should fly out to thank them! They are so wonderful, so valiant!"

Deython's face suddenly altered. There was astonishment and fear in his eyes. He tried to struggle to his feet but fell weakly back, unable even to grip his sword. "It *cannot be!*"

"Their wings! They're all wrong!" Dwynwyn's breath was coming in quick gulps. "It is a new truth . . . a new and terrible truth!"

The remnants of the nightrunner guards encircled the ship. Their swords were drawn. Tired as they were, they were willing to fight one last battle. Each of them knew, however, that it was a futile gesture.

Aislynn cowered behind Dwynwyn. There was no place else to hide.

Ten phalanxes of flying warriors surrounded the nightrunner in a sphere. Their narrow halberds shone in the failing light of the day. They beat the air with their noisy wings, the sound of it rumbling like the thunder of doom in Dwynwyn's ears.

"Winged Famadorians!" Deython yelled over the cacophonous sound as he gasped for breath. "It cannot be! *I cannot believe it!*"

Sympathetic

cannot believe it!" Rhea said, appalled.

"That is what the sword told me," Galen responded, his voice quivering despite all his efforts to control it.

It had taken considerable effort on his part to stand next to Rhea and Maddoc. The combatants in their group had just finished their turn in the arena. Everyone was breathless and sweating freely from the exertion. Now they all gulped air, sitting on the curved stones that formed the sides of the arena bowl.

"No one . . . but *no one* ever returns from these wars." Galen continued to gulp air as he spoke. "They bring the Elect here each fall, they train them for a few weeks, then everyone gets loaded back up on the torusks. We're all supposed to be taken to someplace called Enlund where the next battle is supposed to be taking place."

"And then?"

"And then we . . . then we die."

Rhea shook her head. "That makes no sense! You say this war has been waged for, what, over a century?"

"According to the sword, over four hundred years," Galen replied.

"That's impossible! We're at war? Who are we supposed to be

fighting, and why? All those years and all those dead . . . and no one has won this war?" Rhea became more and more agitated, her words tumbling out of her mouth as she thought. "And just a few *weeks* of training? That's absurd! It takes months to train even the most dedicated warriors, let alone a group of . . . of . . ."

"Of what, Rhea?" Galen demanded. "Group of what?"

Rhea stopped, realizing what she had been saying. She looked directly at Galen as she spoke. "A group who are at *best* afflicted and at *worst* completely crippled by something we know nearly nothing about."

"But they *are* training us for war!" Galen insisted, gesturing down at the arena floor below them. The next two groups had already moved onto the bloodied sand and were exchanging blows.

"Yes, but what *kind* of war? I mean, just *look* at them!" Rhea said with disgust. "Galen, listen to me. Maddoc and I come from a village on the north shore of the Dragonback. My father was part of the garrison there. You Chebon-shore folk don't hear about the north shore much. Occasionally some Vordnara raider will get too bold or too drunk and wander down from Indraholm Bay to attack our villages. The Pir have us organize our own garrisons to push them back into the sea until they sober up enough to leave us alone. I've seen those garrisons training, Galen, and watched them fight. This"—she gestured down at the arena floor as well, having to shout to be heard over the now cheering masses of her own group—"this is nonsense! They've been drilling us in only the most basic of weapons moves! Some of the moves look elaborate, but they are completely ineffective in battle. This training is barely good enough for a traveling bard's theatrical—never mind any actual combat. Could the sword be lying to you?"

"I don't think so," Galen responded, shaking his head. "It's a vicious blade but seems to be rather sincere about . . . just listen to me! Here I am trying to convince you of the sincerity of my sword? I must be insane!"

Maddoc, who had been sitting quietly next to Rhea, suddenly turned to them both, his eyes focused and clear. "No, Galen, not insane, just thinking differently, knowing differently. You've spent your entire life seeing, touching, and knowing what is real. You were wrong, that's all. *Everyone* was wrong. Everything we thought we knew was just a metaphor for the true reality. We were living in a dream—a wonderful dream—and now the dream and the reality are linked in the twilight and one cannot sleep without awakening the other."

"A metaphor? Rhea, what is he talking about?"

"I'm . . . I'm not sure," Rhea responded. "Maddoc, can you hear me?"

"Of course I can hear you, Rhea." Maddoc smiled down at her with warmth and affection. "I missed you so, Rhea. I thought I might come and visit you both."

"Yes, my husband," Rhea said, smiling up at him, nestling herself quickly against his chest. "How I have missed you."

Maddoc gently circled his arms around her. "And I you, my beloved. Still, I've not much time here and I have little time to answer you before I awaken."

Galen frowned. What was this madman talking about?

Rhea nodded, pulling herself away from him with infinite reluctance. "Maddoc, what are you saying?"

The old man smiled through his wild beard. "That I really must talk with Galen. We're old friends now! We have walked the bloodied fields together, he and I. It was there that Galen chose the Circle of Brothers Forged by Galen's Will, now called the Secret Circle of Brothers Forged by—"

"Yes, we understand!" Galen said impatiently.

"Of course." Maddoc nodded quickly. "I . . . I really must apologize for that name, Galen. I'm still working on something more clever. I don't think that such a long title will catch on."

"Look." Galen leaned forward, trying to be heard by his companions alone in the roaring crowd. "The idea of those warriors came from the winged woman, not me! And that was in the dream . . . not here!"

"Of course it was." Maddoc smiled politely. "Here is the metaphor, there the reality."

Rhea's eyebrows arched suddenly.

"What?" Galen shook his head, confused.

"The powers of twilight are sympathetic, Galen." Maddoc spoke calmly and slowly, as though to a child. "What happens there is a metaphor for what happens here. It is a translation of meaning and symbols. It is an entire language of being, and completely symmetrical. You gave your winged woman a set of symbols and she gave you a set in return. The power of the twilight gives them force. How those symbols translate into meaning in this world is all part of the language bound in the metaphor."

"What's a metaphor?" Galen was still struggling to understand.

"A metaphor is like . . . A metaphor is like . . ." Suddenly, Maddoc started to giggle. "That's a good one, Galen! A metaphor is . . . like!"

Galen looked at Maddoc in alarm.

Rhea reached for him. "Maddoc, quiet! *Please!*"

Maddoc stood up. He was nearly apoplectic with laughter. His voice rose louder and louder. In a moment he was up on his feet screaming over the warriors arrayed about him. "A metaphor is *like!* A metaphor is *like!* A metaphor is *like!*"

Several members of the crowd soon joined in with him. They chanted at the tops of their voices, *"A metaphor is like! A metaphor is like!"*

"Rhea! You've got to stop him!" Galen shouted.

"Maddoc! Maddoc, please stop! *Please!*" Rhea pulled frantically at the madman's arm. "Galen, help me! I can't get him to stop! The Pir are starting to take notice. Help me!"

Galen could see them at the top of the arena. Each of the robed figures held a staff, each staff gazed across the arena with the Eye of Vasska. If that eye should turn on them, Galen knew its effects all too well. Already he could feel their attention turning toward them.

He pushed Rhea aside and grabbed Maddoc by the front of his tunic. He cocked back his fist with his weapon arm.

Sound overwhelmed his senses. The swords throughout the arena were screaming at him. Light patterns filled his vision, then collapsed inward with the sounds down a dark and bottomless well.

The towers of Vasskhold stand behind me. I know them well now, but these towers are twisted and deformed. Their stones are loose and they sway precariously back and forth. They are also much smaller than I remembered them. Their doors and windows remain the right size, but it is as if they are less significant and grand in their design. The Temple itself appears to be only two stories high, sagging precariously to one side. I move about the small buildings carrying long lengths of bleached white timber and shoring each of them up in turn. The walls of the city sag as well. These I also prop up with great urgency.

There is danger. I hear the terrible howling of the demons dancing outside the walls. I fear that they will break through and bring disaster to me. My life would end if they were to breach that wall.

I pause at the base of the Temple itself. The great tower rises behind it, Vasska's tower. It, too, slumps badly to one side. I reach down to lay another length of timber against its walls.

The tower sways above me, then steadies. Looking up, I see a light in its highest window. It is the only light I see in all the city.

"Curious, isn't it?"

The voice is all too familiar to me.

"Yes, curious indeed," I reply.

The hooded Pir monk once more stands beside me. He pulls back his hood, running a hand through his straw-blond hair. "It is a strange landscape that we walk together, you and I. Still, I had hoped to find you here."

"I'm just as glad for your company," I reply. "I need your help. The demons are trying to get in. I've been shoring up the buildings and walls with these."

I hold a long white timber out to him.

The monk shrinks away. "I've been shoring up these walls for as long as I can remember . . . far too long. You don't know what you are asking."

I shake my head questioningly.

"Galen," the monk says quietly, "it never pays to look too closely at one's past."

I gaze down at the long timber in my hand.

It is not a timber at all. It is bone . . . human bone. I drop it at once, glancing about.

"Who are they?" I plead.

The monk sighs. "They are the warriors. They are the Elect. They are the ones whose blood flows like a river each fall until all that is left are the bones to prop up this city. They are the dead of many centuries that fertilize the land. They are the ones who carry their secrets to the grave before they can learn to speak."

I dread my understanding. "The Elect!"

The monk nods. "The great army of Vasska, which is formed each fall and marches out never to return."

"No!" I snap. Berkita's face drifts through my mind almost as a ghost of some wonderful past. I cannot give up, for her sake if not my own. "If I am to die, it won't be for this creaking city, or Vasska's pleasure, or your precious Pir Drakonis! I have a life to live—my life—and neither you nor anyone else can have it!"

The monk grasps my shoulder with a powerful hand. "I don't want your life, Galen! I want to help you . . . you and your friends . . . but I need your help, too. I'm trapped just as much as you are! Maybe I'm not under the eye of Vasska or held in the Garden under guard, but I am imprisoned just the same."

"Prison? You?" I scoff. "What enthralls a ruling monk of the Pir?"

"This!" he hisses at me, pain suddenly crossing his face. His arms fling wide, gesturing to the strange, terrible world that surrounds us. "This! This terrible, wonderful place of madness! I hate this place, Galen. I hate it with every fiber of my soul! It is my sin against Vasska; against everything that I have ever held sacred and true! It is destroying my life! Can you understand?"

"How can you even ask that?" I return bitterly. "These dreams have brought me nothing but pain."

"Yes, that's right!" the monk urges, his blue eyes fixed on mine with understanding. "As they have for me. And yet . . ."

"Yet?" I coax.

"Yet there is something . . . something alluring about all of this!" The monk's arms suddenly cross. He rubs his upper arms as though chilled. "It calls to me, whispers to me, and will not be denied. Its tendrils curl around my mind during the day in spite of all else. It summons me to sleep. It seduces me. I love it. I hate it. It consumes me and _will_ destroy me just as surely as the war will destroy you, Galen."

"Then we are both doomed?"

"No, there _is_ hope, and that is why I had to find you." The monk steps toward me, speaking quietly, although I wonder just who it is he is afraid will hear us. "I have seen a vision. If I help you escape from the Garden—get you out of the city and on your way back to this life you say you have lost—will you help me?"

"Of course!" I nod quietly, with no small surprise on my face. "But how can I possibly help—"

"Will you agree?"

"Of course, I agree!" I say quickly.

"Excellent!" the monk replies, shaking my hand. He then once more gazes upward. "Do you suppose she awaits us there?"

"I don't know," I say cautiously.

"Well, there is one way to find out." The monk shrugs, and he steps through the tower portal.

I ponder for a moment, curious not only about the lit window far above us but about this man who appears so amicable in my dreams and denies me when awake. Who is he that he should walk this strange twilight place by my side? His own words, however, resound through my thoughts: _help me and I will help you_.

I step through the portal after him.

The tower changes around us. What appeared moments ago to be a small structure proves, once within, to be extraordinarily exaggerated in size. There are neither stairs nor ladders within its soaring confines.

Far above us, the winged woman drifts at the top of the tower shaft.

"Tell me your name," I say to the monk.

He smiles crookedly at me. "Call me . . . friend."

"Gladly," I rejoin. "But you <u>do</u> have a name, do you not?"

"Yes," he says, turning toward me. His blue eyes look piercingly into mine. "And I promise you shall have it when the time is right. It is for your sake as well as mine that I withhold it. Do you understand?"

"No," I answer. "But I can live with it."

The monk laughs. "That <u>is</u> the idea . . . that we both find a way to live with it! Now, how do you suppose we are to get up there?"

It is my turn to smile. "I promise to tell you when the time is right!"

I summon in my mind a great wind. Suddenly the wind sweeps through the tower, bearing me up from the floor. I soar upward, leaving my monk friend far below. Soon, I drift in the air near the winged woman.

She is sad. Her dark face is lined with worry and pain. As I look about, I find that the entire upper part of the tower is gaudily ornamented in ironworks. Ravens have settled among the rungs of iron. Each in their turn pick at the winged woman with their sharp beaks, tearing at her clothing.

Her eyes plead with me and she opens her mouth to speak!

I quickly hold my hands up before my mouth in warning. She apparently understands me and makes no sound.

I glance about, carefully examining the ironwork. I am looking for a metaphor, not entirely sure—even in myself—what that means.

Something inside me suddenly speaks with deeper understanding than I have ever experienced before, and I know what I must do. I reach upward. Grasping the wrought iron, I easily bend it from the wall fixtures. It heats quickly in my hands, becoming pliable.

I start shaping the iron, pulling more pieces as they are needed from the wall ornaments. The long iron strands begin to take the shape of a great sphere—a cage for the birds that so menace the winged woman.

I offer it to her, and to my surprise she holds it in her hands, bowing her thanks. The cage I have crafted for her disappears, as

*do the ravens. She reaches out, taking me by my hands, and pulls
me upward through the remaining ironworks onto the top of the
tower.*

*We stand under a blood-red sun. Its light is terrible on us: its
heat burns us and its light blinds us. I shrink from it, but the
winged woman reaches out and plucks the sun from the sky. She
cuts the terrible sun in half as though it were a fruit. Reaching inside, she pulls from it a pit of darkness and hands it to me.*

*I hold it in my hand, a seed of black streaked with purple light-
ning. As I hold it, my skin cools and I am no longer blinded by
the light.*

*The winged woman sets the sun back in the sky. Its red rays
stretch over the land, cradled between the clouds that streak the
horizon. The clouds form the head of a great dragon. The sun
winks out its eye and darkness falls around us.*

*I drift downward once again through the tower. The monk re-
mains at the bottom, waiting for me.*

*"You must teach me how you do that," the monk says softly as
the light fails.*

*"And I promise that I will," I respond cautiously, "when the
time is right."*

The blackness falls over us.

"Will I see you again, friend?" I ask the night.

*"Yes, friend, you will," the monk replies from the darkness.
"And we will find our freedom together."*

BOOK OF GALEN

BRONZE CANTICLES, TOME IV, FOLIO 1, LEAVES 39–44

Galen awoke with a start.

"Easy, Galen!" Rhea said quickly. "Lie back and be still! You're
back in the barracks. The dragonstaffs put you out for a long time."

Galen could not relax; there were too many things running
through his mind. He pushed his way up to sit despite Rhea's efforts.
"Please, we've got to get out of here!"

"No one is more in agreement with you than I am," Rhea said

sharply, "but I don't see how that is possible! The guards are suspicious of you. Even if they weren't, we would still have to get you past the Pir monks. They line the walls of the Garden."

"Yes." Galen nodded. "The ever-watchful eye of Vasska, eh?"

"None of the Elect can escape its gaze," Rhea said flatly.

"Perhaps." Galen smiled. "On the other hand—"

Rhea gasped.

Galen held a strange sphere of darkness about the size of an apple in his hand, streaked periodically with purple lightning.

"On the other hand," Galen said, "perhaps Vasska's eye won't *see* us!"

Master and Servant

"I cannot believe it!" Lirry sniffed joyfully as he reclined on the overstuffed chair. "I'm making it, Mimic! I'm finally getting what I deserve!"

Mimic lowered his head in his most servile manner. "Yes, Boss. I believe you are."

"Just look at this, will you?" Lirry said, passing his long green hand about in a grand, sweeping gesture. "Is this not the most incredible fortune? Have you ever in your wildest dreams conceived of such wonders? No, of course you haven't, you're just a technician fourth class, after all. But *I* have, Mimic, and it's almost too good to be true!"

"Yes, Master," Mimic replied. "Almost."

Lirry took in a deep, long breath, relaxing into the soft cushions around him. He knew he was better than anyone he had ever met. Every boss he had ever known had failed to appreciate the specialness of Lirry. Lirry has seen it in their eyes, heard it in their barking voices, and felt it with every blow they had rained down on his head. They were shortsighted, he knew, every one of them. Now he had proof of his specialness. Now they would *have* to acknowledge his greatness! He had a lot of debts to settle, had kept track of each one in a detailed ledger in his mind and was relishing the accounts all coming so spectacularly due in the very, very near future.

Who could contradict it? he thought. Just one look at the splendor and opulence that now surrounded him would bring any common goblin to their knees in awe and envy. He was looking forward to *that,* too.

His quarters had been assigned to him at the behest of Krupuk-chukup, the vice-chamberlain to Dong Mahaj-Megong himself. Located in the middle tiers of the fortress-city of Dong Mahaj-Megong, it epitomized the dreams of every working goblin throughout the kingdom.

The fortress-city had originally been a Titan construct in the ancient days before the Last War. Its original purpose still remained a mystery, but Dong Udang Dibalik Bahtuh, founder of their kingdom, discovered it during a hasty pilgrimage into the mountains at the end of the Last War. Dong Udang's goblin clan was starving and on the verge of mutiny when they came upon the abandoned buildings and heavily damaged mechanical constructs. The discovery was heralded by Dong Udang as a miraculous occurrence: proof that their ancestors were smiling on his leadership and right to rule. He proclaimed himself to be the Emperor of all Goblins and a direct descendant of the goblin god-king Surga, master of all creation before the Titans came along and ruined everything. He then waxed eloquent in a vision that his clan would become the lords of all the clans and rule all of G'tok in power!

It is also known that Dong Udang was suffering from a raging fever at the time. More cynical goblins might have questioned his visions. However, there was plenty of food in the area and the buildings offered shelter from the storms raging across the land in those days. It seemed somehow imprudent for the rest of the clan to question the miracle. Following Dong Udang seemed only as crazy as following anyone else in that dreadful time.

Thus, the legend was born.

Since those glorious days of the ancients, each successive Dong leader of the clan had attempted to bring to pass the prophecy in his own name. Each Dong also wanted to be remembered as the Dong who did it. Thus each successive king had renamed the kingdom and its capital city for himself the moment the preceding Dong keeled over either naturally or with a little help.

As goblins did not read, however, this renaming might have been of little inconvenience. All one needed to know was who was in charge to know the names of places. So the successive Dongs needed some other way of leaving behind a mark that would show all the other goblins their progress toward the world-spanning destiny of their clan.

This took the form of opulence. Riches were an outward sign of an inner and divinely manifest destiny. Anything that was worthwhile, therefore, was sought after, collected, and brought before the Great Dongs in order to enhance their power and glory.

Lirry's quarters reflected this. As part of the royal houses, it was required, by divine decree, to demonstrate the wealth of Dong Mahaj-Megong to any who might enter its confines.

The central chamber was circular, with glorious metal walls, each tastefully streaked with actual rust. These rose impressively overhead nearly twenty feet to a domed metal ceiling with a luxurious fill-valve positioned elegantly just off-center. Large round observation ports with thick glass were fitted into the dome as well, allowing a cascade of natural light to fill the room during the day. The decorator had incorporated the long vertical cooling pipes running up the wall at four corners of the room tastefully into the decor. Crimson cloth hung in great swaths between the pressure relief plugs circling the chamber. The floor itself was a metal grate cut to fit perfectly into the round room. Through its cross-hatching could be seen a collection of tastefully arranged gears, shafts, screws, fans, pulleys, and cables that would make even the most jaded goblin brown with envy.

Large pipes fitted into the sides of this fine dwelling led to the other chambers of the apartment. Lirry's bedchamber itself was nearly as glorious, a spherical tank with an array of viewing ports looking out over the lower tiers of the fortress-city. A smaller pipe led from the central tank to Mimic's servant's quarters, which had been created from an oversized butterfly valve that had been rusted shut.

Lirry reached back over his head, pulling a long strip of red meat from the table at the head of the lounge, and started slurping it with relish. "Mimic, have you checked the Device today?"

"Not this hour, Master," Mimic responded. Lirry had insisted that Mimic call him "Master" ever since they had both been ushered into their apartments. Lirry felt it more appropriate to Mimic, considering his new station in life.

"Then you had better do it," Lirry sniffed. "We have important company coming to take a look at this Device. *Famous* company," he added, his eyebrows arched and the tips of his ears twitching.

"Famous, Master?" Mimic asked simply.

"Yes, *famous,* not that you would understand such things." Lirry yawned. Condescension suited him, he thought. Considering how quickly he was gaining prominence, he needed some place of acceptable superiority from which to address the less worthy. "They are expected and I won't have the moment spoiled by that balky device acting up again!"

"Yes, Master," Mimic said with a gentle smile.

Lirry frowned, a cloud passing over his radiant joy. He never liked it when Mimic smiled. He always felt there was something more going on behind those sharp teeth than placid servile contentment. Still, Lirry could not, as the old goblin saying went, put a nose to what was going on with Mimic. He wished the technician would just fall down a well or something so that he would have an excuse to find another servant.

On the other hand, Lirry knew that losing Mimic was the last thing he wanted. The Device was troublesome and its details still eluded him. He was a master technician and, as such, certainly had more skill and talent than any technician fourth class ever could. His intention had always been to keep Mimic around just long enough to learn the secrets of the Device. Then he could safely be rid of the little maggot. Yet no matter how long Lirry spent with the ticking mechanism, he could not ferret out the underlying workings of the thing. Pieces occasionally fell off, then Mimic would fit them back into places quite different than the ones from which they came, and yet the Device would work. Lirry had even taken key pieces out of the Device—pieces that should have stopped it dead—and still it worked at Mimic's touch. But get the thing more than a few yards away from the ugly little goblin and—boing!—it would stop quicker than a square wheel on a rusted axle.

Lirry hated Mimic because he needed Mimic.

Still, he was confident in his own moral, ethical, spiritual, and intellectual superiority. It was only a matter of time before he understood the Device as well as Mimic did, and then he could drown the little rat.

"Master," Mimic said quietly. "The Device is working perfectly. You will be most proud."

"Of course it is working perfectly," Lirry sneered as he gazed critically at his servant. "Oh, honestly, Mimic! Can't you do anything about straightening that left ear?"

"I am sorry, Master," Mimic said humbly. "I shall do my best not to embarrass you or—"

A cascade of metallic sound rang through the chamber.

"They are here!" Lirry announced as much to himself as to Mimic. "Quickly, get the door! Bring them in!"

Mimic scurried over toward the iron hatch that served as the entrance to their suite of rooms. Lirry struck a pose in the middle of the room, raising his receded chin, and quickly spit on his hands and stroked both points of his ears upward.

Mimic came back through the hatch, barely able to speak. "M-master! I beg to present the Vice-Chancellor Kali-putri and . . ." He seemed unable to continue.

Through the hatchway stepped the imposing figure of Kali-putri. His vest was a deep cranberry over a tunic of the finest wool. The folds of flesh hanging down from his chins spoke of incredible wealth. He was shorter than Lirry by nearly half a foot, his black eyes sunk well back into his flabby head. He even wore shoes, an unheard-of extravagance for any goblin.

Yet, impressive and awe-inspiring as Kali-putri was, Lirry barely took notice of him.

She entered just behind the vice-chancellor. She was nearly four feet tall. Her body was shaped like a pear, huge hips hanging from narrow shoulders. Her mouth was pinched and narrow under over-sized cheekbones. Her almond-shaped eyes were a light jaundice yellow, slanting upward under heavy black eyebrows. Her pointed ears extended a full half hand above her green head on either side. Her linked-metal blouse could not restrain the large breasts that sagged precipitously down to her rounded, pot belly. All of this was supported by spindly legs over enormous feet.

Lirry's jaw dropped.

She was the most gorgeous thing he had ever seen.

Kali-putri could see the effect the girl was having on his host. "Technician Lirry, it is a great pleasure to make your acquaintance at last. I see that you can appreciate my escort. This is Gynik."

Gynik stepped forward, her smile baring a perfect set of razor-sharp teeth. She held out her mottled hand with its perfectly sharp-ened nails. "Lirry, at last, I've been *so* looking forward to seeing your fabulous discovery! I don't know when I've been quite this excited."

"I can vouch for that," Kali-putri said with a deep chuckle. "When I told her about your find, Lirry, she insisted that we come over as soon as possible."

"Hummnnn," was all Lirry could manage.

Gynik smiled once more at Lirry.

Mimic entered the room suddenly with a large chair from Lirry's bedchamber. "Perhaps the lady would care to sit down?"

"Oh, no thank you," Gynik said, dismissing Mimic with the faintest wave of her hand. "We really cannot stay for very long, I do hope you understand, Lirry. Oh, I hope I'm not being too forward! May I call you Lirry?"

"Mmmuhnnunnn," came as close to speech as Lirry could man-age in the presence of this goddess.

"Uh, Master Lirry," Mimic said, "shall I get the Device for our visitors?"

"HunUMMnann," Lirry mumbled while he managed a nod. He could not take his eyes off the woman's incredible figure.

Mimic staggered back through the pipe once more with the chair. He managed to return shortly thereafter cradling the Device.

Gynik's yellow eyes widened at the sight of it. "May we see it operate?"

Lirry finally shook himself from his stupor. "Why . . . why of *course* you may see it operate! Mimic! Set it down on this table! We shall have a demonstration for the lady this instant!"

Mimic nodded. He carefully set the mechanism down on the table.

Tick. Tick. Tick. Tick.

The long hands on the face moved.

Tick. Tick. Tick. Tick.

Gynik's eyes widened at the sight of it.

Tick. Tick. Tick. Tick.

Lirry smiled, though he could not decide if it was with pride or with relief.

"Remarkable!" exclaimed the vice-chancellor.

Suddenly, Gynik looked up. "Kali-sweetie, I really must get back to the district. The day is getting late. Would you please be so good as to call the porters to pick us up now?"

"But, Gynik," the vice-chancellor protested, "we've only just arrived! I've many more questions for—"

"Oh, but I simply *must* get back now! Please be a dear, would you? You wouldn't want my errands to keep me too late into the evening, would you?"

The vice-chancellor chuckled deeply. "I suppose that is that, Lirry. I will recommend you to the court. I would not be surprised if Dong Mahaj-Megong himself asked for you to attend within the week. Perhaps my questions *can* wait until then. If you will please excuse us!"

"Oh, you go ahead, Kali-sweetie," Gynik said, batting her heavy eyelids. "I just want to watch the Device for a few moments more."

The vice-chancellor looked as though he were going to protest.

"I'll just be a moment! You get the porters and we'll be on our way!"

The vice-chancellor shrugged and stepped quickly through the hatchway.

Gynik leaned forward to examine the Device more closely. Lirry watched her breasts sway headily under her linked-metal blouse. "I would certainly just *love* to hear all about how you came by such a remarkable find, Lirry! I think you are a man of hidden talents. I would simply *adore* learning more about you as well."

Lirry swallowed.

Gynik stood up and turned toward the hatch exiting the suite. "Perhaps I might call later this evening and you could regale me with your tales of adventure and conquest. Perhaps you could show me a few of your other things . . . and I might show you a few of mine?"

"Huh?" Lirry blinked. "Of course, I . . . I'd like that."

"So would I! I just love to barter, but I warn you," Gynik said with a smile as she stepped through the hatchway on her way out, "I drive a hard bargain!"

"Hhhnnumminah!" was all Lirry could say.

Traveling Companions

The weapons rested once more in their racks. The long day had drawn to a close, the horns of the Temple rumbling to signal the end of the final worship hour over the city.

The swords in the rack were just as glad for the rest. They spoke to one another in a language that was beyond the understanding of their makers and, for that matter, beyond any real understanding of the swords themselves. They did not know how they communicated, nor did they question much concerning their place in creation. Philosophy was not a part of their world. Swords understood the arts of war and nothing else—insofar as they understood anything at all.

"I hope they don't give me that skinny warrior again," spoke a short-sword by the name of K'thwingsh. *"He gets all excited in combat and keeps swinging my blade into the dirt. I tell you, I get a nick every time he does it. I'm losing my edge!"*

"Aye, it's a sorry lot this time," complained Tshu'shik, a two-handed broadsword known for his temperamental nature. *"They'll not last long enough to make a good showing of it. Not nearly as good as that group we had back seventy-three years ago. Remember that one?"*

"Oh, I wish you would shut up about that group!" rang a dirk named Sni'dinkt. *"Every night we hear how your warrior maiden stood in the midst of three hundred of Satinka's horde—"*

"It wasn't three hundred!" the broadsword clanged.

"One hundred . . . two hundred . . ." Sni'dinkt chimed gleefully. *"Who can keep track when your story grows with every telling?"*

The other blades in the armory rang with laughter.

"I'll cleave your warrior for that one," Tshu'shik rattled with embarrassment.

"If you're fast enough!" the dirk flashed back.

"With any luck you'll be buried with him," the broadsword rejoined.

A shudder passed among the blades at the thought.

"Well, I think the current group is not as bad as all that," a rapier observed, cutting the conversation in a different direction. *"There are several promising warriors in the group who might acquit their blades rather honorably."*

"That may be true, but they all seem to have been claimed." Chi'shishinth, a longsword with an elegant pearl pommel, sighed. *"And by swords which otherwise one might think were rather—"*

"Ugly?" the rapier offered.

"All those shortswords with black pommels," the longsword responded. *"They are all so much alike . . . and so standoffish. I don't recall ever seeing swords like them before, except for S'shnickt."*

"That's right," the dirk cut in. *"Say, where is S'shnickt? Maybe we could ask him about it?"*

Their question rang down through the endless ranks of weapons racks of the armory. In time the question itself came back to the dirk.

S'shnickt was no longer in the armory. For that matter, two other weapons seemed to be missing as well.

The weapons were all very excited at this prospect. Missing weapons meant combat and death were in the offing. They would gladly have alerted the Pir—if for no other reason than they might find themselves pressed into immediate use—but they could not.

There were no Craftis among the Pir.

★　★　★

"Get up!" the quiet voice rumbled.

Galen was having trouble focusing his eyes in the darkness. "What? What do you want?"

"Get up now! Get up and get out!" the voice insisted.

"Galen, I think we had better do as they say." It was Rhea's voice. Galen could just make her out now, standing between bunks. Dim, flickering light from the open doorway to the west was the only illumination. She looked at him with sadness, her eyes those of an animal that had run out of places to hide. She clung to Maddoc with one hand while she clutched a blanket around her with the other. The madman stood stoically next to her, holding the blanket she had apparently offered him over one arm. Maddoc watched the shadows all around them, a grim look of determination on his face.

There were plenty of shadows to watch. Galen could now see the outlines of several Pir monks standing in the aisles around them. All held their dragonstaffs at hand. They stood back some distance from the three, their eyes watching them from the black abysses of their hoods.

Galen pulled his own rough blanket off the bed. His rose doublet, long since ruined, was little protection again the chill of the night. He wrapped the blanket around his shoulders as he stepped down onto the chill floorboards of the barracks.

One of them spoke again, "Out the door—now."

Galen took a long, deep breath and then turned toward the door. Rhea and Maddoc quickly fell in step behind him.

"Who are they?" Rhea whispered urgently from behind Galen.

"I don't know," he said over his shoulder. "We've seen people disappear from the barracks before. Perhaps now we'll get to find out where they went."

"I'm not sure I want to know," Rhea rejoined.

Galen chuckled darkly. "I'm *absolutely* sure I don't want to know. I just haven't figured out how to avoid it at this point."

Rhea shivered behind him. "What do we do?"

"When I come up with a brilliant plan, believe me, you'll be the first to know!" was Galen's only answer.

They stepped out of the open barracks doorway. The night sky overhead was overcast, a broken blanket of clouds shielding them from the stars overhead. Only the occasional torch, sputtering in a stiff night breeze, gave flickering definition to their surroundings. Galen could barely make out the form of the rows of barracks behind them, though they were less than a hundred feet from where he walked. Ahead of them, the darker shape of the arena emerged from the night, a mass more felt than seen.

Now fewer than ten of the Pir escorted them from a distance. Galen could not see their faces, shrouded as they were in their deep hoods, but he noticed that each of them held a dragonstaff, keeping its eye turned away from the prisoners as they walked. The entire group passed quickly through the warrior's arch and onto the floor of the arena itself, a dim open space in the darkness. The vacant seats of the various sections looked down on them in their passing. Galen could smell death in the place.

"Listen, Rhea," he said with quiet urgency. "I met a man in the dream who said he could help us escape."

"It looks like he may be a little too late," Rhea replied gruffly. "Unless . . . do you think this is his doing?"

"I don't know. He appeared to me as the Pir Inquisitas, and these *are* Pir monks."

"The Pir Inquisitas?" Rhea's voice sounded skeptical. "Is this the same Pir Inquisitas you told me about? The one who is responsible for you being here in the first place?"

Galen nodded sheepishly.

"I'm not sure I'm ready to place my entire trust in that one," Rhea said with great sarcasm.

"What's your game, Galen?" Maddoc whispered conspiratorially as they walked across the empty arena floor.

Galen glanced at Maddoc but Rhea answered for him. "It is a mission . . . a mission for the Circle of Brothers who . . . uh, who . . ."

"The Circle of Brothers Forged by Galen's Will?" Maddoc finished for her, patting her on the hand. "Don't you mean the *Secret* Circle of Brothers Forged by Galen's Will?"

"Yes, husband, forgive me."

"Anything for a fellow member of the Circle," Maddoc said, patting her hand.

Galen glared at Rhea. "Is he going to be trouble?"

"Why? Are you expecting any?" Rhea shot back a little too quickly, then thought better of her words. "Sorry, Galen. No, he won't be any trouble. He believes we're performing some noble task for the Circle. He—he thinks we are escaping."

"Oh, great!" Galen huffed, then turned to Maddoc as they walked. "You wouldn't happen to know *how* we were supposed to escape, would you?"

"No, Galen," Maddoc said solemnly. "I do not enjoy that level of trust in the Circle. *You* are the genius behind our escape. You certainly know well how to keep a secret. I'm confident that you will let us all in on your brilliant plan the moment you deem it prudent."

Galen seethed with frustration. "I'll be more than happy to tell you my brilliant plan—the moment I have one."

"And I would love to hear it, too," said Galen's sword.

Galen stumbled in midstride. The Pir monk hoods turned as one to watch him warily. Galen recovered and continued to march across the open arena floor, but he surreptitiously reached down with his right hand along the outside of the blanket draped over his shoulders.

S'shnickt was there, hanging at his side under the blanket.

Galen panicked for a moment. He was certain the sword had not been there when he was dragged out of his bunk. Now, inexplicably, it hung at his side. If the Pir should discover that he was armed . . .

"Can we stop at the armory for a moment?" S'shnickt suddenly asked.

"No!" Galen hissed.

Rhea looked at him in confusion. They were emerging from the opposite warrior's arch in the arena from where they had entered. The Pir guard surrounding them urged them south down the broad curve of Beggar's Lane. Before them, Trader's Gate, one of the original four towers that overlooked the entrance to the Garden, rose into the pitch night, its base illuminated by several braziers roaring with flame.

"Can't we stop just for a moment?" the sword asked once more. *"I*

mean, you wouldn't have to do anything but strike a gallant pose in the door-way while I let the rest of the armory know what is going on."

"I said *no!*" Galen rumbled through gritted teeth.

"Galen? What is it?" Rhea asked urgently. "Is something wrong?"

"Well, it isn't like they can tell *anyone your secret plan,"* S'shnickt groused from under the blanket. *"I mean, none of these Pir are Craftis!"*

"Shut up!" Galen snapped under his breath.

"All right," Rhea responded meekly.

"No, not *you!*" Galen was exasperated.

"I didn't think so," the sword answered mistakenly. *"I'm willing to let things unfold as they come, but Kri-dankt and Swashthok both would like to know how soon we'll be seeing some action out of—"*

"Who?" Galen asked.

"What?!" Rhea demanded, her anger rising.

"Kri-dankt and Swashthok . . . they are the swords with Rhea and Maddoc," S'shnickt answered.

Galen caught his breath. He turned ever so slightly toward Rhea, who was struggling at his side with Maddoc, and spoke in a careful whisper. "Feel down your right side."

Rhea's nostrils were flaring. "Are you talking to *me* now? Because if you are *I've* got a few things I'd like to say to you before we—"

"Later! Just reach down on your right, but try not to be noticed!"

"We're about to die and all you—" Rhea's eyes went suddenly wide. "How?"

"We'll have to work that out later between us," Galen said. "Maddoc, I suppose you are armed as well?"

"A member of the Secret Circle of Brothers Forged by Galen's Will is never without his weapon," Maddoc intoned with a combination of humility and pride.

Their detail was quickly approaching the inner gate. A large torusk beast stood before the gate, an ironreed cage harnessed to its back. The cage was open, waiting for them. A torusk master stood next to the tusks of the beast.

"It looks like we're going on a journey," Maddoc said happily. "How I love adventures!"

One of the Pir—the leader of the detail, no doubt, although

Galen could not distinguish between him and the others—indicated the short ladder laid next to the torusk. Each of them in turn climbed up to the opening in the wicker cage and lowered themselves inside.

Once his prisoners were within, the Pir leader quickly climbed the ladder and secured the cage with several large locks. He then hurried back to the ground and pulled the ladder clear of the side of the beast.

The torusk master clucked.

The torusk slowly began to move toward the gates. As they approached, the huge gates opened wide. They were leaving the Garden, passing the unassailable, impenetrable wall of their prison. The gate soon fell behind them, replaced by the closed, deserted streets of Vasskhold.

Galen quickly looked about. Their escort now numbered only four. One torusk master urged his beast along their course. Three Pir monks accompanied them at a distance, their dragonstaffs at the ready.

Rhea's voice quivered. "Galen, what are we going to do?"

"Remember that brilliant plan Maddoc kept asking me about?"

"Yes?"

"I think I may actually *have* one after all!"

32

Blind Eye

The toruk passed beyond the Trader's Gate into the Caravan District of Vasskhold. Beggar's Lane continued to curve down toward the next tower, Freeman's Tower, and its gate, but the torusk master pushed his baton against the tusk of the beast, turning it to the right off of the large avenue and down a narrow street.

Large warehouse structures lined the street on Galen's left, while the smaller, more ornate structures of the guildhouses were crammed together on the right. The warehouses were dark, their work having concluded with the arrival of the last caravans. The city gates closed at dusk, and with them much of the operations in the warehouses as well.

The guilds, however, were another matter. Their business was conducted well into the night and sometimes into morning as the need required. The lights in the guildhouse windows continued to burn into the street, brightly illuminating the broken stones of the cobbled street as the small procession passed.

"Where are they taking us?" Galen asked, as much to himself as to Rhea.

She could only shake her head.

"To glory, Galen." Maddoc winked. "Where else?"

The guide directed the torusk down several more close and confusing streets. There were ramshackle homes pressed together and leaning outward into the street. They passed a modest Kath-Drakonis at one point, its familiar dome dark against the diffused lights in the streets against the clouds. Then they turned once more down a broad avenue leading away from the Temple of Vasska in a great curve through more homes barely reclaimed from the old ruins.

"I don't think we can wait much longer," Galen said to Rhea. "If they are taking us somewhere in the city, they are sure to have more guards there to help unload us."

"Are you sure the swords can do the job?" Rhea asked.

"We can do our job, if you can do yours," S'shnickt said haughtily.

"We're about to find out," Galen said. "There's a space opening up just up ahead. Everyone knows what they have to do, right? Maddoc?"

"Yes. Escape. Got it."

Galen took a deep breath. He had escaped once before from a cage just like this one, only he still had no idea how he had done it. If they could somehow get out of the cages, they would then have to surprise the Pir monks who were already watchful and were rarely, if ever, surprised by anything. He had to do all this with a woman, a madman, and three swords that would not shut up in his head.

Maybe he *was* crazy after all.

Gendrik, the torusk master, was miserable. Not only had he spent most of the previous night tracking down this Galen prisoner, but now Tragget had put him back on the road with this same Galen and his two companions. He missed his bed. He missed his wife. He missed not having anything to do.

Tragget had called him back to his quarters that same afternoon. It was bad enough that he had to get the caravans ready to leave in less than two weeks' time. Now Tragget had demanded that he make another journey before the departure of the Enlund caravans. It was really too much to expect out of any torusk master—even one in service to the Pir Inquisitor himself.

Gendrik was tired and wondered how he could possibly get

through the night. The monks managed to get the prisoners loaded easily enough and without any protest on their part. Perhaps they knew why they were there and where they were going. Gendrik hoped so—it would make the trip go ever so much more pleasantly.

His route had been very specific: turn off Beggar's Lane and go down Guild Alley. A few difficult turns through the Bard Quarter and then down Ferand Street until it intersected with King's Row. King's Row was the important one: it would bring him into the Old City. Gendrik knew of a path through those ruins that would get them out of Vasskhold without their having to pass through any of the usual gates. Tragget had been very specific about that. He did not want it generally known that these prisoners had left the city.

Indeed, he apparently did not want anyone to know that they had even left the Gardens. Gendrik knew the monks that had been used to bring the prisoners to his torusk. Each of them was specifically in the service of the Inquisitor. Indeed, the three monks that accompanied them as guards on this journey were the most trusted of the Inquisitor's elite. Gendrik had been frankly surprised that there were three of them on this trip; one would have been more than a match for three of the Chosen.

The torusk turned his head, causing Gendrik to pull it back facing forward with his baton. Well, if Tragget wanted to get these people out of harm's way, the torusk master thought, that was his business. It was not Gendrik's place to try to understand the thoughts of the Pir, and certainly not to question the orders of the Inquisitor. Far better for him to just take these people up to Brenna Keep; that was all there was to his business. Brenna Keep was located atop a crag just southwest of Garlandhome and about as far removed from the trade routes as any place in Vasska's realm. It would be an arduous journey to make it there and back, but Gendrik wanted to get it over with. The sooner he finished this little task, the sooner he could enjoy his own warm bed.

Gendrik yawned. He could see King's Row up ahead—a wide avenue that ran straight past the "reformed" buildings of the south side and into the collapsed remains of the northwest quarter. They would have to cross the Victor's Way, the wide avenue that ran between the kneeling statues toward the nine towers of the inner city. They would probably be given little notice there anyway. All they had to do was get out of sight of the city walls before sunup and he could then take his pace as he liked.

The King's Row Cross was absolutely deserted. The rows of tumbledown buildings and their patchwork architecture were all dark and still in the night. Watch fires burned on the corners of the street.

Gendrik pushed the tusk of the torusk to the right. The great beast turned to follow his head, lumbering to the right and heading down King's Row.

Suddenly the beast lurched upward, rearing on its hind legs. Its maw gaped open, baring its double ridges of razor teeth. It howled pitilessly. The terrible sound echoed down the still streets of the city and shook the buildings.

Gendrik leaped back. The thrashing tusks of the suddenly enraged torusk sliced through the air barely a hand's width from his chest. He raised his baton more out of instinct than from any real effort to get the beast under his control again.

It did not matter. The torusk had forgotten entirely about his master, having given over all thought to blind pain and rage. The beast stomped the ground, spinning about in a frenzy. Its thick tail whipped about, bowling one of the monks to the ground as the other two hastily leaped out of the way of the rampaging monster.

"Thon! Thon! Easy, boy!" Gendrik yelled at the torusk. He had never seen one of the beasts this upset before, and though he was one of the most experienced torusk handlers in all Hrunard, even he was uncertain how to calm so enraged a beast.

Thon either did not or could not hear Gendrik through his panic. He spun once more, reared up on his hind legs with a terrible howl, and then bolted at full gait into King's Row toward the south.

"No! Thon! You're going the wrong way!" Gendrik called out.

The massive flanks of the torusk, the ironreed cages bounding on either side, rapidly disappeared down the darkened streets.

The monks pulled themselves up from the ground, giving chase at once.

Gendrik yelled once more in his rage and frustration, then dashed down the avenue after the monks.

The ancient cobblestones still showed through the compacted dirt here and there as Gendrik hurtled down the dark and deserted street. He could hear his booted footsteps rebounding from the walls of the obscure and anonymous buildings as he ran. The sound of the torusk was always before him, seeming to get farther away with each passing howl. Gendrik winced painfully a few moments later when the terrible sound of a crash rolled back toward him from the darkness. Worse still was the silence that followed.

Gendrik pressed ahead faster than before. The shadows of the street were slow to give way to his eyesight. Soon, however, he arrived at the end of the street. King's Row stopped abruptly where Cooper's Lane from the west turns into Southline Alley. The Nine Towers Inn lorded over the end of the street, one of the better-known establishments in the city. Its three-story façade welcomed pilgrims of means to the cleanest lodgings in the city.

Gendrik groaned. The Nine Towers Inn looked to be short a tower or two. The rampaging torusk had been unable to turn in time and slid into the front of the building. The doorway was shattered, buried under a cascade of stone and wooden beams. The front of the building sagged forward toward the street. It was missing its upper corner entirely, and stones lay broken on the street.

Thon, his torusk, was wandering around the street looking somewhat dazed. The creature was bleeding from its flanks. Somehow, the prisoners must have stuck his poor beast back there, inciting it to charge down the street recklessly.

The prisoners! Gendrik realized that the cages were empty. He quickly inspected the separated ironreed strands. They were all sliced cleanly through.

Gendrik swore the worst oath that he knew, glancing angrily about. Several people had spilled out from the inn. They were pointing eastward, down Southline Alley.

Gendrik needed no further urging. These prisoners had been far more trouble than he had expected. They had wounded his torusk. And now they had escaped.

In his mind, Gendrik saw the two portals behind the throne of the Pir Inquisitas. He felt a chill knowing that one of them was waiting for him and that in this moment he was choosing which one. He suddenly ran after the monks in their headlong dash down Southline Alley. He knew he could not return to face the Pir Inquisitas until he had the prisoners safely back in his charge.

Galen struggled to keep control of his breath. It sounded loud in his ears, loud enough to call the entire watch of the city down on them.

Rhea shivered next to him, her sword still in her right hand, her left clinging to Maddoc. "I don't . . . I don't think this is . . . is going very well," she gasped.

They stood in the shadows between two buildings. Galen knew they were trade shops of some kind—smithies like himself or some other business, though he could not tell in the darkness. The lack of stars or moonlight made everything difficult to see.

At least they were off the street. They ducked down between the buildings as soon as Galen had spotted an opening. The terrain behind the shops was more difficult going but offered them far more cover. An open sewer marked their primary course, occasionally meandering under a rickety fence. They scaled, crawled, dashed, and paused as necessary, making their difficult way eastward with all the strength they had.

"Oh, I . . . don't know," Galen said in a hoarse whisper with what breath he could muster. "I think we're making . . . good time!"

Rhea smiled tiredly. "I agree. For not knowing where we are going . . . we're making excellent time!"

Galen smiled into the darkness at her joke. "Not true . . . I know *exactly* where we are going. It's just that I'm not sure we're going to . . . live long enough to get there."

Rhea laughed wearily. "That's not very inspiring."

"You see up over that building across the road?" Galen said, pointing with his sword. "That dark line cutting across the sky? That's the old south wall of the city. Now, follow the line to your left. See where it drops off? *That* is a breach in the wall. *That* is where we are going."

"What's beyond the wall?" Rhea asked.

Maddoc suddenly spoke up. "Death and glory, my dear, that's what is beyond the wall. I can hardly wait!"

Rhea shook again in the chill of the night. "Maybe . . . maybe we had better split up, Galen. You'll have a better chance of making it without us. We'll meet you south of the breach and—"

"No," Galen said flatly. "That's not the plan. We stay together or it won't work. Understand?"

Rhea nodded.

Galen lifted his head. "They're getting closer. We've got to hurry."

Galen pushed Rhea and Maddoc ahead of him. Together, they dashed across the street, hoping to vanish between the structures before anyone else noticed them.

Gendrik lost track of the monks. He did not understand them. They always seemed to vanish just when you needed them the most. Now the torusk master was tired, angry, and frustrated. His initial sprint had slowed progressively to a run, then a jog, and finally a weary walk down the center of Southline Alley. He continued to glance down the black spaces between the shops for the escapees, all the while knowing how impossible it all had become. It was not as though he were looking for a lost boot that he would discover politely waiting in some gutter for him to run across. The prisoners—and the monks, for that matter—had vanished into the night, left him behind to take the blame for it, and none of them were likely to step forward now to save his hide.

He ought to just go back to the inn, collect his wounded torusk, and try to think of some way he and his wife could quietly slip into the night themselves. Of course, that was just a pipe dream. His wife was used to life in court and would never put up with being a fugitive. He would get her to flee the city only by tying a rope to her and dragging her out with the torusk.

He was mulling over this interesting picture in his mind when he saw them.

There they were—his prisoners—dashing across the roadway just ahead of him!

He tried to yell but he was so excited that it came out as a single, inarticulate squeak. He cleared his throat, finding his voice even as his feet once more began to give chase. He could feel his legs shaking under him with the renewed effort, but he could not let them escape him a second time. He called after them. "Hey! Stop! In the name of the Inquisitor, *stop!*"

He dashed between the broken-down shanties, desperate to keep his quarry in view. They were elusive but he was calling on reserves from unknown depths. His alternative to capturing them was to face the displeasure of both his wife and the Inquisitor. These were powerful motivators. He doggedly stayed nearly fifty feet behind them, following step by step as they ran splashing down the thin sewer behind the shacks. He cleared the same low fences they threw themselves over and vaulted the obstacles they pulled down in his path. Several times he lost them among the chaos of the shacks, but each time he managed to find them again. With each moment the escaped prisoners were putting more distance between themselves and the torusk master, but still he did not give up. He could not give up.

Suddenly the hovels gave way. Gendrik saw the great breach in the southern wall that Vasska had made during the siege of the city more than four centuries earlier. Now great stones lay scattered across the landscape, with broken visages of ancient Rhamasian kings lying among the maze of blocks and debris. The ruins seemed to glow with a halo of light. Gendrik could see in the distance a large moon shining down through a break in the clouds, illuminating the wide plains to the south. The River Zhamra shone like a silver ribbon cutting across the Southern Steppes

The prisoners were running through the debris field toward the open land. The pain in Gendrik's side was terrible. "Stop!" he gasped in faint hope. "Stop!"

To his amazement, they stopped!

Then the torusk master saw, silhouetted against the steps, a Pir monk with his staff raised.

Gendrik could not believe his luck. The prisoners—all three of them—were in a large clearing among the rubble from the wall. They turned away from the monk, trying to escape by another route, but as if by some miracle a second monk appeared atop one of the broken blocks directly in their path. The prisoners backed away from this new threat, their swords raised in their defense.

Gendrik could only smile through his wheezing breaths. Their swords would be useless against the dragonstaffs.

The third monk walked past Gendrik, holding up his own staff. The prisoners, back to back, were now in the center of the sandy clearing. One of them, the young man, had sheathed his sword, at least, and was holding his hands up in the air. Sensible, Gendrik thought, although it would do him no good.

As though of one mind, the monks turned their staffs to face the Elect. Gendrik smiled once more, slumped over as he was, sucking for air with his hands on his knees. They had asked for it.

The three prisoners screamed and fell writhing on the ground. In moments they lay in an unconscious tangle. Gendrik had seen it before. The Elect can never escape the eye of the dragon.

The monks relaxed and lowered their staffs. It was over, Gendrik reflected as he moved forward. This lot had given him a scare, it was true, but not so bad really now that he thought about it. For that matter, he might be able to get those cages repaired quickly enough to get them all back on the road before anyone was the wiser. They would be certain to frisk the prisoners a bit more carefully this time. All in all, he thought, it had not turned out so badly after all.

He approached the prisoners with the monks. They lay motionless before him: a careworn woman, a man about her same age, and a younger man. What had they in common? Why had they behaved so badly? You would have thought they *wanted* to go to the war.

"Master Gendrik," one of the monks said. "If you will help us get these prisoners back to the torusk, I believe we can complete this task without further delay."

"My thoughts exactly," Gendrik replied. So the monk wanted to cover all this up, too, eh? Things were going to work out after all.

Gendrik reached down to grab the young man's arm.

The young man grabbed his first.

Gendrik looked down in shock.

The young man was looking back at him.

In that instant, Gendrik was kicked backward by the young man's booted foot. He fell back flat against the hard ground, what little breath that was left in his lungs pressed out with painful suddenness.

The prisoners were all on their feet. The monks stepped back as well, lifting their staffs quickly to their defense. They were useless. The young man held aloft in his left hand a strange globe that flared with purple lightning.

The Eye of Vasska was blinded.

Gendrik's eyes went wide. He was witnessing evil in its purest form, a power that challenged the holy Vasska. His legs pressed uselessly against the sand, trying to push him farther from the terror before him.

The woman's blade slashed outward, cutting the dragonstaff in two. The monk, shocked at being disarmed so readily, stumbled backward over a stone and fell to the ground. The woman was on top of him in a moment, driving downward with the hilt of her sword.

The older man stood over the second monk on the far side of the woman. Gendrik watched as he casually picked up a broken dragonstaff and swung it downward. The monk's sandal kicked once against the dirt and then went still.

Someone yelled to his right. Gendrik turned and could see the final monk running through the rubble back toward the hovels at the edge of the city. The young man whispered something to the sword, then threw it with all his might.

The blade spun through the air, its hilt striking the monk squarely in the back of the head. He fell behind the stones, Gendrik for the moment uncertain of his fate.

Then, inexplicably, the blade was back in the hands of the young man.

It was then that they all turned to face Gendrik.

"Please," Gendrik said, his voice wavering on the edge of a sob. "Please! Don't kill me!"

The young prisoner turned toward the breach in the great city wall. The open plains beyond seemed to beckon him. He did not speak to Gendrik but only to his own companions. "Are you hurt? Can you travel?"

"As far as you take us, Galen," the older man said.

"Then the road is open before us. Let's go home."

The prisoners turned toward the breach.

"Excuse me," Gendrik called.

The young man turned toward him. "You want something?"

Gendrik nodded. "If it wouldn't be too much trouble, would you do me a very small favor?"

The young man turned away once more, called by some vision beyond the horizon, perhaps, or a road he was anxious to travel.

It was the woman who answered. "What do you want?"

"The monks have an excuse," Gendrik pleaded, his voice small in the night. "Would you leave me here with none?"

The young man turned back to look at Gendrik.

Gendrik smiled meekly and pointed vaguely at his own head.

"Very well," the young man said, drawing his sword.

"Oh, thank you!" Gendrik replied.

The last thing he thought of was the glorious welt on his head he could display to the Inquisitor. Then all his thoughts went truly black.

Obsessions and Confessions

I am not interested in your excuses or your problems, Master Gendrik!" Tragget raged. The Inquisitor's voice echoed through the Hall of Truth until even the polished stone in the walls shook. "You have had three days. Three days of my good pleasure. Three days of the full resources of the office of the Inquisition. Three days of searching and you have come up with *nothing?*"

Gendrik rubbed the lump still prominent on his forehead as much for his own satisfaction as to subtly remind his master that he, too, was a victim—albeit a willing one. "Lord Inquisitor, we've done everything you have asked. Your Pir monks have searched all the routes from the city. The crossings have been watched since the first dawn, and the monks seek the roads night and day. Others at Your Lordship's word are watching the ports of both the Northreach and Cebon seas. Perhaps if we notified the priests of each Kath-Drakonis they could help us search the cities—"

"I will *not* have the Nobis order apprised of our failure, Gendrik!" Tragget was livid. "We will clean up our own mess without having the Aboths breathing down our necks. *No one* beyond the Inquisition is to know about this, is that clear?"

"Yes, Lord Inquisitor!" Gendrik spoke respectfully, his eyes averted.

The door at the back of the hall closed. A robe-clothed monk moved silently down the length of the hall toward the throne.

Tragget looked up, his eyes blinking furiously. "So, Brother Lyndth! Do you have news for me?"

"I do, Lord," Lyndth intoned in a reedy voice. "Does the Lord Inquisitor wish to hear the current report?"

"I would not have asked, otherwise," Tragget said through clenched teeth. "Have they been found?"

Lyndth shook his head, then spoke evenly. "The traveler monks have found no trace of the prisoners anywhere on the roads or along the banks of the River Zhamra from Gateway east as far as the Leeside Bridge and south as far as Homage. Reports of their inquiries among the towns and settlement farms have yielded no results."

Tragget was trembling.

"No one has seen them," Lyndth concluded.

"I have seen them!" Tragget screamed, his body straining forward suddenly, the veins on his neck standing out starkly. His hands went white as they squeezed the carved arms of the throne. The outburst was so sudden that both the monk and the torusk master started visibly. "Don't tell me they are dead, I *know* that they are not! Don't tell me they have vanished, I *see* them out there in the world laughing at us! I do not care how you do it, who you injure or how far you must go; they *must* be found, is that clear? *Is that clear?"*

Gendrik looked at Lyndth as if for help. The monk took a deep breath before continuing.

"There *is,* however, a curious development."

Tragget was still breathing heavily from his outburst, struggling to bring himself back in control. "What development, Brother Lyndth?"

"One of our brethren, at your behest, traveled the east road along the northern branch of the River Zhamra. He thought the prisoners might attempt to reach Tempus or one of the eastern ports through

Hynton Pass. While in Burk's Cove, this good brother heard talk of a dwarf in the village who had come out of the Dragonback."

Tragget raised his eyebrows. "The Dragonback? There are no dwarves in the Dragonback!"

"Which is why the report interested our Inquis brother," Lyndth intoned. "This blind dwarf was traveling in the company of a human woman. They said their objective was to come here—to Vasskhold—that they might seek redress for some wrong. They started out from some small town named Benyn some weeks ago during—"

"Benyn?" Tragget blinked. "Did you say *Benyn?*"

"Yes, Lord, but—"

"Did they leave around the Festival of the Harvest?"

Lyndth nodded, his eyes narrowing. "Yes, My Lord. Is that significant?"

Tragget preferred not to answer. "Where is this dwarf now, Lyndth?"

"The dwarf and his companion were stranded in Burk's Cove when they were discovered. Our brother thought it prudent to forward them to you directly, Lord Inquisitor," Lyndth replied evenly. "They are in the antechamber awaiting an audience at your pleasure."

"That *is* most interesting indeed," Tragget replied, leaning back in his chair more easily now. "Our brother has done well. By all means, Brother Lyndth, grant them audience." He then turned to the torusk master. "Gendrik, I am finished with you for now. By all means, take the right hall exit."

The torusk master bowed, swallowed, and walked gingerly through the right hall archway, hoping that his luck would improve.

Berkita sat as motionless as the stone in the antechamber around her. The stillness helped because a part of her thought that if she moved, her life would tumble out of control and into a chaos from which she might never return.

Berkita's life had been a tranquil, pleasantly controlled existence. She had known that each day would be much like the last and that tomorrow would be a satisfying, serene variation on today. The tablecloth in her home would be pressed in just such a way and placed on its shelf. A pleasant morning would see her walking into Benyn to the markets and entering into determined negotiations over the relative value of sharp tools to fresh fish. Afternoons would carry the chores of maintaining her household in strict order through hard work, with a place for everything and everything in its place. Her life was ordered to her will and obeyed her whims. Even the selection of her husband had been of her own design. She loved her father but also knew well just what to say and how to say it to have her choice become his.

But now everything in her life seemed to be moving, swept onward as though a dam had broken and the tranquil waters had emptied into a raging river. Her life now bounded between the boulders of one town after another; from Bayfast to Vestuvis to Lankstead Lee, drifting in the eddies of each for any sign of her Galen. Searching the torusk caravans of the Elect dragged them down the "Blood Road," as Cephas put it, like whitewater through the thieves' dens of the Hynton Pass. At last their money ran out in Burk's Cove, a whirlpool of a town where many others had given up hope and never managed to escape.

Yet Berkita held on, determined to get back her beloved and return order to their upside-down lives.

She was working tables at an inn called the Torusk's Tale, nearly starving herself as she struggled to save enough money to continue, when the Pir Inquisitas came for her. Now the river that had swept her into lands she had only heard about in her youth had once more picked her up and, miraculously, brought her to the place she had struggled to reach.

She knew that somewhere, not a few steps or the distance of a shout from where she sat, was her beloved Galen. So she sat as still as she could lest that terrible river of fate pick her up once more.

If only the dwarf next to her could hold still, too.

"Er now, Lady," Cephas rumbled gently as he sat next to her on a long bench. Cephas's legs swung freely, a good half foot short of the floor. "Relaxed be ye. Cephas great audience with Lord soon er is. Right again soon all be."

Berkita looked down at herself. Her traveling dress was dirty and stained at the hem, and there was a large tear under one arm that she had not had time nor the thread to mend. She knew even without a glass that she was far from being presentable before the Lord Inquisitor of all the Pir. "Cephas, I don't know if I can go in! We're in the courts of Vasska himself, and I wouldn't be presentable at a mud carnival in this dress."

"Er! What talk be this is?" The dwarf stuck his hat firmly back on his head, a sign of assertiveness. "Pretty enough for our need er is! High Lord Inquisitor fancy be but dull metal next to Lady Arvad!"

Berkita smiled thinly as she spoke, her eyes fixed on the door before them that led to the man who could give her the answers to everything she sought. "I'm getting court fashion advice from a blind dwarf, but I thank you, Cephas, all the same . . . for this, and so much more."

The dwarf shrugged. "Thanks wasted on Cephas. Save thanks and smiles. Looks no matter. Galen's eyes see Berkita soon. You be beautiful to Galen then . . . no matter if ye be hair lumpy like Cephas. Cephas know."

Berkita shook her head sadly. Getting used to dwarven compliments had taken her the better part of two weeks. Now when Cephas mentioned Galen's affection as gently as he knew how, the thought of it lifted her heart.

The stern monk appeared once more through the double doors. "The Lord Inquisitor has granted you audience. Enter and be judged."

Cephas hopped off the bench, adjusted the red binding across his eyes, and then reached out with his right hand. As she had done more and more often recently, Berkita took it to guide him. Cephas never bumped into a wall more than once, but Berkita's guidance was an expedient whenever they were in a new and unfamiliar place.

"Ready er is?" the dwarf asked.

"This is why we came, Cephas," Berkita answered. "I am ready er is."

She felt the river of fate pulling her forward once more.

★　　★　　★

He watched them approach down the length of the Hall of Truth, both of them looking the worse for the road. The dwarf wore an oversized leather hat with a long feather in it, showing a hint of gaudy affluence without any of the quality. He wore a hooded traveling cloak but no shirt, his carpet of chest hair jutting out around the straps of his traveling pack. His hard boots echoed across the floor as he walked, leaving marks in the fine polished finish. The woman leading him wore a dress that was coming to rags. Brother Lyndth escorted them as they walked, keeping a distance that offered respect to the dwarf's smell.

Tragget watched them approach with rising anticipation. The last few days had taken their toll on him. The demand for the early departure of the Enlund caravans had forced him into trying to save Galen and his associates, but Galen had spoiled it by escaping. He had even managed somehow to use the power of the madness to elude the Eye of Vasska itself. Now, *there* was a power for which Tragget had a real and immediate use. That Galen had managed to discover it and make it work in the world outside his madness was tantalizing and intoxicating just in its thought. That Galen had used that same power to escape Tragget's control was frustrating beyond endurance.

For three days, Tragget had been in torn agony. Each night, he managed to find Galen and Maddoc in the madness of his dreams, although they endeavored to avoid him in that ever-changing landscape of the familiar and the bizarre. He begged them—Tragget, the Inquisitor, actually *begging*—to teach him their knowledge, show him the way of their mastery and let him taste its sweet power. But they remained distrustful and refused.

Then each day they would elude him in the waking world. It was as though they were traveling only in the realm of madness and had eluded the bonds of reality. Some part of him knew that was not true, but another part of him wished that it were—hoped for the kind of freedom it would represent and the possibilities it would offer for his own escape.

Tragget had nothing to offer them for their knowledge, and they had every reason not to give him what he craved. He had to find them, had to make them see that he only wanted to help them—

force them to understand his position. Everything he had tried, however, had failed. What he needed now were not better hunters but a better understanding of his prey.

"Lord Inquisitor, I beg to present to you two supplicants who entreat your time and judgment," Lyndth intoned with formal solemnity.

"Present them and I shall hear their petition," Tragget said with all the restraint he could muster.

Lyndth bowed, turned toward the dwarf, and gestured with his open hand. "May it please the Inquisitor, I present—"

The dwarf decided he had had enough ceremony. He took two large steps forward and began speaking over his own introduction. "Cephas Hadras I be! Dwarf smith best er is. Who be ye?"

Brother Lyndth bellowed with outrage, "How dare you! You do *not* ask questions of the Pir Inquisitor!"

"Aye, then ye *er* the Pir Inquisitor, eh?" Cephas smiled beneath his crimson bandages, then stomped his foot in approval. "Good er is! Great wrong were done er Benyn! Right making be ye, Sire Inquisitor. Right making sure er is! Sire Inquisitor just, er?"

"Master Dwarf! You will hold your silence while—"

"It's . . . it's all right, Brother Lyndth." Tragget squinted at the dwarf as he spoke, not entirely understanding what the short man was saying. "I believe I will conduct this audience with some leeway. Am I to understand that you are from Benyn, both of you?"

"Aye, sire," Cephas intoned boldly.

Tragget glanced at the woman. Nice figure beneath her ruined dress. Her hair was a bit unkempt but she had a fine face. The most striking thing about her was her violet eyes. They looked directly at Tragget and never glanced away.

"I was in Benyn recently," Tragget said easily. "It is a beautiful little town."

"Aye, beauty as er is," Cephas said, his face lifted up in pride. "Though Cephas n'er seen it. Know I each stone in Cephas's heart."

"May I call you Cephas?" Tragget asked gently.

"Cephas name er is!"

The dwarf then spat on the floor, much to Lyndth's dismay.

Tragget decided it was some part of dwarven introduction customs that he did not understand and simply went on.

"Very well, Cephas, thank you. And your companion? What may I call her?"

"Berkita," Cephas asserted.

"Berkita, yes. Well, Cephas, I am most interested in your town. I am looking for a man who lived there."

"Er?" Cephas cocked his head, trying to understand. "Sire Inquisitor, *Cephas* look er friend to free."

"Yes, I understand, dwarf," Tragget said, trying to hold his impatience in check. "But you see this man that I am looking for was an ironsmith—"

"Yes!" Cephas interrupted. "Yer Sire Inquisitor understands old Cephas! Here Lady and Cephas er looking fer ironsmith!"

Tragget stopped for a moment. "Cephas is looking for—"

"We are both looking for a man by the name of Galen," Berkita said suddenly, her voice strong and insistent. "He was taken in the Election two weeks ago in our town of Benyn."

In the periphery of his vision, Tragget could see Lyndth turn his shocked and surprised face sharply toward him. Tragget put his hand up to silence any comment from his brother monk but never took his eyes off the dwarf.

"His name is . . . Galen?" Tragget said slowly. "Galen . . . Arvad?"

The woman stepped forward, her quick words edged with desperation. "You know his name? I am sorry for coming before you in such a state, my lord, and for speaking out of turn, but our need is urgent and time works against us. Please, sire! I am . . . I was his wife, Lord Inquisitor, and I believe there was a . . . an irregularity in his Election. Do you truly know him, my lord?"

Tragget sat back slowly on the throne, his mind spinning, trying to grasp what was standing before him and all the possibilities that it implied. The silence in the room lengthened as he considered his answer.

"Yes," he said at last. "I know him well."

A cry caught in Berkita's throat. Tragget could see that she was swaying slightly where she stood. Her jaw had the barest of quivers as she carefully asked the questions she longed to know the answers to and dreaded each night. "Is he well, sire! Is he here? Please, Lord Inquisitor, might I just see him for a moment or—"

"Please, Berkita!" Tragget said gently, his voice calming. "Please be calm and assured. It was Berkita *Arvad*, was it not? Galen was your husband, wasn't he?"

Brother Lyndth's eyes shifted to the woman with great interest.

"Yes, sire. Galen and I are married . . . were married until his Election." Berkita's violet eyes narrowed slightly as she looked at the Inquisitor. "Have we met?"

Tragget shook his head. "No, Lady Arvad . . . it's just that Galen has spoken of you so often and with such fondness."

"He has?"

"Yes, I should have known you at once," Tragget continued. "My apologies for my oversight, especially in light of the difficult situation regarding both you and your husband."

"Difficult?" Cephas said harshly. "What is difficult?"

"Well, it is all rather complicated," Tragget said with an inflection of perhaps too much concern. He had to be careful not to overplay this part. "Your husband was taken during the Festival of the Harvest. He gave every indication at the time that he was one of the Chosen . . . the Elect of Vasska. When that happened—as with all other such cases since the beginning—your marriage was dissolved."

"Every Pir knows this," Berkita said evenly, her eyes still fixed on the Inquisitor.

"Human nonsense!" Cephas rumbled.

"Brother." Tragget gestured to his assistant. "Please explain to the dwarf."

"Yes, my lord," Lyndth said at once. "Since the Festivals were instituted, it has been the compassionate will of Vasska that marriages and all bonds of family are dissolved in the Election. This is done so that those not Chosen may be relieved of all burdens the Elect may impose upon them in deeds, contracts, and nonsubstantial obligations as well. It is the mercy of Vasska toward all those who lose loved ones to the Election that their losses may be assumed by Vasska and his Pir."

"He is still mine, even if the marriage was dissolved in the eyes of the Pir." Berkita spoke it as an unquestionable fact.

"As of the moment of his Election, that is correct," Tragget said quickly. "But, there is glad news in all of this if you will but hear me out."

Lyndth shot a questioning look at Tragget but said nothing.

Berkita nodded. "Go on."

Tragget thought for a moment. It was important that he weave as much truth into the lie as possible. No lie stands up well on its own without the support of at least a little truth. "Galen was convinced that there had been some mistake made—that he was not of the Elect. No one would listen to him. He was so desperate to get back to you, Berkita."

"How know you?" Cephas asked suspiciously.

"I *am* the Inquisitor," Tragget said evenly. "We spoke many times. Indeed, he was so desperate that several days ago, he escaped while we were moving him."

"Escaped?" Berkita snapped. "You mean he's no longer here?"

"That's correct," Tragget said. "We've been looking for him ever since."

"If only we'd gotten here sooner!" Berkita moaned.

"There now!" Cephas said, stepping toward her carefully and taking her hand. " 'Tweren't so! Lady Arvad been doing more than needful!"

"I should have done more! If I were here just a few days earlier—"

"It would have been a tragedy," Tragget said quickly.

"What?"

"His escape has caused the Inquisition to reexamine his case more completely. If you had come earlier, he might not have escaped and we would not have discovered the truth."

"What truth?" Cephas and Lyndth asked at about the same time.

"That Galen is not legitimately of the Elect," Tragget said, setting the hook. "It is a unique circumstance—and one which I feel we can quickly clear up—but we *must* find him first before he does harm to himself or anyone else."

Berkita took in a long, shuddering breath.

"Will you help me find him?" Tragget leaned forward on his throne. "Will you help me bring him home?"

Berkita looked up, hope in her eyes for the first time since Tragget had looked into them.

"Yes," she said.

Cephas nodded. "Both shall help cr is!"

Tragget stood up and stepped down from the dais. He extended his open arms toward Berkita and the dwarf. He ushered them gently toward the left archway. "Brother Lyndth will show you to your quarters. They are the best that I can offer you. From this moment on, you are under the protection and grace of the Pir Drakonis. With your help, I am sure that we will be able to find Galen and bring him back among us."

"Then he truly is *not* mad?" Berkita asked hopefully.

"No." Tragget smiled comfortingly. "No more than I am."

Kyree

Dwynwyn stood protectively close by Aislynn as they gazed down over the side rail of the nightrunner. She knew there was probably nothing she could do on behalf of the princess should their enemy make a determined effort, but she stayed close all the same.

The winged Famadorians held fast to the harnesses of the airship, dragging it with their noisy, fluttering wings down toward the courtyard of Kien Werren. Only now as they drew closer could Dwynwyn get an understanding of how the great tower had fallen.

The main tower itself was intact. It rose above the rocky shoreline at the farthest apex of the hexagonally shaped outer wall. The beautiful ornamentation around the spire swirled upward in continuous grace, supported by five delicate flying buttresses arching upward from the smaller towers at the remaining points of the wall. The top of the main tower resembled the petals of a flower opening high above the crashing waves of the sea at its base. It was still beautiful there in the moonlight.

But they could see the terrible damage inflicted upon the tower. Its pure white glazed finish was marred by dark and splattered stains.

As the nightrunner glided into the courtyard, Dwynwyn also saw great dark patches in the carefully kept grass.

Several of the winged creatures grabbed Aislynn and Dwynwyn by the arms, dragging them roughly out of the nightrunner. Aislynn started screaming, beating her wings as fiercely as she could, but the creatures held her fast. "Help! Guards!"

"Stop, Aislynn!" Dwynwyn tried to make her voice both urgent and calming at once. "Please, calm yourself!"

Aislynn relaxed into the biting grip of the winged men that held her. The beasts were pulling them across the ground toward the elaborate arched door of the keep. Dwynwyn noted that the beasts had already begun to stake down the nightrunner in the courtyard. The wounded captain was also being dragged from the gondola, though the creatures carrying him were headed toward one of the lesser towers. Dwynwyn knew that she was Aislynn's only remaining protection.

"Where are they?" Aislynn whispered harshly to Dwynwyn as they walked. "Where are the guardians of the keep? There were nearly five hundred faeries stationed at this posting. How could they have failed?"

"Your Highness," Dwynwyn said as they walked across the ground between their captors, "I don't know, though I hope to find out. For now I must ask you to remain silent. I will speak for us. Do you understand?"

"Yes, but why—"

Aislynn's words stopped in her delicate throat.

At the top of the wide curve of the beautiful stairs, the double doors to the keep of Kien Werren stood closed.

Two sets of faery wings, dismembered from their owners, were pinned with daggers to the door.

Dwynwyn could barely breathe.

The two faery women were propelled through the doors by their captors; strong-armed males by the look of them, Dwynwyn noted. They wore fitted black tunics with silver panels and trim. Their hair—the color of harvest wheat—fell long and free down their backs, with the exception of a single long braid hanging from their right temple. Their ears were pointed like the faeries and at a distance one might even mistake them for one of the Fae. Their builds, however, were larger and more muscular than any of the faerykind, and their wings were patterned after the eagles—feathered rather than membraned. That they were Famadorians—recognized by all the Fae as the lowest caste of creatures—was certain. Yet they were a new truth for Dwynwyn and, she suspected, for all other faeries as well.

The main hall of the tower was a great open space that rose thirty feet up to a domed lattice. This, in turn, supported the upper floors of the tower, each subsequent level supported by another lattice of shaped stone. The arrangement was typical for faery constructs: different levels accessible by flight and each level offering its own declaration of station one above another. It was also one of the safest designs. Famadorians were ground-bound creatures who typically did not possess the gift of the sky. Their armies could invade and even gain access to the buildings of the faeries, but in the end the faeries would be victorious from their secure heights.

Until now, Dwynwyn realized. Looking up into the chamber, she shuddered to see these winged Famadorians noisily flapping about the overhead lattice. No doubt they had gained access to the upper chambers and taken them as well. It was dawning on the Seeker just how perilous their situation truly was: all the defenses of Qestardis—and all the other faery realms, for that matter—depended upon their ability to stay out of reach of their foe.

Their guards pushed them forward into the center of what had been the grand rotunda. The grasses under their feet were trampled flat, as were many of the flowers that had been cultivated here, a chaos no faery would allow into a tower of Qestardis. By the looks of the plants on the main floor, the tower must have been taken several days before.

No word had reached them that the tower had fallen to an enemy. There must have been no one free to convey the message. No escapees. Everyone had been caught, and, by the looks of the wings mounted on the entrance door, killed.

In the center of the rotunda, one of the creatures was hunched over a large, crude table. It must have been built by the Famadorians, as the wood had not been coaxed into shape as the faeries do, but was rather hacked and forced together. Several tapestries lay across the surface, as well as thin rolls of dried wood pulp. The Famadorian rested with both his hands spread wide on the table, his muddy brown wings stretching wide for a moment in the creature's listlessness, then folded back into place. He was intently studying whatever was on the table before him, his head bowed down.

The winged guards stopped just short of the table, their grip still harsh against Dwynwyn's skin.

"The female faeries, Master," announced Dwynwyn's guard. "You asked that they be brought to you at once."

Dwynwyn glanced at the rough man in surprise. "You speak our language? You speak the faery tongue?"

The winged man at the table looked up at last, his light golden hair pulled straight back from his high forehead. His eyes were narrow but of a piercing pale blue color. His face was angular, with a strange, dangerous smile playing on his lips. Dwynwyn feared that smile more than anything she could remember.

"Well, will you listen to that, Sargo? *We* speak *their* language!" He straightened up to stand erect, crossing his arms over his chest as he stood casually observing his prisoners. "What arrogant presumption we find in these faery folk. *Their* language! *Their* culture! *Their* glory! Everything they say just seems to make you want to tear their wings off, doesn't it?"

"Right you are, Master!" laughed the one named Sargo.

Dwynwyn noticed Aislynn blanch next to her. "Who are you?"

The master chuckled as he spoke. "We are the Kyree. More precisely, since I just *know* that you'll want me to be precise, we are what remains of the Aerie Kongei of the Jhunthong Province, loyal servants of the Greater Empire of Kyree. Does that help?"

Dwynwyn blinked. "The Kyree?"

"No, I can see that it doesn't help at all." The master shrugged. He stepped casually around the table as he spoke, his narrow eyes never leaving Dwynwyn. "Yes, we are the Kyree, of whom you know absolutely nothing. Nothing at all. Although, if you *did* know something you might even concede the possibility that it was *you* who learned your language from *us.*"

"You are Famadorians, then," Dwynwyn said, her calling as Seeker driving her to ask the questions burning inside her. "You are winged Famadorians?"

The master laughed out loud. He spoke to the guard but his eyes remained fixed on Dwynwyn. "Sargo, can you believe it? These faeries are amazing. Everything that isn't faery must be Famadorian!"

Sargo and the other guards laughed darkly. "Right you are, Master!"

"Such arrogant conceit!" the master said, shaking his head, his voice suddenly speaking as though instructing a child. "They play in their little nursery with all their pretty little toys. They bicker—not about who is superior because they all know that they *are* superior—but rather about which of them is *more* superior to the other superior faeries! Anything outside their careful little world is 'Famadorian' and therefore worthy only of their disdain."

The master leaned forward suddenly, his face only inches away from Dwynwyn's.

"No," he said with a quiet, biting voice. "We are *not* centaurs. We are *not* satyrs. We are *not* mermen or harpies or griffons or hippocampi or unicorns or dragonmen. And, by oblivion, we most *certainly* will *not* be conveniently lumped by you into any sack of entrails called Famadorians! We are the *Kyree!*"

The master leaned back once more, leaning comfortably against the table.

"Please, sir. Master," Dwynwyn continued, unfazed by his hostility. "You are new to us and we do not understand. What are your intentions? Tell us what you want from us."

"No," the master said through a large smile.

Dwynwyn was confused. "But surely you have demands! There may be a way that I can communicate that with the court at Qestardis. Let us return to the capital with your problems and I will return with their answer."

"No," the master replied simply.

"At least tell me your name!" Dwynwyn demanded.

"No, I won't even give you that satisfaction, madam," the master said, placing his hands on his hips. "Sargo, I thought I asked you to

bring them here to answer my questions! Faeries! Who can understand them? First you can't get them to talk, and then, when they finally *do* talk, all you want is for them to shut up."

The guards laughed deeply once more.

"It's my turn," the master said, leaning forward once more. "What
is your name?"

"I am Dwynwyn."

"Very good, and what is your station?"

"I don't understand."

"What is your . . . what do you call it . . . oh, yes, what is your
caste?"

"I am a Seeker," Dwynwyn said quietly.

"And your companion, is she a 'Seeker' as well?"

Dwynwyn blinked. Being a faery, it was beyond her ability to
speak or think anything beyond what was real and observed. The
problem was that she knew this creature's questions would very
quickly touch on subjects whose truthful answers would bring ruin
on herself and everything she loved. She could not let this thing—this
Kyree—know Aislynn's name and station. Dwynwyn had only one
choice when confronted with a direct question that was too dangerous to answer.

Dwynwyn answered nothing.

The master raised an eyebrow. "You see what I mean, Sargo? You
did hear me, didn't you, Dwynwyn?"

"Yes, I heard you," Dwynwyn answered carefully.

"I see . . . but you're not going to answer me?"

"No, I cannot."

The master nodded. "You came with a large and armed contingent. Do the faeries know that we are here?"

Silence.

"Who are the faeries fighting now?"

Silence.

"Why have you come?"

Silence.

"Who is your companion? Where did you begin your journey?
How long did you travel?"

Dwynwyn glared back.

"Bah! This is hopeless!" the master said, waving his hand dismissively as he walked back around the table to resume his musings. "Let all faeries die in their own silence. Sargo, kill them both and dispose of them as with the others."

"At your command, Master," Sargo said, casually pulling his sword free of its scabbard.

"No!" Aislynn yelped. "Please, Dwynwyn!"

Dwynwyn put her arms around the princess, hiding the girl's face in her breast. She closed her eyes, not wanting to witness her own approaching death. She retreated in that moment into her own thoughts; wishing she had something—anything—to delay their deaths, to buy her time to think . . .

In her mind, she recalled the wingless man giving her a gift.

"Yeow!"

Dwynwyn opened her eyes.

Through a gray flickering veil, she could see that Sargo was holding his bleeding arm. She and Aislynn were inside some sort of extraordinary and inexplicable bubble that shimmered darkly around them. She thought that there was something familiar to it, as though she had seen it somewhere before, but had no idea where it came from or what had caused it.

The master was once more moving around the table toward them. "Sargo! What is it?"

"I . . . I don't know, Master!" Sargo grimaced, wincing through his pain. "I swung my sword and—I don't know."

"Plutich," the master ordered, "hand me that pole."

The guard addressed as Plutich reached over and pulled a long staff from where it was leaning at the side of the rotunda. He handed it to the master and took a pair of careful steps back. The master grasped the pole and carefully slid it toward the gray sphere throbbing around Dwynwyn and Aislynn.

No one in the room was more astonished than Dwynwyn at the result.

The pole entered the sphere, only to emerge thrusting back in the direction from which it had come. The master, both eyebrows now raised, pushed and pulled on the staff. It slid easily in and out without resistance. It moved normally in every respect—except that its sharp point threatened to stick its wielder. The master then moved around the sphere, testing the pole at various points. Each time the pole pushed directly at Dwynwyn, and each time it stuck back out pointing at him.

The master pulled the pole back and stood considering the problem for a moment.

"What is it?" Sargo asked.

"I don't know," the master responded, somehow amused by it all. "What do you think?"

"I think I cut myself with my own blade, Master," Sargo said ruefully. "It's the power of spirits, but I'll be plucked if I know whether they're good or bad. What are your orders, Master?"

"Well," the master said, leaning on the staff as he eyed Dwynwyn in the sphere. "My first order is to not use any spears or arrows on these faeries or everyone in the room will be dropping like sparrows!"

A chuckle ran through the room.

Aislynn spoke quietly. "Dwynwyn! What do you think it is? Where do you suppose it came from?"

"I don't know," the Seeker replied. "I think . . . I think it is a new truth."

"A new truth? What kind of new truth?"

Dwynwyn reached her hand out to touch the sphere with her extended finger. She expected some resistance but her hand passed through, only to bend suddenly back through the wall of the sphere with her finger pointing directly back at her.

Aislynn closed her eyes. "Please don't do that!" she begged. "It makes me ill just to think of it."

Dwynwyn stared in amazement. She opened her hand and moved her fingers. There was no pain or unusual sensation of any kind . . . just her arm folded back through the edge of the sphere. She pulled it back and smiled. "All right, it's all right now."

None of this had escaped the attention of the master. "Well, Sargo, if our weapons can't get in then I am left to wonder if anything else can either. We may not be able to harm them for now, but they don't seem to be going anywhere either." He then turned to the sphere. "In there! Can you hear me in there?"

"Yes," she replied, still testing the properties of this incredible new truth. "Can you hear me?"

"I can, indeed," the master responded. "I am curious as to how long you can keep this marvelous defense going."

"As am I," Dwynwyn replied.

The master sat down on the ground, his legs crossed. "Then I believe we have some time to continue our discussion after all. By the way, I won't harm you or your companion now: you have shown me something that I very much want to have. I suspect I'll need you alive in order to get it."

"I am glad to hear it," Dwynwyn replied coolly. The air in the sphere already was beginning to taste stale. It was getting difficult to breathe.

"Now that we understand each other," the master said through a thin smile, "perhaps we can continue our discussion? What was your name again?"

"Dwynwyn," the Seeker answered. Her head was beginning to hurt. "And you?"

"Xian," the Kyree master replied sweetly. "My name is Xian."

Dwynwyn shook her head. Her vision was beginning to blur. She wondered if this strange globe protecting them would remain after the shadows closed around her mind. She thought for a moment that she was somewhere new. She could see a thin, wingless man in a hooded robe walking through winter grasses of a high mountain meadow. She could see small, wicked creatures, Famadorians no doubt, who darted about in the grass behind the thin man, hiding their gleaming sharp-toothed smiles. Atop a nearby hill, her more familiar wingless man waved at the robed man, who saluted him back. The wicked creatures licked their lips.

Xian's voice was distant and fading. "Dwynwyn?"

Dwynwyn reached out toward her wingless friend in that other world, and fell into darkness.

Beholder

Rhea lay back on the large, flat rock, her head cradled in her hands behind her head. The rock was still warm on her back in the late afternoon. It eased her pains despite its unforgiving surface. She relaxed into it as though it were the softest of beds and every bit as welcome.

The afternoon sun flickered over her eyes, dappled by the shifting leaves of the oaks that towered over her. The leaves drifted down toward her, each careening in a spinning eddy of the cool afternoon breeze. She watched their gentle approach with calm satisfaction. The peace of a warm fall day had settled over her, removing her from the cares of her life for a time and granting her rest. It was an enchantment of its own, she thought as she lay there, as powerful as anything Maddoc or Galen was dreaming up. She was grateful to her ancestors for providing it and hoped that her thankful face could be seen by them as they looked down from the sky.

The rock rested next to a brook that tumbled down the cleft between two hills. Behind it was a small cavern, their shelter for the night. It was a fortunate find; Rhea did not relish the idea of another cold night under an open sky.

She turned slightly to gaze down the small canyon. Its cheerful brook continued downward through the trees until it was obscured completely by the Talwood Forest and the broadening plain of the Southern Steppes. The brook was an insignificant tributary to the River Zhamra, one of hundreds that fed the river's course. Even from here through the trunks of the whispering trees, Rhea could see the winding course of the river cutting a vibrant, twisting course across the plains and fields. It ended at Lake Evni, now a brilliant plate of fire as it reflected the vibrant salmon color of the evening clouds overhead. Closer by, to the west and but a few miles distant from the base of her comfortable seclusion, columns of smoke were rising from the hearths of the village of Talwood. Those were the evening fires that welcomed the farmers to their homes and their rewards for the labors of the day. Those were the signs of simple peace and the comfort of unchallenged routine.

How she longed for them. She closed her eyes and allowed herself to remember, if just for a moment, the quiet of what such a life was like. She swept the floor of her neatly kept and simple home. She instructed her darling little girl on the geography of her homeland so that she might not be lost. She prepared supper for her husband and daughter as she had each night. She took satisfaction in the joy and comfort it brought them. With Dahlia safely in bed, she read the histories next to Maddoc as they sat by the light of their hearth each night. She rested in his arms, cradled securely in his undying and unquestionable love.

Rhea opened her eyes, a tear coursing down across her nose as she lay gazing once more at the town that seemed more and more distant from her as she watched. It had been a simple life and a good life and now it was gone. For several years now, her husband had gone mad in ways that she did not comprehend. He was Chosen. He was of the Elect. She did not know what it meant, and the more she learned the more puzzling and frightening it became. Maddoc had told her that there was no mystery so dark that it could not be understood under the lamp of knowledge. Dahlia was sixteen when the suspicions of their neighbors forced them to leave their home on the north shore, moving with Maddoc from place to place, never staying in one town long enough to attract attention or, worse, attend the local Festivals of the Election. Over their years of flight, Rhea and her daughter had been shining that lamp on the problem of Maddoc's madness. The mystery had become a dwarven mine into which they were all walking deeper and deeper with each step. The farther they walked, the darker it became, until it seemed that she and the lamp were all that were lit in this black and unfathomable, bottomless place.

Dahlia—their gifted, beautiful girl—had already contracted the madness. She understood what was happening in Maddoc's world of dreams far better than Rhea. There was a pattern to it, their daughter would say, a rhythm like a song that she could not quite hear. Unlike her husband, Dahlia seemed to accept the madness with a calm and almost dispassionate clarity. It was something she wanted to study and dissect, as her father had taught her to do in all her learning from childhood. Rhea felt that perhaps through Dahlia's guidance, they were coming to the end of the long darkness at last.

Then, by accident, Maddoc had been discovered during one of his more violent fits. Rhea could not get word to Dahlia but knew her daughter could survive alone where her husband could not. She chose in that moment, and wandered far from her hearth and her daughter and that simple life that had once seemed so mindless. Now she longed for the mundane life in that little village of Talwood that was as far from her as the other end of the world.

Hearing the snapping of twigs down the small canyon, she rolled quickly off the back of her rock. She was not expecting the intrusion on her solitude, but some caution was in order. It would hardly do for her to be discovered here by some errant hunter while she waited.

Two figures moved through the trees and up the draw next to the brook. Both carried cloth sacks over their shoulders. Even through the trees at a distance, Rhea could see that one of them wore a faded rose doublet. She smiled to herself. Galen's outfit was not entirely well suited for stealth.

"Welcome back, you two," she said cheerfully as they approached. "Meet with any success?"

"Yes we did, thank you," Galen rejoined, his words a little winded from his exertions. "We bear all manner of delights . . . as long as you are not too particular. Could you spare some accommodations for the night?"

Rhea snickered. "If that is the case, then you may have the best in the house . . . in fact, you may *have* the house if you can find it."

"Thank you, good lady," Maddoc enjoined most seriously. "I should like a room with a southerly exposure and a private bathing room, if you would be so kind."

"Well, Maddoc, you may have it," Galen said, dropping his sack down on the rock. Relieved of his burden, he stretched as he turned toward Rhea. "I don't think he actually *knows* which way the southerly exposure is, so I guess you are safe."

"Nonsense!" Maddoc scoffed. "I know exactly where we are!"

"You do?"

"Of course!" Maddoc replied. "This is Talwood Forest on the western slopes of the Rheshathei Range. We are about seven or eight miles southwest of the Ghrumald Pass, I should think."

Galen turned to Rhea with surprise on his face. "Is he right?"

Rhea laughed as she leaned back against the flat rock. "Not often about much, but he *is* right about this. Geography was one of Maddoc's favorite subjects. He has a collection of maps that seemed to always be underfoot at home. Most of them cover just about every corner of the Dragonback, and there are a number of rather detailed maps of Hrunard as well. He used to study them endlessly at home, telling Dahlia and me about all the different places on the map. He would even . . ."

Rhea's voice trailed off and she fell silent.

"Even what?" Galen encouraged quietly.

"Dahlia has an insatiable curiosity. 'I don't know' would simply never satisfy her. So, when Maddoc came to a place on the map that he did not know about, he would make things up just to keep her happy." Rhea looked down at the ground, her voice thick and her words suddenly difficult. "It was . . . it was a happy memory."

Galen nodded. "How old is she?"

"Now?" Rhea looked up, trying to look casual as she wiped a tear from her eye. "She is twenty-three and far too independent for the men in our village. I wish you had met her."

"I will," Galen asserted. "You can introduce us when you visit me at home."

Rhea caught her words before they came out. Galen was important. She felt that he was somehow the key to this entire mystery of the Elect and the madness that had robbed her of her husband. Through Galen she might just find the bottom of that dwarven mine after all.

But that meant keeping some things to herself for the time being. For many years, the only home she had known was the one she carried in her heart. She had come to understand that she could never return to her old village and neighbors. But the idea of going back to his former life was what drove Galen, gave him his reason for getting up each morning, breathing from moment to moment, and allowed him to sleep each night. Rhea knew that Galen could never go home again . . . not in any sense that Galen would understand. It was better for them all—including Galen—if he were left with his wonderful delusion for a while longer.

"I look forward to it," was all she could bring herself to say.

"Well, it can't come soon enough," Galen said with a smile. "Do you and your scholarly husband have any idea how we get there?"

Rhea looked away, then nodded. How could she tell this man? When would it ever be right to speak the terrible words: that the world would never be the same for him or for any of them? How could she show him that their future could be both different and beautiful when she herself could not see it?

"Of course we have a plan," she said brightly. "There is a pass to the south through the range. The Old Empress Road runs through the mountains there. It is far less traveled than the Ghrumald Pass, especially this late in the year. That will take us east over the Rheshathei Mountains. We'll then follow the River Celborsil eastward. There are small farming settlements along the river that we can use to scavenge for food. That should take us as far as the sea."

"Yes," Galen said, nodding eagerly. "That sounds good."

"You understand: we have to avoid the major ports," Rhea said. "Any passage that we arrange will be illegal in the eyes of the Pir and therefore expensive if we can obtain it at all. If we cannot find passage on a ship, then we may have to turn south and follow the coast all around the Chebon Sea until we reach the Dragonback. It could take months to get to your home . . . possibly a year."

"I don't care, so long as I put this nightmare behind me!" Galen snatched up the sack from the rock and stomped back toward the cavern.

Rhea sighed loudly, her exhaling breath carrying with it as much of her burden as possible.

"I know that sound," Maddoc said easily. "Rhea always made that sound when she was displeased and frustrated. I always feared that sound more than all the invading hordes of Vordnar."

Rhea smiled sadly. "Am I that fearsome, husband?"

"You always were," Maddoc replied, walking up to her. He suddenly cradled her in his arms. Tears welled up in his eyes. "How I miss you."

Rhea held him long, reluctant to let him go.

"Galen misses his wife, too," Maddoc said. "Doesn't he?"

"Yes," Rhea replied. "He does. He longs for his wife and home . . . and he cannot let them go."

"I understand." Maddoc nodded as he held her. "More than he knows."

The sounds all shine in colors I have never heard. Their expression tastes sweet as they fold over me in great, warm waves. I let them flow over and around me, caressing me in their delicate embrace, exploring their vibrancy even as they drift behind me and into silence.

The glorious expressions of heightened thought and experience emanate from the flame creature dancing before me. It writhes seductively, consuming itself continuously and being reborn at once. I watch it with fascination, reveling in its power, life, and sensuous call.

How Rhea would have marveled at this. I weep oceans at the thought, threatening to drown out the flame before me in the sorrow that engulfs me. Losing my beloved is a vast ocean of pain

*that can never be emptied; only crossed, and the far shore lies past
the horizon of ice.*

*My wife to me is dying . . . will die . . . is dead. Time flows in
strange eddies about me; all time is one time. All death is the
same death. All hope is one hope. The future and the past con-
verge in the great and eternal choice that is now.*

He comes.

*He, too, burns with the flame of creation and destruction. I
have seen this one before wandering the landscape of forever. He
speaks with Galen when he dreams, but never before to me. Our
infinities collide in this now, for he speaks to me.*

*"Sir, can you hear me?" he speaks and forever binds our fates
together.*

*"Of course, I can hear you," I reply. "Are you enjoying your
journey?"*

*"It has been a long one, sir, and appears to be longer still." He
appears before me in the robes of his office. They are shabby and
cheap, as is his power here in the Grand Truth. I pity him that he
has not cast off the trappings of that other place of dreams he
calls his life. "You are the one they call . . . Maddoc, are you
not?"*

*I bow out of courtesy. There is no call to upset the poor monk
who still believes his robes and his titles have any power or authority. "I am, indeed, sir."*

*"Then you can help me." He is too excited and too anxious. "I
am searching for Galen. It is imperative that I find him. Have you
seen him?"*

*I am bemused. Their fates must be forged together somehow. "I
would love to help you, good sir, but it seems you have me at a
disadvantage."*

*"My name is of no consequence," the shabby monk replies
stiffly, "but my need is urgent."*

*"Well, in that case, I wish you the best of luck in your search,"
I reply, casting my arm about me. "The world of our experience is
vast indeed. We are drawn together by our fates, it would seem—
fates which include our wills in some mystic fashion. Galen is out*

there in all of time and place. I doubt very much that you will find him until he wishes to be found."

This, the monk considers for a moment.

I turn back to my revels with the fire.

The monk's voice is quiet behind me.

"My name is Tragget."

I turn to him. "Indeed? I have heard of a Tragget . . . he was the Lord Inquisitor of the Pir. His life was to discover the madness of the Elect and hurry their fate before their time. Only it seems that perhaps the Elect were not so insane after all. Still, that Grand Inquisitor Tragget would not know anything about that. Are you, then, this same Grand Inquisitor Tragget?"

The monk shrinks as I speak. I expect him to vanish into smoke and blow away in a breeze but he looks at me instead and speaks with gaining strength.

"I am. I am that Tragget, and I am mad, truly mad! Yet I think that there is some purpose in this madness, some great design that I cannot see." Tragget grows taller with his words. "The Dragonkings wish to destroy us and have been destroying us for centuries. They fear us, Maddoc!"

"As well they should!" I reply with a laugh.

"I'm living a lie—I know that—and I need Galen's help," Tragget pleads with conviction. "I need to learn this mystical power that he is mastering. Imagine it, Maddoc! A power higher than the Dragonkings! Perhaps it is the evidence of the ancient gods returning to men. Perhaps it is the power of a new, higher god in search of followers who are strong enough to serve it. Whatever its source, I must learn how to wield it, and I need Galen's help to do it."

"He won't help you." I laugh. This Tragget is quite comical in his naive earnestness. "He hates the Pir for what they have done to him. Now that he is free he appears to have little use for exploring the mystic powers and their use in the world of the dying. I do not think he will help you."

"But I can help him . . . I can help him return home."

I shake my head sagely. "No one can ever return home."

"Galen can, if he will help me," Tragget replies.

Suddenly the fire erupts and spreads all about us. It is a forest of flame suddenly cooling into a charred wood. Beyond its blackened branches, I espy a ruined tower on the western slope of a hill.

"I want you to give Galen a message for me," Tragget continues. "Tell him that I am leaving the Pir, that I wish to join him and learn all that he knows of this mystic power of the Elect."

"This is an interesting place," I remark, gazing at the ruin. "Does it have anything to do with us?"

"Yes," Tragget replies. "There is much to tell, so listen patiently. I need you to tell it to Galen just as I tell it to you."

"I always liked a good story." I smile, sitting down.

"First of all, his wife, Berkita, is here with me . . ."

THE CONFESSIONS
BRONZE CANTICLES, TOME VI, FOLIO 3, LEAVES 14–16

Tragget lay in his bed, his breath shallow and quick. His eyes rolled beneath their lids as he dreamt, fitfully shifting under his bedding. His lips moved, though he did not voice the words. His head shifted occasionally in quick jerks from side to side.

All about him as he slept, the candles of his bedside sputtered in the room. Their flames were not tall nor their light all that bright. Still, they were a gift and he had never preferred sleeping in the darkness. He feared the darkness still. He always felt there were eyes in the darkness watching him. The light helped keep those demons at bay.

The smoke from each of the candles curled upward toward the ceiling of his bedchamber. They drifted through the eddies of the air, coiling one about the other in the stillness over his sleep.

Here was a face in the smoke.

There was a forest in the smoke.

There, again, was the ruin of a tower.

The smoke from the dragonwax was special indeed.

And the eyes were watching, as they always had, from the darkness.

Gynik

M imic! Keep my cape out of the mud!"

Mimic dutifully obeyed, raising the end of Lirry's cape off the ground. They were parading down through the marketplace, as they did twice each day, in search of something new to purchase. Normally this meant that Mimic would have to follow along behind Lirry while carrying the Device. It certainly was too valuable to just leave anywhere out of Lirry's sight. Awkward as this was, it was now compounded by Lirry's cape, which was entirely too long for him and required that Mimic both hold the Device and keep the cape from dragging along the mud-churned central avenue of the market.

Mimic tried to shake himself out of his reveries. He had been thinking about a place far from here—so far he could not say—where there was a ruined tower. There was a woman with the wings of a bug caged atop it. She seemed so terrible and so real in his thoughts, sitting inside a glass ball. There was that tall robed fellow with the light hair as well. He was made of brass with a clockwork mechanism inside him that never stopped. Such was the nature of his strange imaginings. They were sometimes so compelling that he forgot all about what was going on around him. It seemed more and more as the days wore on in the great fortress-city of Dong Mahaj-Megong that he was having trouble keeping his mind on his work.

Not his work for Lirry, of course. *That* particular work was a mind-numbing repetition of groveling tasks to support his master in the manner to which he was rapidly becoming accustomed. Anyone would be bored into forgetfulness trying to keep up with those particularly mundane chores. It was backbreaking and often needless work.

Lirry delighted in giving orders. Now that he had risen to a more prominent station in the goblin community, he had more goblins to boss around than ever. Mimic had hoped that this would mean his boss had less time to order him around, but such was not the case. There seemed to be no end to Lirry's sense of inferiority, and therefore no end to his need to remind anyone *else* that they were inferior to him.

Sometimes Lirry would have him take out each of the treasures under the floor grating for cleaning and oiling. The oiling especially was sheer ostentation on Lirry's part. None of the gears or mechanisms in his treasury were actually connected or required oiling at all. Still, it was a sign of wealth that one not only had the gears but cared enough to oil them as well. There was a period of three days, however, when the fad went about court that mechanisms that *looked* old and antique were all the rage. Lirry then told Mimic to dirty up every one of his treasure mechanisms to be in step with the latest fashion. Mimic just barely managed to convince Lirry not to do so with the working Device, but submitted with the rest of the treasures. Just about the time Mimic finished corroding and messing up Lirry's collection, the fad passed. Mimic spent the next three days cleaning up the treasures he had just dirtied.

It was no wonder to Mimic that his mind wandered from time to time as he performed his chores.

That was not the work that he needed to concentrate on. His real work was for him alone; a somewhat quieter and secret thing. It required that he be diligent and alert. He knew there would only be one chance for him. He knew what to do. The critical question was not what but when.

It was not easy. His musings during the day took a different turn. He might be standing next to the clockwork man in the robes, opening him up and contemplating the mechanisms within . . . with Gynik standing at his side. Or he might build a great winged device that flew like a bird in the air . . . with Gynik holding him in an enraptured embrace. The dreams and visions were constantly in flux, changing as his imagination shifted, like eddies in a slow stream, but Gynik was more often than not at the center of them all.

It certainly did not help that for the last week she had rarely been more than ten feet away from him. Ever since that day when she had accompanied the vice-chancellor to Lirry's residence, she had become a fixture of Mimic's life. They were almost constantly together.

Not that Gynik took a moment's notice of Mimic. Indeed, the miserable little goblin was barely acknowledged by the ravishing beauty. It was on Lirry's arm that Gynik hung and his attentions alone that she curried.

"I'll smack you if you let that cape fall again!" Lirry screamed.

"Yes, sir," Mimic responded automatically as he lifted the garment once more. He staggered backward slightly under his awkward load, trying to pull the slack out of the cape.

"It is so difficult to get good servants," Gynik said to Lirry with sad resignation. "It is so wonderful of you, Lirry, to keep your servant on out of your generous heart!"

"Well," Lirry said with far more magnanimity than he had ever actually felt, "I feel that it is a responsibility that comes with wealth and superior position."

"Oh, you are *so* right, Lirry!" Gynik smiled, her sharp teeth flashing in the sunlight. "You are such a generous creature!"

"After all," Lirry continued, "keeping lazy and stupid servants employed shows character and upbringing. I think all truly superior individuals should have one."

"You are so sensible," Gynik cooed. She reached over and ran her fingers through Lirry's sparse hair. Lirry smiled dumbly.

"Well, a little understanding and patience with indolent servants will— Ouch!" Lirry yelped. "Mimic, when I get you home I'm going to smack you so hard that you'll be using your teeth for a gearbox!"

"Yes, sir. Sorry, sir." Mimic sighed. The cape had been dragging again in the mud. Gynik had insisted that they purchase the cape for him even though it was far too long for his squat body. It was, however, the most expensive in the shop and that had impressed Gynik.

"You are going places, Lirry," Gynik said casually as they walked between the stalls of the marketplace. "I think you should give more thought to your image . . . how others think of you."

"Really?" Lirry said. "I thought I looked pretty good!"

"Oh, you do! Of course you do," Gynik responded at once. "It's just that a person of your stature and wealth, there are appearances that you have to keep up. You are about to be presented before Dong Mahaj-Megong himself! You can't just be great, you have to *appear* great as well."

Lirry nodded. "You are so right. What do you suggest?"

"We should buy me something," Gynik responded.

Gynik had explained days ago that since she was being seen with Lirry in public, her appearance would be a direct reflection on his status. Therefore, anything that he could buy her that showed her as being wealthy and prosperous reflected indirectly on him as well in the most becoming manner. To be overdressed and lavish presents on oneself was ostentatious. To overdress and lavish gifts on one's date was the most becoming generosity.

Of course, Lirry did not have two stones to put together in terms of actual wealth. Aside from the gifts that he had extorted from goblins coming to gawk at the Device, he was still just the supervising technician and really had no wealth of his own. Gynik was, to put it mildly, an expensive friend to have. The only alternative for Lirry was to put his entire appearance of fortune on the accounts and promises rapidly adding up at every one of the merchants in the fortress-city.

None of this was of great concern to Gynik. As she so often reminded Lirry on their long, luxurious evenings together—accompanied by the ticking of the Device and the ever watchful Mimic—Lirry's wealth was assured as soon as he was presented at court. All Dong Mahaj-Megong had to do was take a look at the Device and Lirry's debts would be satisfied a hundredfold.

"What do you think of this?" Gynik asked Lirry. She was holding up a staff with a spinning governor mechanism on the head. The small brass balls of the governor would shift out every time she spun them. "It's almost magical, isn't it?"

The shopkeeper was a little gremlin named Knikik. Lirry had dealt with him just the day before. The necklace he had secured for Gynik was still around her green neck. Knikik was eyeing it as though he still should be owning it.

"That staff be worth a hundred cogs," Knikik intoned defiantly.

Lirry's eyes bulged out of his head. "A *hundred?!*"

"Aye! One hundred cogs and not a screw less!" Knikik stomped his foot for emphasis.

"*Nobody* has a hundred cogs!" Lirry growled.

"Nobody's got that staff, either!" Knikik responded, somewhat erroneously, as it was obvious that at least one person had that staff— namely, Knikik.

Gynik did not appear to be taking notice. She was too absorbed in the staff itself. "Oh, Lir-Lir! It reminds me of your darling Device so! It would be the perfect reminder for me—and simply *everyone*— of you and your wonderful Device."

Mimic rolled his eyes. She had used her pet name for Lirry. It was a weapon of formidable persuasion.

"But Gyki," Lirry responded with his own pet name, causing Mimic to feel queasy. "That's a lot of cogs!"

"Oh, nonsense! What are such considerations to my Lir-Lir? Show the little gremlin your prize and work out your silly little business details," Gynik said, charmingly batting her yellow eyes. She once more smiled as she spun the rotating governor. "If you do, I promise to spin for you later."

Lirry grinned foolishly, then waved Mimic forward.

Mimic was a little uncertain as to what to do. If he moved forward, the cape would once more fall into the mud. There was not enough room to swing wide to either side; he would simply end up standing in someone else's shop. After a moment's thought, he balanced the Device in one hand and grasped the cape in the other. In a single motion, he flipped the cape over his own head and then stepped carefully forward, holding the Device out from under the cape.

He could not see a thing but could hear well enough.

Tick. Tick. Tick.

"Ah!" exclaimed Knikik.

Lirry cleared his throat. "Do we have a deal on my account?"

"Very well," Knikik sniffed. "But no more, Lirry. Your account is already too high as it is."

Gremlins and goblins have perfect memories when it comes to processes and accounts. Every merchant knows exactly what is owed to them and by whom. Even so, it was beginning to get difficult for Lirry to keep track of all the debts he had accrued throughout the fortress-city.

From under the blanket of Lirry's cape, Mimic heard the sweet and alluring voice of Gynik. He could imagine himself controlling one of the great war machines of the ancients, destroying his opponents with breath of fire and hurling destructive rocks great distances. Lirry would be receiving all his terrible wrath and Gynik would be there at his side speaking as she was speaking now . . .

"Lirry! Ooh! Look! You should buy me some of *those!*"

The Bargain

The leaves from the aspens drifted down around Rhea in a soft yellow cascade. The morning chill was leaving her as she made her way through the trees, her breath coming in steaming puffs. Galen picked his way ahead of them, searching through the thick copse as they made their way along the hillside. Maddoc struggled along behind Rhea, his breath labored with his exertions.

It was difficult to keep up with their friend. Rhea had told the man that they were going home, and now he walked the hills with a fanatic determination. Nothing in the world existed for Galen except the road home, and there was nothing that she could say or do that would hold him back. Besides, the difference in their years was being demonstrated in the spring of their steps.

Rounding another ridge, Galen stopped. The gentle slope gave way to a deep canyon cutting back into the Rheshathei Mountains. The rushing sounds of a stream could be heard from somewhere far below them. Rhea and Maddoc struggled to catch up.

"Now what?" Rhea puffed as she reached Galen.

Galen looked around, considering. Something caught his eye and he pointed. "See that? Farther up the slope . . . that outcropping of rock. It juts out clear of the trees. I think we'll get a better vantage point up there."

"Up, down, all around," Maddoc recited in a singsong voice. "Walking to the grave we're bound."

"He's cheerful this morning," Galen said dryly.

"I think he needs a little break," Rhea said, her voice sounding winded. "You go up and take a look. If you find a path for us, we can join you in a few minutes."

Galen nodded. "Good idea. You wait here and I'll be right back."

"Don't you worry, we'll be right here," Rhea said as she sat down heavily on the ground, pulling Maddoc to sit next to her.

Galen was already moving out of sight, his faded and stained rose doublet moving quickly through the white tree trunks.

"That is one determined young man," Rhea observed, stretching her aching legs. "How much farther until we reach the Empress Road, do you think?"

"The Empress Road . . . a heavy load," Maddoc said, his head bobbing lightly over his shoulders. "A mile or two and then we're through."

Rhea sighed and closed her eyes as she lay back among the carpet of fallen leaves. "That close? Well, that's a relief. I think I might prefer the dangers of the open road to this torturous route through the hills. How far is it through the pass to Tokfield?"

"The Empress Road will not be taken, lest our Galen be forsaken!" Maddoc giggled as he finished.

"What?" Rhea said sitting up. "What are you talking about?"

"Tragget holds the master's fate with Galen's wife behind his gate and we must act before too late!" Maddoc laughed with pleasure at the foolish rhyme.

"Galen's wife? Berkita?" Rhea became alarmed. She grabbed her husband with both hands by his shoulders where he sat. "What about her? Maddoc, talk to me!"

Maddoc's eyes focused suddenly on her. A sad smile erupted on his face, his eyes filling with tears. "Oh, it is so good to see you again, my beloved."

"Oh, Maddoc!" Rhea's words were clipped in her ambivalence. "What about Galen's wife?"

Light dawned in Maddoc's eyes. "I have a message for him, a very important message!"

"What message?" Rhea's eyes narrowed slightly. "When did you get a message for Galen?"

"I have to find him right away," Maddoc said brightly, standing up suddenly. "We've got to change our course . . . find a new destination. A new destiny."

"Wait!" Rhea stood up with him, clasping her hand around his arm. "Change our course? Where are we going?"

"South. Southwest to ruins older than Mithanlas," he said. His eyes were focused on a distant place. "That's where we are to meet him. That's where everything will be made right."

Rhea shook her husband again. "Who, Maddoc? Who are we to meet?"

Maddoc turned to his wife. "Why . . . Tragget, of course."

"Tragget?" Rhea squawked. "Grand Inquisitor of the Pir? *That* Tragget?"

"Why, yes!" Maddoc smiled with delight. "How very clever of you to know! He has a proposition for our friend Galen. He wishes to meet with him, learn from him, and join us on our adventures!"

"Oh, my poor husband." Rhea sighed. "I've lost you again."

"Nonsense," Maddoc snorted. "I'm still here. You just aren't listening. Tragget is one of the Elect. He's a bit odd, perhaps, and seems to feel entirely too guilty about his being one of us, but I suspect it's just a matter of his upbringing. In any event, he has Galen's wife with him."

"He's captured her?" Rhea said, shocked.

Maddoc shook his head. "No . . . nothing like that. She came looking for her husband. That's one thing you've got to say about that Arvad family, they are a determined clan!"

"Like us, I suppose." Rhea nodded, but her brow was still knitted with troubled thoughts. "It doesn't sound right to me, Maddoc. The Grand Inquisitor of the Pir just wants to toss aside his faith and join us? For what? For something that we barely understand ourselves? It just doesn't ring true to me, dearest."

"Oh, what do you know of truth," Maddoc sniffed. "You're dead. All of you are already dead."

Rhea held her tongue for a moment, choking back the anger and frustration, before she continued. "I know enough not to tell Galen. Not yet. This may be a trap, my husband. We need to know more before we can decide. But trap or no, if Galen hears that Tragget has his wife, there will be no holding him back!"

Maddoc nodded for a moment. "So you don't think I should tell Galen?"

"No," she said clearly. "Not until we are sure."

"Sure of what?"

Rhea turned around sharply. Galen was stepping down the slope toward them. She had been so concerned about what her husband was saying that she had not heard him approach.

She opened her mouth to answer him with some vague and meaningless statement . . . but Maddoc spoke first.

"Sure that Inquisitor Tragget is with your wife, of course," Maddoc said with an odd smile. "He wants to talk to you about her."

I stand in a small clearing. Turning, I can see the ruins of the tower behind me bathed in twilight. Around me, the forests are made of ice, their leaves burning with brilliant flame. The crumbled foundations of a long-dead village cast multiple shadows around me in stark relief. The grasses here are green, tall and supple.

I can see the winged woman floating above the ruined tower. She is surrounded by a clear, glowing heart that will not free her. The light shining up from the tower is holding her at bay. She would help me if she could. I will help her if I can. I am filled with hope. She is filled with despair. Yet neither of us knows what to expect of this encounter.

A small demon sits on one of the foundation stones. It holds a lantern that is filled with a blue light. I try to speak to it, and it responds, but its sounds are all ugly and gibberish. I remember this vile little creature. He was one who was dismembering Maddoc so long ago in another of my dreams. Now he sits patiently on the ruined foundation at the edge of the clearing.

We have not long to wait. From the ice-wood forest they come, first one and then the other.

"Maddoc," I say. I know that my voice is too full of hope—perhaps too full of desperation as well.

"Galen, how good of you to come!" Maddoc says pleasantly as he steps forward, extending his hand. I grasp his arm at the elbow as he grasps mine in return. "I've someone who has much to say to you."

I see him more clearly now. I know him too well.

"Hello, friend," I say cautiously.

"My name . . . my name is Tragget," he replies. "Hello, friend."

"This is a strange place indeed," I say, my arms crossed in judgment on the man standing awkwardly before me. "I am your friend here but you did not seem so when you took me from my home, my wife, and my life."

"I was more friend to you then than you know," Tragget answers. "Your Election was due to a power greater than either of us, Galen. You could not avoid it. I could not prevent it. I see now that our only hope lies in accepting it."

"Accepting it?" I cannot believe what this man is suggesting. 'This 'power' has done nothing but ruin my life. It has destroyed my every hope of happiness, torn me from my life's blood and soul, and you ask that I <u>give in</u> to this monstrous curse?"

"There are bigger things . . . bigger issues involved—"

"Not for me!" The anger and rage, the fear of the years instilled in my bones, seems at once to find a voice. I cannot stop my words as I speak, the emotions forcing the blood to my hot face and tears from my eyes. "I want nothing to do with this . . . this mystic power! The only things I care about are my wife and the beautiful life that you and the Pir and this curse have stolen from me! That's all that is important! That's all that matters!"

"Yes, that matters! Of course, that matters!" Tragget agrees, his voice calming and careful. "I know you better than you think, Galen! I'm one of you . . . I, Grand Inquisitor of the Pir, am my-

self one of the Elect. I know what it is to hide from the eye of the dragonstaff, perhaps even better than you. At least you have a life that you want to go back to . . . all I have is a life from which I want to escape!"

Tragget suddenly steps closer, extending his hand. "I can give you back your life—but I _can't_ do it without your help. You know that. I can put everything else to rights for you—get you back to your sweet little forge in your backwater town with your beautiful wife and you can forget all about this . . . but _only_ if you trust me."

He pushes his open hand toward me.

I shake my head, my arms tightly folded across my chest. "Trust you? You, who took everything from me, who would not acknowledge me outside the dream, who dragged me from my homeland and tossed me into that meat grinder you call war training . . . I am supposed to trust you?"

"I tried to save you!" The frustration wells up in his voice.

"Oh," I reply in disbelief. "Is that what that was?"

Tragget glances about in frustration. "You don't understand, you can't possibly understand."

"I understand that I have something you want . . . but trust is something you aren't going to get." I turn from him, looking to escape, to get away from this man somewhere else in the dream.

"Would you trust her?"

I stop, uncertain.

"Would you trust me for her?" Tragget says. "I've seen her, Galen; I've seen the way she aches for you. She weeps nightly and is inconsolable."

My breath comes hard and is loud in my ears.

"She followed you, Galen. She used everything she had to find you, and when the money ran out, she worked any little task she could just to find a way to come one step closer to you," Tragget says harshly. "If you won't trust me for yourself, couldn't you have pity on your own wife and trust me for her sake!"

I look up. I cannot keep the tears from coming. The words come hard in my throat even as I am desperate to know the answer to my soul's yearning. "My wife . . . is she . . . how is she?"

Tragget's face softens. "She is well. She is in the towers of Vasska's citadel in Mithanlas. She is well cared for, but she is desperate for news of you."

I release a great, shuddering breath. My beloved is alive and still searching for me. "Will you . . . will you tell her that you have word from me? Will you tell her that I love her? Will you tell her that?"

"Yes, friend, I will," Tragget replies earnestly. "And her dwarf friend will be pleased to have word as well, I believe."

"Cephas?" Just saying the name gladdens my heart. I laugh. "So he came, too, did he? Well, there is no stopping a determined dwarf!"

"So it would seem." Tragget smiles shyly himself, and then looks pleadingly into my eyes. "I need you to teach me what you know about this . . . this mystic power. I can use it to help you, Galen. It can purchase your life back. Will you help me?"

Once more, he extends his hand.

This time, I extend my own. We grasp each other's forearms just at the elbow.

"I still do not trust you," I say.

"You don't have to," Tragget replies. "I'll prove myself in time to both you and your wife."

"Yes," I say, "I will help you, for her sake."

Maddoc smiles next to us, and then places his own hands on both our shoulders. "And I'll do what I can to help. We'll be mystics of this great power together, at least until we die. You can't hope for a better bargain than that!"

I glance to the side. The demon smiles back at me with sharp teeth reflecting the flaming light of the leaves. He reaches up and hands me the blue lantern to seal the bargain.

BOOK OF GALEN
BRONZE CANTICLES, TOME IV, FOLIO 1, LEAVES 49–52

Deep Magic

numanthas?" Rhea furrowed her brow in the rising light of a new day. "He wants us to go to Mnumanthas?"

The journey down the western slope of the Rheshathei had been a particularly difficult one the day before. The foraging had not been nearly as good as they had hoped. What additional supplies Galen had scavenged from Talwood were carefully being rationed for the trip over the pass. It had made for an unsatisfying supper when they finally made camp in a canyon near the head of the South Zhamra. The river cascaded in a tremendous fall from the towering cliffs at the back of the box canyon. A grassy clearing spread near the pool at the fall's base and down the whitewater of the river as it continued down into the Talwood Forest. The eddies of the canyon winds had promised to disperse the smoke from the fire that originally had given them some cause for the hope of a warmer sleep. But the ragged group was exhausted and there was no one to tend the fire through the night. The embers had gone cold by the deep of morning, so the night had been a chill one.

Now Rhea had awakened stiff and aching, only to be confronted by her unusually lucid husband and a suddenly cheerful Galen who was anxious to drag them all in what Rhea thought to be an entirely senseless direction.

"He'll meet us there—with Berkita," Galen said earnestly. "Then he'll provide us with whatever papers we need to get back to Benyn: Absolution, Pardon of the Election, Reinstatement of Marriage . . ."

"Meet him?" Rhea squawked. "But why Mnumanthas?"

"I don't know." Galen shrugged, then turned to Maddoc. "Is it far from here?"

Maddoc pondered for a moment. "Several days' journey, I should think, at least. It is on the northern slopes of the Ghnemoth Peaks."

Rhea considered for a moment what she knew of the area from what she remembered of Maddoc's old maps. "That's miles away from any Pir settlement, actually from any settlement of any kind. It also takes us *farther* from home, not closer."

"Tragget says it's the safest place for us to meet," Galen rejoined.

"Galen, I just don't trust the man." Rhea leaned forward, clasping her hands nervously. "Why should he do it? Why risk everything . . . his position, his life, his entire faith—"

"Because he is one of us, Rhea," Galen interrupted. "Think of it! The Inquisitor of the Pir Drakonis being as mad as any of the Elect he is charged with destroying."

"It's not a madness, Galen," Rhea said, shaking her head. "It's . . . it's something bigger than us . . . bigger than our minds can understand. Dahlia tried to explain it to me once and I didn't understand her then. She said it is something so powerful, so incredible and magnificent, that it drives those few upon whom it calls *into* madness."

"It is the power of the Mad Emperors." Maddoc spoke in rapturous tones. "They had mystics whose dark powers were crushed by the Dragonkings anciently. The Deep Magic it was called. The Deep Magic of Rhamas brought madness to the Emperors and caused them to be cruel and unjust. It was to protect humanity from themselves and their own Deep Magic that the Dragonkings fought the Mad Emperors and brought humanity under their protective eye."

"Then this is the Deep Magic that we have?" Galen was astonished. "The power that destroyed the rule of men in all Rhamas?"

Maddoc considered for a moment, then looked Galen straight in the eye. "Perhaps. It would explain a great deal. Still, we know so little of that time, and everything that we *do* know comes from the records passed to us by the Pir."

"Well, now I've heard entirely too much about what it *might* be," Galen said, crossing his arms impatiently over his chest. He was anxious that they get on their way. "Could you possibly tell us anything about the madness that is *certain?*"

"It is certainly a power—how great a power we cannot possibly tell," Rhea said, standing. She began to pace despite the aching in her bones. It was an old habit whenever she was thinking through a problem. "I wish Dahlia were here. She understood all this so much better than I do. She tried to explain it to me but I just don't think I'm any good at this. She was always telling me to organize what I knew and look for the pattern in it." She stopped and looked squarely at Galen. "This place that you go . . . where you meet each other . . . is something beyond dreams. You communicate through it with each other as well as with creatures that you do not even recognize."

Galen nodded. "Yes, that's how we got this message from Tragget."

"Yes," Rhea agreed quickly. "A message that comes to you from a man who is over fifty miles from where you sleep. But you do more there than just speak. The warriors of the brotherhood; their swords are real and they came from the dream. You said yourself that it was the winged woman from the dream that set you free from the torusk cage. And what about that sphere that blinds the dragonstaffs? The things that you experience in the dream are somehow coming into the waking world, too."

"I think you've got that backward, my dear," Maddoc softly corrected her.

"What?"

"The experiences in this illusion we now are sharing find their manifestation in the reality of the other world," Maddoc said. "It's all a matter of perspective. Being dead, I would not expect you to understand. Still, you are right in that what happens in one world affects the other. They are linked sympathetically, you see. The symbols in the illusion being a metaphor for the reality of another."

"What is he talking about?" Galen said, shaking his head in frustration.

"Wait a moment, Galen," Rhea said, her eyes narrowing as she watched her husband. "What are you saying, Maddoc? How is the Deep Magic a metaphor?"

"It's a language—actually a translation of a language, to be more precise," Maddoc explained, at once the picture of his old scholarly self. Rhea remembered him suddenly as he had been before, excited to teach something new. "Everything in that world is connected to this one and vice versa. They are linked as symbols for each other, each having alternate meanings in the other incarnation of our world."

"The black sphere that closed the eye of the dragonstaffs," Rhea said slowly, trying to understand the implications of what her husband was saying. "Galen . . . didn't you tell me that you got that from the winged woman in one of your dreams?"

Galen nodded. "Yes. In my dream she reached into the sky and pulled it from the sun and handed it to me."

"The sun." Maddoc smiled. "The eye of the day. The eye of light. The eye of the dragon. That's it, Galen!"

"What?" Galen shook his head. "What are you talking about?"

"The power . . . there is a direct connection between your powers in this world and the other," Maddoc said quickly, his words tumbling out in his excitement. "Whether it is a dream or a real or magical place, I don't know. What I *do* know is that what happens there translates somehow symbolically into mystic power here . . . and possibly the other way as well."

Rhea nodded enthusiastically. "It *is* like a language then, an incredible, complex language that we have lost or forgotten. It is like your winged woman who speaks and you cannot understand what she says."

Galen shook his head. "I hardly see how a language we do not understand is of any use to us."

Maddoc turned casually toward Galen and then pointed at the charred logs within the ring of stones nearby. The embers had gone cold under the dim twilight. "Son, does that remind you of anything?"

"It's a dead fire, Maddoc," Galen returned.

"Yes, but *look* at it; *consider* it."

Galen stopped, sighed, and then looked at the log. As he did his face became thoughtful. He shifted his weight slightly and brought his hand up in front of him.

"Can you *feel* the connection?" Maddoc smiled as he quietly spoke. "Your body conforms to the Deep Magic. Your mind senses the connection between them. Your words utter the sounds that are in sympathy with the true reality."

Rhea held her breath.

"It reminds me of the fire in the dream," Galen murmured, shifting as he considered the ring of stones. He gestured toward the dead fire, his eyes focused on the ashes. "There was some pointy-eared demon creature that handed me a blue lantern—"

Brilliant blue flame erupted from the log, a keening chorus of high-pitched sound reverberating through the air. The flame shot skyward, towered directly overhead to the height of the trees. Rhea had to look away from its intensity, her arm rising instinctively to shield her. The glade shone under the severe illumination. No heat came from the mystic flame. No smoke curled into the sky. There was only the screaming wail of the flame and the unbearably bright luminance radiating over the glade and shining against the waterfall beyond.

"Maddoc!" Rhea called out. She could not see him in the brilliance. "Maddoc! Galen!" Blinking furiously, she tried to see into the unnatural flame. There were shapes in the vivid light and they appeared to be dancing.

Then, just as suddenly, the light vanished.

A thunderclap shook the air around them, cascading leaves from the trees at the edge of the glade. For several moments the three of them stood around the ring of cold stones, listening as the thunder reverberated down the walls of the canyon.

"What was *that?*" Galen gasped when the words at last came to him.

Maddoc looked up at Galen sharply. "It is a language; a language you have to learn."

Galen shook his head. "No. It's the language of madmen."

"It's the language of the Deep Magic, Galen!" Rhea said.

"Is *that* what Tragget wants?" Galen said sourly. "Then he is welcome to it. Let *him* fight the Dragonkings if he wants. It isn't *my* fight; I want nothing to do with it!"

"You *have* to learn it, Galen!" Rhea snapped.

"Why?" Galen said, stepping threateningly toward her. In a moment his face was inches away from hers, looking down into her eyes with fierce determination. "Why do I *have* to master the one thing that has destroyed my life?"

"Because it is the only thing you have to bargain with," Rhea said, holding her ground, staring right back into Galen's eyes. "Tragget thinks you can teach him what he needs to know. That knowledge is the only thing you have to purchase your life back—to purchase your *wife* back. When Tragget comes to collect, you had better have something to offer him that is worthy of his price!"

Galen's face softened as he took a step back.

"If Tragget can be trusted," Rhea said, shivering in the morning cold, "you can be *sure* he will want to be paid . . . and your wife will come at a dear price."

High in the tower, a hundred feet above the courts below, Berkita stood on the balcony of the Temple of Vasska and gazed out over the brightening morning.

The light of dawn was rising over the grasslands to the south. The Temple and its city remained in the shadow of the Lords of Mithlan and would not receive the warmth for another hour. But the wide plains to the south were already bathed in bright light, the dawn having crested the Rheshathei Mountains that lay in purple shadow.

Berkita gazed on that southern horizon. It was the last direction she knew her husband had taken. Somewhere in that broad expanse, he walked the ground. Somewhere in the breaking day he arose and was looking for his way home. Somewhere, she knew, he sought her as she sought him.

"What to see er is?" the gruff voice rumbled behind her.

"The dawn, Cephas," Berkita replied distractedly. "The hope of a new day."

"Nay, lass; in the darkness hope er is." The dwarf stumped toward her, adjusting his blindfold. "Light brings no need for hope. What look ye for in the light?"

"He is out there, Cephas," Berkita said quietly. "Somewhere he is out there."

"Aye, out there Galen er is." The dwarf sniffed loudly. "And *we* in *here* er is!"

Berkita turned from the balcony and came back into the sitting room. "At least it is a lot nicer than every other place we've stayed since we crossed the sea."

"Nicer?" Cephas spat on the floor, wetting the delicately woven rug. "Soft er is! Frilly drapery! Plump beds—aye, soft er is! Hate it, Cephas does!"

"Well, at least I've been comfortable," Berkita said with the slightest disdain.

"Comfortable for the lady er is . . . but Cephas can smell a cage, decorated or no." He stomped about the room listlessly. "It a lovely prison be . . . but prison still!"

"But Lord Tragget said that—"

"Lord Tragget, my ax!" the blind dwarf bellowed. "There be false pyrite as er is! Cephas would trust Lord Tragget nor further than—"

The door from the staircase suddenly opened.

"Just how far would that be again," Lord Tragget said as he stepped quickly into the room. "Forgive me for overhearing you, Cephas, it could not be helped. Your voice does carry quite some way." He turned toward Berkita and bowed. "Miss Kadish."

"Arvad," Berkita replied stiffly. "Lady Arvad."

"My apologies," Tragget said smoothly. "Although technically Kadish—your maiden name—would be correct. But, then, we are going to remedy all of that . . . and sooner than I had hoped. I have news which— Are you all right, m'lady?"

"I'm sorry," Berkita said, feeling suddenly tired. Tragget quickly reached out and guided her to a large chair. "I haven't slept well lately."

"Your troubles, no doubt, or the weariness of the road," Tragget replied comfortingly. He knelt down before her chair, looking into her pale face. "Are you sure I cannot summon someone to help you?"

"It will pass, Lord," Berkita said uneasily. "You said you bear news?"

"Yes, great news indeed," Tragget said quietly. "It is about your Galen."

"Galen!" Berkita held tightly to the arms of the chair. "Is he well? Do you know where he is?"

Cephas stepped impatiently forward. "Speak, Tragget! What news?"

"Calm yourselves and be at ease," Tragget said, his voice still low. "He is, indeed, fit and well . . . as you yourselves shall soon see."

Berkita closed her eyes, a grateful prayer to Vasska on her lips.

"I do not know where he is," Tragget continued, his voice quiet, his words quick, "but I know where he will be. We will go to meet him."

"When?" Berkita said, tears of joy welling up in her large violet eyes.

"Soon," Tragget said. "It will take a few days to prepare everything, but I need you to be ready to depart in an hour's notice—both of you."

"Where?" Cephas growled.

The Inquisitor turned to the dwarf. "Excuse me?"

"Where er we meet Galen?" Cephas said flatly.

"It will take us several days' journey to get there," Tragget responded quickly.

"Bah!" Cephas spat again on the floor, then stomped his boot onto it: a sign of great dwarven displeasure. "Question simple er is! Where er we meet Galen?"

Tragget eyed him for a moment before he spoke. "It's a little-known place far to the south. Its name would be useless to you."

"Show me for ignorant, then," Cephas persisted. "Name little-known place where Galen er is!"

"Mnumanthas," Tragget said casually. "Does that name help you, Master Cephas?"

The dwarf stood as still as a statue for a time before he spoke. "Nay, Lord Tragget."

"I am not surprised, Master Cephas," Tragget replied, standing. "It is, however, vitally important that you keep this conversation a secret between us. There is considerable embarrassment surrounding Galen's unfortunate Election. There are those among the Pir who would take terrible advantage of the knowledge of our plans. Indeed, they might destroy any hope of our success in restoring you to your former happiness should they discover us before we have completed our purpose."

"Vasska forbid!" Berkita breathed.

"Indeed," said Tragget, "Vasska forbid. So let us tell no one of our plans . . . no one at all regardless of their rank . . . or all may be lost. Do you understand?"

"Aye," Cephas rumbled. "Cephas understand well."

Berkita nodded. "Of course."

"Then I shall leave you with this glad news." The Inquisitor turned toward the door, opening it quickly. "Take heart . . . it is the will of Vasska that we shall repay you for all you have suffered."

He slipped out of the room. Cephas and Berkita both waited quietly where he had left them, speaking not a word. The time stretched long between them as they remained in their places. At long last, Cephas turned toward Berkita, his voice speaking words like gravel.

"Cephas trusts no Inquisitor," he grumbled. "Mnumanthas er no place to meet!"

"But Cephas, Galen may be out there right now—"

"Cephas knows Mnumanthas," the dwarf continued. "Ruins of Rhamas er is! Far, too, from aid er is! Trap as er is could be."

"Perhaps." Berkita blinked, suddenly unsure. "But even if you're right, what can we do?"

"*We* do nothing! Cephas do all." He turned quickly around and disappeared into his room. He reemerged almost at once, his traveling sack once more slung over his back, his large hat pressed onto his head. "Cephas go to Mnumanthas *now*. Beat Galen *and* Tragget both to ruins. Cephas make safe *afore* trap sprung, if er is."

"Cephas! You're leaving me? Here?"

The old dwarf clomped toward the chair where Berkita sat. He extended his large hand. She understood and took it in her own.

"Berkita safe here as er is," Cephas murmured softly. "Where Cephas goes, dangerous for Berkita as er is. Tragget needs Berkita well, he harms you not."

"But, the stairway outside," Berkita replied. "You said yourself it leads only to three places: this room, Tragget's audience hall, and the dungeons below. There's no way to get out."

"Nay, Lady Arvad. *You* say no way out er is. *I* say them dungeons below were *dwarven* built er long ago. *Dark* er is!" The dwarf tugged at his blindfold and smiled.

He laid an ear against the door and, hearing nothing, opened it. Then he turned back to Berkita and smiled. "We meet again er long, Berkita in Galen's arms then er is. That day all right again er is."

With that, the dwarf vanished down into the dark.

Farther
to Fall

Mimic was in awe. He had never imagined the courts of the great goblin king Dong Mahaj-Megong. From what little he could observe from beneath Lirry's cape, the court was more magnificent than anything he had ever seen.

The vice-chancellor himself had ushered them into the room. Mimic suspected he was feeling a little hurt over the loss of Gynik, especially since she was hanging on to Lirry's arm when they showed up at court. There was no hope for it, however: the importance of Lirry's Ticking Device had trumped even the pride of the vice-chancellor. Talk of the great working mechanism had spread throughout the kingdom. Goblins, gremlins, gnomes, and imps from one end of the empire to the other—some more than ten miles from the center of court itself—were already whispering the name of Lirry with jealousy and bitter envy. There were few higher positions to which a goblin could aspire.

The Grand Palace of Dong Mahaj-Megong was a magnificent edifice of corrugated steel plates fitted over arching steel beams. The beams were elegantly holed throughout their entire length and were strong enough to span the entire forty-foot width of the structure without the need of any extra support. Great panels of glass were fitted into sections where the steel plates had been removed. These were painted over to reflect the long history of Dong Mahaj-Megong and his ancestors—whoever they might be. The elegance of these pictorials was that they were so entirely generic in nature as to apply equally well to any particular story the current ruling Dong might wish to tell. Thus the integrity of each ruler was assured down through the ages, even if the accuracy of the story might be otherwise suspect.

All of these things alone would have been enough to impress Mimic with the power and magnificence of the Dong. But yet more wonders awaited him as they walked down the hall, his limited view from under the cape revealing more marvels the farther they progressed.

Down the length of the great throne room of the Dong, riches beyond measure were tastefully displayed in alcoves between the arching support beams: gears and screws of every size, coils of copper tubing forming uniform loops, and rolls of copper sheeting gleaming smooth. There were a number of intricate mechanisms and devices that included fitted pistons, push rods, and their matching shafts. There were no fewer than three boiler tanks in the room, complete with their original twisted piping. The thought of exploring them made Mimic's mind reel with wonder.

So excited was he that he nearly ran into Lirry's back when he and Gynik stopped before the throne of the Great Dong.

Mimic was tasked this time not only to hold both the Device and the cape but also to make sure that the cape dramatically billowed from time to time in order to impress the Dong. This had been considerably difficult to achieve while walking down the hall, although their walking motion helped. Mimic was primarily relegated during that time to hanging on to the Device, keeping the cape over his head, and occasionally blowing a puff of air up into it with his face. It was not particularly effective, but he hoped Lirry was too impressed with actually being in the throne room of the Dong to take any notice.

Now that they were stopped, however, Mimic could take a step back, hold on to the Device with one hand, and pump the cape up and down with the other.

The sight that greeted him when he stepped back nearly made him drop the cape.

The head of a Titan—complete except for a large dent on the left side and its missing jaw—rested directly over the throne of the Dong. Its bronze metal was polished in places to a bright shine, while in others the natural patina of the metal was allowed to remain, with tremendous artistic effect. Three great gears of decreasing sizes lay on their sides, forming the elevated platform for the throne, while two large rocker gears sat on either side, framing the throne itself.

Atop this dais, two large chairs were set, and on them sat Dong Mahaj-Megong, goblin king, and Ebu Sihir Putih, his current queen.

Mimic was overwhelmed by such grandeur.

Dong Mahaj-Megong was a squat, toadlike goblin whose girth fully equaled his height. He had the look of a goblin who had perhaps been made of clay and then pushed down to be more squat than was natural. He wore elegant armor made of tin squares two inches across that were linked with rings. Over this was draped a robe of the finest towel material Mimic had ever seen. His crown—the famed Crown of All Goblinkind—was a brightly oiled beveled cog with a towering spindle in its center of bronze. Mimic knew that it was one of only ten famed Crowns of All Goblinkind, and he felt privileged just to have lived to see it.

The Dong's current wife, Ebu Sihir Putih, was something of a beauty in her own right; she had a lovely pot belly of her own and hair actually growing out of her ears. Mimic had heard the story of how the Dong had become bored with his first queen many years ago and instituted a policy of rotating queens in the kingdom as a public service. As he put it, his subjects should not be burdened with coming to him with their homage, only to have to look at a less than magnificent queen. It was a measure of the Dong's magnanimous nature that he changed queens often.

Ebu Sihir Putih glared down from her throne at Gynik with open hatred. It was a well-known fact at court, whispered to Mimic by the grumpy kitchen staff, that the Dong had been trying for the better part of a year to convince Gynik to be his next queen. Gynik had, however, repeatedly refused. The rumors in court ran into two lines of thinking: either Gynik had someone else on her string that was richer and more powerful than the Dong, or Sihir's family was strong enough to ensure that Gynik would very quickly move from being the heralded current queen to being the lamented *late* queen. Most who knew the current queen subscribed to the second theory. These same courtiers also subscribed to the additional theory that if Gynik could find a way around the current queen, she would do so without hesitation.

This was as much of court politics as Mimic knew; that Ebu Sihir Putih was a beauty, no one doubted. That her beauty paled next to Gynik was also just as quickly accepted as fact. Mimic certainly could see it even from beneath Lirry's cape. Now, as he watched the bald hatred glaring out from Sihir's yellow eyes, he knew that Gynik truly was the fairest in the court.

The vice-chancellor had been introducing Lirry now for some time. Mimic reminded himself to concentrate. The most important moment in Lirry's life—for Mimic's life, too—was about to take place. Mimic had to be attentive and not let his mind wander. He certainly did not want to miss it.

Lirry tugged at his collar. The robe kept yanking at him from time to time. It was Mimic, of course, who was tugging at it. Lirry had specifically told the little speck to billow the cape majestically, not yank it around. He made a note to smack Mimic soundly for this insult when they got home. For now, however, he just wanted to get through the introduction and get on to his audience with the Great Dong.

He had been imagining this moment his entire life; the moment when he would no longer just be Lirry. He would instead be *Lirry:* Lirry the Great, Lirry the Magnificent, Lirry the Powerful. He knew there was greatness in him, had often wondered why others did not acknowledge it, and cursed everyone either above him or below him for not giving him his due. But today he would finally be vindicated.

He would stand here—right where he was right now—and the Dong would say, "Lirry, your discovery ain't like anything I've seen ever! Every goblin in the world will know that it was you—*you*—that did this thing! Then they'll all be sorry for what they said about you. They'll all suffer for what they did to you. They'll all grovel at your feet . . . and if they don't, I'll smack 'em so hard that they won't stop hurting *ever!* It'll be great!"

And now here he was, Lirry, standing in front of the Dong Mahaj-Megong with the greatest discovery in the memory of the goblin kingdoms. It was all going to happen for him just the way he imagined it.

". . . in long service to your Majesty as Technician Supervisor First Class of the North Western Salvage unit. I have the honor therefore to present before your most glorious and beloved Majesty . . . Lirry."

Lirry tried to bow deeply, but the cape only allowed him to bend over so far before it started choking him. He managed to rasp out a hoarse, "Your Majesty."

Dong Mahaj-Megong was not even looking at the supervising technician. He was leering at Gynik and wiggling his pudgy fingers in her direction. His pointy teeth glistened through his broad smile. "Hello, Gynik! So good to see you in court."

Sihir continued to glare, but Gynik ignored the current queen.

"And I am simply *thrilled* to be here, Your Majesty." Gynik's smile was dazzling; her creaking voice sent a jolt of either lust or envy through everyone in the throne room. "I am escorting my good friend—Lirry, here. We have something very interesting to show you, sire!"

"Oh, I'll just bet you could show me *plenty* that would interest me," the goblin king leered.

Queen Sihir reached over with her long, willowy staff of office and smacked the king with it. The king growled back at the queen menacingly.

Gynik pretended not to notice. "Indeed we *have* brought plenty that would interest the King of the Goblins. Lirry, present your discovery to the King."

Lirry nodded. This was it and he knew it. He turned around to Mimic and whispered harshly, "Give me the Device!"

"Just a moment, sir. I have to stick the cape back over my head before—"

"Just *drop* the cape, idiot, and *give me the Device!*"

"Whatever you say, Lirry."

Lirry snatched the Device from Mimic's hand.

Tick. Tick. Tick.

He turned toward the Dong.

The Dong leaned forward, suddenly keenly interested in the treasure Lirry had in his hands.

Gynik smiled.

Sihir's eyes narrowed.

Lirry reached forward with the Device.

Tick. Tick. THUCK. Whhhrrrrrr . . .

The Device stopped.

The Dong frowned.

Gynik's eyes narrowed.

Lirry smiled gamely. "Sorry, Your Greatness. Hehe. The Device is somewhat sensitive. It occasionally will stop of its own accord."

Lirry shook the Device gently.

Silence. Nothing moved.

"Mimic!" Lirry grumbled under his voice. "Get over here!"

Mimic dutifully obeyed.

"Make it go!" Lirry growled at the technician fourth class.

The Device was still as a rock.

Lirry, holding the Device with both hands, slammed it down on the metal dais. Several small wheels bounced out of its inner reaches and rolled across the floor.

"Your Majesty," Lirry said, his hands shaking. "If you'll please indulge me. I'm sure that I can get it working for you in just a moment . . ."

"Sire, he lies."

Lirry looked up, appalled.

It was Mimic.

Dong Mahaj-Megong turned toward the little technician. "What did you say?"

"Sire," Mimic said. His voice was quivering in his boldness, as though he were afraid of the very words he was speaking. "Sire, Lirry cannot make this Device function. He never could."

"Shut up, Mimic," Lirry growled, "or I'm going to give you such a smacking that you'll never wake up!"

Mimic took another step forward, continuing the plan he had practiced before his mirror at every available moment for weeks on end. "It was me, sire, just me."

Lirry screamed, lunging for Mimic.

He dropped the Device.

Mimic had taken too many smackings from his boss. He knew Lirry's moves. In a flash, he ducked out of the slower goblin's way, and Lirry fell flat against the dais. When he rolled over, he saw Mimic standing over him, holding the Device.

Tick. Tick. Tick.

Gynik's eyes shifted to Mimic. She stepped forward at once, the staff that Lirry had purchased for her in one hand, her other hand sliding around Mimic's arm.

"Sire, I believe that you, in your infinite wisdom, have discovered the *true* Master Technician of all Goblins!"

As Lirry watched from the floor, the governor at the top of Gynik's staff began to spin on its own. Several of the devices around the hall creaked, groaned, and slowly began to move as well.

A ripple of amazement ran through the goblins, imps, and gremlins in the hall.

"Mimic, you shall be rewarded as no other goblin in the history of our kingdom has been rewarded," the Dong intoned. "You are, indeed, the Master Technician of my entire kingdom!"

Mimic bowed his gratitude.

"How may I show you my admiration," Dong Mahaj-Megong asked through a wide smile, "and demonstrate my benevolent support?"

"If you please, Your Majesty, I would like to take ownership of

Lirry's apartment and its possessions," Mimic said with practiced ease. "After all, he only acquired them because of *my* talent."

"Why, that seems almost fair! So be it and so I decree. However, what do you suggest we do with this Lirry idiot?" the Dong asked Mimic.

It was Gynik, however, who answered the Dong. "I believe this Lirry idiot has a huge number of debts in your city, sire. Perhaps we should just turn him over to his creditors?"

The guards grasped hold of Lirry.

He was about to get everything he deserved.

Tower of Mnumanthas

We walk across a blasted plain. Everything is illuminated with crimson light under a flaming sky. The clouds overhead are ablaze with deep salmon light ignited by a fiery dawn. The place is familiar and foreign all at once. The ash under our feet billows up as we walk, only to be swept away in the hot breeze that blows gently past us. We stop for a moment at the edge of a ravine, the gray waters at the bottom of it flowing sluggishly around a bend in its course.

"Where are we, Tragget?" I ask of my companion.

"In another place or age, perhaps," he replies. The Inquisitor turns and points to the north. "Those are the Lords of Mithlan, or so I would swear. I've lived at their feet all my life. Yet the mountain is broken and spews fire and smoke. If, however, they are the Lords of Mithlan, then we should be standing on the Southern Steppes. Were that so, then we should be wandering among the fertile farms of the Pir. This river should be the River Indunae . . . indeed, it is the Indunae in its course as I remember it."

"Perhaps it is our distant past that we are seeing," I suggest, more as a guess than an observation, "or could it be our future?"

"Or perhaps it is neither." Tragget shrugs. "There is so much about this that we do not know, Galen. It is hard to know where to begin."

I shake my head as I look about. "Well, perhaps wherever we start will _be_ the beginning. There certainly doesn't seem to be anyone around to tell us what we are doing wrong."

Tragget laughs at this; hearty and relaxed.

"Now _that_ is progress right there," I remark. "I didn't know you could laugh. I think I rather like it."

Tragget looks down shyly. "I think I do, too."

We walk eastward toward a line of statues on the horizon. They appear to be tremendous wrecks of iron and bronze in the shape of men that lie scattered across the plain.

"How is Berkita?" I ask cautiously.

"She is well, considering," Tragget replies easily as we walk across the dusty, bald ground. "She is feeling lonely since the dwarf abandoned her. I suppose that typical behavior for his kind. I've never really met dwarves before him, though others have told me that they are not to be trusted. Do you want me to find him? Is it important?"

"No. I'm sure he has his reasons," I reply with as much honesty as I can force into my voice. I most certainly do not want Tragget to look for Cephas and desperately want to change the subject. "What do you make of those iron men? Are they statues?"

Tragget stops, his brow furrowed.

"What is it?" I ask.

The Inquisitor opens his mouth, hesitates for a moment, and then speaks. "Galen, I've lived a curious and guarded life. I was raised in the Temple itself, my parenting secret and my childhood a deception. I've had companions and playmates, each of whom was brought in for that purpose and none of whom knew who I really was." He shrugs and looks off to the horizon. "I guess _I_ never really knew who I was either. It's hard to live a lie."

Is that what I have been doing? "I know. We all do."

"I guess it's just that, well, I've never really felt able to trust anyone or be completely at ease." Tragget looks back at me, his

face a little sad. "There was always a part of me that was afraid I
would be discovered, so I was always on my guard. Do you know
what I'm saying?"

"Yes, I do." I, too, look toward the horizon. "It is strange that
we should come to such a bizarre and foreign land just to find
some peace at last. I used to hate this place—wherever or whenever it is—and now it seems to be the only place we can be honest
men."

"Yes," Tragget says, then turns to face me. "Isn't it all disturb-
ing?"

"Definitely!"

"Still, we have much to learn." I sigh. "Let's try something, a
little gift as it were. Do you remember a night when we were in
Vasskhold, only it wasn't really Vasskhold?"

"Yes," Tragget says. "All the buildings were smaller and they
were falling down. It was a dark night."

As we speak, the ashen plain beneath our feet erupts with tall
grasses. The fiery mountain to the north heals itself once more into
the quiet Lords of Mithlan. The flaming sky slips quickly into a
deep night as the sun is banished from the heavens.

"We were standing at the base of the tower. The bones of the
dead held up the walls . . ."

The world flows around us. The mountains fly toward us and
settle to the east. The crumbling walls of Mithanlas rise up around
us. The tower sags next to us.

"I wondered if the winged woman would be inside. We went in
through the door."

The doorway shifts around us, engulfing us until we stand inside the tower now as we did before.

I turn toward Tragget. "I asked you your name, do you remember?"

"Yes. I told you I couldn't give it to you."

"You said you would give it to me when the time was right."

"Yes, and I have given it to you."

"Then," I answer easily, "the time is right!"

The great wind comes as it did before, but this time it catches us both. It lifts us both into the tower, yet something has changed. The winged woman is there, but she is sleeping inside the iron ball that I had fashioned for her. I wonder at this as I grasp Tragget's hand. I lead him up through the remaining ironworks and onto the pinnacle of the tower.

Tragget and I now stand under the blood-red sun. The light burns and blinds us. This time, however, it is I who reach out and pluck the sun from the sky.

"How did you know to do that?" Tragget speaks with awe in his voice.

"It is hard to explain. I look at the thing here in this dream and somehow within myself I just know. This is what you are looking for," I say, cutting the sun in two and handing the black pit of it to Tragget. "There is much that I can tell you; much more we both could learn. Still, this is where I started. I suppose it is where you may start, too."

BOOK OF GALEN
BRONZE CANTICLES, TOME IV, FOLIO 1, LEAVES 53–55

The ancient tower of Mnumanthas rose above the trees, framed by the Ghnemoth Peaks beyond it to the south. Galen's heart felt light as they approached through the deep woods. They were at last near the end of their troubled journey.

It was a welcome sight to Galen. He and his two companions had cautiously passed the Empress Road three days before. Their path led through the forest of Mnumath, a wilderness long since abandoned by men. According to Maddoc, the only settlement beyond Mnumath was the Pir outpost of Waystead at the farthest tip of the Rheshathei Range. Beyond that the lands of the Pir ended, and Enlund and the Forsaken Mountains—the domains of Panas and Satinka—began.

Rhea had had difficulty leaving the Empress Road behind and had expressed her displeasure in no uncertain terms. While they were relatively close to civilized lands, there was the occasional opportunity to find sustenance from the castoffs of trade and travel. Now, far from any settlements, their supplies continued to dwindle and the deep forest of Mnumath offered little hope for forage. Galen, however, set aside her concerns; Tragget would join them in Mnumanthas. He would bring food, clothing, supplies for their journey, and, most important of all, his dear Berkita.

Galen ran lightly down a gully and dashed up the opposite side. He still could not see the base of the ruins through the trees and underbrush, despite being able to see the tower itself through the canopy of fall leaves. He lay his hand on his sword hilt, peering eagerly through the trees, hoping for a glimpse of their goal.

"Galen! Wait!" Rhea called after him. She was struggling with Maddoc on the far side of the gully. Her husband had grown more recalcitrant over the last two days. Today he was nearly impossible.

"*I think you should leave them here,*" S'shnickt said. "*We should scout ahead and make sure it is safe!*"

"That's a good idea," Galen agreed, "but we don't want to get too far ahead of them. I'm not sure I could find them again in this undergrowth."

"*Well, at the very least you should draw me out of the scabbard and brandish me as you advance,*" the sword huffed. "*You are woefully unprepared for the dangers ahead and would live longer if you exercised a little caution.*"

"You are *always* telling me to draw and brandish you," Galen said in mock derision. "I rather think you *like* being threatening."

"*It isn't a question of threatening,*" S'shnickt countered, "*although I do enjoy a good dramatic pose now and then. I just think a little more caution could prolong the periods I experience between different owners. Just when I get them trained, they usually die on me. It's rather discouraging.*"

Rhea struggled up the slope next to Galen, Maddoc leaning heavily on her arm. He was pale today, his eyes unfocused. Rhea was breathing hard.

"Galen, we need to stop and rest. Just for a little while."

"Well, I understand. Just sit down here," Galen replied anxiously. "I think I see a brighter space up ahead—not too far. Perhaps it's a clearing. I'll go take a look."

"Galen," Rhea said through her labored breathing as she collapsed to the ground. "Don't go too far. Please."

Galen smiled. "I won't. I'll be right back."

He waved and trotted off into the woods, moving smoothly through the underbrush with a carefree air. The sunlight fell on him in dappled patches through the autumn leaves above. Their fellows who had fallen before lay as a golden brown carpet under his feet. He could smell the rich aroma of fall in the air and it lifted his spirits as he walked, bubbling over into a nameless tune that he whistled.

Suddenly, he stopped.

A thin column of smoke curled into the sky next to the tower. Galen realized that he could smell it now on the breeze. It looked to be coming from a clearing just a few dozen feet ahead of him.

Galen smiled with relief. "It must be Tragget. He's here early!"

"You know, a little caution never killed anyone," the sword yelped, *"but the lack of it has done in men a lot better than you!"*

"If you don't keep quiet," Galen said happily as he plunged forward toward the clearing, "I'll be forced to toss you back in my sack and you'll miss everything."

"Oh, as though I've missed much thus far," the sword complained. *"Tromping around the woods and hills. Picking berries. Where's a good fight when you need one?"*

Galen broke through the trees at the edge of the clearing. Several stone walls stood at varying heights before him. One low foundation carved a large circle through the small clearing, vanishing in places before reemerging and continuing in its arc through the glade. A gentle autumn breeze stirred the tall grasses.

Galen saw the campfire; a ring of carefully placed stones rimmed the fire itself, while the dried grasses and brush surrounding it had been cleared away to a safe distance. Its smoke drifted up, carried on the breeze up around the abandoned tower that pierced the sky above him. He could smell the burning wood.

There was no one in sight.

Galen drew his sword.

"It's about time!" S'shnickt sniffed.

Carefully approaching the fire, Galen knelt down to examine it closer. The ground around the ring of stones was hard-packed and he could not discern any footprints.

"Where are you?" Galen muttered as he looked about him. "You're here somewhere, but where?"

Carefully, he stood up and started backing toward the woods. The quiet of the ruins in the afternoon unnerved him. Most of all, he wished he were out of the open and back in the protection of the forest.

The long moments passed, undisturbed except by his own shallow breathing. At last, after many glances about him, his back reached the woods. Galen turned to run. He had to get back to Rhea and Maddoc, had to—

"Galen! Behind you!" his sword yelped.

He turned, but not soon enough. The heavy body slammed into him, knocking him off his feet and driving him down onto the ground. The air rushed out of his lungs from the impact and his sword bounded from his hand. He gasped for breath as a thick hand closed around his throat. His vision blurred. He was dimly aware of something sitting on him, a rock raised up to strike him.

"Prisoner mine yer be!" the deep, enraged voice yelled. "Speak yer name and business er dead you be er is!"

Galen blinked furiously, struggling to catch his breath. All he could utter were gulping sounds.

"Speak say I!" The thick hand gripped Galen's throat all the tighter.

"Cephas!" Galen managed to squeak out.

The dwarf relaxed his grip. "How know yer Cephas name er?"

Galen chuckled through his coughing as he struggled for air. "It's me, you old dwarf forger! Galen!"

"Galen! True er is? Yer no *smell* like Galen . . ."

"Maybe not," Galen coughed. "But you sure smell like Cephas!"

"Galen!" the dwarf howled, huge tears welling from under his bandages. Cephas threw himself down on the supine human, wrapping his massive arms around him and squeezing the air out of him again as he sobbed uncontrollably.

Galen nearly passed out.

★   ★   ★

"Good er is!" Cephas bellowed. "Lord Tragget spoke Galen at Mnumanthas er is! True he were! True er is!"

The fire blazed at the center of their celebration. Rhea was astonished at what an amazing host the dwarf turned out to be. Somehow this blind little stump of a man had brought down a deer and found an amazing amount of late fruits, wild vegetables, and berries for a feast. Now, in the dark of the evening, they warmed themselves next to the fire, their appetites satisfied for the first time in days. Even Maddoc had much improved under the influence of Cephas's hearty meal.

The light of the fire reflected off the remains of the broken walls that lay about them, most of which had nearly been reclaimed by nature and time. In the blaze's warm light, the evening passed pleasantly. They talked of home, of the journeys of Cephas and Berkita as they chased Galen across both water and land until they were brought to the Temple of Vasska and before Lord Tragget. It was on the subject of Tragget that they settled at last.

"One has to wonder what his game is," Rhea said as she contemplated her answers in the flames of the campfire. "He obviously wants to develop more than just an understanding of the Deep Magic. He wants to master it as well. He claims that it is the one thing the Dragonkings fear. If so, why would a member of the Pir Drakonis want to master such power?"

"Perhaps Tragget challenges this dragon-god?" Cephas grumped. "Dragonkings' defeat means Pir triumph as humans er is!"

"I can't say that I wouldn't welcome the loss of the Dragonkings," Rhea said absently, "but to put such power in the hands of the Pir— in the hands of the Lord Inquisitor no less—I'm not entirely comfortable with *that* thought either."

"Rhea, I thought you were one of the Pir," Galen said with surprising seriousness. "Your ancestors honored the Dragonkings and now they are beyond the Veil of Sighs. You talk about challenging the gods themselves. You risk not only your spirit in the next life but theirs as well."

Rhea gaped at him. "After all they have done to you—all they've taken from you—you still believe?"

"Tragget says it was all a mistake and they'll make it right by me."

"Tragget." Rhea shook her head. "I never want to meet the man."

"I, for one, will be glad to see him," Galen said, as he leaned back against a foundation stone and stretched. "We've been studying this . . . this Deep Magic or whatever it is nearly every night. He's made some good progress. I think he's getting what he wants."

"Is he," Rhea mused. "What about you, Galen? Are you getting what you want?"

"Absolutely," Galen replied. "I get to go home."

"Get home?" Maddoc scoffed. "Oh, we can't go home, can we, Rhea? None of us can."

Rhea looked away.

"What does he mean, Rhea?" Galen asked suspiciously. "What is he talking about?"

Rhea looked back at him, their eyes locked. "Galen, we cannot go home. Not Maddoc, not me . . . and certainly not you. Not ever."

Galen crossed his arms over his chest. "No . . . I'm going back. That's all I care about. That's the only reason I'm doing this! Look, Tragget promised me—"

"Galen," Rhea said with slight impatience, "that is just not possible—no matter what Tragget promises! You may be able to return to the Dragonback. You may even get letters or papers from Tragget that say nice things about you and that your Election was all some mistake, but no matter what, you will never go back to the life you had. The Pir know that you are one of the Elect. Everyone in your village saw your Election. Did you think they would just forget about it when you returned?"

"They are my friends . . . my family!" Galen protested. "They wouldn't . . . they couldn't . . ."

"All of them, Galen? I've thought about this a long time and it's time you thought about it, too." Rhea pressed on mercilessly. "I've been trying to find a way home every moment of the day for over six years. Who will you be when you get back? Everyone in that village has lost someone to the Election, and you are the first one who has returned; the first one who knows their fate. What do you tell them? That their sons, daughters, husbands, and wives have been sent to their deaths for centuries? Who will come to your shop then, Galen? Would *every one* of them believe you over the Pir . . . the very religion that forms the foundation of their beliefs, their life, and their civilization? Who would come to your shop then, Galen?"

"I won't tell them," Galen said with determination.

"So you won't tell them, you'll lie to them and perpetuate the lie that the Pir have been telling them for centuries," Rhea responded vehemently. "Maybe you won't tell them and maybe they won't ask—but *you* will know. More than that, the Pir will know that you know. With all Tragget's promises and all his papers of retraction, nothing can take back the fact that you know. Tragget may be the most powerful man among the Pir Inquisitas, but he is only one man. The Inquisitas will not abide the thought that someone still breathes in the world that knows this secret. If any of us stop running just long enough . . . well, they wouldn't wait for the formality of the Election to take our lives!"

"Listen to Rhea," Cephas rumbled sadly. "Rhea speaks truth er is. Cephas knows. Cephas wanders the face of Aerbon . . . a blind dwarf under the light of men. Why? Because no one can go back to a lost home. Truth er is."

"Then what are we doing this for?" Galen cried.

"We are doing this because we must!" Rhea said sharply. "We are doing this for your lost wife and for my lost child and for my husband who is here but is lost nevertheless. We're doing this for whatever home lies ahead of us. I don't know where this road is taking us. Maybe we don't get to choose the road. Maybe the road chooses us."

"Well, I don't want it!" Galen spat the words with disdain. "What kind of a life is this? Nightmares and visions! Dreams made real! Mystic power straight out of a dead Rhamasian nursery story! It's unnatural, it's wrong, and it has taken everything from me that I love. I've spent days in that strange place helping Tragget for no other reason than to get my life back, and now you tell me its knowledge is the very thing that will keep me from going home? I hate it with all my heart! I hate it, Berkita!"

"I'm Rhea," she said quietly.

Galen caught his breath.

Rhea sighed. "Galen, wake up! You're heartsick for your past and the lovely life you had? Well, get over it, Galen, because it's gone! It's just gone! All our yesterdays are as dead as the Mad Emperors of Rhamas! This is who you are—one of the Elect chosen by who-knows-what to receive this gift, this strange, powerful gift. You didn't choose the magic, the magic chose you, and now *that* is your life!"

Galen stood, quivering with rage. "You're wrong, Rhea! I'm going home. Tragget will be here with Berkita in just a few days. When he comes, I'm taking my wife home and leaving this mystical curse behind me forever!"

"Don't you see, Galen?" Rhea said, forcing her voice into a steady calm. "You can't go home. *This* is who you are. You're trying to run away from yourself—from who you really are. No man can run that fast or that far."

41

Heretics

G endrik!" Tragget shouted through the door. "Where are you?"

"I am right here, Master," the torusk master said quickly, his head peering around the door frame. "I haven't gone anywhere."

Gendrik's eyes went wide. "My lord, what happened to your rooms?"

Tragget chuckled to himself. Gendrik had been to his private chambers before at whatever odd times his assistance was required. Each time, no matter the hour of the day or the shortness of his notice, these rooms had always been in impeccable order. Now, however, the room into which Gendrik peeked was in complete disarray. Although several traveling cases had already been removed by porters, the discarded dross remained where it had been hastily tossed.

What's more, Tragget did not care a whit.

Tragget smiled. "Nothing to worry about, Gendrik. I'm sorry; I guess I'm just anxious to get going."

"I can't imagine why, Master," Gendrik said distractedly. "I've seen an odd trail now and then in my life, Lord, but this one is the strangest of all. An entire caravan outfitted while hidden inside a trade warehouse! The trade guild master was so upset I wondered if even your great name would be enough to buy his silence."

"He agreed to it." They always agree to it, Tragget thought.

"All of the torusks loaded down while still in their stalls. It ain't natural, they'll be gettin' skittish for sure!"

"They won't be there long, Gendrik. We are leaving directly," Tragget said, examining a set of heavy bound books. They were the *Pir Inquisitas Desment*—the books that spelled out the faith of the Pir and the godhood of the Dragonkings. He pushed them aside. He would not need them where he was going.

The heart or the head, he thought. Magic comes from the heart . . . no wonder the Emperors were mad!

"Yes, my lord," Gendrik said, his head still bobbing comically at the side of the doorway. It looked like it was disembodied and nodding on a string. "I'd feel much better about this trip, though, my lord, if I knew where we were going. I mean, it's hard to pack a caravan when you don't know the destination or the road or how long it will take to get there."

"Don't question me, Gendrik," Tragget said without looking back. "I'll let you know once we are under way. Now get back to your torusks and keep them calm until we can get there. I've got just a few last things to address."

Gendrik's eyebrow rose. "Who else is coming?"

"Do as you are told, Gendrik!" Tragget snapped. "I've known men who have been hung by their own tongue for less."

The torusk master swallowed before he answered. "Yes, Lord Inquisitor! At once!"

Tragget listened for a few moments to the retreating footfalls as Gendrik ran back down the corridor. Gendrik had served him well over the years; a skilled man who knew when to be discreet. The Inquisitor had used him more than once for delicate journeys that were best completed without anyone else knowing they had ever taken place. He was a good man—a bit weak-willed, perhaps, but a good servant. Tragget actually felt sorry for what he was about to do to him.

Now satisfied that he was alone, Tragget looked about his chambers. They had been his home for many years. In many ways this wing of the Temple had been the only home he had ever really known. He considered it for a time. Here about him were all the things that he had thought important. The icons of Vasska stared back at him from the stone walls, their ornate carvings filled with shadows. His books that spoke of the orders of the Pir and the greatness of their cause lay next to the bed in a pile. Who, he thought, would read them when he was gone? Would they be put away by some other hand, or would they remain here, forsaken and moldering? Would they somehow miss his gentle hand and long to be opened and read with the interest he once had felt and now had pushed aside?

Tragget was suddenly unsure. What was he doing? He was safe here, safe even from the insanity that was consuming his soul. What could possibly be so great a thing to induce him to leave his home, his mother, and everything that had been so important to him?

He sat down on the edge of his bed. The thrill of the adventure had suddenly waned in him. The heart or the head, he thought. Am I running toward one or just away from the other?

He gazed at the fireplace next to his bed. On either side of the hearth stood two iron dragons, more icons of Vasska, guardians over the now-cold fire. They represented the faith taught to him by his mother, the reason for his existence and his justification for every life he had seen taken in the greater cause of the Pir.

Tears streamed down his face as he studied them. The iron faces of Vasska had been his most constant companions throughout his life, and he was planning to leave them.

But then he saw other things in his mind. The Deep Magic welled up unbidden within him. He reached out toward the iron statues.

The dragons began to move.

Tragget wept but did not turn away. Choked sobs were wrenched from his throat, dragged unbidden through the half-smile on his lips. The power of the Deep Magic coursed through him, glorious and thrilling.

The iron dragons spread their wings. They began to glow as their wings beat the air.

Tragget's tears flowed freely from his fever-bright eyes. The magic burned away his doubts. He laughed and sobbed at once, hysterical in his confusion of emotions. He could not leave the magic. It would never let him go. It was splendid and shameful but it was the truest thing he had ever experienced in his life.

The iron dragons leaped into the air, flying high into the room . . .

The eyes in the darkness spoke.

"You have done well, my son!"

Tragget turned quickly in shock and fear.

The twisted forms of the iron dragons plummeted to the stone floor of the bedchamber, landing with a ringing clank.

"Mother! I . . . It is . . . it is part of my investigations! You asked me . . . the Pentach asked . . . that I discover the false and deceptive powers of—"

"Hush, my child." Edana smiled as she stepped into the room. She wore breeches and a tunic of leather under her traveling cloak. Tragget recognized them as the flying gear she used each time she rode the back of Vasska, but to where? "There should be no secrets between us! There is a time when the darkness serves us well, but here, between a mother and her dutiful son, there should be a little truth at last, don't you think? Perhaps we could start with you?" Her voice grew quiet and dangerous. "I'm sure there is something that you would like to tell me; something that is a secret that I do not yet know."

Tragget felt the blood drain from his face. "I . . . I don't know what you mean! I've always tried to be honest with you . . ."

"Tried, yes, I'm sure you have tried," Edana said, stepping closer to her son, "as I have tried for many years to shield you, take care of you, and keep your little secret safe from so many others."

Tragget blinked. He could barely find his voice when he spoke. "My secret?"

"Yes," Edana continued. She stood looking down on Tragget where he sat on the edge of his bed. "Your secret. That you are one of the Elect, my son; that you are as mad as the rest of them."

Tragget could not control his shaking. "I . . . I d-don't know what you're t-talking about!"

"Oh, don't disappoint me, son, not after all I've gone through for you—for both of us!" Edana's voice was sharp-edged as she spoke. "I've known you were of the Elect for years now! How is it that you have always had special dispensation to be absent anytime the Eye of Vasska is passed? *I've* seen to that! Your position is uniquely suited to keep you from suspicion; who inquests the Inquisitor? *I've* seen to that, too. Oh, yes; your mother has watched over you, son, and now it is time for you to fulfill all the dreams your mother has had for you."

"Mother," Tragget said meekly. "I don't know what I am supposed to do."

"Do? You are supposed to stand up and fulfill your destiny!" Edana snapped. "You are supposed to take this strange power and subjugate the dragons as fate intends! We need no longer serve them; *they* should serve *us!* The Pentach only suspects that this power exists; they know nothing of you! Together we can become a saving force for all the Pir! Think of it! Your destiny has been written in the dreamsmoke of Vasska himself! Now you've learned the power from that fool Galen, it is time to finish him and his companions before they challenge you."

"Challenge me?" Tragget yelped. "They are no threat! All they want is to go back to their homes and live out their lives in peace!"

The back of Edana's gloved hand stung Tragget's cheek. "Live their lives in peace? With power like this? How long do you think it would be before they were no longer satisfied with just living their lives in peace? How long before they showed up at the gates of the Temple with their own trained Elect, mystics intent on bringing down the greatness of the Pir! We alone must possess this magic or we will spend the rest of our days watching our backs!"

Tragget slumped before her. "Yes, Mother."

Edana considered him for a moment, and then looked down at her hands, tugging at her gloves as she spoke. "I've known for days now of your little trip to Mnumanthas. I watched you each night, read your dreams and listened to your murmured words as you slept.

Galen and his companions have been traveling for days toward that old ruin—and so have my cadre of the Aboth-Sek."

Edana looked up. Tragget sat broken before her. "Now tell me, and consider your answer well, my child."

The head or the heart, he thought.

"You were going somewhere tonight. Where were you going tonight?"

The head or the heart?

Tragget spoke his words to the floor. "I was going to find Galen. I was . . . I was going to bring him back."

"Good child! Bright child!" Edana took his wet face in both her gloved hands, turning it up toward her. "You are the destiny of the Pir, my son. I have seen it! You no longer need the fool. We shall see that he and his friends are cared for as destiny intended."

Tragget heard the scream of the dragon high above the Temple. Vasska was awake and abroad in the night.

"You will keep your promise to go to Mnumanthas," Edana continued through a terrible smile, "and you won't need the caravan. I have a much quicker means of travel."

Berkita stood at the balcony.

She clutched the short message that had been delivered to her as she looked out into the night. The Southern Steppes were dim to her sight but she looked anyway. It was there she would be traveling. It was there her Galen awaited her.

She wore her traveling cloak. Such things as she had were packed in a sack and laid carefully by the door. Tragget would come to collect her and then the nightmare would end. She would be on her way to Galen and they would be on their way home once more. Perhaps then the sickness that she had felt for weeks now would be at an end, too.

She gazed into the night, waiting for the knock at the door.

I stand once more on the shores of Mirren Bay. It is painful for me to see it again as I contemplate what is so far from me. My little village, however, has been replaced with a great city of glass and lace. It is too beautiful for me to look upon. I walk away from it on the shoreline toward the east.

The winged woman floats above the sands of the shore over a blue, heatless flame. The stones that I had given her lie in a circle about her feet. It is well, for there are a dozen demons screaming in a rage about her. They wish to destroy her but the stones keep them all at bay.

The demons, however, are clever. They cannot pass the circle of stones but they can touch them. They are rolling them closer and closer to the winged woman, hoping that they will reach her when the circle is small enough.

I reach for my sword. S'shnickt is in my hand and I charge the demons on the shore. I leap inside the circle, wondering for a moment why it would let me pass and not the demons. The winged woman grasps my hand, plunging my sword into the blue flame, where it glows with a strange aura. As each demon approaches, I strike from inside the circle. Before my blade can connect, however, the blue flame leaps from it, crashing into the demons. The flame explodes against the demons and their arms fly from their sockets, their heads topple to the ground, their bowels fall out from their stomachs. Each collapses in a gruesome stain on the sands.

In my victory, I see Tragget. He stands on the shore. "Tragget!" I call out. "I've something new for us!"

He turns and starts walking away.

I do not understand. He has always been so eager to join me before.

"Tragget!" I start running down the shore after him. The world is getting darker as I run. "Tragget! Wait!"

BOOK OF GALEN
BRONZE CANTICLES, TOME IV, FOLIO 1, LEAVES 56–57

Galen woke with a start

"Galen! Wait! Don't move!"

It was Rhea's voice. He was still confused. He tried to sit up but felt the immediate bite of several swords' tips at his throat. He lay back slowly.

"She is quite right, Galen. It would be best if you did not do anything at all."

He knew that voice from the Election, a voice that still haunted him . . . Priestess Edana! His mind raced. How had she found them?

Tragget!

"Where are the others?" Galen asked quietly. He could not see the hooded faces of the Aboths about him, all holding their swords ready to strike.

"Oh, they are waiting for you . . . you and this woman both, in fact," Edana said softly. Her face glowed in the light of their campfire. "The dwarf gave us a little trouble but he is none the worse for the exchange. I wish the same could be said for two of my Aboths."

"Sorry," Galen responded. "We weren't expecting to entertain guests."

"Ah, how droll." The High Priestess smiled.

"Why wake us at all?" Galen asked, despair seeping into him like the cold from the ground he rested on. "Why not just kill us as we slept?"

"Murder?" Edana replied. "It is a sin against all the faithful to murder one of our own, no matter how tempting. No, I've come to thank you for your great service to the Pir, Galen. You have secured our rule for generations to come."

Galen's eyes swept over the swords ready to slit his throat. "You have an odd way of showing your appreciation."

"Then may I introduce someone else who would like to show their appreciation?" Edana said. She turned from him, her voice changing as she uttered strange and terrible sounds.

Fear descended over Galen.

From the darkness, the great shape emerged. It towered behind Edana. Even the Aboths quickly backed away from the massive shadow. The leathery wings unfolded in the light of the campfire, dimmed by their great height. The massive chest hove into view, its scales glistening. Atop the long curve of the scaled neck, the head bent down from the darkness of the night. It alone was fully ten feet tall from its bladed lower jaw to its horned ridges. Its dull, lifeless eyes—at least two hands high—swiveled forward to gaze through Galen. Then the terrible maw opened, and Galen saw the double rows of razor teeth, the long tearing fangs top and bottom, and the shredding gullet, all inviting him with the stench of death.

Rhea started screaming.

The dragon's chest drew a great breath, then the colossal beast roared. It was a sound unlike any Galen had ever heard or dreamt of. The sound shook stones loose from the ancient foundations around them. It ran through his bones and into his head. It seemed never to end.

A dead silence followed.

"Vasska thanks you personally for your service in his great war." Edana smiled thinly as she spoke, though Galen could barely hear her words. "While necessarily delayed, it is, after all, time that you die in glorious battle—and the sooner the better!"

The Mystics

Pieces
in Play

Dwynwyn woke to a pounding headache.

She pushed herself up from the bed. The coverlet was soft and warm. The bed beneath it was inviting. It seemed to pull at her, begging her to collapse once more into its welcoming folds. She fought the desire to give in, however, to its opulence. The waking world around her seemed treacherous, and she felt the need to face it with open eyes.

The curved room was sparsely furnished. Aislynn lay quietly on one of the two large and ornately shaped beds, her beautiful wings curled protectively around her. The princess trembled occasionally where she lay in fitful sleep. The oval entrance to the room was flanked by columns coaxed into a pattern that reminded Dwynwyn of climbing roses. The exit itself, however, was closed with a series of roughly hewn wooden planks banded together with iron. It was an abomination of a door, offensive for its obvious violence against the wood. The long curve of the outer wall was a brilliant alabaster shaped into delicate curves resembling waves near the shore. These arched over a wide window. There, a window seat was fitted to a low balustrade which protruded out in a gentle bow into the sky beyond. Yet even this idyllic perch was ruined by long, thick bands of iron only inches apart that spanned the opening from top to bottom.

The room was a luxurious cage and the prisoners had a visitor.

"Ah, my guests awaken at last," Xian said dryly.

"Where are we?" Dwynwyn asked, her hand rubbing her forehead in a desperate and partially successful attempt to subdue the pain.

"You are in the tower rooms of . . . what did you people call this place?" Xian considered for a moment. The Kyree master was leaning against the wall near the columns, his wings neatly folded behind his back. "Oh, yes, Kien Werren Keep. I have had these rooms remodeled just for you. What do you think of it?"

"Confining," Dwynwyn responded at once.

Xian smiled. "Excellent. I knew you would appreciate it."

"I don't remember coming to this room," Dwynwyn said as she closed her eyes for a moment. She was disoriented and needed time to get her mind in order.

"I shouldn't wonder," Xian replied, crossing his arms over his chest. "You were unconscious at the time. Apparently your little trick last night worked too well. It kept us from harming you, to be sure, but it apparently wouldn't allow any of life's breath to come in either. You were quite entertaining toward the end, just before you passed out and collapsed to the floor. You said the strangest things."

"What did I say?" Dwynwyn asked, a chill edge to her voice.

Xian raised an eyebrow. "It was unimportant. Perhaps I will tell you about it some other time." He stood away from the wall in an easy move. His hands clasped behind his back. "You understand that, don't you, Seeker. What does that mean, 'Seeker'? Is that your title or rank or some designation of function?"

Dwynwyn stared back at him. With his pinched face and hideously deformed abomination of wings, he was repulsive to her. She would not allow herself to tell him anything.

"What does a Seeker do?" Xian asked, shaking his head for emphasis.

Dwynwyn kept her silence.

"I see this is pointless." Xian shrugged, turning toward the blocked doorway. "I should have had you both dispatched while you were unconscious!"

"Why didn't you?" Dwynwyn asked suddenly.

Xian stopped and considered her for a moment before he answered. "Because it pleased me not to."

"That is a lie," she replied.

His eyes narrowed for a moment. "Excuse me?"

"You did not spare us simply on a whim," Dwynwyn said. "What I have seen of the master of the Kyree would not support such an assertion."

"You are wrong, faery," Xian replied through a thin smile. "I do *many* things of my own pleasure."

"I believe that you *kill* of your own pleasure," Dwynwyn said factually, "but you would not *refrain* from killing without a reason."

"You know nothing of my reasons," Xian said quietly. "You know nothing of my people or our pain. Until you understand those, Dwynwyn of Qestardis, it is *you* who are lying." He again turned his dark face toward the door. "Guard! Open the door! These mongrels no longer amuse me!"

Aislynn awoke with a start. Seeing Xian, the princess caught her breath, pushing herself backward until she cowered against the headboard.

A metallic rasping sound shivered through the door, then it swung wide. Xian strode toward the open portal.

"Wait!" Dwynwyn said.

Xian half turned in the door. "What is it, bug?"

"You are correct; there is much about you that we do not know," Dwynwyn said quickly, her mind racing. There were so many questions she needed answered. The Kyree were a complete mystery to her and, so far as she knew, to any of the faery. They seemed to be in the service of the Famadorian cause and yet vehemently denied having anything to do with the Famadorians. Qestardis was threatened by the Famadorians from the north and by Lord Phaeon from the southwest. What was this unknown threat from the southeast? She had to know. "For instance, do you play games?"

"Do I what?" Xian snorted.

"Play games, Master Xian," Dwynwyn continued. "Games are symbols of greater truths. They teach us things that we might not have previously supposed. They teach us of the mysteries."

"The mysteries?" Xian hesitated in the doorway. "I'm listening."

Dwynwyn spoke quickly. "There are many mysteries between us, Master Xian. I am your prisoner here and I do not understand why. That is a mystery to me, would you not agree?"

Xian chuckled. "I know why you are my prisoner. What I do not understand is why you came here in the first place."

"Of course not," Dwynwyn said more earnestly. "That is a mystery to you. We both of us have our mysteries, Master Xian. But, in my experience, the patterns and rhythms of a game often provide an opportunity for two beings to come to an understanding—a place where each may share their mysteries."

"You want to play a game?" Xian chuckled.

"Yes, Master Xian."

He stepped back in the room, the heavy door closing and quickly locking behind him.

"What do I win?" he asked.

"What do you mean?"

"Is answering a question with a question part of this game?" Xian asked. "I mean, if I win this game, what do I get out of it?"

Dwynwyn blinked. "Well, you get the knowledge of the patterns and strategies that prove successful during the course of the game. Of course, it will also provide us with time to address the mysteries between us as we converse."

Xian shook his head. "Not enough. I want higher stakes."

Dwynwyn chewed at her lower lip. "What do you propose?"

"If I win," Xian said, pointing his long, narrow fingers at the Seeker, "then you will teach me how to perform that trick from last night."

Dwynwyn considered for a moment. When she spoke, it was with deliberation. "It is impossible to teach you because I do not understand it myself. But if you are willing to play this little game with me, perhaps we can get to a place where we will both understand each other better."

"Not enough." Xian shrugged and turned back to the door.

Dwynwyn glanced at Aislynn and saw the terror in her eyes. "If you win," Dwynwyn said desperately, "I will answer one of your questions."

Xian spun around to face her, his narrow eyes keen. "Any question I like?"

"Yes!"

He took a step toward her. He looked like a predator. "And you will answer it fully and completely to my satisfaction?"

Dwynwyn hesitated. Xian had apparently dealt with faeries before. It was dangerous, but she had questions of her own that had to be answered.

"Yes," she said, "but if I win, you will grant me the same boon."

"Done!" Xian chuckled. "What is to prevent me from cheating?"

"Nothing. I fully expect you to cheat, but I will be watching to correct you when you do."

"And how do I know that you will not cheat?"

"Because faeries cannot deny the truth."

"You truly *do* amuse me, Dwynwyn!" Xian laughed. "Very well, what is this game of yours?"

"Sylan-sil, Master Xian. Your servants will find it among the things in our cloudship."

"Is it a game of war?"

"Yes," Dwynwyn answered honestly, for she knew no other way. "I believe it could be."

He smiled. "Then let's have them bring your game to me!"

Galen managed somehow to open his eyes, only to shut them once more. The sight that filled them terrified him and burned into his memory.

The wind roared through their ironreed cage. Vasska's huge wings scooped through the air in long, slow beats. They flew through the dark of the early morning, their cage clutched in the dragon's talons. Now, as the cheerless dawn was breaking, they had left Hrunard far behind. They were deep in Enlund, of that he was sure. S'shnickt had told him it was the land of the enemy. Now they had taken his sword from him and they were in the land of war and death.

"By the Claw," Rhea shouted. "Look at that!"

Involuntarily, Galen looked. They were lower now and the sight caught by his tearing eyes made him hold his breath in wonder.

Through the woven cage he saw it: a great undulating plain. The long streams of torusk caravans split into veins as they ran between the hills, eventually emptying their cargo of the Elect onto the edge of a great hollow many miles across among the hills. There, thousands of the Chosen stood, prodded from their cages out onto the field, their weapons in hand. They formed roughly into ranks, their backs to the Pir monks, who herded them with their dragonstaffs. The Elect of Vasska were an army carpeting the edge of the great open space before them.

He had seen this place before, had *been* in this place. He remembered the dead lying across these same hills as though cut down by a scythe. It was the place from his dream. He remembered walking these same hills with Maddoc and Tragget and finding Rhea on the hilltop.

He glanced at Rhea next to him. Her face was pressed close to the woven strands of their cage, searching the land that passed below them.

He remembered her dead.

"Over there!" Rhea shouted over the wind, her arm pointing into the distance.

From their great height, they could see other armies now, each being arrayed at the other sides of the wide hollow, each at the foot of a tall hill. Enormous creatures moved atop each of the hills.

"Who are they?" Galen shouted.

Maddoc lolled back in the cage, uninterested, yet answered the question anyway. "Satinka and Panas, I believe. Dragonkings of the Forsaken Mountains and Enlund, although I should think that Dragonqueen would be a better title for Satinka. She's the cause of all this, you know."

"What?" Galen asked, but the cage bounced suddenly as Vasska soared over a rise, wheeling over the battlefield. Galen shuddered and closed his eyes once more. To him, the dragons far below looked like deadly, terrible toys.

The toy monsters were giving Mimic trouble.

"Honestly, Mimic." Gynik sighed. "I wish you would put those things away for a while and pay attention to me!"

Gynik lay on the cushioned bench. Her breasts and stomach both sagged over the side seductively. It had never failed to arrest any other goblin cold in his tracks, but for some reason Mimic was so absorbed in his little devices that he wasn't affected by her charms, which troubled Gynik immensely.

They were in the main room of Mimic's apartments, but she barely recognized the place. Mimic had pulled up part of the floor grating last night and since then had been pulling out cogs, gears, wheels, rods, springs, screws, plates, and anything else he could find and sticking them together. Now the floor was covered with an amazing array of little mechanisms. The smallest of them looked like little goblins made of metal. These were quite charming, Gynik thought, and seemed to work remarkably well. It was the larger ones that seemed to be giving Mimic so much trouble, and were taking his attention away from more important things—namely, Gynik.

"Can't stop," Mimic muttered, connecting a second spring to one of the long brass sheets on the wing. "No time! I've an audience this afternoon with the Dong to show him this army."

"This afternoon!" Gynik cried as she sat upright on the bench. "But I haven't got a thing to wear!"

"Actually, my dear," Mimic sputtered as he tightened down a screw, "I think the king would prefer you that way."

"Well, I wouldn't give the old fool the satisfaction," Gynik sniffed. "Why did you have to make this appointment so soon?"

"I saw it all in my dream," Mimic replied with a grunt as he gave the screw a final twist. "I saw this entire mechanical army below me as though I were standing on a high tree or maybe a mountain. Not just these little men but these winged monsters as well. I saw the king, too, and he was standing in the middle of the armies, towering over them. He was laughing and clapping as they moved about him. Then I saw him handing me a great treasure—although I couldn't see it very clearly. Anyway, I don't know why, but I've just got to show these devices to him and it has got to be this afternoon."

"Oh, Mimi," Gynik pouted. It was not a great nickname but it was the best she had come up with. Gynik regularly changed her allegiances to suit the situation, but things had been moving along a little fast even for her these last few days. "I don't think the Dong expected you to build him Titans immediately!" She picked up one of the little miniature metal goblins that had wandered clicking and whirring over to her and looked at it. "Besides, I rather think he wanted Titans that were a bit 'bigger' than this."

Mimic smiled as he continued to work, sweat pouring down his brow. "Goblins are little creatures, Gynik. I think that the Titans overlooked us and that's why they fell. You would be surprised at how big a little thing can be!"

True Blades

Vasska wheeled over the Enlund Plain. The warriors on the field below scattered in his wake, fear of the creature clutching at their souls with icy claws. The dragon shifted in the air. The leathery wings pressed hard against his path of flight, slowing the enormous monster as he neared the ground. He gripped a small cage with the talons of his powerful rear legs, holding it forward. Plumes of dirt roiled into the air under the beating of his wings and warriors of the Election tumbled out of the way. In moments, however, he was airborne once again, his burden left behind on the plain.

Tragget watched everything numbly as he lay next to Edana in the Talker's pouch behind the dragon's head. Vasska needed his Dragon-Talker to communicate with humans when he traveled beyond the confines of his lair. The pouch provided a means by which the Dragon-Talker could ride with the dragon wherever he went. When Vasska permitted it, the Aboth would strap on the leather assembly just behind the crest plates at the rear of the dragon's head, far out on the neck. This had the advantage of allowing the Talker to communicate with the dragon while they were in the air. The disadvantage was that dragons were constantly craning their heads in flight, thus making the ride in the pouch a wild and dangerous one.

367

Worse, the dragons all hated the pouch. It struck them as demeaning and they occasionally made their displeasure known to the occupant by shaking their heads violently.

The leather pouch was designed to make rider and dragon as comfortable as possible under the circumstances. The back of the pouch was, indeed, a pouch—a hard leather sack whose interior was lined with padding for the warmth and protection of the Dragon-Talker. In the front, handles with long leather thongs were fitted just behind the high ridge that ran across the pouch's front as a windbreak. Talkers could grip the handles and then wrap the straps around their wrists and forearms for some measure of safety. By pulling themselves up to rest on their elbows, they could look forward over the ridge past the dragon's head, but few bothered. The view on the open sides was frightening enough.

"It is a historic day, my son!" Edana said loudly to Tragget, the excitement evident in her voice. She lay next to the Inquisitor, the air roaring over them both as the pouch bucked and swayed beneath them. "Today we begin the true battle for the Pir!"

Tragget did not move. He no longer cared.

"You'll look back on this day, my son," Edana continued, her enthusiasm unchecked. "We both will! We'll look back on this day and mark it as the first day of a great new order in the world!"

Vasska circled the hilltop once and then wheeled sharply toward it. His wings beat back from the approaching ground, slowing him quickly, billowing the dust up out of the tall grasses beneath him, and obscuring his passengers' vision for a moment. He settled down on the top of the hill, his neck craned high over the field of battle arrayed below him. This left the pouch nearly vertical. Edana spoke to the dragon with a few clacking sounds. Reluctantly, Vasska lowered his head to the ground.

Edana quickly unwound the leather straps from her wrists. Seeing that Tragget was making no move to do likewise, she reached over and untied him, speaking all the while. "There is a destiny in all this, Tragget; your destiny and mine. Many of the things that are demanded of us are hard and distasteful. We may not like doing them. They may not even seem right at the time. In the end, however, they are justified by the knowledge that we purchase contentment and progress for the Pir and for humanity itself. You'll see. It may seem wrong now but, in the end, you'll know I'm right."

Tragget slid to the ground. He gazed out over the field below him. Five thousand warriors of the Pir stood below him, prepared for battle. "Is that why we fight this war, Mother; to purchase contentment and progress for the Pir and humanity? Is that why the dragons have fought for four hundred years?"

Edana stood next to her son, chuckling. "No, of course not!"

"Then why are the dragons at war?" Tragget asked.

"To settle their bets," Edana said easily.

"What?"

"I guess it really is the clearest way to put it," Edana returned. "You see, dragons just don't think the way we do, their minds work differently. What is important to them may seem trivial to us. You're the Grand Inquisitor. You've dealt exclusively with the problems of maintaining order within the Pir itself. It's time you learned something of the true nature of the larger world. Defend, conquer, glory, and spirit, eh? Those are human ideas, my son; the dragons only care about themselves. They have an honor, to be sure, but it is their own. We are little more than a way of keeping score for them and a ready source of meat. *That* is why the dragons fight these wars: to settle their petty arguments. Now—thanks in no small part to you— we know another reason: it is also the dragons' way of keeping any of us with a talent for this magic power safely and conveniently *dead*."

Edana sat down on the hillside, gazing down over the great field below. "On the other hand, *we* have been forced to allow this senseless river of blood each year to purchase peace for all the rest of the Pir. What are a few madmen sacrificed to the whims of our flawed and unfathomable gods, if their deaths purchase everyone else's peace for a season? That, at least, is what we have told ourselves each night so that we might sleep. Now, it seems that we have been killing the very means of hope, bleeding it from our bodies year after year until we are weak and frail before our dragon tyrants. But all of that is about to change: the wheel of destiny turns and on it we are ascending."

Tragget gazed down at the army below. He could make out Galen's open and empty cage. The man and his companions were now out among the sea of yelling warriors and Tragget could not find them. "So what of them, Mother? What of the Elect? They have the magic that threatens the dragons, too. Why do they die today?"

"Because that is *their* destiny." Edana sighed. "If this power of magic threatens the dragons, then it must be powerful indeed. The Pir is more than just some nonsense about worshiping a Dragonking. Such power should only be in the hands of those who are capable of understanding it, harnessing it, and directing it toward the greater good."

"Better our greater good than theirs?" Tragget said coldly.

"We don't need rivals," Edana replied. "Power is strongest when it is wielded by only one side in a conflict."

"The rest of the Pentach doesn't know about the magic, do they?" Tragget said with fearful astonishment.

Edana smiled. "I've told them you haven't found anything yet and, I suspect, you never will."

At distant other points around the field, Tragget could make out the other dragons perched atop their own hilltops.

"Look there, my son!" Edana said, gesturing out over the battle plain. "The prophecy will be fulfilled. The fool who taught you will die, the magic will be yours alone, and you will claim our destiny! I have done it all for you, my son!"

"I've done it all for you, my Dong!" Mimic said nervously. "I beg . . . er, hope . . . I mean, I desire that . . ."

Dong Mahaj-Megong leaned forward on his throne so far that his feet almost touched the floor. Sihir was affecting a studied lack of interest, but the Dong was wide-eyed in wonder at the display on the floor. "Relax, Mimic! Don't be so formal . . . we've been friends for, what?"

"Since three days ago, Your Dong-ness," Mimic said.

"Exactly!" The Dong never let reason get in the way when making a political point. "In all those years you should have learned that I only expect ceremony out of toadies, lackeys, and regular subjects—

not from wealthy and important people like us. What *have* you brought for me today?"

"Well, er, I have brought something that may interest you a great deal," Mimic said. He had practiced this speech since early this morning, but was still too nervous to deliver it properly. "It has long been a question in the minds of the technicians as to what destroyed the Titans in the Last War. I have brought before you today a representation of that war which may answer that question decisively."

He stepped back to the side, gesturing with his hand grandly over the floor of the throne room. On the floor, arrayed in a circle, were a collection of the most magnificent small mechanisms anyone had ever seen. They were little metallic goblins, each only a foot high, organized in three groups. Their metal was polished and oiled, reflecting brightly the light in the room.

Behind each of these groups sat three larger metallic creatures the likes of which neither the Dong nor anyone else in all the goblin realms had ever seen. Each looked like some sort of bird, with long wings made of metal sheets. The creatures' necks were far too long for their bodies, and each sported a long barbed tail. Moreover, they had arms as well as feet, all of which were fitted with long, sharp claws. The heads were sharp and covered with spikes. Each of the three looked slightly different but all of them had a terrible aspect.

The Dong loved them all. "So this is going to answer the question . . ."

"Of how the Titans fell, yes, Your Dong-ness. It will simulate mechanically what happened."

"Is this based on strict interpretation of history and science?" the Dong demanded.

"No, sire," Mimic replied at once. "I just made the whole thing up."

"Good," the Dong replied, slapping the arms of his chair with both hands. "I hate it when facts get in the way of a good story." He tried to lean forward farther but found himself in danger of falling onto his very fat face. He restrained himself, out of respect to his office as the Dong. It was difficult, however, because he was absolutely fascinated by the little mechanical goblins.

There were thirty-six of them in all. Each held a sword in one hand that was beautifully crafted with a single black bead in the hilt.

"Rhea! Maddoc!" Galen shouted. "Are you all right?"

"Yes," Rhea replied, wincing against the noise around them. Several of the mad warriors were screaming for the war to begin. Rhea held close to Maddoc. "We're fine . . . for now, at least."

"Where's Cephas?"

"Cephas er here!" the dwarf cried out behind Galen, his voice shaking.

Galen had never known him to be afraid of anything. "Cephas! What's wrong?"

"Cephas lost er is!" the dwarf moaned. "Blind and lost! Cephas the rock and dirt have lost. Ground smells different er is! Oh, blind and lost!"

"By the Claw!" Galen swore.

"What is it?" Rhea asked.

"The dwarf is lost!" he shouted back.

"I thought the dwarf was *never* lost!"

"It must have been the flying," Galen said, looking frantically about them, trying to see over the heads of the other warriors. "Dwarves sense the passage of the ground under them as they walk or the sea on those rare occasions one can coax them onto a boat. They know where they are because they know where they've been. How far do you think we've come?"

"I don't know." Rhea glanced around. "Two hundred miles . . . maybe more."

"The dwarf doesn't know that; he didn't feel the ground pass under his feet," Galen said, then took his old friend by the shoulders. "Cephas! We're in Enlund. We are on the Enlund Plain!"

Cephas still shuddered under Galen's hands. "Enlund! Lost still er I but Enlund be a bad sign! Blood er is! Blood and danger, Master Arvad!"

"We've got to do something," Rhea cried. "We've got to get away!"

"Away, yes, but *how?*" Galen shouted. "If we had weapons, maybe we could—"

"*Always nice to be working with you, Galen,*" S'shnickt said cheerfully at his side.

Galen's eyes went wide. He reached across to his waist with his right hand.

It closed around a cool hilt of leather-wrapped steel.

"Rhea!" Galen said. "Do you have your sword?"

"Galen, they took our weapons when they—" Rhea stopped suddenly. "Yes! I do! How did you . . ."

"*This sure is going to be a great war today!*" S'shnickt said gaily. "*You are quite privileged to be participants. I don't know when such an important issue has been decided by one of these contests in ages.*"

"Important issue?" Galen said puzzled. "What issue?"

"*All the other weapons are ringing with it. The reason for the war today,*" S'shnickt answered brightly. "*By the gods, would you just listen to them? Some of them just won't shut up about it, either, which is really annoying when you think about it.*"

Maddoc pulled out his own sword, which had appeared just as magically as Rhea's and Galen's. He was jumping up and down while shouting excitedly.

"S'shnickt, *what* issue?"

"*Well, today we're fighting over the question of paternity. Satinka, the female dragon on northeast hilltop, wants a clutch of eggs for a new brood. Neither Vasska nor Panas want to father the clutch, of course, so the war this year is to decide who will be forced to mate with Satinka. It's nice to know you'll be dying for something important this time!*"

"We're fighting this war," Galen shouted in outrage, "just to determine which dragon mates with another?"

A strange, awkward silence descended over the warriors immediately around Galen, all of whom were staring at him dumbfounded. Rhea's mouth fell open. Cephas stuck a finger in his ear, trying to clear it, for he was sure he had heard wrong. Galen looked about him, horrified.

Maddoc turned to the warriors and shouted, "Our dragon's gonna win!"

The warriors suddenly cheered all the louder.

"These wars are fought over all kinds of things," S'shnickt went on. *"One year it was who could fly higher than the other dragons. Another year it was over who got to eat the spoils first. At least this year you'll be dying for something that will cause the dragons some discomfort. Dragon mating is tricky at best, dangerous at worst, and always painful to them. They haven't made a bet like this in over five centuries."*

Galen turned to Rhea. "We've got to get out of here."

"You can't," S'shnickt interjected. *"Those are not the rules. You are selected to become warriors. You come to the war. You fight the war and then you die. The positions of the dead on the battlefield determine which dragon is the winner, or in this case the loser. Those are the rules. They've been the rules for centuries."*

Galen held the sword up in front of him in frustration, yelling at it. "No! I will *not* die! Not for you, not for this dragon, and certainly not today!"

He heard Rhea's voice speaking his name.

As once before, the Elect had cleared away from him, leaving a circle of warriors. Each of them saluted Galen with their swords, their black stone pommels glinting in the morning light.

"Galen!" Cephas shouted. "Thank ye! Cephas a sword now er is!"

Galen looked at his blind friend next to him.

A sword with a black stone pommel had appeared in the dwarf's hand.

Galen looked about him. There were thirty-two men and women standing at attention. With Rhea, Maddoc, Cephas, and himself, they made thirty-six. The magic was with them, though he wondered what difference thirty-six could possibly do against the dragons and their hordes.

"S'shnickt," Galen said. "I think it is time we changed the rules."

New Rules

Your games are meaningless, Dwynwyn," Xian muttered as he examined a polished black stone in the shape of a cube. "Do the pieces represent anything at all?"

"That is a lie, Master Xian," the Seeker responded, selecting her own pieces from the game case. "They are symbols that the mind may interpret as patterns."

"You don't see them as warriors on a great campaign?" Xian mused. "Or as birds in the air vying for food?"

"No, Master, I do not," Dwynwyn replied, "although sometimes my inner eye assigns values to them as representative of other values. It is considered a fault in most castes, but it is a redeeming quality in Seekers."

"Remind me, then, to associate only with Seekers." Xian chuckled darkly. "May we begin?"

"Well, start it up!" the Dong demanded. His excitement was uncontainable. "I want to see the war!"

"Your Majesty." Mimic nodded as sagely as he could manage. "I will do so at once. All I need is someone to play the most important part of the demonstration."

"You need someone to play?" Dong Mahaj-Megong was puzzled.

"To participate, Your Majesty, to witness firsthand the demonstration, and not just anyone, Your Majesty!" Mimic asserted with conviction. "I need someone of undeniable honesty, bravery, and stature. In short, I need a goblin of such character, such importance, and such power that they could represent one of the Titans themselves."

"That sounds like someone very important!" the Dong considered as thoughtfully as was possible for him.

Mimic nodded. "Yes, indeed, Your Majesty. The more important the better!"

"But no goblin is more important than Dong Mahaj-Megong!" the Dong shouted.

"Why, that is brilliant, Your Majesty!" Mimic sounded in awe of the monarch. "I am flattered that you would volunteer!"

Dong Mahaj-Megong frowned. "I am not sure. I wonder if the Dong is *too* important to be a Titan!"

Mimic leaned forward and spoke under his voice. "You'll get a much closer look at the mechanical goblins if you help."

The Dong leaped off his throne. "Where do you want the most important goblin to stand?"

"Right over here," Mimic said, gesturing toward the mechanisms on the floor, "near the center."

Dwynwyn and Xian both tossed the stones at once, scattering them across the board on the table. They bounced across the field, rebounding from the sides of the game board and off each other. In moments, however, they had settled on the surface, Dwynwyn and Xian both eyeing them from opposite sides of the board.

"That's an odd pattern," Xian observed with a frown. "Is there something wrong with your dice? You wouldn't be trying to cheat *me,* would you?"

Dwynwyn looked startled, then leaned forward, examining her

pieces with a quiet intensity. The pieces, with two or three exceptions, had settled into three groups in a ring pattern. Most of Dwynwyn's own red-colored pieces were in one group on one side of the board, while Xian's black pieces had settled in a second grouping across from him. A third, more chaotic grouping of both red and black had rolled to a stop near the corner on Xian's side.

"This *cannot* happen," Dwynwyn replied in concern. "I have *never* seen such a pattern in a game before!"

Xian reached out across the board. "Well, if it bothers you, we could just toss them again—"

Dwynwyn's hand stopped his.

"No," the Seeker said. "We will play the game as the fates have determined for us. There is a destiny in this that I need to understand."

Xian pulled his hand back. "I'm not even going to pretend to understand what that meant. I thought you said this was just a game?"

"It is, but perhaps you did not lie after all," Dwynwyn said, pointing at the board. She was gazing at the pieces, but her eyes were unfocused, and her voice seemed far away. "Look! Here are three armies, great and powerful, all meeting on the field of battle."

"I'll be the Kyree," Xian said smartly.

"No," Dwynwyn said. "None of these armies are the Kyree . . . or the faeries or any of the Famadorians."

Xian frowned. "I thought you said these pieces didn't represent anything."

Dwynwyn looked puzzled and confused. "They *don't*, Master Xian. I mean they don't *normally* mean anything . . ."

"Well, if they don't mean anything to *you*, then you shouldn't mind that they mean anything to *me*," Xian said. "To me, they will be the Kyree!"

"As you will, Master Xian," Dwynwyn replied, but her mind was racing as her eyes darted about the pieces on the board. She could see them, see them all, in the eye of her mind. It had never before been so vivid, so intense. The board of her game had become a plain surrounded by rolling, grass-covered hills. The pieces she knew only generally, but there were three that were familiar to her. The large black stone was power and flight. A smaller stone nearby was someone she had met; a man in ill-fitting robes.

In front of the black stone grouping, however, and near the center of the board, there was one stone she knew very well. It was the wingless man from her dreams. She could not take her eyes off the piece. It was he who had given her the vision to find the pearls that still hung around Aislynn's neck. Now here he was, about to be destroyed utterly in the battle which would take place on her table.

She realized that she was playing the wrong side. If Dwynwyn won her game, then the wingless man would die, and with him the last hope she had to save her queen and her rule. If she lost, then she would be forced to give up the only power she had over Xian; her guarded truth.

What she needed was a new truth.

"I think it's time we changed the rules!"

Dwynwyn blinked at the thought. New rules?

"Master Xian," Dwynwyn heard herself say, "I believe there is a rule that I have forgotten to tell you about."

Xian looked at her skeptically. "A rule . . . you *forgot?*"

"Yes," Dwynwyn said, not entirely sure where the thought was coming from or what it meant. It was a new and not entirely comfortable sensation.* "It may seem like a small rule, but it is an important one. You see this piece . . . here!"

She pointed at the piece representing her wingless man.

"This is a special piece in the game," she continued, her voice odd in her own ears. "You may, whenever you move it, change its upturned face to any adjacent face."

"Won't that change the strength of the piece?" Xian said. "I thought you said that the abilities were fixed once all the pieces came to rest?"

"For all the other pieces, that is true," Dwynwyn said quickly,

---

* Humans would ascribe her experience to "making it up" in her imagination. Faeries, however, have no imagination. The sensation she is describing would be an uncomfortable one and is conveying knowledge to her through the magic.

"but for this piece on your side you may change its abilities whenever you move it. Use it wisely, however, because if *this* piece is lost to you, then I win the game at once."

"And how do I win?" Xian demanded.

"By getting that one little piece off my side of the board any way you can," Dwynwyn replied. "Do that, and you win."

Xian smiled. "Do *that,* and I get the truth from you at last."

He reached forward and moved his first three pieces toward the center of the board.

He ignored the special piece.

The dragons on the hilltops craned their heads skyward. As one they trumpeted. The sound rolled across the field of battle, cutting through the shouts of the warriors and ringing in their ears. It was the signal to which they had been trained to respond.

"What do we do?" Rhea pleaded. "The battle! It's begun!"

"Their battle, but not ours," Galen responded quickly. "We've got to protect ourselves. Stay out of the battle until we can fight our way out! Maddoc! Get those men around us to crowd in closer! Tell them to hold here with us!"

"But the trumpets!" Maddoc looked at Galen, his face in confusion. "That's the signal to charge! That's how it all begins!"

The great horde around them started to move, a stampede of fury, swords, and death.

"Listen to me!" Galen shouted over the crowd running past them, charging across the plain toward the onrushing armies of the other dragons. The Circle of Brothers turned at the sound of his voice. "We are not going to blindly march to our deaths! We are *not* to charge! Understand?"

"What of the Aboths?" said one of the Circle. "Their dragon-staffs will force us!"

"Stay close to me," Galen said, "and hold your ground!"

The armies of the Elect roared across the plain with a great shout. Whether they were the Elect of Vasska, Panas, or Satinka did not matter; each army charged because that was what they were trained to do. The dust rose from their anxious footsteps, their hearts quickened, and they ran headlong toward the opposing armies. Their eyes shone with zealous invincibility; they all screamed hoarsely the rightness of their cause; and their footfalls thundered across the ground, for their god stood behind them against their evil enemies.

The forces of Vasska managed to reach the Yanisir Stream first, crossing it against the screaming hordes of Panas on their left. The armies crashed into one another like the confluence of two rivers, merging with the sounds of steel and rage, each unit prodded by monks who pressed them forward or released them at the orders of their Dragonkings through the Talkers.

Satinka slowed her own forces until the armies of Panas and Vasska were fully engaged with each other. Satinka hated both of the males vying to sire her brood and would vanquish them both if she might. However, she held a particular hatred for Vasska, for he had taken Mithanlas as his prize when Rhamas fell—a city she considered to be hers by right. So she held back her forces for a time, considering the flow of the battle and how she might best Vasska and humiliate him first.

It was then that her gaze fell upon a small group of warriors behind Vasska's line of attack. This concerned her, for it was not the usual arrangement, and she considered anything out of the ordinary to be a threat. She gave the word, then, to her Dragon-Talker—a Pentach named Evabeth. Evabeth, in turn, gave the orders to her Aboth, and in short order the army of Satinka wheeled to its left. It crossed the Yanisir downstream of the main battle, engaging and pinning the flank of Vasska's force as it fought two armies at once. Then Satinka's warriors turned again and started a frenzied run around the rear of Vasska's line.

Only one thing stood in their way: a small group of thirty-six warriors left standing alone on the plain.

"Aboth!" Edana shouted. "Rein in that right side! We're being flanked!"

Tragget could hear the frustration in her voice. The battle was not going as she or, more importantly, Vasska would like. From atop the hill, they could see that the battle was fully joined at the Yanisir Stream. The Panas forces were scrambling backward with terrible losses, trying to extricate themselves from the bloody banks of the stream. Vasska was making them pay for every step, however, with their own blood. The line was weakened but holding as it advanced. The army of Satinka, however, was still unbloodied. They had delayed their engagement and now were charging around the end of Vasska's forces.

It was then that Tragget saw them; a small group standing alone on the plain behind the lines of battle. They stood at the bottom of his hill, only about a thousand feet ahead of the line of monks controlling the battle. They had not moved forward when prodded by the dragon's eye in the staffs.

Tragget smiled. Of course they did not move. The staffs would have no effect on them, if Galen were with them. If they could stay out of the battle, somehow, they might manage to survive.

Then he saw it. Satinka's army broke around their right flank and, in a fury, charged.

Edana saw it as well. "So your Galen is indeed resourceful! Well, we may lose this battle, but at least I'll have the satisfaction of being rid of *him* and his Circle of Brothers!"

Satinka's army screamed its rage. They raised their swords into the morning sun.

"Galen!" Cephas shouted. "Death coming er is!"

Galen turned to his old friend. "What is it?"

"Cephas feels through er boots!" the dwarf roared. "A thousand steps er is and more!"

Galen cast frantically around the plain. Then he saw it, the billowing dust just over a slight rise in the distance. Satinka's entire army of Elect warriors was bearing down on his circle.

He glanced down. It was faded and soiled nearly beyond recognition, but he still wore his rose-colored doublet. He had wanted to impress his wife so much that day. All he had had to do was get through the Election. Yet this magic had chosen other fates for him. He once had a life, and it was gone. Now the horde would rob him of his breath, and that would be the end of Galen. Did the magic do this to him or was this his fate from the beginning? Perhaps, he thought, the magic was his true self, and that happy life before was the illusion.

He did not choose the magic; the magic chose him. Now he would die for the magic. Perhaps that, too, was what was fated for him all along.

He raised his sword and yelled.

"Berkita!"

45

Tin
Soldiers

A most interesting move, Master Xian," Dwynwyn said casually. She knew that she was playing two games at once, and only one of them involved the pieces on the board. "I wonder that the great leader of the Kyree has time to play a game with a faery at all."

"You wonder too much," Xian grumbled as he looked over the pieces on the board once more.

"It is my calling to wonder," Dwynwyn replied. "We are always in search of truths which have not yet been discovered. You, for example, are a truth which is new to us."

"Are you trying to annoy me?" Xian answered. "We are not some 'new truth' to you . . . unless there is something very wrong with your memory *or* your records."

"Our records are very complete, I assure you."

Xian snorted.

"I have seen the histories myself," Dwynwyn said carefully. "They are shaped into the trees of the tower of Qestardis and are complete all the way back to the founding of the Seven Kingdoms."

"The Seven Kingdoms?" Xian shook his head. "What arrogance! You think there was nothing before your Seven Kingdoms? You faeries are all alike! Self-centered, self-important—you think that nothing existed before you gathered out of your forest hiding places and called yourself a nation!"

"Before the Seven Kingdoms there was only chaos!" Dwynwyn asserted.

"No," Xian answered back, his hand slamming a piece down farther up on the board. "Before the Seven Kingdoms there was a *different* order."

"No. The histories are clear on this. The faeries fled the chaos of the east and established the Seven Kingdoms in the west. This was the beginning of the Age of Light when reason and truth ruled—"

"Reason and truth?" Xian snarled. "Before your precious Seven Kingdoms were a forbidden hope in any faery heart, our empire spanned a continent! We soared over the Cliffs of Kagunos where the gods of Halehi blessed the centaurs of the eastern shore. We slept in the Glades of Magrathoi after we conquered their fortresses on the southern isles. Our armies stood guard over the clouds off the western Aeries on the shores of Dunlar! The glory of our cities filled the crags to the very peaks of Mount Isthalos, our monuments touching the face of the sky itself! We flew over lands ten times the size of all your kingdoms combined. We hunted you for sport, faery. We are not a new truth; we are just an old truth you chose to forget."

He snatched another piece and smacked it down on the game board.

Dwynwyn considered the board. Xian's pieces were vulnerable on the left side. She reached forward tentatively, and then pushed three pieces forward, threatening the left side of Xian's line as she spoke. "Your nation must be great indeed."

"We were great," Xian said roughly, "and we will be again, with your help."

Xian reached his hand toward the wingless man.

"No," Dwynwyn said sharply, cupping her hand over the piece on the board. "You'll get no help from me."

*　　*　　*

His sword extended, Galen stood with Cephas at his right side, his face grim. Rhea and Maddoc were on his left, Rhea's face a mask, while Maddoc's lips were curled in a snarl. Around them the other warriors of the Circle anxiously handled their swords, their fingers playing against the hilts.

This is the reflection of death, Galen thought. This is what we look like when we face our end. He thought about the beautiful winged woman and wondered what she would think of all of this. Was she a goddess of Old Rhamas? After years of worshiping the Dragonkings, would it do any good to call on her now?

Then he felt it; the power welling up inside him. There, in the back of his mind, hovered the winged woman from his mad dreams. Her hair flowing about her, she was submerged, sinking away from him into deep, green waters. Her hand was closed around something; holding it out toward him. Hope and pleading filled her large, beautiful eyes, and he reached for it in his mind.

He knew what she wanted him to do.

"Your swords!" Galen cried urgently. "Present their hilts!"

"What?" Cephas roared. "Mad er is!"

Doubtful faces turned toward him.

"You do remember how I'm supposed to work, don't you?" S'shnickt demanded.

"Hold your weapons with the pommel out!" Galen commanded in a voice filled with resolve. "Do it now! Do it and we'll live!"

He held up S'shnickt with the blade pointing down. The polished black stone in the pommel glinted in the sunlight of the morning sun.

It was joined at once by thirty-five others.

Tragget could not take his eyes from the small group at the bottom of the hill. The deafening rush of Satinka's army rolled like a tide across the undulating landscape of the Enlund Plain, flattening a wide swath through the tall grass in its wake. Her warriors were frenzied in their bloodlust for Vasska's army. Tragget was sure that the small cluster of Galen's so-called Circle could not help but roll under its headlong stampede like a pebble beneath a flash flood.

Still, he could not look away. That might have been him down there, he realized. He could have been down there awaiting his own death, for he was as insane as Galen, and in the eyes of Vasska, he knew, the more culpable. Yet his mother had seen the signs in the dreamsmoke; his destiny was to take the magic forward and save mankind. He would be the father of a new future for humanity, and the price was this man's blood. The heart of the fool would be taken here as the prophecy had foretold. Perhaps this one man's death was the price the magic demanded, he thought, perhaps greatness comes at such a cost.

So Tragget watched as this small group would pay the price for his glory and humanity's future.

There was a glint and a flash among the Circle warriors. A flickering, pale light shone around them, making it difficult for Tragget to see. The light grew brighter and became steady. It was Galen, Tragget knew; one last trick before he died.

Satinka's warriors approaching the Circle pressed forward their weapons and screamed as they charged.

Two dozen warriors of Satinka's frontline troops collided with the Circle . . .

. . . *and vanished.*

"Just stand right here, Your Majesty," Mimic said with contrition. "You'll be the Titan in our demonstration. You'll see everything more clearly from here."

"Wonderful!" the Dong croaked as he waddled in among the small mechanical goblins. "Where ever did you get such an astonishing idea, Mimic?"

"Well, Your Majesty," Mimic responded with a knowing smile, "that *is* why I'm the new Chief Engineer!"

Xian stood up suddenly, his anger flashing into fury. "Who are you to tell me *no?* Who are you to deny me *anything?* You know *nothing* of the world beyond your petty little kingdoms and your petty little intrigues in your petty little courts!"

Dwynwyn stood suddenly in fright, stumbling backward from the fierce onslaught. "What do you mean? What has happened in the world?"

Xian yelled in his fury, the back of his hand sweeping across the table and sending the game and its pieces flying across the room.

"Great kingdoms are *dying* in the world—passing into the cold night of history—and *you want to play games?*"

The board crashed to the stone floor, the pieces tumbling.

Tragget screamed curses to the sky, to himself.

Satinka's army continued its charge, but in the center the rampaging warriors were vanishing as they came in contact with the brightly shining hemisphere of light. The line of the attack surged forward for a few moments on momentum alone, the army being cut neatly in half where Galen's Circle held its ground. Then in a spreading swath, the charge began to falter. Warriors trying to leap around the devastating and terrifying globe ran afoul of the warriors at their sides. Some fell underfoot, trampled, while others knocked into their fellow warriors, sending them all sprawling to the ground. Others attempted to stop or flee backward in midcharge, so that the line of attack bent backward in the center.

Then the hemisphere began to widen slightly, at which point Tragget noticed the noise, and the wind.

The glowing circle was not just absorbing those who came in contact with it, it was drawing bodies into it. A mystic whirlpool, it was pulling warriors into its shining vortex and dragging them out of existence.

Satinka's Aboths on the opposite hill began to understand the enormity of the disaster below them. They struggled to pull their warriors out of the charge and back toward their hill to regroup, but they had already lost control. Parts of Satinka's army were scattering across the battlefield, while others continued their charge in weakened and unsupported pockets. These slammed into the rear of Vasska's troops, causing terrible damage but failing to break through his line. Vasska's troops turned to engage on both sides. The careful lines of battle were disintegrating into chaos all across the battle plain.

Suddenly, a single screech tore over the land. Tragget looked up toward the terrible sound.

It was Satinka. Tragget was not nearly as proficient in dragon-talk as his mother or any of the rest of the Pentach, but the single word Satinka bellowed in her outrage rang clear in his mind.

"Cheater!" the dragon spat at Vasska.

Satinka vaulted into the air, her enormous, sleek body arching over the field. She straightened out, her wings pulling her, it seemed, toward Tragget. Her venomous eyes, however, were locked behind the Inquisitor.

Tragget heard a terrible sound and felt the tumult in the air behind him.

Vasska, standing behind Tragget, was rising into the air to meet Satinka.

The rules of their war had been broken.

For the first time in four centuries, the dragons would do battle themselves.

Then Tragget realized his mother was still in Vasska's pouch.

Mimic stood back from the display on the floor. With the Dong standing at the center, it all looked exactly as Mimic remembered it from his dream. It looked as he had seen it in his mind three days before and as the fiery, hooded creature had given it to him in a vision.

He walked over to Gynik. She was holding his book—the book from the Titan—and looking rather self-conscious about it. Mimic took the book and opened it to the middle. The symbols on the pages had power, he knew, though they were otherwise meaningless to him. He placed his hand on the book and concentrated on its pages for a moment.

Ping! The mechanical goblins chimed.

Zing. Whirrrrr . . .

The little goblins slowly turned on their little legs.

Dong Mahaj-Megong was beside himself with delight. He bounced up and down in the center of the devices, clapping his chubby hands together. "Wonderful! Wonderful! No other kingdom can come close! I'll shame them all with this! They'll all bow down to me!"

Tick. Tick. Tick.

The mechanical goblins raised their bright little swords, their keen edges gleaming in the throne room light. One foot after the other, the devices clanked around the Dong in a circle.

"You see, Your Majesty," Mimic began, "when the—"

Sproing!

One of the strange winged figures bounded into the air. Its wings extended at once to a three-foot length and began flapping smoothly with a whirring sound. It wheeled in the air and turned.

Mimic was dumbstruck. The mechanism was actually flying in a circle around the Dong.

The Dong giggled. "Mimic! You are a *genius!*"

Mimic was confused. The mechanism was not supposed to behave this way. "Your Majesty, it's not supposed to . . . I mean, it wasn't meant to—"

Sproing! Whirrrrr . . .

A second winged monster bounced into the air, unfolded its wings, and soared around the Dong in pursuit of its partner.

"Your Majesty," Mimic shouted, trying to be heard over the noisy mechanisms tromping about the room. "There seems to be something wrong with—"

The Dong was laughing too hard to hear him. "I'll bring every kingdom in the world under my thumb with this!" he bellowed. "There isn't an imp, gnome, gremlin, or goblin that won't sell their masters out in a snap to be a part of this!"

The third creature leaped up into flight.

Mimic took his hand off the book. He tried to concentrate on stopping the mechanisms as he had stopped the Device before, but the power had taken on a will of its own. It had heard Mimic's inner voice, known his inner desires, and moved to comply.

The flying monsters wheeled as one to attack each other. . . .

With the Dong standing between them.

The razor-sharp talons tore at the other creatures, but the Dong was in the way; they ripped gashes in his face. The serrated teeth in their little mouths snapped at one another, but the Dong was in the way; they gouged chunks out of his flesh.

"Stop, Mimic!" the Dong shouted. "I see the point of your demonstration—how the Titans fell! You can stop it now! Stop it!"

Mimic panicked. He waded in among the mechanisms, frantically trying to bat the flying creatures away. Then he looked down.

The metal goblins had turned and were converging on the Dong.

Queen Sihir tore the air with a shrill scream.

Mimic kicked at them, knocking several of them to the floor. They righted themselves almost at once and turned once more toward the Dong, their little swords pressed forward for the attack.

The mechanical goblins sprang as one, burying the Dong under an avalanche of whirring gears, rods, and springs. Mimic frantically pulled at them, trying to pry them loose. He was still tugging at the metal goblins when they all fell over into a heap on the floor. Mimic fell with them, ending up lying on top of them.

Only the Dong's crown rolled free, spinning circles on the stone floor until it came to a noisy stop.

Tick. Tick. Click! BZZZzzz . . .

The entire pile stopped.

Looking down past his gleaming mechanical warriors, Mimic saw the dark stain slowly seeping from under the heap of mechanisms.

Gynik saw it, too. She looked from the deadly gleaming pile of metal, to the empty throne, and then to Mimic. Then she turned and, in quick steps, mounted the dais of the king.

"Sihir," Gynik sneered, looking down on the horrified current queen. "I sincerely hope you stole liberally from the kingdom while you could, for I believe your position has just been terminated."

Sihir glared at Gynik for the last time, then she leaped from the throne and fled the room.

Gynik descended the dais and stepped quickly over to where the

Dong's crown had come to rest. She snatched it up off the ground. She then turned, stepped over the pool of blood, and stood next to the mechanical pile.

"May I present my *husband*"—Gynik's voice dared anyone in the throne room to contradict her—"the Dong of our new kingdom, a kingdom whose name shall be determined at a later date! Dong Mimic! King of the Goblins!"

With that, she placed the crown on Mimic's head where he still lay shaking with his hands closed over a pair of bloodstained mechanical goblins.

Small Sacrifices

D wynwyn hastily stepped backward, her wings pressed suddenly to the closed door.

Xian threw the table over in his rage, his own wings quaking behind him. In two powerful strides, the Kyree master reached the Seeker, his large, rough hand grasping her by the throat. "You want to know why I have time to play games with you, you little bug? Because I've already *won!* You faeries are all so unfailingly *predictable!* Lord Phaeon made the same mistake—he lumped the Kyree in with all the other unwashed masses you call Famadorians. He thought we were all alike; as though some horse-assed centaur were even *remotely* akin to the Lords of the Sky! He came to us. He was arrogance and superiority and we nodded like the polite little Famadorians he wanted, all the while knowing that it was *him* who needed *us.*"

"Please! Stop!" Dwynwyn cried. "You're hurting me."

"Oh, am I?" Xian seethed, his words dripping vicious sarcasm. "Am I hurting you, little bug? Why would I want to do that? You're just one little bug, just like the one little bug that came to our land some years ago. He was a Seeker, too, if one believes the frantic few reports we got near the end; a little Seeker bug just like you. He had powers, too, that one." Xian's words suddenly turned dark and threatening. "And now they're gone, all gone! The glory of a thousand years fallen with such speed that all there was left to us was to flee before its terrible darkness!"

A single tear coursed down Dwynwyn's cheek.

Xian tightened his grip. "Now I'm done playing faery games! You'll give me the answers I want or I will tear your wings off with my bare hands! Before I am finished with you, you will beg for your own death! So, who are you? Who is your friend? Why were you traveling here under guard?"

Dwynwyn trembled under his coarse touch. She looked at Aislynn, and kept her silence.

"You like 'new truths,' don't you? Well, I'll tell you something you may not have known," Xian said, his free hand reaching up and seizing the top of her wing. "If you grasp a faery by the upper wing vein just about two feet above the back sockets, you can snap it with a single hand. It makes a particularly chilling sound, too, like a bundle of straw breaking. It isn't a particularly fatal break, but it *is*—and I was told this by those who *know*—an excruciatingly painful one that may not heal completely."

Dwynwyn cried out as Xian bent the brittle vein.

"One of us is about to learn something," Xian sneered.

A voice spoke suddenly behind him.

"Aislynn," she said, standing now. "I am Aislynn, daughter of Tatyana, Queen of Qestardis."

Xian turned in surprise. "Princess Aislynn? Lord Phaeon's Aislynn?"

"That is only Lord Phaeon's assertion," Aislynn replied quietly.

Xian chuckled. "Lord Phaeon's troops are marching on Qestardis as we speak. He is expecting a wedding when he gets there, though he'll find that difficult since I am holding his bride prisoner!"

"Please," Aislynn said, bowing her head submissively. "You have your answer, now let Dwynwyn free."

Xian considered for a moment, then shook his head slowly. "Not just yet. We have so many more things to talk about now. So many more possibilities! Still, I feel the need for more conversational sur-roundings. *Guard!*"

The metal latch rasped against the door.

"It's time to say good-bye," Xian whispered into Dwynwyn's ear. Then, with a growl in his throat, he pulled her away from the door and opened it.

"No, please," Dwynwyn begged. "I've got to stay with her! Please!"

His hand was still on Dwynwyn's throat as he dragged her from the room. In her frantic flailing, Dwynwyn's foot kicked at the bro-ken game board, sending the pieces skittering across the floor.

"It's time to leave!" Galen shouted. "Which way do we go?"

Rhea was still intently holding the hilt of her sword forward. They stood in a circle of calm surrounded by the storms of war. The battle continued to rage all around them, but at a distance. An occa-sional combatant drew too near their magic and was whisked into nothingness. "We're hundreds of miles from anywhere, Galen! *Any-where* is better than here!"

"South!" Cephas yelled. "We go south!"

"South?" Maddoc bellowed. "There's nothing to the south!"

Cephas spat on the ground. "Forsaken Mountains er is! Desola-tion er is! Forest and food; caves and hiding er is!"

Galen nodded. "South it is! We charge the Aboth line."

Maddoc yelled back. "What happens to this spell if we move?"

"It will fail—but the Aboths won't know that!" Galen called back. "Stay together, cut through the line, and keep running! Don't stop until we get to cover! Everyone understand?"

The grim-faced warriors of the Circle nodded.

"Now!" Galen shouted, twisting the sword in his hand as he turned.

A chill went through him.

To the south was the hill he had seen in the dream, the hill where he had seen Rhea dead. At its crest, beyond the line of Aboths, stood the lone, robed figure of Tragget.

The Warriors of the Circle were already starting their charge. It was too late to change their plan.

Galen raised his sword and charged with them.

Edana screamed into Vasska's ear, desperately trying to get the dragon to hear her words. *"Stop! Defend! Omen ill Dragonking war blood! Perch and guard!"*

Vasska answered her back with anger and suspicion. *"Edana vision clouding! Mad-kings live below! Unforeseen the vision-smoke their coming is! Mad-kings must die!"*

They careened through the sky. Vasska twisted in quick, jerky motions as he tried to position himself against Satinka. The two dragons were nearly at an even altitude, with Panas well below them both, desperately scooping at the air with his great wings and trying to join the fight.

Edana held with a death-grip to the straps of the pouch. She slammed over on her right side as Vasska spun suddenly before pulling up in a tight turn toward Satinka, his talons extended. They thundered past one another, barely missing a collision. For a moment, Edana caught a glimpse of Satinka's pouch. It was empty. Edana wondered for a moment if Pir Oskaj had managed to get out before Satinka vaulted into the sky, but she doubted it. Everything had happened so quickly; Oskaj could not have had time. It meant that Satinka was in a blind rage and without a Dragon-Talker to calm her down.

Vasska flipped over twice, spinning Edana wildly in the pouch, then reversed himself, wheeling hard to the left. As they turned, Edana caught sight of the battlefield below.

Amid the chaos, she caught sight of them—a small band moving up the hillside toward the south.

Suddenly she crashed forward. Satinka and Vasska were tumbling through the air, locked in a clawing mass. Their wings beat frantically at the air, and their clawed feet tore at each other's scales. Vasska breathed a plume of flame as he spun out of the sky toward the ground below. Edana felt the bloom of the heat on her face.

Vasska pitched suddenly upward, throwing her back into the bottom of the pouch, snapping one of the straps. Edana had a quick look at the Enlund Plain rushing up at her before everything blurred, replaced by the morning clouds. She frantically grabbed another strap and wrapped it around her free wrist, then pulled herself up once more to the forward ridge of the pouch.

Panas had fallen on Satinka from behind. Now they were careening through the sky against each other, affording Vasska a moment to pull away and maneuver to a better position.

Edana knew it was her only chance.

"Vasska true! The mad-kings must die! Vasska sight below southward running! The mad-kings! The mad-kings must die!"

Vasska paused a moment, then turned and dove down toward the small band of warriors charging up the southern hill.

Aislynn watched the door for what seemed to be a very long time. She did not know the fate of her old friend but guessed that her death was most probable. But she did not know it as a fact and so sat for long minutes waiting for her friend Dwynwyn to return to her, and waiting, she also knew, in vain.

She was alone.

"I'll take care of you," Deython had said. Yet he would never take care of her again. An eternity of moments and heartbeats would never change that terrible truth.

Now Dwynwyn was gone. Dwynwyn who would have given her life to protect her as well, who now most likely *had* given her life, and what had it accomplished? Aislynn would be bartered to Lord Phaeon by this horrible Xian creature, and she would still be forced into a marriage of political expedience. Deython was dead, Dwynwyn would be dead, and she might as well be dead, too.

Aislynn settled onto the window seat, pressing her head against the bars that kept her from the free sky beyond. She gazed sadly down the side of the ancient tower to the crashing surf below. The sea was full of the dead, she thought. Why could it not swallow her as well?

She moved to rest her chin on her open palm, and her fingers brushed the necklace of jet black pearls. She ran her fingers along their smooth, cool surface, then unclasped the chain and held them in her hand.

A gift from Dwynwyn, she remembered, holding the strand of pearls in her hand. They were supposed to protect me, she thought as she grasped them tightly.

The strand broke in her hand. The pearls spilled into her palm.

A tear coursed down Aislynn's cheek. Everyone she had ever cared for had sought to protect her. Each of them, in their turn, had failed.

She looked back through the barred window. She missed her mother. She missed Dwynwyn. She missed and ached for Deython.

They had taken everything from her but these. At least these few things she could choose for herself. Perhaps, wherever Deython now was, he could put them to better use than she did.

Her head pressed once more against the chill bars, Aislynn held a pearl out the window and released it. She watched it fall down the length of the tower and vanish into the surf so far below. She shed a tear for each one . . . until there were none left.

The
Warriors

The Aboths lifted up their dragonstaffs each with its Eye of Vasska facing toward the small cadre of warriors rushing up the hill toward them. Galen smiled; he had already called the mystical globe that negated the power of the Eye from the recesses of his memory. He screamed as he ran, his sword swinging before him in the rising sun, his brothers and sisters of the Circle charging with him, their own voices rising in an unholy chorus next to his.

The line of Aboths disintegrated in the face of their charge. Knowing their dragonstaffs were useless against Galen's magic, the Aboths, who were used to herding the Elect like cattle, were left powerless and vulnerable. They sensed that flight was better than death, and scattered before the charging group like surprised birds taking flight.

The slope increased slightly, but in their enthusiasm the warriors' speed was undiminished. Onward they rushed, their cries still in their throats, for over the hill lay hope. Over the hill was freedom. Over the hill was their destiny.

Galen came over the rise first, knowing who awaited them there. "Tragget! Tragget, where are you?"

A searing bolt of flame slammed into him, burning through his doublet at the shoulder. He gasped in pain. The stench of his burning flesh filled his nostrils. The power of the blow stopped his momentum, and he staggered backward.

"Stop! Stand where you are!" Tragget yelled. His hands were raised, his fingers cupped slightly over the palms that faced toward Galen. There was a red glow gathering in them, spinning flame curling back in on itself. The Inquisitor was forty feet away, just down from the ridgeline, waiting for them.

Galen held his hand up behind him as a sign for his companions to stop. Maddoc and Rhea halted their momentum and managed to hold Cephas back from continuing headlong forward. The rest of the Circle slowed to a stop as well, their blades raised as they watched warily.

"I haven't seen that one before." Galen winced as he held his damaged shoulder. "Learn something new?"

"I'll teach you worse if you come any closer!"

Galen spread his hands wide and low, his palms down. "It doesn't have to end this way, Tragget."

"Yes it does!" the Inquisitor answered back, his voice high and strained. "It cannot end any other way for us, Galen! This is where it must end. This is where it is *supposed* to end!"

"No!" Galen insisted, stepping carefully forward, his hands still facing down. "There is a tomorrow, Tragget. You can come with us! We can find a way to master this mystic power. We can do it together; you and I."

Galen took another step toward the Inquisitor.

Tragget blinked, licking his lips. "But the prophecy . . ."

"I don't know about any prophecy," Galen replied evenly, his gaze fixed on Tragget's eyes. "All I know is that this is the life fate has dealt us. Maybe it's a curse, or maybe it's a gift—I don't know. But I know that it is as much a part of us as the sky, the sun, and the earth. We can no more deny it than we can deny breathing. I don't know why or what ends these things portend. Perhaps mortal eyes aren't meant to see so far. But we'll find our way, Tragget, I promise you! We'll forge our own fate!"

Tragget lowered his arms slightly. His breathing was fast and shallow.

Galen took another step. Slowly he extended his right hand. "We are brothers, you and I. We are all of us brothers."

Tragget looked down at the offered hand.

A shadow passed over them, blocking out the sun.

"Galen!" Rhea screamed.

Galen looked up. Vasska had returned, his wings blotting out the sky. The wind beneath them kicked plumes of dust up into Galen's eyes; its force threatened to blow him off of his feet. Involuntarily, he started backing away from the maelstrom of dirt, dried grasses, and wind. The Dragonking hovered in the air—an incredible feat of strength—as he rotated around to face Galen and his companions. Then, with a booming thud that shook the earth under their feet, Vasska landed on the hilltop, his forelegs straddling an astonished Tragget.

Vasska trumpeted his outrage. His yellow eyes narrowed in their deep sockets.

The Circle quickly rushed to Galen's side. He felt them come near, even as he kept his eyes on the cold stare of the dragon. He knew they looked to him for direction, for it was his magic that had saved them from the battle. They would expect his magic to save them now.

"Galen?" There was both awe and fear in Rhea's voice. "Maddoc? What do we do?"

Galen looked within himself, and found nothing. He ill understood the strange ways of his power, felt all too keenly the blundering blindness of his attempts. It was powerful—more powerful than he had ever imagined—but it was raw and uncontrolled. It all depended upon a connection that was tenuous and ephemeral.

The connection was not within him.

The winged woman was gone from his mind.

The magic was not there.

Galen saw a figure rise up just behind the dragon's head. It was

High Priestess Edana, and she was speaking to the dragon, though Galen could not hear her words, nor, he suspected, would they have made any sense to him anyway.

Her meaning, however, was clear enough.

Vasska reared back, his chest expanding with a terrific inhalation of air. His wings extended, his talons flexing as he prepared a great, flaming breath.

A shadow passed over him. Distracted, the dragon looked up, but too late.

Satinka dove down on her enemy from behind, her powerful rear talons catching Vasska's outstretched right wing. A wet ripping sound filled the air as her claws raked through the membrane of the wing until they caught on the upper leading tendons. The speed of Satinka's flight matched her bitterness; Vasska lurched upward from the force of the blow, which lifted him completely over the astonished Tragget. He flailed against Satinka, tearing himself loose from her grip and tumbling forward. The dragon's jaw slammed against the ground, the grasses erupting before the great inferno of breath gushing from his mouth.

The attack had cost Satinka her speed in the air. All four of her legs caught the ground rushing up to her, sending a second shudder through the rock of the hilltop. She turned at once, her cold eyes fixed on Vasska. Galen could see that one of her wings hung lower than the other and moved awkwardly; it must have been damaged in the attack. Her head was low and her spiked tail was raised. Her voice shook in her wrath.

Galen looked quickly back to Vasska. The Dragonking dragged his forelegs out from under him and crouched, preparing to spring. His right wing was bleeding black ichor from the gaping hole Satinka had torn through it.

The dragons were earthbound. They would continue their battle and finish their differences here, on this hilltop.

And Galen and his companions stood squarely between them.

Galen grimaced. "Where's an army when you need one!"

"Well, you just made one disappear!" Rhea responded grimly.

"Yes, and now I wish I knew where it went!"

★   ★   ★

Dwynwyn stood between her Kyree guards, their rough hands holding her arms so tight that her fingertips were going numb. She gazed
sadly at the floor of the rotunda. She had never grasped the tenuous
new truth that she had sought. She was the cause of Aislynn's being
discovered by these monsters. She had made sure that her queen
would be forced to abdicate her throne and upset the delicate balance
that existed between the Seven Kingdoms. She had failed them all.

"This is your lucky day," Xian said simply.

Dwynwyn could not bring herself to look up.

Xian bent his head a little lower, trying to look into her eyes.
"After some more thoughtful consideration, I am setting you free."

Dwynwyn looked up in disgust at his vile humor.

"Oh, no, I assure you, I am quite sincere." Xian looked away as
he spoke. "The truth is that I need your services as a messenger. I
need *you* to tell Lord Phaeon that I am holding his bride safely for
him, and that I would be delighted to ensure her safe passage to . . .
What *do* you call that city of yours again?"

"Qestardis," Dwynwyn said quietly.

"Yes, this Qestardis," Xian continued, "as soon as Lord Phaeon
properly demonstrates to us his generous gratitude for this favor."

Dwynwyn glared at Xian. "And just *how* would you like Lord
Phaeon to express his . . . 'generous gratitude'?"

The Kyree master looked down at the table before him. A large
tapestry map of Sine'shai lay across its surface. "In addition to ceding
all the lands east of these Cendral Hills, I think it would be most appropriate for him to grant us the lands of the Suthwood."

"He will not do it," Dwynwyn stated flatly.

"I think he *will* do it," Xian said, looking up. "His alternative is to
lose his only chance at fathering an heir to the Qestardan throne,
fragmenting his hold on Qestardis and having to fight me for the land
anyway."

"How can you be sure—"

"—That you'll deliver my message?" Xian finished for her. "Because you are a faery you will tell the truth, and because it is a message you *want* to deliver. Your famed faery silence will only purchase

your mistress's death. You'll deliver the message because it is in your best interests to . . . What is that noise?"

A distant cry had drifted into the rotunda from beyond the great doors. Now another cry sounded, followed at once by more noises and the clatter of armor and weapons.

"By the Gods of Isthalos," Xian swore, moving quickly around Dwynwyn and her guards. "What now?"

He had not taken three steps before the doors to the hall burst open.

"To arms!" Sargo cried. *"To arms!"*

The Kyree in the rotunda fluttered instinctively into the dome, drawing their weapons noisily.

Xian laid his hand on the hilt of his own sword. "Sargo! Report!"

"An army, Master Xian!" Sargo was having trouble catching his breath, whether from exertion or excitement, Dwynwyn could not tell. "Faeries, but different. They are all shadows and gray, Master, and terrible in their aspect. They are at the walls even now!"

"How is that? Why were we not warned of their approach?" Xian shouted angrily. "I ordered watches posted over all the lands north and west!"

"They are not coming from the land, Master," Sargo said, his eyes wide. "They are marching *out of the sea!*"

Galen turned to the others. "Get out of here, all of you!"

"Where can we go?" Rhea wailed.

Vasska bounded in their direction.

"Watch out!" Galen yelled.

The front left claw shattered the ground underneath them. The group scattered frantically out of the way, leaping in any direction that might afford some safety. Satinka circled around, closing in as well. Galen found himself in a forest of gigantic scale-shrouded dragon legs that were pounding the earth around him. Between the dust they raised and the smoke from the grass fires, his vision was obscured and he lost track of his companions. He tried to break for the east ridge of the hill, only to face the raking curve of a dragon's tail. He tried south, then west, but the thunderous stomping of the dragons' legs made his gait unsteady as the earth itself rebounded from their footfalls.

He lost his footing and dropped to the ground on his back. He looked up past the shoulder that hung twenty feet above his head and saw the empty pouch just behind the spiked ridge of the dragon's crest. It was Satinka. She turned her gaze at once on Galen, her lips curling back.

He struggled to get his feet under him, as Satinka raised her foreleg, her talons quickly flexing over him, then plunging downward.

Suddenly, Galen was struck from the side, bowled out of harm's way. Dazed, he turned looking for a place to run . . .

Rhea lay facedown nearby, one of Satinka's talons thrust down through her side, pinning her to the ground.

"*No!*" Galen screamed.

The dragon turned her malevolent gaze toward him once more.

Bolts of blue fire suddenly exploded against Satinka's jaw. She turned toward them in rage.

"Get away from her, you damn bitch!" Maddoc yelled, as blue flame burned about the blade of his sword. "Your time is done, you just don't know it yet! This is where it starts! This is where it ends!"

Satinka leaped up into the air, drawing her sharp, bloody talon out of Rhea's side. She screeched at Maddoc, outraged at the insult of this magic fire, then dropped back to earth on the other side of him, her head recoiling and her fangs bare.

Galen stumbled quickly back to where Rhea lay, falling next to her. She was still alive, her arms struggling to lift herself up, but she managed only to turn over on her back. She seemed unable to move her legs.

Galen took her head in his hands, trying to support it. Tears flowed down his cheeks. "Oh, Rhea! Why did you do it? Why?"

She looked up into his eyes, a thin trickle of blood running from the corner of her mouth as she smiled. "Dahlia," she said carefully. "Promise me you'll find her. Promise me you'll tell her about us . . ."

"Quiet! Just rest here and we'll . . . we'll figure something out!" Galen pleaded as he gently set her head back into the grass.

"My daughter! You've got to take care of our daughter!" Rhea moaned, clutching at Galen.

"Yes! Of course." He glanced frantically around for help.

Maddoc was raising his sword, facing down Satinka.

"Maddoc! Come here!" Galen yelled. He drew his own sword, searching within himself for the magic to save his friend. It had failed him before, but he had to try again. He found it. The mystery was there; it was only an elusive and feeble light somewhere within, but it was there just the same. "Maddoc, come to me! We'll face it together!"

"*Dragon-slaying?*" S'schickt said with pride. "*You* are *ambitious, Galen!*"

Galen fumbled with his sword, then presented the hilt. He could see that other place in the back of his mind where the magic came from. The winged woman was there once more . . . a shadow and vague but there nevertheless. He pictured the ironwork he had made for her protection. She was offering it back to him in return for something.

"Maddoc!" Galen yelled frantically. "Come quickly! Rhea needs you!"

Galen saw Maddoc turn. The scholar's gaze fixed on his wife lying on the ground. He started to run toward Galen.

Two front claws suddenly straddled Galen. Vasska! Galen looked up past the twenty-foot-high massive shoulders of the beast. High Priestess Edana, still holding fast in the pouch, was yelling to Vasska just behind his head. She looked down at Galen below, every line of her face conveying hatred as she held to the single remaining strap.

Galen turned back to Maddoc. The scholar ran madly toward them. "Rhea! My beloved! I am coming!"

Satinka lowered her head behind him, her maw gaping open!

Galen opened his mouth to yell, but there was no time.

The conflagration boiled out over Satinka's jaws, rushing with hurricane force toward them. It enveloped Maddoc in moments, engulfing him completely in a deadly inferno.

Galen clutched at the hilt of his sword, tears of rage flowing down his face. The magic reacted as he felt it would, the great sphere forming a shield around him.

The furnace fires of Satinka blasted into the mystic sphere . . . and emerged again bent at an angle sharply upward.

Vasska was prepared for Satinka's blast. He had lifted his well-plated chest to protect himself against her breath. The deflected fires, however, were unexpected. They towered up past his shoulder, burning at his wing sockets and curling down his tender back. They would not do much damage, but they startled him.

Edana, too, was caught unprepared. The flames roared about her, burning her hand. She cried out in pain, loosening her grip.

Vasska lurched upward at just that moment.

Edana tumbled down the shoulder of the dragon, its horned ridges slowing her descent. She plunged toward the sustained flames of Satinka's fiery breath, catching a glimpse of Galen below her, kneeling safely within his protected space. She fell toward it, hoping for a moment that it might offer her some refuge as well.

She fell against the sphere . . .

. . . *and it reflected her back outward!*

Edana rolled behind the hind legs of Vasska, embroiled in the flames. She dragged herself behind his hind claw by her arms, desperate to escape the agony of the blistering phosphorous fires raging around her, searing her flesh.

There Edana stopped, ablaze in the fires of the Dragonkings.

Enmity's Fool

They walked out of the sea.

First came eighteen tall faery warriors unlike any truth known to the Seven Lords. They were smoke gray with turquoise-tinged foam running through their skin, and their gray wings were mottled in black. Their eyes gleamed like black pearls. Each of them wore gray armor and held a long curving blade in their powerful hands. They were slightly taller and a good deal wider than most faeries, their arm, wing, and leg muscles bulging with strength. Stepping from the rocks at the base of the tower at Kien Werren, the white foam of the waves breaking around them, they stretched open their wings, then flew as one up the face of the cliff behind the tower. They then broke into two groups of nine to either side of the tower, landed atop the cliffs, and turned to face the sea. With their arms raised above them, they called in deep voices out over the waters.

With the breaking of the next wave against the base of the cliff, their call was answered. Another rank of their brothers emerged from the sea. These were lesser creatures: a lighter gray with gray eyes, and sized as other faeries. Their features were each unique, for they were patterned after faeries who had once been taken by the sea. Some were sailors and some were merchants, and many of them had been lost not so long ago. Their bodies had been cast from these same battlements but days before.

Each successive wave crashed against the shore and brought with it another rank of the gray warriors.

The sea was giving back its faery dead.

Xian drew his sword as the shadow faeries stormed the rotunda. He barked his orders to the Kyree in the hall. "Form up! Keep them at the door and we'll take them as they come!"

The Kyree's wings rumbled in the air as they tried to form a pocket around the doors into the rotunda. If they could contain the onslaught—confine it to a single narrow entrance—Xian knew they had a good chance of holding here until they could either beat back the assault or just bleed them through attrition.

The large gray warriors led the charge, and Xian was startled at the sight of their shining black eyes. What I could *do* with such warriors! he thought as his wings beat against the air furiously. He raised his sword as the first of them rushed toward him.

Their swords met with a tremendous ringing. The gray warrior's blow was so strong that it pushed Xian backward in the air. Xian pressed back, however, raining a quick series of blows against his opponent. The gray warrior met each with quick defense. Xian gained a little headway, pressing his foe backward slightly, but was frustrated in his attempts to land *any* blow, let alone a telling one.

The Kyree master dodged a sudden lunge, spinning in midair. He reversed and swung his blade in a sideways arc toward the gray warrior's exposed neck with all the strength he could muster.

The blade passed cleanly through, severing the gray warrior's head. It fell to the ground below, rolling to a stop near the feet of Dwynwyn and the astonished guards who still held her there.

Xian smiled as he looked on the body that still hovered before him. The cut was flecked with turquoise foam. It was his first clean kill of the day.

The headless warrior surprised him. It dodged once in the air, and then swung again.

Xian barely managed to block the blow. The decapitated warrior pressed the attack forward with renewed fury, and Xian was forced once more to give ground. He suddenly backed against one of his own warriors just as his opponent—still stubbornly alive—feinted to the right and then slashed to his left.

Xian did not feel the blow itself but instantly experienced its effects. The wingtip on his left side was severed, causing him to fall suddenly into a spin. He flapped frantically, barely managing to right himself before he smashed into the floor of the rotunda.

The headless guard settled down on the floor nearby.

Xian scrambled to his feet, backing away from the gray horror that stalked him. In doing so, he passed Dwynwyn and her guards. The guards, finally coming to their senses, drew their weapons, releasing the Seeker to her own fate. They closed ranks before their commander, backing up with him.

The headless warrior stalked them as far as Dwynwyn, then paused. It reached down with its free hand, snatched its head from the ground, and placed it once more on its shoulders. Bluish foam seemed to ripple around the wound as it healed.

"By the Gods!" Xian exclaimed, his eyes wide.

The gray warrior turned its eyes once more on Xian and strode forward. The first of Xian's guards swung but the warrior arrested the blow with its free hand. Xian heard the guard's wrist snap as the warrior casually tossed the smaller Kyree aside. A second guard lunged with his blade, but the warrior blocked the blow and countered with his own thrust. Xian saw the blood on the blade as it emerged from the guard's back.

"Yield, Xian!"

It was Dwynwyn's voice.

Xian backed against the heavy table, causing the parchment maps to spill to the floor. The gray warrior reached forward for Xian's throat, its weapon arm pulling the sword blade back for a final, telling blow.

"I said yield!" Dwynwyn yelled.

Xian bent backward over the table. The gray warrior held him with an iron grip.

"I yield!" Xian shouted.

The gray warrior froze with his blade at Xian's throat.

"Stand down!" Xian called into the room. "We yield!"

A silence descended on the rotunda. Only Dwynwyn's footsteps cut through the sudden quiet in the vast room.

Xian glanced over at Dwynwyn as she approached. The gray warrior still held him awkwardly over the table.

"I see you have found a new truth, Seeker!" Xian exclaimed.

"Yes," Dwynwyn answered, "as you are about to find a new truth, Master Xian."

Xian struggled uncomfortably under the gray warrior's iron grip. It continued to stare at him from its shining black eyes. "I don't suppose you would care to enlighten me, would you? I would be delighted to hear it!"

"I would be delighted to tell you," Dwynwyn said evenly. "Lord Phaeon will *not* be taking Qestardis, either by force of arms or by marriage. It appears that Queen Tatyana will have a larger force at arms than Lord Phaeon had previously supposed."

Xian nodded as best he could. "You're saying that I have bet on the wrong unicorn."

Dwynwyn puzzled over the phrase for a moment. "I'm sure I don't know what you mean."

"It means that I would very much appreciate the opportunity to extend my heartfelt apologies to your queen for any misunderstanding that may have existed between us," Xian said quickly. "And offer to withdraw from her lands under terms of a truce."

"And?" Dwynwyn prompted.

"And . . . and as a token of my good faith, I will release you . . ."

"And the princess . . ." Dwynwyn coaxed.

"*And* the princess Aislynn at once."

"Yes." Dwynwyn smiled. "I see that you *have* found a new truth."

Vasska lunged toward Satinka, but the female dragon managed to pull herself into the air. Vasska was not about to let her go so easily. He, too, pressed himself into the air in pursuit, his torn wing shivering with the effort.

Tragget observed none of this. He had seen Edana tumble from Vasska's pouch and had watched in horror as the flames enveloped her. He ran across the scarred hilltop, screaming her name into the smoking, charred grasses.

He reached the mystic sphere.

Galen still knelt there, gripping his sword with the hilt turned upward and his eyes tightly shut.

There was something else there, too. He did not recognize it at first, it was so deformed. The hair was gone from its head, its legs were shriveled, and what remained of its clothing still smoldered. Yet as he gazed at it, the form resolved itself in his mind into an image that would haunt him forever.

Tragget fell to his knees next to his mother.

She had been everything to him . . . his entire world before the magic had tempted him away from her. She was his life. She was his center. She sustained him.

She was his heart!

A guttural scream of agony rose in Tragget's throat. It was punctuated with a wrenching sob and words that were barely coherent, but some of them Galen understood.

"Mother! Oh, Mother . . . no!"

She moved.

Tragget did not know which was more horrifying, that he had thought her dead, or that she still lived in this condition. Her head twisted slowly toward him, her blistered, distorted lips parting as she spoke in slow, rasping tones. "Tragget . . . my son! Is it you?"

The mystic sphere shattered, its pieces vanishing. In that moment, the bent remains of Edana straightened on the ground. Galen stared in disbelief for a few moments, the horror of what had happened to them overwhelming him. "Oh, Tragget! There was nothing I could do . . . nothing any of us could do."

Tragget looked up at Galen. *He has taken on more than he knows,* he thought. *The magic is bigger than he is . . . stronger than he is . . .*

"See? The figure wears robes that are too large for him."

Tragget choked back a sob, then laughed sadly. "Am *I* the fool?"

Galen shook his head quizzically, not comprehending what Tragget was asking. "No, Tragget . . . you're no fool!"

Tragget was looking at Galen, but his mind saw only the visions of the dragonsmoke. *It reached out with its hand, plunging it into the chest of the fool, tearing out the fool's heart.*

Tragget gazed down at his mother. She had looked at the dreamsmoke with a mother's eyes. She had seen two men. She had seen the man Galen would be and had mistaken him for the man she wanted her son to be.

"We don't have much time. Please, come with us," Galen said, offering his hand once more. "We'll figure out what to do next. We'll find a life for us both."

"Tragget!" his mother croaked.

Tragget looked down at her. He reached out with his hand for her reddened, peeling hand, not daring to touch it. He could not look at her as he spoke. "I'm here, Mother."

"Help me. Don't leave me!"

Tragget's gaze cast about the broken hilltop. Rhea Myyrdin lay dead at Galen's feet, her arm stretched out over her head as she reached for the blackened corpse of her beloved husband. Beyond them, the rest of Galen's Circle awaited him. The dwarf looked anxious to leave.

Farther still, down the hill, the battle that had begun so long ago continued. Panas had already begun to feed on the carnage. Satinka and Vasska continued to threaten each other but were not willing to allow Panas all the spoils of the war. They, too, had begun feeding on their own armies, and no longer felt obliged to eat only the dead.

He had hoped to stop it. He had hoped to put an end to the senseless war with its senseless deaths. He had hoped to end the tyranny of the Dragonkings. He had seen it in the dragonsmoke . . . a great and noble destiny.

"Come with us," Galen pleaded. "There's nothing more you can do for her."

Nothing more I can do? The Inquisitor looked up into Galen's face. The head or the heart? He was the fool . . . and now the horror would go on.

"No!" Tragget jumped up with a cry, his hands cupped in front of him. Orange bolts of searing flame leaped from his hands. They smashed into Galen, exploding against his chest and lifting him off the ground.

Galen tumbled backward through the air, falling chest-first into the ground. Tragget marched purposefully toward him, the deadly bolts forming quickly and roaring through the air into his opponent.

"It is *my* destiny, Galen," Tragget raged through eyes blurred with tears. "You cannot have it . . . you cannot take it from us! Your magic and dreams and powers . . . what has it gotten me? Where has it led me? *You* did this to me . . . to *her!*"

The bolts were not finding their mark, but still Tragget pressed forward, his voice edged with violence. "I've got your wife! I've got your dreams! I'll take it all . . . for everything you've taken from me!"

Something was in his way. Tragget blinked to clear his vision, and only then saw them.

The Circle. They had rushed forward, gathering between Tragget and Galen. Each of them presented their sword hilt first . . . and Tragget's bolts could no longer reach the object of his hatred.

Galen stood up among them. His gaze locked with Tragget's pain-filled eyes.

"I am not your fool, Galen! I *will* fulfill my destiny, and not you nor any of your clan will survive to stop me."

Tragget turned and strode back to where his mother lay. Removing his robe, he wrapped it as carefully around her as he could and picked up what remained of her pain-racked body. She screamed once in his arms and then fell gratefully silent.

"I will hunt you, Galen," Tragget shouted.

"South," said the dwarf. "While still we can!"

The Circle moved off warily down the slope. When they deemed themselves safe enough, they turned and ran toward the wild lands to the south.

Tragget continued to yell after them from the hilltop.

"It is *my* destiny, not yours! Mine! . . . *And I will hunt you until the end of time!*"

Destiny

Dwynwyn stood on the walls of Kien Werren. Aislynn was at her side with her face buried in Dwynwyn's shoulder.

Below them on the plain stood their army of shadow faeries; nine thousand warriors prepared to march into battle in the service of Queen Tatyana.

"They frighten me," Aislynn said.

"I should think they will frighten Lord Phaeon more," said Xian as he stepped up on the battlement to join them. "This is certainly a development, or—how would you say it?—a new truth that none of his generals have anticipated."

"Is our nightrunner prepared?" Dwynwyn asked without comment.

"Yes, indeed it is," Xian said easily, "and you may depart at your leisure."

"We have no leisure," Dwynwyn replied. "We will depart at once."

"I expected as much." Xian crossed his arms. "You *will* forward my regrets to your Queen Tatyana over the taking of this tower, along with my vow to give it up at once."

"As I said I would," Dwynwyn replied.

Xian nodded. "As well as my desire to negotiate an alliance at Her Majesty's earliest opportunity?"

Dwynwyn arched a questioning eyebrow at the Kyree master.

Xian shrugged and smirked. "I like to back a winner. Besides, you said yourself we have a lot to learn from each other. Perhaps we Kyree could even teach you faeries a new truth or two, eh?"

"If you are ever admitted to the queen's audience," Dwynwyn returned, "I should very much like to be there. It would be an event worth experiencing. In the meanwhile, I suggest that you pull back your forces well to the northeast. I would not want to find you here when I return with this Shadow Army."

"Nor would I want to be here when you did." Xian smiled. "Farewell, Dwynwyn. I trust we shall meet again."

Dwynwyn gave no reply. She pulled Aislynn around under her arm and led her down to the nightrunner. The eighteen largest shadow faeries lifted the craft and propelled it over the wall. In moments they were drifting over the great army below. As they passed the front lines, the army began to move as one.

Nine thousand warriors floated into the night. They would fulfill Dwynwyn's promise of a new truth.

A change in goblin leadership is so common a thing that it rarely occasions much comment from those who toil in the service of the kingdom. It is primarily a function of knowing which name one is supposed to curse. It certainly would do no good to complain about someone who had been assassinated or tossed out of power; one had to be up on who did the assassinating or the tossing.

This time, however, there was a difference that had everyone talking. Even before they knew the name of the new Dong, they knew about his first royal decree. It seemed foolish and stupid and a general inconvenience to everyone in the goblin realm, giving them cause to complain for weeks on end.

The burning of books was banned—and all books were to be brought to the new Dong at once.

★   ★   ★

Galen stood at the top of a hill and gazed to the north as the sun set on the day. He had done the same every day for a month since they escaped the Enlund Plain and found refuge in the wooded foothills to the south. It had become almost a ritual for him of remembrance, regret, and resolve.

Behind him, the Circle was together for their evening meal in a meadow among the thick trees. Galen and his followers found it far easier to pool their resources than to try to make do on their own. The mystic power—this "magic"—was also proving to be a useful tool in their survival, although not always one on which they could count. It remained a rather chancy proposition to use the magic; it was still nearly as much of a mystery to them as to anyone else. Still, they were exploring it as best they could with what little free time they could find in their day. Survival was a full-time proposition.

But at the end of the day, Galen always took the time to slip away and claim a moment for himself. He then considered his fate and wondered how it had brought him to this strange and terrible place. Thoughts of home were painful still, but he knew with terrible certainty that he could never go back. He had caused the death of the High Priestess of the Pir Vasska; his name was no doubt notorious throughout the Dragonback and spoken with either anger or loathing. He longed for Berkita but knew that he would most likely never see her again. That life, it seemed to him, had ended indeed.

So what was there left, Cephas had said to him, but to go forward? Perhaps, as Rhea had said, this was his true destiny all along. If so, then its price was too high. He should have known, he supposed, for the magic itself had tried to tell him back in the beginning, in the dream he had on his last night with his beloved wife.

The river drags me backward. I roll among the water spirits, their voices laughing as they scurry about me. My body merges with the river and now I am clear as the stream, flowing with it, pulled helplessly down its course. Resigned to my fate, I am transformed. A spirit of the water myself now, I cascade over the crest of the falls. The water spirits leap about excited and triumphant. I tumble through the air and water, smashing against the rocks and ex-

ploding into a thousand drops of blood. Each drop is my shat-tered self, diffusing among the waters of the river and the foam of the water spirits. The crimson waters rush outward into the bay. I am scattered farther and farther apart—thinner and thinner until there is no more left of me to gather up. Nothing left of me to be me. Lost forever among the waters of the bay, lost forever to my home now dark under the smoke of the dragon . . .

BOOK OF GALEN
BRONZE CANTICLES, TOME IV, FOLIO 1, LEAF 4

Thrice upon a time . . .
A man accepted a destiny that was larger than himself
A winged woman found strength in a new truth
And a small thing rose to greatness.

Thrice upon a time . . .
An ancient lie would be laid bare . . .
A precarious alliance would be forged in the sky . . .
And the power of magic would corrupt the innocent . . .
But that is another tale . . .

Song of the Worlds
Bronze Canticles, Tome I, Folio 1, Leaf 29

THE END OF PART ONE

Appendix A
Translation

The Bronze Canticles as we know them today—or, more properly, the Tales of the Bronze Canticles—is not the original. It is a compilation from texts that are believed to date from 436 F.A. to 30 E.A. (457 D.R. through 923 D.R.). However, most scholars believe that the compilation itself was made sometime around 225 E.A., long after the events had taken place and certainly well outside the direct knowledge of the compiler.

There has long been some confusion regarding the work. The Bronze Canticles themselves were a magical relic long sought after by the Mystics of Aerbon as the key to their understanding of the ancient craft. The Tales of the Bronze Canticles, on the other hand, were based not on the Canticles themselves but on the events surrounding the rise of the Mystic Dynasty and their quest to achieve the knowledge of the ancient Bronze Canticles, as well as their relationship to the faery and goblin realms and the Binding of the Worlds. Over time, events have overshadowed the Bronze Canticles themselves, while the tales of that terrible and tragic time remain.

Less is known about the compiler, who is usually referred to simply as the Chronicler. What little we know comes from the clues of the text itself. He (or she) is thought by most scholars to be human, quite probably a descendant of the Mystics from the Southern Crescent along the Sea of Rhamas. Most of the dates listed in the Canticles appear to have been adjusted to favor the Rhamas Empire dating system, which was later adopted for use by the human Mystics. Further, the text itself has a distinctly human bias to it both in its language and its selection of texts. The language of the text has a distinctive Lehman Coast flavor, yet is written in a Qelaran script unknown in Uthara. The identity of the Chronicler has spawned numerous debates. The text, however, makes no direct reference to this mysterious person. All we have is inference and our own imagination.

Original Translation Problems

The Chronicler faced daunting problems in compiling the texts. It is evident that he or she drew not only from human sources, but also translated extensively from both faery stories and goblin transcripts.

Of these, the faery stories are perhaps the most suspect, as explained in the marginalia of the Chronicler (included in this edition). Faery thought is so markedly different from human construction as to be difficult for humans to comprehend. Indeed, prior to the Second Epoch, faeries had no stories among themselves as humans would understand the concept. Faery stories evolved later out of the need to communicate in terms to which humans could relate. As such, there could be no contemporary recorded accounts of events as depicted during the First Epoch of the Binding. Famadorian texts, however, were apparently most helpful in drawing a more familiar framework to the events of the First Epoch as it related to the faeries.

Goblin transcripts were taken from their oral histories and are nearly as suspect as those from the faery realms. Goblins' basic outlook belies anything but an empirical reality. As such, truth for them is entirely subjective and regularly altered to suit the purposes of the moment. The Chronicler was well aware of this and assures us (again in his marginalia) that the account in this text is a compilation of a number of different transcripts concerning concurrent events. As such, it is perhaps the best hope for any sense of objectivity concerning goblin events—something of a consensus view of reality from numerous (and admittedly self-serving) observers.

Human and dwarf texts from the early ages of the Mystics are also suspect, though less so than the first two sources mentioned above. The Chronicler's own human bias, as we have noted, is evident in the selection of texts. However, numerous contemporary sources were extant, and the Chronicler goes to great pains to assure us of their veracity.

Translation Issues in This Edition

In translating this work from the original Gerandian, we are acutely aware of the inadequacy of language. Words in translation are often only the shadow of the original intent of any text, and more so here, as we present essentially a translation of a Gerandian translation compiled from various other language sources.

Nevertheless, we have tried to be true to the Chronicler's noted intent: to "convey the essence of what was in words that resonate truth in the mind of man."

Appendix B
Pir Drakonis

The Pir Drakonis was the center of thought, worship, justice, might, and government in all the land of Hrunard and throughout the Dragonback.

The origins of the Pir Drakonis church—its rituals, liturgy, and practices—lay obscured in the smoke of the fallen Rhamas Empire.

According to the church liturgy, the seven divine dragons—Vasska, Ulruk, Jekard, Panas, Whithril, Ormakh, and Satinka—descended from the heavens in order to stop humankind from utterly destroying their creation. Their advent marked a new era for humanity—Drakonis Regiva—in which all people would come to understand the divinity of the dragons and their own humble place in the celestial spheres.

The opening of this new age came when each of the dragons sought out and discovered humans who held within themselves "the gift." This "gift" was no less than the ability to read and interpret the smoke emanating from the nostrils of the dragons as they slept. Such chosen individuals were then patiently instructed in the complexities of dragon speech and brought into service of the divine dragons as interpreters and prophets of the smoke.

The Drakonis Pripha, or First Dragon Voice, convened secretly in 172 D.R. This council of Dragon Voices brought together for the first time the priests and priestesses who acted as voice for the dragons of Hramra. With the ascendancy of the divine dragons Whithril and Ulruk, the Drakonis Pripha renamed itself the Pentach, or the Five.

Doctrines

The first known formal doctrines of the Pir were the Rules of Five, which were established primarily as the five major points to be remembered at all times by the Dragon-Talkers. These formal doctrines were later practiced and taught only to the Pentach.

The doctrines of the Pir center on the four major aspects of Vasska. All other aspects (known as the minor, or lesser, aspects) sprang from these four central concepts. Each aspect was divided into two major divisions, known as left aspect and right aspect. Right aspect was that which encompassed the greater Pir as a theocratic organization and deals with church government and the conduct of the general organization. The left aspects were those which related to the individual members of the Pir and their obligations under the doctrines of the church.

Defend (Outer Knowledge)

"The Enemy hides in the night: The Breath of Vasska is bright."

The aspect of defend encompassed how the Pir related to the ideas, philosophies, arguments, and sophistries of those outside the Pir. The center of this aspect was rooted in the idea that because the Pir were led by Vasska—a divine being—their understanding of the universe was the correct one. Therefore, as they had the only true view of the universe, all other ideas that were found in the world might only be judged on the merit of how closely they adhered to the doctrines of Vasska. Ideas that were not in accordance with the doctrines of the church were deemed heretical and evidence of evil or dark-heartedness.

Right aspect. It may have seemed paradoxical to those outside the religion of the Dragonkings, therefore, to note that the Pir maintained a very active system of ambassadors and spies who were tasked to gather as much information from the world outside the Pir as possible. The objective was to "shine the light of Vasska's hot breath" on those ideas and either promote them or destroy them depending on how "correct" they were with doctrine.

Left aspect. The individual was responsible for banishing all thought or knowledge that was not in accordance with the aspects of Vasska. Ignorance was fine but vanished as soon as a petitioner heard something new. Should any concept, thought, or knowledge that was new come to the attention of any member of the Pir, and its status regarding doctrine be unknown, it was the petitioner's duty to bring such ideas before the local priest and any member of the Pir Inquisitas in order to ascertain its standing with the church.

One might readily understand, therefore, how the question of what exactly *was* doctrine became paramount among the Pir clergy and membership alike. This question, of course, fell firmly within the province of the fourth aspect.

Conquer (Outer Strength)

"Death judges all: The Claw of Vasska is sharp."

Physical strength manifested itself in both left and right aspects of conquer.

Right aspect. Military strength was a core belief of the Pir Drakonis. The rightness of the cause of Vasska and the protection of the Pir dictated not only a strong military but also the active use of the military in enforcing the rightness of the Pir on her enemies—enemies being defined as anyone who professes thought outside the doctrine of the Pir.

Left aspect. Just as individuals were responsible for the purity of the doctrine under the first aspect, so, too, were they responsible for exerting the physical might of the Pir whenever called to do so.

The doctrine of death itself, as established by the fourth aspect, was either a glorious affirmation of one's faith or the ultimate in condemnation. Those who died with hearts that affirmed the second aspect may use their deeds to purchase from torment relatives or loved ones who failed the Pir in death and whose souls were in torment. There were numerous other degrees of fate that awaited those who died without knowledge of the aspects of Vasska, each of them chilling and terrible. The enemies of Vasska who never knew the greatness of his aspects and truth fell deep into the ground below into the belly of the world, where they were forever being digested by the world but never consumed. Those who died failing Vasska in their appointed task (who are defeated in battle or died before fulfilling a quest, for example) suffered an even worse fate: they were sent to dwell among the spirits of Vasska's enemies, who would torture them even as they themselves were tortured. This was because their crime was greater: for they knew the aspects of Vasska and yet their faith turned away.

Thus it was better to die in battle affirming the greatness of Vasska and his aspects than it was to retreat. Failure was without forgiveness.

Glory (Inner Strength)

"The body is of many parts: The Heart of Vasska is steadfast."

The physical and organizational aspects of the Pir were largely dealt with under this aspect. The body of the Pir was constituted from the individuals of whom they were a part. No individual part was of any importance except insofar as it served the greater good of the Pir.

The inner strength referred to in this Aspect was twofold: inner strength of the individual in being steadfast to the doctrines of the Pir (left aspect) and inner strength of the Pir itself as an organization serving Vasska (right aspect).

Right aspect. The priests of the Pir were the most recognizable manifestation of this aspect. They served locally as both secular government and ecclesiastical authority. All matters of civilization came under the purview of the priests: community harvests, festivals, local defense, jurisprudence, taxation, welfare, and education, to name a few. The priests were also concerned with controlling the doctrine and knowledge of the petitioners under its purview.

Left aspect. The individual had to support the Pir. As part of the body of the Pir, the individual petitioner was to respond to any task required of him by the clergy from any branch of the Pir organization. Most such tasks were menial, simple, and easily satisfied. Occasionally, a pilgrimage was requested and the person made the journey to the Temple of Vasska. Some had been called to work on the reconstruction of the Temple without any knowledge of when they would be released from their task. Accepting and, more importantly, completing these tasks were the highest form of worship, and their rewards toward one's past family sins were great. The penalty for failure was dire (*see* second aspect).

Spirit (Inner Knowledge)

"Bright faces hide dark hearts: The Eye of Vasska is vigilant."

Right aspect. The purity of the doctrine and the destruction of opposing doctrine was largely the province of the Grand Inquisitor and the monks of the Pir Inquisitas. Judge, jury, and often executioner all rolled into one, the Pir Inquisitas roamed the lands of the Pir in search of heresy and impure doctrines.

Left aspect. The doctrine of the Pir as it related to the individual was one of penitence for the folly of humanity and the Mad Emperors of Rhamas, and a search for favor in the eyes of Vasska both for the individual and for those who had departed before them.

The doctrine states that the world was created by the Dragonkings from the smoke of their dreams. Into this world, also from their smoke, came the beasts, with man chief among them. But man, in his madness, rebelled against the greatness of the Dragonkings. The Mad Emperors of Rhamas built citadels that defied Vasska and his kind high in the mountains so that they, too, could reside among the clouds. The Dragonkings were angered by the madness of the Mad Emperors and came down to earth with vengeance and power. Man had proven himself willful and insane with pride. Only a chosen few, the Talkers, heard the words of Dragonkings and knew their justice.

Thus came the Cleansing War, or the War of the Dragon Siege. The dragons, their Talkers, and those who would follow them in their righteous anger—the people, or the Pir—made war against the Mad

Emperors of Rhamas and brought low the might and folly of humanity. The souls of the damned sank deep into Aerbon beyond the caverns of the dwarves and into N'Kara—the belly of the world. Only through the penance and devotion of the Pir could the souls be purchased from the belly of the world to become part of the Dragonkings in the land of Surn'gara—the Veil of Sighs found beyond the sky.

Rituals and Worship

There were many ways to serve and worship Vasska, each prescribed in the *Pir Inquisitas Desment,* the multivolume doctrinal work that was the touchstone for all the Pir. First was the knowledge that none of the Pir could approach the greatness of Vasska on their own, for such presumption mirrored that of the Mad Emperors and was to invite similar folly. All devotions were to be done through the authority of the Pir Drakonis and were to be strictly maintained.

The Kath-Drakonis

The heart of each Pir community was the Kath-Drakonis. This place of worship varied greatly from place to place in terms of its construction, although invariably it was the finest and largest building in any community. In most villages this simply meant a larger structure than those around it. In some of the larger communities, these buildings were the size of cathedrals and were tremendously large, though none came close to rivaling the Temple of Vasska itself.

All the Kath-Drakonis, however, were built along the same basic plan. Each had four naves reflecting the four aspects of Vasska, and each portrayed the basic principles of proper penitence and worship for the Pir. At the nexus of the four naves was an Eko-Drakonis, an iconic image of the great Iconograph of the Temple. This item was the center of worship, for it represented the image of the great Iconograph itself.

The Festival of the Harvest

Also known as the Festival of the Election, this Pir-wide celebration of the rule of the Dragonkings took place every Leavenmonth of the Pir calendar. It was a community celebration which formally began with the Supplicant Dance. The call to Election, the Reveler's Trump, and the Mad King's Parade followed in that order. The local priest then conducted the Election over the entire assembled community, culling out the Chosen to be taken care of by the Inquisitas. The event culminated with the casting of the coins of blessing over the crowd.

The origins of the Festival were as old as the Pir.

The Temple of Vasska

The center for worship among the Pir Drakonis of Vasska's lands was the Temple of Vasska.

This edifice was originally the Temple to Kel during the Rhamas Empire and was kept largely intact following the Pir sacking of Mithanlas, which was renamed Vasskhold. Vasska took the Temple as his home—more accurately, he took the caverns underlying the Temple as his home and determined to rule from there. After that time, the Temple of Vasska, as it was renamed, was the center of Pir rule, law, and faith throughout Hrunard and the Dragonback. In later years, extensive efforts were undertaken to "restore" the Temple. These so-called restorations, while they involved rebuilding those parts of the Temple that were damaged during the ancient assault, were more aimed at eliminating any icons or vestiges of its former function or reworking them into icons that favored Vasska and the Pir.

The Temple of Vasska was the great pilgrimage temple of the Pir. Devout Pir journeyed from the far reaches of Vasska's lands to come into this structure and worship at the center of spiritual power.

Appendix C
Mystics

In the early days of the mystics, the fundamentals of magic were little understood. Down through succeeding generations, the principles would be analyzed, codified, and refined into exacting relationships and effects. In the beginning, however, the mystics felt their way clumsily into the power of magic . . . its metaphor and analogy . . . and were doing so by instinct alone.

One of the most basic principles of magic —especially in that first Age of the Mystics—was that of reciprocity. All things hold within themselves a power; a power of presence, potential, and force. The magic, too, has a momentum of its own. It then imparts this momentum to the people and objects in the world that it affects. However, it only does so in a great cosmic balance between the worlds. Heat in one realm becomes cold in another. Light in a third realm dims two others. Greatness borrows its power by diminishing another sphere. No magic in any world has any impact without affecting in reciprocity one or another of the others.

All of this was still part of the great mystery in the First Age of the Binding, unknown and unsuspected. Massive, chaotic magical effects were enacted without consideration of their direct impact *on other realities. The results were often unexpected and profound in their implications. One need look no further than Galen and the Battle of the Enlund Plain for an example. The Magic of the Stones caused much of the army of Satinka to vanish in a cataclysmic abyss of destruction. Yet no thought had been given to the reciprocal: the army had vanished but the power that army represented had imparted a momentum of its own to the magic. To Galen and those on the Plain, the army had disappeared, but its reciprocal momentum still existed within the magic and searched for its release . . .*

THE COMMENTARIES OF IGNASTUS
BRONZE CANTICLES, TOME 21, FOLIO 12, LEAF 17

Overview of Magic

Magic in the Bronze Canticles is commonly referred to as either Surface (or Common) Magic or Deep Magic—even though the two are related. All magic, in its various forms and regardless of cultural custom, appears to be linked to one or both of these forms. Further, it is important to understand that while the nature of magic remains constant throughout the Binding of the Worlds, the methods by which it is employed change over time due to the altering conditions of the Binding itself.

Magic in the Bronze Canticles is thought of generally as *reciprocal and metaphoric magic*. It is reciprocal in that creative events in one world translate into magical effects in another world, often greatly amplified in power. It is metaphoric because the causal translation of the creative and subconscious mental energies involved relies on icons, metaphors, representations, symbolism, interpretations, similes, and parables.

Magic is also transtemporal in nature. Within certain limits, the timing of magical cause and effect between the worlds of creation is flexible. A mystic in the world of the humans who draws upon a faery Seeker may meet that other in the dream (the ethereal realm) while they are both asleep, even though the passage of time in their respective worlds since their last encounter may be counted differently. This is true of both Deep and Surface Magic, as Surface Magic naturally compensates for the power of Deep Magic.

Surface (or Common) Magic

All the worlds have always had Surface Magic, also known as Common Magic. It is a power that is tied to the Deep Magic, and both operate in tandem, although this fact was not fully understood by the mystics until late into the Binding of the Worlds.

Each of the different incarnations of the world utilized Common Magic in some form or other, although always with different names and processes. The faery were the most adept at this form of magic and incorporated it unquestioningly into the very fabric of their society. The Famadorians used it also, although without nearly the subtlety of the faery and most often through shamans. The Kyree used it through what they called Oracles. The Dragonkings and their Pir priesthood utilized a rigid form of it to actually suppress the burgeoning Deep Magic. This was the source of the magical properties given to the Eye of Vasska staffs utilized by the monks or the visions in the dreamsmoke of the Dragonkings. The dwarves had totems which were imbued with Common Magic. While the Titans themselves had spurned all forms of magic—Surface or Deep—their servants and slave gnomes, goblins, imps, and ogres often had societal shamans or even simple superstitions which drew upon the Common Magic.

Coincidence, Reality, Cause, and Effect

One of the important effects of the Common Magic as it related to the Deep Magic was in the area of causality or cause and effect. The Common Magic permeated all of creation in all incarnations of the world. It was a leveling force that helped keep the worlds in balance while it was being acted upon by the more dynamic and focused forces of the Deep Magic. Thus a great many "little coincidences" in one world could translate through the Deep Magic into dynamic and powerful effects.

Deep Magic

Creative expression in many diverse forms is the medium by which magical force and change is generated on the world of the ethereal, also called the dreamworld or thoughtscape.

As it is this ethereal plane by which all magic is created, the basic and fundamental principle is that all magic results in an iconic or metaphoric translation of action or thought from one realm to powerful incarnation in another. Thus any magical action can only have effect if it draws its power from reciprocal thought or action in another version of the world.

Reciprocity

One of the most basic principles of magic—especially in that first Age of the Mystics—was that of reciprocity. All things hold within themselves a power; a power of presence, potential, and force. The magic, too, has a momentum of its own. It then imparts this momentum to the people and objects in the world that it affects. However it only does so in a great cosmic balance between the worlds. Heat in one realm becomes cold in another, Light in a third realm dims two others. Greatness borrows its power by diminishing another sphere. No magic in any world has any impact without affecting in reciprocity one or another of the others.

Abstract Translation

The exact form in which the provided energies take shape is controllable but naturally tends toward representational or abstract translation. Visions in the dream, for example, rarely, if ever, depict a clear and exact representation of either the source of power or its ultimate form. Rather, inside the dream, these are represented by icons that are similes, analogies, or parables to the actual source or result.

More importantly, each participant in these visions may experience different perceptions of the vision itself. This is due to the metaphoric nature of the magic; different mystics perceive the metaphors in different ways. Thus while two mystics may meet in the ethereal realm, their observations of events taking place there may be different. In general, mystics in the same world will find their metaphors closer to one another than those from different worlds. Thus two humans who meet in the ethereal realm may experience the encounter with nearly identical observations, while a faery joining them might perceive the encounter with an entirely different set of metaphors.